HUNLAF'S JOURNEY

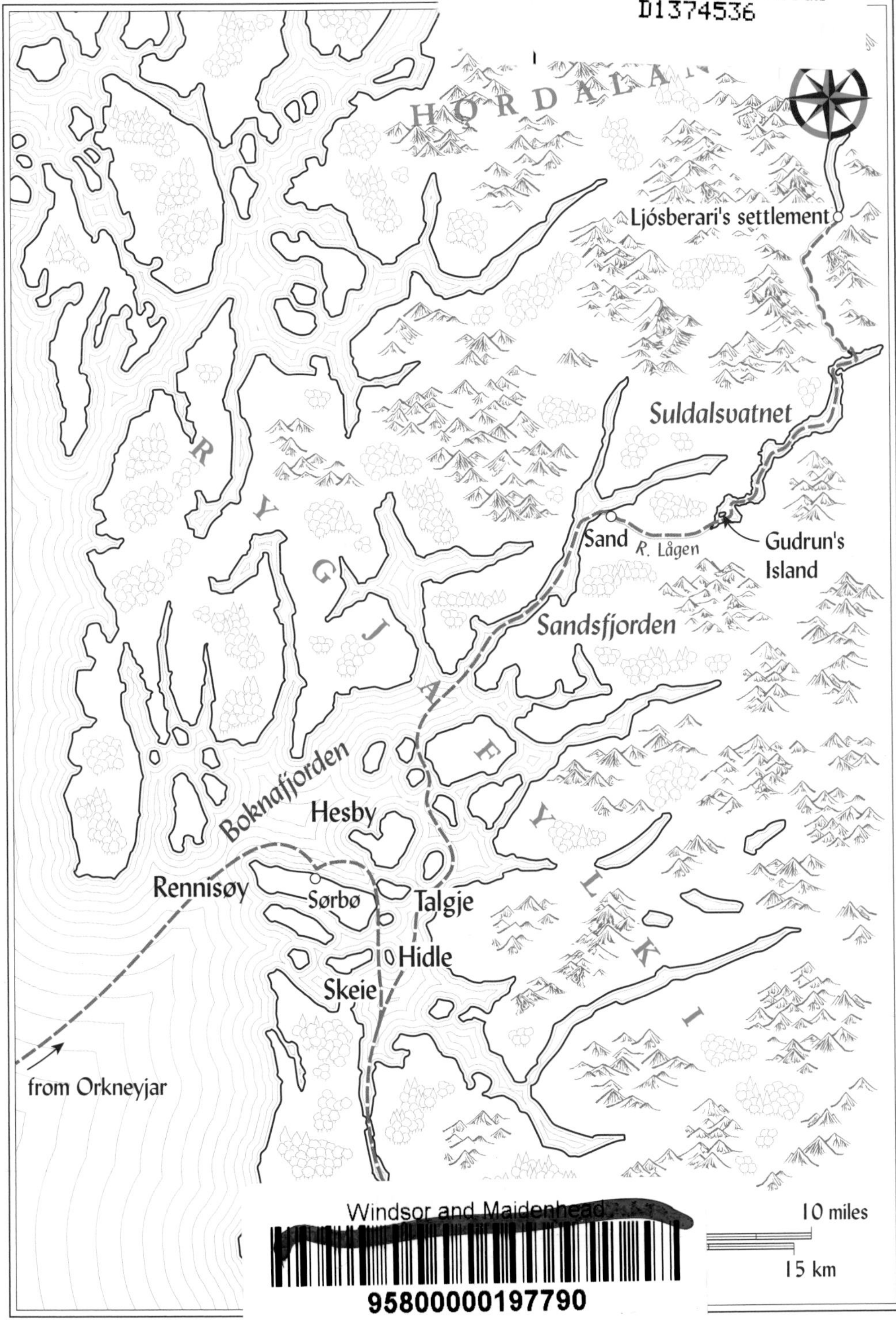

Praise for

MATTHEW HARFFY

'Harffy is a master of the Dark Age thriller... *A Time for Swords* is a bold opening to yet another enthralling series. It promises to be one heck of a ride.'

Theodore Brun,
author of *A Mighty Dawn*

'Terrific white-knuckle action, absolutely gripping storytelling... Can't wait for the next one. Highly recommended!'

Angus Donald,
author of *Robin Hood and the Caliph's Gold*

'Nothing less than superb... The tale is fast paced and violence lurks on every page.'

Historical Novel Society

'Harffy's writing just gets better and better... He is really proving himself the rightful heir to Gemmell's crown.'

Jemahl Evans,
author of *The Last Roundhead*

'A tale that rings like sword song in the reader's mind. Harffy knows his genre inside out.'

Giles Kristian,
author of *Camelot*

BY MATTHEW HARFFY

A Time for Swords series

A Time for Swords
A Night of Flames

Bernicia Chronicles

The Serpent Sword
The Cross and the Curse
Blood and Blade
Killer of Kings
Warrior of Woden
Storm of Steel
Fortress of Fury
For Lord and Land
Kin of Cain (short story)

Other novels

Wolf of Wessex

A NIGHT OF FLAMES

MATTHEW HARFFY

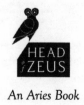

HEAD of ZEUS

An Aries Book

First published in the UK in 2022 by Head of Zeus Ltd,
part of Bloomsbury Publishing Plc.

9 7 5 3 1 2 4 6 8

A catalogue record for this book is available from
the British Library.

Typeset by Divaddict Publishing Solutions Ltd

ISBN (HB): 9781801102278
ISBN (XTPB): 9781801102285
ISBN (E): 9781801102308

Printed and bound by CPI Group (UK) Ltd,
Croydon, CR0 4YY

FSC www.fsc.org MIX Paper from responsible sources FSC® C171272

Head of Zeus Ltd
5–8 Hardwick Street
London EC1R 4RG

WWW.HEADOFZEUS.COM

A Night of Flames
is for Derek and Jacqui
(More mead?)

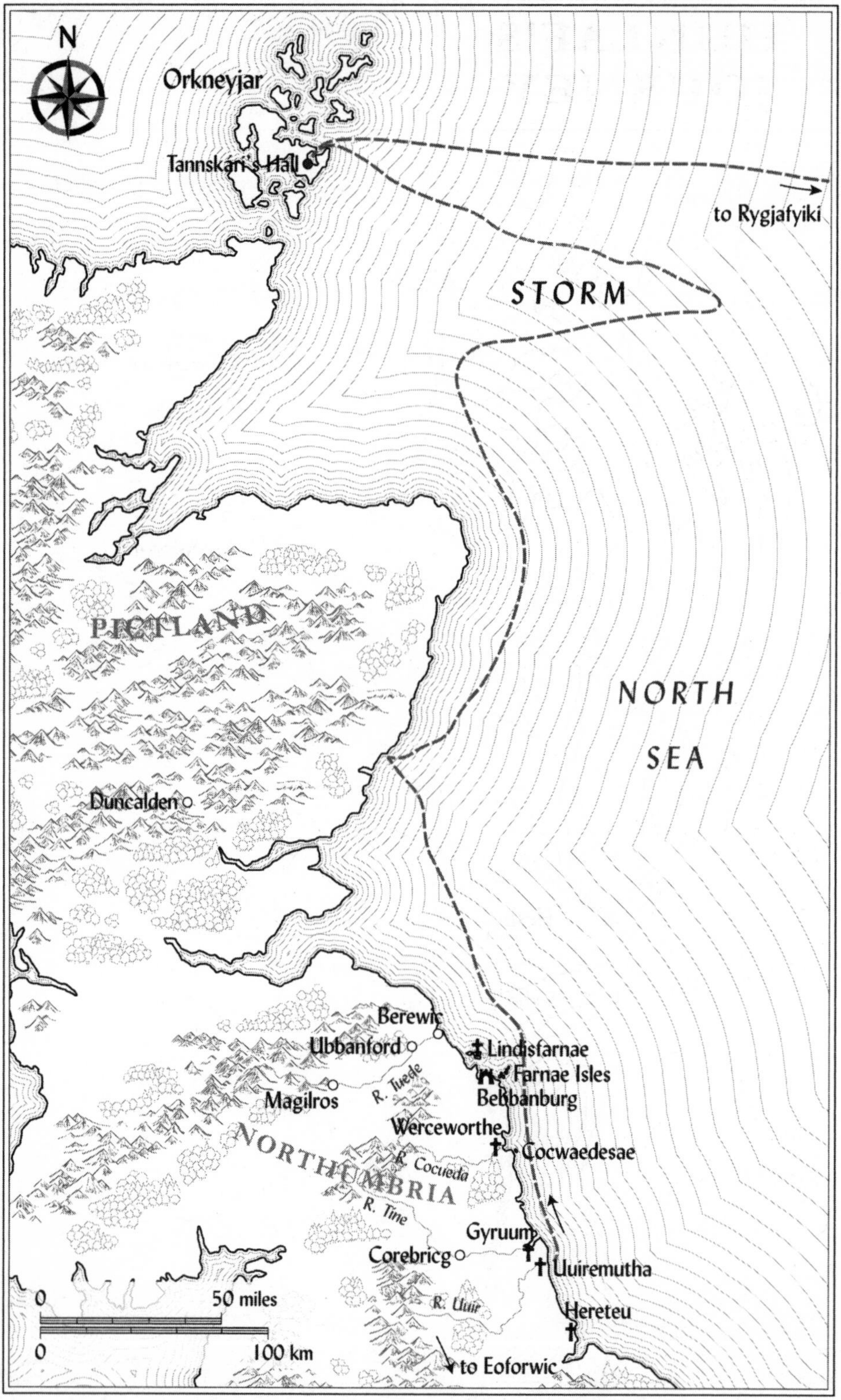
N
Orkneyjar
Tannskári's Hall
to Rygjafyiki
STORM
NORTH
SEA
PICTLAND
Duncalden
Berewic
Ubbanford
Lindisfarnae
Farnae Isles
Bebbanburg
Magilros
R. Tuede
Werceworthe
Cocwaedesae
NORTHUMBRIA
R. Cocueda
R. Tine
Gyruum
Corebricg
Uuiremutha
R. Uuir
Hereteu
to Eoforwic
0
50 miles
0
100 km

HUNLAF'S JOURNEY

Legend

○ Settlements
✝ Holy sites
Fortresses
– – – Hunlaf's route

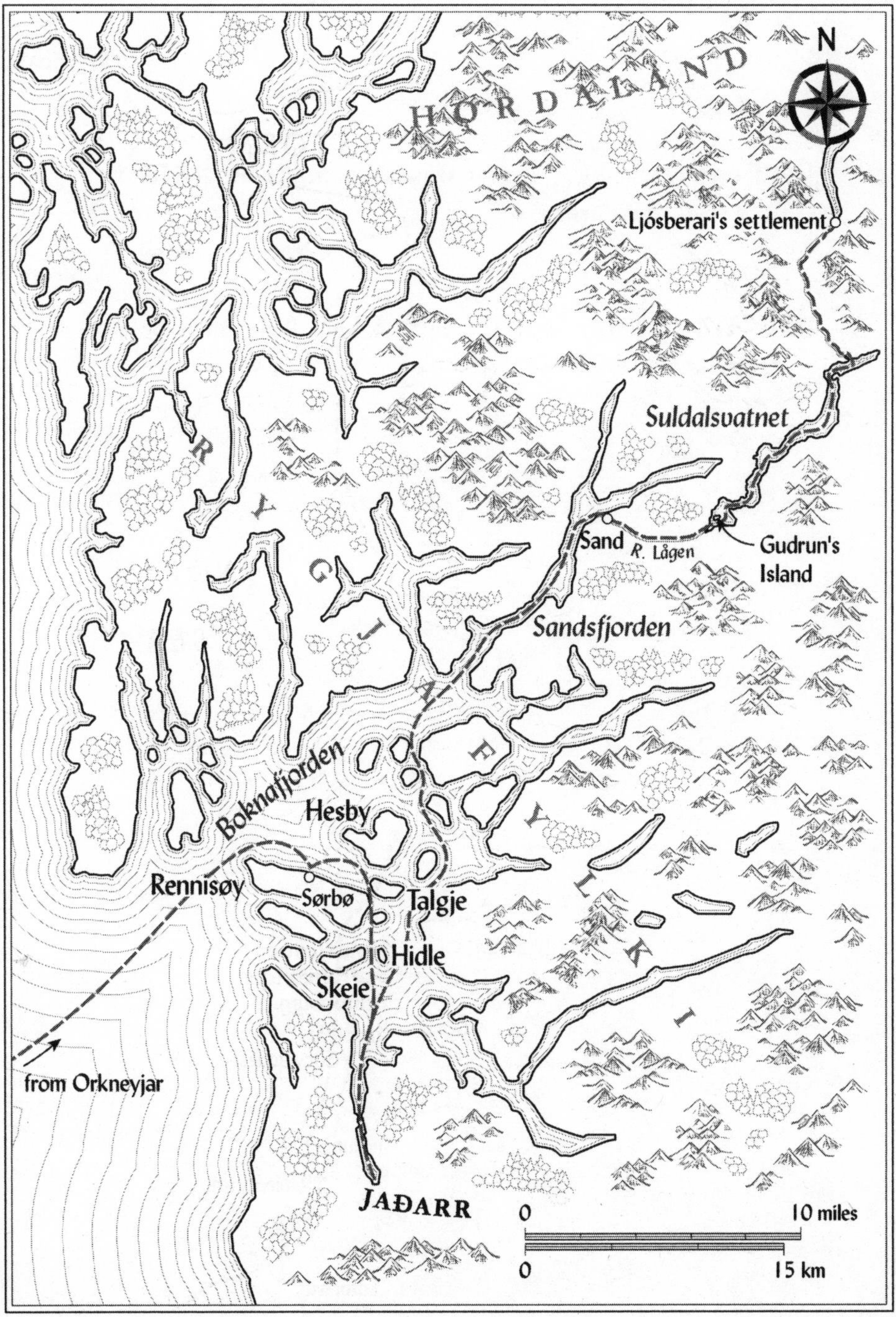

And God saw the light, that it was good: and God divided the light from the darkness.

Genesis 1, verse 4

Take heed therefore that the light which is in thee be not darkness.

Luke 11, verse 35

Place Names

Early medieval place names vary according to time, language, dialect and the scribe who was writing. I have not followed a strict convention when choosing the spelling to use for a given place. In most cases, I have chosen the name I believe to be the closest to that used in the late eighth century, but like the scribes of all those centuries ago, I have taken artistic licence at times, and, when unsure, merely selected the one I liked most.

Some of the place names also occur in my Bernicia Chronicles novels with different spellings. This is intentional to denote that this is not part of that series and also to indicate the passage of time and the changes to language that occur over the centuries.

Alabur	Aalborg, Denmark
Al-Andalus	The Muslim-ruled area of the Iberian Peninsula
Al-Askar	The capital of Egypt from 750 – 868
ar-Raqqah	Raqqa, Syria
Bebbanburg	Bamburgh
Berewic	Berwick upon Tweed
Boknafjorden	Bokna Fjord, Norway
Byzantion	Constantinople (Istanbul)

Cocueda, River	River Coquet
Cocwaedesae	Coquet Island
Cordova	Córdoba, Spain
Corebricg	Corbridge
Danapr	The Dnieper
Duiblinn	Dublin
Duncalden	Dunkeld, Scotland
Eoforwic	York
Fossa, River	River Foss
Farnae Isles	Farne Islands
Gwynedd	Early medieval kingdom, now a county, situated in the north-west of modern-day Wales
Gyruum	Jarrow
Hereteu	Hartlepool
Hidle	Sør-Hidle, Norway
Hǫrðaland	Hordaland, Norway
Ifriqiya	Area comprising what is today Tunisia, western Libya and eastern Algeria
Išbīliya	Seville, Spain
Jabal Tāriq	Gibraltar
Jaðarr	The traditional district of Jæren, Rogaland, Norway
Hesby	Hesby, Norway
Lågen	Suldalslågen river, Norway
Lindisfarnae	Lindisfarne
Loch Cuan	Strangford Lough, Northern Island
Magilros	Melrose
Madīnat as-Salām	The City of Peace, Baghdad, Iraq
Oguz il	(Oguz Land) Turkic state located in an area between the coasts of the Caspian and Aral Seas
Orkneyjar	Orkney Islands

Powys	Early medieval kingdom, now a county, situated in central modern-day Wales
Quentovic	Frankish trading settlement. The town no longer exists, but is thought to have been situated near the mouth of the Canche River
Rennisøy	Rennesøy, Norway
Roma	Rome
Rygjafylki	Rogaland, Norway
Sand	Sand, Norway
Sandsfjorden	Sandsfjord, Norway
Skeie	Skeie, Stavanger, Norway
Sørbø	Sørbø, Norway
Suldalsvatnet	Lake Suldal, Norway
Streanæshealh	Whitby
Talgje	Talgje, or Sør-Talgje, Norway
Tine, River	River Tyne
Tuede, River	River Tweed
Ubbanford	Norham
Usa, River	River Ouse
Uuir, River	River Wear
Uuiremutha	Monkwearmouth
Vestfold	Vestfold, eastern Norway
Volga	The Volga
Werceworthe	Warkworth

One

Weeks have gone by since I last took up a quill. In spite of my infirmity, I am pleased to find my hand has not forgotten how to form letters. The words on the vellum may not be as perfectly aligned and bold as my writing once was, but they are clear enough and still better than many a scribe's scratchings. My eyes, though, water constantly, and I need to dab at them to prevent the tears running down my cheeks like a man grieving for a loved one. But of course, I am mourning. I weep not just for the loss of all those I held dear, but selfishly, for my youth and the time that has trickled through my hands, like the fine burning sands of ar-Raqqah or the cool waters of the mighty Volga.

But I must not allow myself to become maudlin. Our Heavenly Father has granted me more time, so it is my duty to put it to good use. For many days, I believed I would never be able to return to telling my tale. I thought the Lord might take me. Or that the Almighty had forsaken me, and perhaps the Devil would come for my soul, as I lay trembling and moaning alone in my cell. I cursed my weakness, and on more than one occasion I needed to beg forgiveness, not just of God, but of His young servant, Coenric, who brought me food and tended to my needs. Coenric came to me every day. He spooned thin pottage into my mouth when I had no hunger, and he held me steady so that I could piss and shit in a pot, even when I was too weak to rise from my stinking pallet. The sallow-faced lad put up stoically with my whimpering fury, cleaning me, feeding me, and fetching more of the potion of woundwort, mugwort and wormwood that the old cunning woman from the village made to blunt the talons of the beast that scratched at my innards.

Coenric sat beside me as the foul liquid dulled my pain. Outside my cell, the long warm days of summer became ever shorter, as the year slipped inexorably towards the darkness of winter. My aged ears strained to hear the whistling song of the redwings and the chirrups of the fieldfares as the summer grew old, and I often wished that Coenric would sit in silence. Instead, he read from the Scriptures and prayed. On the few occasions when Abbot Criba came to visit me, the boy explained that he was doing all he could, and that I needed rest. He would offer me a small smile as he ushered the abbot out of my noisome room, and this lifted my spirits somewhat. Coenric knows how I detest the supercilious abbot. If Criba should ever read these pages, I can barely imagine how furious he would be.

Coenric is as different from Criba as steel is from cheese. I have known many men in my long life, both good and honourable, and loathsome and evil. And yet I do not recall having encountered any more Christlike in their compassion than young Coenric. I may sometimes berate him and he may not be the brightest boy in the world, but as I am sure he will read this, I would have him know that no matter my ill-temper, I know that I owe him much. I have oft been told I am a difficult man, quick to judge and fast to anger. I have clashed swords with dark-skinned Berbers in the forge-heat of Ifriqiya and pale-eyed screaming brutes in the snowy wastes of the north, sailed in Runolf's great ship to lands beyond anything most men can imagine. I have walked the shadowed streets of Byzantion, and traversed the swollen rivers of the Baltic. It is not easy for one who has lived such a life to accept aid from anyone. But I am old now, and I know that Death has his skeletal hand on my shoulder. I loathe the decrepitude that has wrapped itself around me like a sodden cloak. I rail against the grip of time and the approach of my end, but I am not insensible of Coenric's sacrifice these last weeks. And I am thankful for his patience and his ministrations.

One grey drizzled day, when the ache in my guts had been made distant by the cunning woman's brew, I asked Coenric why he endured my poor humour and barbed words.

"Why, to make you well again, so that you can write the next volume of your annals," he said, seemingly genuinely surprised by my question.

I looked out the small window at the leaden sky and listened to the constant drip of the rain from the building's eaves. The smell of smoke, perhaps from the forge or a cooking fire, came to me on the breeze. The weather and the smoke sent me instantly back to that day long ago, when Skorri and his Norsemen brought chaos and death to Werceworthe, and my life changed forever.

I had not imagined that Coenric had read what I had been working on all those months. Clearly, he had not divulged my secrets to Criba, who still enquired regularly whether I would be well enough to continue with my transcription of the *Vita Sancti Wilfrithi*.

I began writing the story of my life and adventures so that a record of certain events might not be lost. I have many tales still to tell, if the good Lord sees fit to spare me for long enough. I never expected to have any readers of my work while I yet lived, but I would not wish to add lying to my numerous sins by saying that I am not gratified that at least one reader might be satisfied with the marks left by the scratching of my pen.

There may be those who read these pages and think they recognise other tales within them. Know then that these are the events as I remember them, but I am old, and perhaps my memory is not as sharp as it once was. Of course, it is also true that other stories may have been told before now by men or women who also witnessed these events, and they would surely resemble my own recollections. But each man can only see with his own eyes and remember that which his mind recalls, so what I offer here is my truth and that of no other.

I feel the curse of my age and illness hanging over me, an ever-present cloud, and I know that I must not squander any of the time given to me. Since Lady Day, the gnawing pain in my stomach has dwindled. I know not why. Whether this is a short reprieve, or an answer to Coenric's prayers, I do not know. But as the acute agony has become a dull ache, so my mind has begun once more to wander the dark paths of my memories. To the days when I was not much older than Coenric. To the time when I arrogantly believed I would never grow old and die. I think back to the rain-soaked autumn and the frost-riven winter that followed the savage attack on Werceworthe.

I recall the sadness and grief, and then the rallying of the folk to rebuild what they had lost.

I remember marvelling as Runolf, the huge Norseman that many considered a brute, created a thing of exquisite beauty and power: a ship the likes of which no free Englisc man had voyaged in before.

And, although I do not wish to follow them down those dark trails, my memories pull me towards events I wish I could forget. To a river winding through towering trees that echo with the screams of the damned. To the vacant eyes of dead friends, staring unseeing at the flame-streaked sky of Hǫrðaland.

And, with a dreadful sadness and guilt, I remember as vividly as yesterday, the warmth on my cheek of the dying breath of the first truly innocent man with whom I crossed blades.

Two

His name was Wistan and though he was perhaps four or five years older than me, he was no fighter. I remember staring into his eyes as the sun rose over the North Sea on that summer's morning long ago, and all I saw there was a righteous burning fury. In his hand he held a sword that Runolf had lent him. It was a well-made but simple weapon, with wooden grip and iron pommel. It had belonged to one of the Norsemen who had attacked Werceworthe the year before, and in the hands of a skilled warrior, despite its lack of adornment, that sword would kill as well as any other. But Wistan held the sword's grip so tightly in his fist that his knuckles were white. He had no battle-skill. His talents lay in working wood, toiling and learning in his father's shadow. Wistan's arms were strong from chopping, splitting and planing timber, but strength alone does not win a sword fight.

On his left side, much of Wistan's body was concealed behind a circular, iron-bossed shield. The hide that covered the board was painted the red of blood. Upon that crimson field, the shield bore the sigil of a black bird. A raven, Runolf had said, for they were the sacred birds of Óðinn, the father of his people's gods. Most of the shields we had taken from the Norsemen had been repainted. My own was now daubed in white, with a scarlet cross to show my faith in the Lord. Runolf had left the pagan symbol on the shield he had taken. Though baptised, he seemed to enjoy shocking the rest of us, flaunting his heathen ancestry.

"Put aside that sword and walk away," I said, stepping to my left, circling around so that Wistan would have to stare into the rising sun. It was early summer and the sun blazed bright beneath a brooding bank of dark clouds far out over the sea. The view was dazzling. The sun's rays reflected from the waves, as if the water had been fashioned from polished patterned steel.

With practised ease, I drew my own sword from its plain leather-wrapped sheath. Like Wistan's, it too was unadorned. The metal was clean and burnished, but it did not bear the patterns like water or a serpent's skin that came from the twisted rods of metal being beaten together by a master bladesmith. There was little difference in our swords, but there was much to separate the men who wielded them.

"You must pay for what you have done," Wistan said, his voice wavering with the passion he felt. "What you have taken from me."

I sighed.

"You cannot beat me," I said. My words were arrogant, but we both knew them to be true. He met my gaze and did not flinch. He was brave. I respected that. He knew he would die, but could see no other way out of this without being branded a coward.

He had every right to be furious. I am not proud of it now, but I was young then, and I revelled in my newfound strength and ability. I had found my purpose it seemed to me, and as my skill with a blade increased and my muscles hardened, so I embraced the new life I had seized for myself. A sharp seax hung from my belt across my loins, and a deadly sword was scabbarded at my side. No longer did I wear the coarse woollen habit of a monk. I had a blue kirtle trimmed with yellow and red tablet weave, and when I trained, I donned a heavy byrnie, the iron rings as light as a second skin to me now. I was a warrior, and with my new status came a swagger and self-belief that now, looking back with the eyes of an old man, makes me both envious and ashamed.

"Go on, Hunlaf," came a shrieking voice from the throng that had gathered around us, "cut him!"

Both Wistan and I flicked a glance over at the rosy-cheeked woman. Her hair was the colour of spun flax, and her eyes the green of summer clover. Her dun dress was cinched at her narrow waist, accentuating her shapely hips and the swell of her breasts.

She was lovely, of that there was no doubt, but her tone was as harsh as the croak of a crow. I longed for Wistan to step away from this fight. I didn't wish to kill him; didn't want the blood of a good man on my soul. Over the years I have seen how often the affections or rejections of a woman cause bloodshed. Leofstan used to say that it all stemmed from the original sin that has resided in mankind since Eva partook of the forbidden fruit from the tree of the knowledge of good and evil. I have never been so sure, but what I know for certain is that men, both young and old, can find themselves acting like fools around a comely woman.

And I was no exception.

I had given up the rigours of life as a monk and thrown myself fully into the ways of the warrior. For a few weeks after the Norse attack, whilst we had remained at Werceworthe, the minster that had been my home for the past years, Brother Leofstan's calm presence had kept my more lusty behaviour in check. He had still prayed with me at least once a day, encouraging me to think of Christ and his teachings.

That changed when I moved south to Uuiremutha with Runolf and the others. We left Leofstan behind and, with his absence, I took another step away from my past and grasped my future with both hands.

Wistan had found me with those hands full of his betrothed's breasts.

It had been going on for several days before he caught us, and I had grown increasingly brash about it. I was full of self-importance. We had newly come from Eoforwic with orders from King Æthelred himself and I swaggered about, overseeing the construction of the ship, or at least relaying Runolf's orders to the carpenters, smiths and labourers who helped with the work.

Cwenswith smiled at me whenever I passed by, and her pretty green eyes followed me as I sauntered past. I knew that she was promised to one of the carpenters, but I did not care. As soon as I had seen her interest in me, I could not push her from my thoughts. Whenever I saw her, I puffed out my chest like a robin, and grinned. Just as my demeanour and inflated ego seemed to rankle the older men, my very disdain for them appeared to be what fanned the flames of Cwenswith's desire.

When she first followed me into one of the storage huts, I was as powerless to resist as if I had tried to halt the tides. I had never lain with a woman before, and when she caressed my skin, her tender touch made me tremble with excitement.

I wondered whether she had ever stroked Wistan like that.

As he looked back at me, for a heartbeat I saw a new emotion there in his dark eyes. Gone was the fury. It had been replaced by abject sorrow.

"Cut him, Hunlaf," Cwenswith screamed again, and the sound of her voice, breathless and filled with excitement, made me flinch. Such was the tone of her gasps when we had been locked together, as she clawed at my back and I grunted and thrust. Did the prospect of seeing Wistan's blood arouse her?

The crowd about us was hushed. Only Cwenswith made a

sound, shouting for me to kill her betrothed. All the talking had been done the day before. Gwawrddur and Hereward had made me offer weregild for my offence, but Wistan, also young, proud and foolish, had refused my silver. I spied Wistan's father, grim-faced and silent, like a man attending a funeral. His wife's face, gaunt and thin from a life of hard work, was tear-streaked.

I do not know how Cwenswith thought that day would end. Did she truly wish to see me kill the man she was intended to wed? Whatever she thought, the final betrayal of her taunting words snapped Wistan's head up. The day before, as he had raged at me, he had convinced himself that Cwenswith was innocent, that I had forced myself on her. The sadness in his eyes was burnt away now by his ire; his anger at me, and surely at Cwenswith too.

With a roar, Wistan leapt forward, swinging his sword clumsily overarm. There was great power in that swing. Years of hewing oak and ash, and the sudden realisation of Cwenswith's duplicity gave Wistan a terrible strength. If his blade had connected, it would have cleaved me from shoulder to navel. But he was no swordsman. So ponderous was his attack that I did not even need to raise my shield. I took two darting steps backwards, keeping my stance long and my balance low, as I had been taught.

With a great effort, Wistan managed to keep his sword under control, avoiding slicing into the gravelly earth at our feet. For a heartbeat he was leaning forward, his head, shoulders and neck exposed. I could have slain him then, but truly, I did not wish to take his life.

I waited for him to right himself. I do not know whether he understood that I had spared him. If he did, it made no difference to him. He bellowed and rushed at me again, this time scything his sword from my right. I twisted my body, catching his blade on my shield's rim, and deflecting it away.

He carried on forward, and again I could have killed him. Once more, I held back. His shield clattered against mine, the bosses clanging like anvil and hammer. Bracing myself, I shoved him back, hard. He was stronger than I, but unbalanced and untrained, so he staggered away.

"I do not wish to slay you," I hissed at him. "Drop your weapon. End this."

"There is only one way to end this now," he yelled. His face was pallid, his eyes glimmering in the bright early morning sun.

Unless he turned away from this course, he was right. I could not defend against him indefinitely. If I waited too long, his brawn and rage would overcome me at last. He was unarmoured, so I had not donned my byrnie. One strike from Wistan could easily prove fatal.

Springing at me again, he attempted a feint, but he signalled his intention with his eyes and his footwork, so my shield was there to parry the attack. This time, I flicked out my sword and opened up a gash on his side, beneath his shield.

I skipped away, seeing the pain reach his eyes.

Behind him, Runolf met my gaze. The huge Norseman was grinning, clearly enjoying the excitement of a duel, or hólmgang, as he called it. He had paced out and marked the fighting area with hazel stakes, smiling wolfishly all the while at the prospect of a fight. Beside Runolf, the shorter Gwawrddur was sombre. At my look, he shook his head. I saw the disappointment on the Welshman's features. There was no honour in defeating a foe who is not able to defend himself. The night before, Gwawrddur had told me to do all in my power to dissuade Wistan from fighting.

"I cannot flee, if he wants to fight," I had said.

"No, you cannot," he'd replied. His eyes were sad as he sipped his ale. "But when you laid with his girl, you surely knew this could happen."

I nodded. I had been flattered by Cwenswith's attentions, and of course I had enjoyed our fumbling, panting trysts in the store hut, but I had never thought our actions could lead to someone's death, and certainly not at my hand.

"What if he refuses to step aside?"

"Then you must answer for your actions, just as Wistan must answer for his."

Wistan now stood breathless before me. He looked down and seemed shocked to see the blood soaking through his kirtle. I had not cut him deeply, hoping the stinging pain would bring him to his senses.

At the sight of blood, someone in the crowd gasped.

Cwenswith screamed, "Finish him!"

Wistan's eyes narrowed at the shrill sound of her voice. His shoulders tensed and I knew he was preparing to attack once more.

"Don't," I said, but too late.

He ran at me, and I retreated. He beat his sword against my shield over and over until the hide covering was tatters and the linden wood splintered.

With a growl, I pushed him back. There was nothing for it. I could not dissuade him, and if I waited any longer, I would be the one to lose my life that day. I sprang forward, holding his blows away from me on my splintering shield and lunging beneath his guard. I felt my sword blade make contact. Wistan grunted and staggered.

The morning air was filled with the sudden screaming of women. The men quickly added their voices to the din. I recognised Runolf's booming voice over the clamour of the crowd, but I could not make out his words.

For a heartbeat, I was confused, but I remember it now, as vividly as if the events of that morning had occurred yesterday and not decades ago.

But wait, my aged mind is meandering like the great rivers

that flow out of the snow-capped Norse mountains. I have not yet told you of how we came to be there at the mouth of the Uuir. Before I recount more of what took place that early summer's day at Uuiremutha, and the darkness that came after, I must take you back to the winter before, when we were still at Werceworthe.

Three

After the battle for Werceworthe, there had been tears and wailing; grief for the dead and for what had been lost. For a long while, the land had reeked of the rotten corpses of the Norsemen, but as the sun came out in those last days of summer, the stink became too much and we summoned up the energy to bury our fallen enemies. And with that, as the air cleared of the stench of death, the rebuilding of the minster and the settlement began.

There was much to do. Most of the buildings had been destroyed by fire, so there was no time for anything more than the hard labour of construction. Several of the men had been killed in the defence of their homes, so all the survivors had to help, if they were to have shelter for everyone in time. Although the days were often warm, they all sensed the approach of winter, like an unseen wolf snuffling at the hall door at night.

Once again, having helped bring us victory in the battle against his kin and countrymen, Runolf proved his worth, overseeing the felling of trees and the splitting of the logs into manageable planks.

One afternoon, I found him staring along the river towards the sea. The sun was low in the sky, and the waters of the Cocueda were the colour of burnished bronze.

"Do you think more of your people will come?" I asked in his native Norse tongue.

"Not this year, I think." He spat into the wood shavings at his feet. "But anything is possible."

I snorted at his use of the phrase that so infuriated Drosten. Runolf did not smile. I could sense the tension in him. I shared it too. We both wanted to put to sea. Runolf longed to seek out his wife, Estrid. He had not put into words what his intentions were when they met again, but I did not believe Runolf to be a forgiving man. When I had tried to enquire of his past and his kin across the Whale Road, his face clouded, his jaw setting hard.

I too was desperate to search for my cousin, Aelfwyn. She had been taken by the sea wolves who had descended on Lindisfarnae before midsummer. There was also the matter of the strange book that brother Leofstan had become obsessed with. It was called *The Treasure of Life*. I had only seen the tome briefly, and had become enamoured of the jewel-encrusted cover and the meticulous artistry of the words and resplendent images on its parchment pages. Leofstan had spent a day and a night with the book, and he spoke of its contents in hushed tones of fear and awe. This was a work of heresy. Most men of the church would seek to destroy it, but Leofstan sought to study it. The destruction of such a thing would be as bad as heresy to him. I agreed with him then. I was bereft at the destruction of so many books in the conflagration of the scriptorium of Lindisfarnae. It was only later, after I had witnessed the darkness such teachings could unleash, that I would come to believe that perhaps some books are best consumed by purifying flames.

"As soon as we have roofs over their heads," I said, looking across the fields to the scattered buildings and half-finished frames, "we can begin work on the ship."

He hawked and spat again. In silence, we watched as the Pict, Drosten, stripped to the waist so that the whorls and swirls of his tattoos could be clearly seen on his sweat-slick muscled chest, carried a couple of long planks across his shoulder. I struggled with one such plank, but the Pict made two look effortless. I had wondered whether Drosten would head north into his homeland after the battle, but he made no effort to leave, instead throwing himself into the rebuilding of the houses, as willingly as he had stood in the shieldwall against the Norse.

Runolf gazed up at the sky, where a skein of geese flew over us, honking as their creaking wings bore them southward.

"If I do not start to build the ship soon," he said, "I will not finish in time for us to sail next summer."

"So long?" I was shocked. We had spoken little of Runolf's shipbuilding plans since his revelation in the smoke-wreathed aftermath of his brother, Skorri's, defeat. There had been too much to do, and for a time, we had little appetite to look to the future. But at such times when my thoughts had drifted to ideas of heading across the North Sea in search of Aelfwyn, I'd had a vague idea that it would be in the spring. It was a long time to wait, unknowing of her fate, but I told myself I had believed her to be dead. Surely whatever life she had as a thrall was better than death.

"Crafting a sea serpent is not like sowing crops, boy," Runolf growled. "I need timber, lots of it. Hundreds of rivets. Pine tar. And where do you think we are to find a sail and ropes?"

"We can sell what we took from Skorri's men."

Runolf sniffed.

"We will need the byrnies and the weapons for the men who will man the ship I build. And where do you think you will find the crew? And the men I will need to help me with the building?"

I frowned. I had promised I would find a crew, but it was becoming clear this would be no simple task.

"The Lord will provide," I answered. Picking up one of the heavy planks so that my journey was not wasted, I trudged away.

When I looked back, Runolf had not moved. His features were starkly lit by the setting sun, his golden-red hair and beard burning like fire against the ruddy glow of the molten sky. Standing there, unmoving, his bulk and height made him appear like a carved statue of one of his people's pagan gods.

For the next few days, as the nights grew ever longer, my mind turned over the problem, the way a song thrush twists and flicks a snail this way and that, to crack it open and feast on the soft flesh within its shell.

I was no longer a member of the brethren of Werceworthe. There was no sign now of the tonsure on my head, but at times I yearned to join the brothers when the sounds of their liturgies wafted from the newly constructed chapel. For years, my life had been governed by the different offices of the day, and I still found myself waking with the monks in the dead of night to celebrate Vigils. But I was a warrior now, and I would not turn back from the path I had chosen. Or that the Lord had chosen for me.

Gwawrddur, still sporting a bandage across his back and over his right shoulder, was not of much use to the builders, but he helped where possible, carrying nails and trenails, and passing hammers and axes to the workers with his left hand. The Welsh swordsman was a man of action and, like Runolf and me, he carried the burden of his frustrations with little grace. I had half-expected him to leave once he was well enough to travel, but, despite his desire to once more be able to test himself against an enemy, he knew he needed to recover fully before swinging a sword in battle again. Besides, perhaps he sensed that staying by my side would reap the most opportunities for him to challenge himself. If so, he was not wrong.

At the end of each long day, Gwawrddur took a seemingly perverse pleasure in continuing my training with sword and shield.

"Expand your stance," he snapped, rapping my shin with the long stick he carried for the purpose of helping me not to forget his lessons. "Come now, Killer," he said, "you can do better than that. I am still injured, and yet I am faster than you. Where is your youth?"

I practised the parry, feint and lunging attack he had explained to me once more, pushing my aching body to the extreme of its endurance. I had been lifting heavy beams of oak all day and every day before that, and my muscles screamed in protest at the lack of rest.

And yet I did not halt or complain. The flames of battle had burnt away my childish notions of glory. I had witnessed the truth of it, and knew that the instruction Gwawrddur provided might well keep me alive when next I was called to stand against an enemy.

I missed Cormac. The Hibernian had been a good sparring partner and a better friend. He was headstrong and foolish, but also brave and honourable, and I would have given anything then to have had him standing with me before Gwawrddur's piercing glower. Tears stung my eyes as I remembered Cormac. No matter how much I wished it, I would never again hear his musical voice, or clash blades with him as we vied to prove who was the better swordsman.

I cuffed the tears away. I would cry no more. I had shed enough tears for Cormac when we had laid him to rest. I was a warrior now, and men who lived and died by the blade did not weep like women.

Gwawrddur pushed me to exhaustion, but when I finally shrugged off my byrnie, wrapping myself in my cloak to sleep, my mind was full of thoughts that swirled like one of the vast murmurations of starlings that drifted over the moors, rising and falling; a living cloud. Sleep was slow to embrace me on those nights, and I wished Hereward was yet at Werceworthe. The Northumbrian warrior would have given me good counsel. Perhaps his lord, Uhtric of Bebbanburg, might have offered us help with the building and equipping of the ship. But Hereward had done what his lord had commanded of him when we defeated the Norse invaders and shortly afterwards, as soon as the rains subsided, he bade us farewell and rode northward in search of his master, and the war that still raged in Pictland.

I prayed that Hereward would be safe, and wondered at what drove such men to seek out battle. Such men, I thought grimly. Was I not one? Cormac's face came to me then, as sleep began to murmur and whisper at the edges of my mind. Just like Hereward and the rest of us, Cormac had never fled from danger. Instead, he had chosen to rush towards it. He had been rash and foolhardy, but his bravery could not be denied. And yet his impetuous nature had caused the most pressing problem that faced us. If Cormac had not burnt Skorri's ships, we might even now be planning to sail to the kingdoms of the Norse, rather than fretting over how to construct a seafaring vessel.

I had thought little of it at the time. I had been filled with the terror of impending battle and my almost certain death, and I had been in awe of Cormac's audacity. But lying in the darkness and fearing for the fate of my kinswoman far away across the Whale Road, I cursed Cormac's rashness. I understood now that he had destroyed something of incredible value: ships that would cost as much to build, or perhaps even more, than a king's great hall.

The next day I went about the now familiar daily routine, but all the while, my mind was elsewhere. I carried lumber until my back screamed for respite, and then, when the sun was close to its zenith, it was time to hoist one of the heavy wooden frames into place. This was always a delicate task, and a mistake could cost someone crushed fingers or worse. I was distracted, my thoughts churning like so much milk in my mind. And just as churned milk produces curds and eventually butter, so my ideas were tantalisingly close to solidifying. I was so lost in my concerns that at first I did not hear the shouts.

"Hunlaf! Be careful!"

It was the tall monk, Brother Eoten, who always supervised each building's construction. He was a giant of a man, but usually quiet and measured. So it was with some shock that I saw his face was flushed, the cords of sinew in his neck bulging.

Immediately, I realised what was amiss. I had not taken up the slack on the rope I was holding, leaving most of the considerable bulk of the timber for Eoten to bear. It was too heavy for any one man to hold aloft, even using the rope and pulley that Eoten had rigged for the purpose, and the tall monk was struggling. If the beam was dropped, the two men who stood beneath it, ready to guide it into place, might well be injured, and the frame of the building, a new house for Wulfwaru and Aethelwig, would surely be damaged.

"Sorry, Brother," I mumbled, quickly tugging on the rope to bear my portion of the weight.

Eoten replied with a grunt.

Moments later, the joints, expertly shaped with axe and plane, were guided into the slots cut for the purpose. The beam fell into place with a satisfying thud. At the same time, my tumbling thoughts settled.

I knew how to get the shipbuilders and crew we needed.

Four

"We must travel," I panted, breathless from running across the fields.

Runolf and Drosten both continued hammering with their wooden mallets, driving wedges further into the grain of the long trunk of oak.

"Careful," said Runolf, gesturing for me to stand back.

I stepped away through the sawdust and wood shavings, then stood, holding my knees while I caught my breath.

With a final strike of their mallets and a splintering, tearing sound, the trunk split along its length, neatly following the grain. The two halves fell away and rocked on their curved, bark-covered exteriors and then were still, resting in the dust and shaved remains of the trees that had preceded them.

"Travel?" asked Runolf, wiping sweat from his brow. "Where?"

"To Eoforwic. To see the king."

Runolf eyed me for a time.

"Why would he see us?" he asked at last.

"We have saved Werceworthe, and I have a proposition for him that will get us what we need for your ship."

That caught his attention.

"Lord Uhtric won't like it," he said with a frown.

"Uhtric is not here."

"No, but I am his man. I swore my eiðr to him. If your cunning mind has thought of a way for me to build my ship, I think Lord Uhtric would wish to hear it first."

I sighed. Now that I had my ideas clear, I wanted to rush south to Eoforwic and Æthelred, but Runolf was right. Uhtric had taken a chance sparing Runolf's life and bearing him to Eoforwic after the attack on Lindisfarnae. Runolf was his man, and if he was to build a ship, we would need to seek Uhtric's permission.

Drosten began chopping into one of the sides of split log, cutting grooves into the bark where he would later place the wooden wedges that would split it further, creating a plank.

"But Uhtric is in the north," I said. I was disappointed and frustrated. It has ever been thus with me. When I have an inclination to do something, I want nothing to stand in my way. Our Heavenly Father often has other plans. Perhaps it is His way of teaching me humility. Alas, in this I have been a poor student. "North is in the wrong direction," I went on, angry to be so quickly deviated from the course I had foreseen.

"It is not the wrong direction," replied Runolf, "if that is where we need to travel."

I shook my head in annoyance. I had been convinced that I had come to the right conclusion.

"We don't even know where he is. He could be anywhere in Pictland fighting Causantín. Hereward left weeks ago and we have heard nothing since."

"I know where he is," Drosten said in his gravelly burr. He stretched, pushing his meaty hands into the small of his back with a grunt.

Runolf and I both turned to look at the Pict. Drosten rarely spoke and it was easy to forget that he was listening to everything. He was quiet, but sharper than most men I have known. His speed of thought and muscular physique made him a formidable warrior.

"You do?" Runolf asked.

"Aye. Lord Uhtric. Hereward too."

"How?" I enquired. I wondered if he was jesting with us. I waited for him to begin laughing at our expense. But Drosten was seldom jovial and it seemed this was no jest.

"I spoke last night with Onuis."

It took me a moment to place the name.

"The pedlar who visited yesterday?"

"The same."

A wizened man had arrived just as the sun fell the day before. He had called for the ferry, and Copel had grumbled at having to leave his cup of mead. The pedlar looked as old as the hills, his legs as spindly as rush lights and his back bent. A burly brute with a neck as thick as a bull's had silently pushed a laden handcart behind the old man.

"He seemed a grumpy sort," I said. I had asked the old man after his health, and he had snarled at me like a dog. His massive servant had glowered beneath his heavy brows, and I had looked away. Travellers were usually a source of tidings. They were welcomed with hospitality, but this pair had appeared churlish and rude. They had been gone when I rose the following morning.

"Oh, Onuis is not a bad man," said Drosten. "He travels far that one. He doesn't like strangers though."

I thought it an unusual choice to travel widely selling your wares out of a cart for one who did not like to meet people, but I held my tongue.

"But you are no stranger to him?" I asked.

"No, no. Quite so. I have known him since I was a lad." This was a surprise to me and Drosten smiled at my expression, which unnerved me somewhat. His tattoos always gave him a monstrous aspect, and when he grinned, the impression was heightened. "We enjoyed a few cups of mead last night. He told me much of what goes on north of here. He spoke of the land of my people and how they fare against the Northumbrians. And he told me of Hereward and the lord of Bebbanburg."

"So where are they?" growled Runolf, clearly as frustrated with Drosten's rambling as I was.

"Oh," replied Drosten, raising an eyebrow at Runolf's terse tone. "They are at Bebbanburg."

"Uhtric has returned?" I asked.

"Yes, the fighting season is over. Causantín mac Fergusa has retreated to his stronghold at Duncalden and the Northumbrians have come back home."

Runolf clapped his hands and turned to me.

"Good. Tell us your plan, then."

So I told them, and the next morning, just after the dawn, we had Copel carry us and our mounts across the Cocueda, and we rode towards Bebbanburg.

Five

The great hall of Bebbanburg was dark and sombre. When I had last visited, I had been in awe of the rich decorations, the sumptuous, draped hangings, carved and painted columns, and the weapons, armour and standards of defeated foe-men that adorned every surface. It had been a place of warmth and lively noise. I was yet a monk then, living my days in silence. The destruction of Lindisfarnae was still fresh in my mind, and, despite the exhilaration I had felt to at last step foot in this famed hall, the feasting had seemed somehow obscene so soon after the murder of dozens of innocents on the holy island that could be seen from the ramparts of the fortress.

There was no laughter in the hall now. It was as quiet and still as a barrow.

The hazy gloom was punctuated by candles, and a large metal bowl on a tripod near the central hearth fire belched out sweet-smelling smoke. I sniffed the air, as the steward ushered us in. The incense that smouldered in the bowl almost covered the stench of decay and death that hung thick and pungent in the hall.

Almost.

I glanced at Drosten. He shook his head. The message was clear. Onuis had mentioned nothing of this.

"He is very weak," whispered Hereward. He had entered the hall with us and now led us past the censer and the fire crackling on the hearth stone, despite the warmth of the day outside. "We should not tarry long."

Hereward had met the four of us in the courtyard. He had seemed pleased to see us, but his eyes were dark and his expression pinched. He had offered us a warning about the lord of Bebbanburg's injury. It seemed he had taken a small wound in their final confrontation with the Picts. They had thought nothing of it. The wound had been bound and, at first, Uhtric continued with his usual verve and energy. But soon, the cut became inflamed, painfully red and swollen.

"Elf-shot," Hereward had said, his tone hushed and bleak.

I had made the sign of the cross. Drosten, Gwawrddur and Runolf said nothing, but their expressions were grave. We all knew that an infected wound often led to death.

Despite Hereward's warning, I had naively thought it could not be so bad. Surely Uhtric would not be slain by an infected scratch. But as we walked slowly towards the shadowed far end of the hall and the stink of corrupted flesh grew stronger, I made the sign of the cross again and offered up a silent prayer for the lord of Bebbanburg.

"He is dying?" I hissed, my voice louder in the gloom than I had anticipated.

"Hush," growled Hereward.

Runolf, Gwawrddur and Drosten were silent.

"Of course I am dying," came a rasping voice from the shadows. From the flickering tongues of the candles' flame, I made out Uhtric, skin sallow and sweat-sheened, propped up in a bed that had been placed where the high table had stood on my last visit. Beside him sat a woman. Her eyes glistened, the candlelight limning her austere beauty. Despite the dancing shadows and dim illumination, there was no hiding the pain and exhaustion on her slender face.

Uhtric shook his head. “You never could keep your thoughts to yourself.” He began to chuckle, but the laughter quickly became a cough. The woman leaned forward, clutching his hand and patting him gently on the back. She whispered soothing words I could not hear.

When the coughing subsided, Uhtric met my gaze. His eyes were bright, liquid and febrile. “You’re a clever one, Hunlaf. I don’t suppose you have brought me a cure for what ails me.”

My throat was dry. I swallowed, but could find no words. Slowly, I shook my head.

Uhtric snorted, as if amused by my reaction.

“Leave us now, my dear,” he said to the woman.

“You must not tire yourself,” she said.

“I can think of nothing better to do with my time,” he said, an edge of sarcasm in his tone. “It is not as if I have anywhere else to go. Not until the Almighty deems it to be my time.”

Abruptly, the lady stood. Her body was rigid, her anger apparent as she looked at us.

“My husband needs his rest. Do not tarry.”

Uhtric reached for her hand. She allowed him to grasp it for a second, and then she pulled away and strode from the hall.

As her footsteps retreated, Uhtric surveyed us all. He offered a curt nod to Runolf, and sized up Gwawrddur with a glance. Spying Drosten, with his blue-painted cheeks and oiled plaited hair, Uhtric frowned.

“What’s this? You bring my enemy to see me laid low? Is this how you fulfil your oath to me, Runolf? By bringing a Pict to gloat over me as I waste away?”

“I am not your enemy, Lord Uhtric,” said Drosten, his thickly accented voice low and respectful.

“Both Gwawrddur and Drosten, here, fought with us at Werceworthe,” said Hereward. “They are brave men. They risked everything to protect the minster.”

Uhtric glared at Drosten for a few heartbeats, then allowed

himself to fall back into his pillows, as if being angry had exhausted him.

"Well," he said at last, "if you have not come to heal me, or to watch me die, what do you want?"

Runolf turned to me. Again, I swallowed. My mouth was so dry, I was sure that my voice would crack. I looked about for something to drink. There was an earthenware jug on a small table beside Uhtric's bed. I thought it might contain water, and I looked at it longingly. But there was only one cup, and even if I had been bold enough to request a drink, the thought of sipping from the same cup as the dying lord turned my stomach. Here, this close to the injured man, the incense did little to disguise the odour of his putrefying wound. The cloying stink of rot was thick in the warm air. I could barely imagine how the lady of the hall could stay by his side without gagging.

I wished we had not come here. If only I could have convinced the others to head directly towards Eoforwic, I could have avoided witnessing the ignoble end of this lord of Northumbria.

"Well, do not tarry," Uhtric said, a twisted smile on his emaciated lips. "As my good wife said, I am tired, and, as is apparent to us all, even to her, bless her, I do not have time to waste."

Hereward nodded and Runolf pushed me forward. I scowled at him, before turning to Uhtric.

"As you know, lord," I said. My voice broke as I had feared it would, and I cleared my throat before continuing. "As you know, we defeated the Norse who attacked Werceworthe, thus saving many lives and valuable treasures of the minster." I thought of the great trench we had filled with the dead and realised with a stomach-twisting shock, that the smell permeating the hall reminded me of the miasma that had hung over the bloated corpses. Uhtric was staring at me, but he said nothing, so I went on. "What you may not know is that we wish to travel whence the Norsemen came. To the land of Rygjafylki, across the North Sea."

"Why?" Sensing this might be Runolf's doing, Uhtric's eyes flicked away from me and towards the Norseman. "Do you wish to return to your home, Runolf?"

"That is not the reason, lord," Runolf said.

"Then what is it?"

"The jarl who led his ships to Lindisfarnae and Werceworthe was my brother."

Uhtric waved a thin hand.

"Yes, yes. Hereward told me as much. But you killed him, did you not?"

Runolf's face clouded. Perhaps he was remembering fighting his brother; severing his head and holding it aloft, wide-eyed and gore-dribbling, to show the Norsemen that their leader had been defeated.

"I did. But I also learnt of my wife's treachery."

"She yet lives?"

"As far as I know."

"And you would have revenge on the wench?"

Runolf hesitated, and again I wondered what thoughts swarmed in his mind.

"I would look her in the eye. Perhaps then I would understand."

Uhtric sighed. Grimacing, he closed his eyes, as if a sudden pain gripped him. After a time, he reached for the cup at his side. Hereward stepped forward quickly, filling the vessel from the jug and handing it to his lord. Uhtric took a deep draught of the liquid and shuddered.

"If this wound doesn't kill me soon, this God-accursed potion will," he said, setting aside the cup with trembling hand. I was glad I had not asked for a drink. "I can understand the desire for revenge," he continued, "but I do not see why this interests me."

"There is more," I said.

"Go on, young Hunlaf."

"Along with many others from Lindisfarnae, my cousin, Aelfwyn, was taken as a thrall by the raiders. Before Runolf's brother died, he told us where Aelfwyn was. I would bring her back to safety."

Uhtric nodded slowly, carefully, as if his skull weighed more than normal.

"This is a laudable plan," he said, "though I am sure not as simple as you make it sound. However, you do not need my blessing to undertake such a daring quest. You are not oath-sworn to me. Rather you were a member of the clergy, so you should seek out the permission of Bishop Hygebald."

"I am a monk no longer," I replied. "I have left the brethren."

Uhtric raised an eyebrow.

"Even so, how you choose to lead your life is not my concern."

"There is also a book."

"A book?" Uhtric asked, confused at the sudden shift in the conversation.

I thought of the heretical text of *The Treasure of Life*, and its gem-studded, ornately decorated cover. Uhtric would have little or no interest in the contents of the vellum pages.

"The Norsemen stole many artefacts from the holy isle," I went on. "Gold, silver and some books that are worth a king's hoard. Beyond price, really."

At the mention of treasure, Uhtric's focus sharpened and he sat up straighter.

"And?"

"We wish to recover what treasure we can from those who stole it."

Uhtric shook his head and sighed.

"You will never find that treasure. It will have been melted down, or sold to merchants from other lands, or buried." He delicately shook his head again. "This is folly."

Runolf looked down at the rushes on the floor. He was not a man to easily admit defeat, but I could see in the slump of his shoulders that he feared we were no closer to being able to build his ship than we had been when we left Werceworthe. I could feel the weight of Hereward, Gwawrddur and Drosten's gaze on me, but I did not look away from Uhtric.

"Perhaps you are right," I said. "But there is more that we had hoped to offer King Æthelred beyond treasure."

"You wish to speak to the king?"

"With your consent, and in your name, of course," I replied. "I believe that we can achieve what we want and also bring more power, wealth and even stability to the kingdom." Uhtric was an ambitious man and despite his sickness and the pain that racked him, he leaned forward, grasping the timber frame of his bed.

"And how is it that you propose to achieve this?"

"In return for men and materials to build a ship, we will—"

"A ship, you say?" Uhtric interrupted me. "You wish to build a ship?"

"Yes. Runolf is a great shipwright. He will build us a wave-steed to carry us across the Whale Road."

"There are ships in Northumbria," replied Uhtric. "Why spend months building a new ship when there are vessels already in Berewic, Gyruum, Hereteu," he waved his hand weakly, "all along the coast? By Christ's teeth, I even have a boat that would serve here, in the bay. You could be aboard it tomorrow."

Runolf raised himself up to his considerable height. He was taller than all of us and towered over the bed-bound Uhtric.

"The boats you speak of are not fit to ride the waves of the Northern seas," Runolf gnarled. "They are like wallowing mules. I will build you a stallion, such as no man of Northumbria has ever sailed in before."

Uhtric stared at him a while, before nodding.

"But to build such a ship will be costly. I do not have such quantities of silver to pay enough men for such an endeavour."

"I imagine the king does," I interjected.

"I am sure Æthelred could finance such a venture," said Uhtric. "But why would he want to? I do not believe the king would care for your cousin, your wife," he looked at Runolf, "or stolen books."

"Perhaps not, but he must care about his kingdom. Runolf will teach the carpenters and shipwrights of Northumbria the secrets of the dragon ships of his people. No longer would we need to face the Norsemen at a disadvantage. We could build ships to rival theirs. Northumbrian warriors could patrol the coasts in sea serpents, ready to confront any ship that approaches our shores. Perhaps the king might even wish to send his own ships to raid his enemies, just as we have been raided." I left that idea hanging in the air. I could see that Uhtric was thinking hard. He nodded slowly, appreciatively, at my words. He could see that Æthelred might well accept this plan.

"And I have not told you the final, most important part yet..."

Uhtric listened intently as I laid out the reason I believed the king of Northumbria would agree to my terms. When I had finished, he settled back with a groan. He held out his hand and Hereward poured him more of the stuff from the jug. Uhtric sipped and grimaced.

"You are a clever one, that's for certain," he said. "Very well. You have my leave to travel to the king with this proposal."

My heart leapt. I flashed a glance at Runolf. The huge Norseman stared back at me, his thin smile hidden behind his thick beard. Drosten and Gwawrddur both looked shocked. Uhtric held up a hand, drawing our attention back to him.

"I have one condition," he said.

"Yes, lord," I replied, fearing what he would ask.

"I truly believe that you will do this thing you speak of. Runolf here will build his ship, and you will sail far away." He put his cup down, staring into the flame of the candle that guttered on the table. "Oh, what I would give to see the things you will see. But the Lord will take me soon. I will never again leave Bebbanburg. I will not see Crístesmæsse." When he said these things, his gaze drifted. Tears brimmed in his eyes. As I watched him then, the darkness of the hall threatening to engulf us, all I could think about was that he had granted us leave to petition the king. I hung on the words he spoke, hoping he would say nothing that would hinder our plan. Now, looking back through the mists of memory, I feel great sorrow for Uhtric. He was a much younger man than I am now, and an unlucky scratch would soon cost him his life. And lying there in his stench and agony, he knew it. We all live with the certainty of our own mortality, but it is only when Death breathes on the nape of your neck, that the true horror of it, the impending limitless darkness that yawns before you, becomes solid and true. Then, it is all we can do to meet our creator with dignity.

Uhtric pulled his gaze away from the flame and stared directly into my eyes. His eyes were blue, his pupils tiny, like pinpricks in silk.

"You must make me a promise. Upon my death, you will be free of your oath to me, Runolf. But if you succeed, as I believe you will, you must give me your word that half of the treasure you glean for yourselves on your adventures, you will bring back here."

"Here?" asked Runolf.

"To Bebbanburg. My son, Uhtred, will be lord then. And after him, his son, and I would have my kin gain riches from this venture." He let out a shuddering breath that caused the candle flame by his bed to flicker. "There is nothing more important than kin."

I thought of my brother, Beornnoth, and my father at Ubbanford. I was in no hurry to see them again. But they were kin. Then I imagined Aelfwyn, far across the sea, frightened and alone. Perhaps she was suffering, maybe she was even dead. Runolf's brow furrowed, and I was sure he too was thinking of his kin. The wife who had left him, the brother he had slain.

"You have my word, lord Uhtric," said Runolf at last. He reached out his massive hand and clasped Uhtric's forearm in the warrior grip. They met each other's gaze for a few heartbeats, before Uhtric released his grip and lay back.

"Hereward," he said, his eyelids beginning to droop. "You are to go with them."

"Lord?" Hereward sounded shocked. "My place is at your side."

"Your place is where I say it is," snapped Uhtric, the force of his will adding strength to his voice. "There is nothing for you to do here. I would have you keep an eye on my interests. Besides," he went on, his voice lowering to little more than a whisper, "you only live once. Never turn your back on adventure, for your tomorrow will come too soon."

I recall Uhtric's words now and they speak to me through the years since his death. I do not know if Hereward was glad of his lord's command to join us, but it seems to me all of us listened, and each in his way sought to obey the lord of Bebbanburg's dying wish. That somehow, by heading into the unknown and always facing the dangers we met, we were honouring him.

Hereward knelt by Uhtric's side and his lord placed a pale hand on the warrior's bowed head.

"Godspeed," Uhtric said with a sigh. "Leave me now. I am weary and would sleep. Perhaps I will dream of your ship and the adventures that await you."

As we walked away, leaving Uhtric to the darkness and his dreams, Runolf cuffed at his cheeks. When I cast a look at Hereward, there were tears streaming down his face.

As we stepped through the carved double doors and stood blinking in the light of day, the lady of the hall brushed past us, hurrying to her husband's side once more. None of us said a word, nor met her gaze.

Six

"And if I help you to get this ship built, you say you can broker an agreement with Runolf's people?" King Æthelred's eyes narrowed as he stared at the three of us standing before him in the great hall of Eoforwic.

Runolf, his bulk, height and fiery red hair making him stand out from everyone else in the building, was to my right, Hereward, sombre and subdued in the presence of the king, stood silently on my left. We had thought it best not to bring Drosten and Gwawrddur to the audience. Æthelred's suspicious nature was infamous and we had reasoned that it would not help our cause to have a Pict and a Welshman amongst our number. Looking at the king now, seated on his grand oaken chair, clutching the elaborately carved arms, and leaning forward like a heron about to strike an unsuspecting fish, I was sure we had made the right decision. Only months had gone by since I had last seen Æthelred, but he seemed older, his hair more streaked with silver, his face gaunter, his eyes more full of suspicion.

After making us wait for an audience for the best part of a day, we had told him of our visit to Bebbanburg and Uhtric's support of my plan. Outside the hall, a cold autumn rain fell on Eoforwic. The hissing roar of the downpour had been a constant sound for days. We were dry now, having been allowed to warm ourselves at a fire in one of the small buildings that dotted the royal enclosure. Thralls had brought us warmed ale and some good, rich pottage. We were glad of the food and warmth, but what we most looked forward to was a dry bed and a good night's sleep.

As we had ridden southward, the rain had followed us. Clouds had formed far out over the grey North Sea, the air beneath them streaked and smudged with the driving rain. As the rain reached us and quickly drenched our cloaks, I'd look over at Hereward. The water slicked his face and I remembered his tears. As our horses carried us south, leaving the fortress of Bebbanburg behind to sit silent sentinel over the Whale Road, we all knew we would never see Uhtric again. Hereward was at first sullen and angry, but as we travelled further from Bebbanburg, so his spirits seemed to lift. We were wet and cold, but it was as if the darkness and sickness of the hall had infected his soul, and as he rode through the daylight and the downpour, his sour mood was washed away.

I thought then that Uhtric had done Hereward a great service. The warrior who had led us to victory at Werceworthe was prone to brooding. To sit and watch his lord die would have been a terrible torture for one such as he. To be active, in command of men, with adventure and the unknown ahead of them, this was a gift for Hereward. Neither gold nor silver would have been of as much value to Hereward as this final gift from his lord.

And yet, as Hereward's humour had improved, the closer we had got to Eoforwic and the king, the more nervous I had become. Æthelred was not a man to suffer fools and there were always rumours of the intrigues and murders amongst his retinue. If there was any truth to what was whispered about him throughout the realm, the king would think nothing of having us all slain, if my words did not please him, or if he suspected some insult or attack on his power.

I swallowed back my fear. I was a warrior now. I had killed men and should not be afraid to speak before any man. Even a king.

"Yes, lord king," I said, fighting to keep the tremor from my voice. I spoke in the soft and even tone of one speaking to a skittish animal that might at any moment turn on me and sink its fangs into my flesh. "With your blessing, Runolf would build the ship, teaching others to do the same, and then we would sail to Rygjafylki to agree terms of peace and trade with the people there."

"And you wish to do this in my name."

I nodded, though it was not a question.

The king tilted his head, as if he had heard something far off, though I could hear nothing but the thrumming of the rain.

"And why would I back such an endeavour?" he asked.

"I believe such a pact would bring Northumbria peace and wealth."

Æthelred licked his lips at the mention of riches. His avarice and ambition were as well-known as his violence and volatility.

"You do, do you, Hunlaf of Werceworthe? How so? You think Causantín will declare a truce with me?" Some of the men seated around the king laughed. "Why would the Picts care for what these Norsemen agree or do not agree?"

My mouth was parched and I clenched my fists at my sides to avoid trembling. I cleared my throat. The faces of the counsellors and advisors who sat beside the king stared back implacably. Some seemed bored, others vaguely amused. One man, whom I recognised as Daegmund, the priest who had baptised Runolf, sneered at me. What was I doing here? I had been so full of certainty in my plan, but despite my newfound self-assurance that came from bearing a sword and having survived my first battle, I was but a young man. Nobody of import. No matter how much I told myself I should not be afraid, I could feel fear welling within me. The last time Æthelred had spoken to me, I had been a novice monk. Why should he listen to me?

I felt foolish for believing I could convince the king of this course of action. But a small, prideful voice inside whispered that I had persuaded him once before. And I had been proven right. My actions had saved Werceworthe, and the king was no fool. He knew as much.

"I fear it is beyond me to gain peace with the Picts, lord king." I forced my fear down and smiled. After a heartbeat, Æthelred grinned back, and I released my pent breath. "But the Norsemen have attacked your coastline twice this year alone. We have shown that we can beat them, but once the foxes have a taste for the hens, they will always return."

"And with the ships Runolf can build, we can better defend our kingdom from these Norse foxes?"

"Yes," said Runolf, his voice rumbling in the hall like distant thunder. "My ships will make your people into wolves. And with such wave-riders as I can build, you will be able to raid your enemies too."

Æthelred's eyes gleamed, and I could see him warming to the idea. Every king wishes to have the ability to keep his people safe, but more than that, he wants to possess the means of inflicting pain on his enemies, and, perhaps most of all, to accumulate more treasure and power.

I met the king's burning gaze, blowing air onto the flames with my words.

"It is as Runolf says. We have seen with our own eyes the devastation that just a handful of these dragon ships can bring to our shores. People said that perhaps it was the Almighty who sent the Norse to attack the minsters." Æthelred frowned, his face clouding. Many had blamed the sins of the king for the attacks on his shores and the slaughter of the men and women of Christ. I carried on quickly. "Who can say what is true? But I say that it was surely God who sent us Runolf. His knowledge and battle-skill helped us to save the minster of Werceworthe, and now his skill in the construction of ships will help us once more. Northumbria will be the only kingdom in Britain with such dragon ships, and, if you permit us to sail to Rygjafylki, that we might broker a deal with the king there, yours will be the only kingdom whose coastline will not be harried." The king had begun to nod slowly, the spark of interest returning to his eyes. I pressed on, hammering home my points. "Lord king, with this decision you will profit from the power of these new ships, peace with the Norsemen, and new trade that would bring riches to your coffers."

Æthelred sat up straight in his ornate chair. He stroked his long moustache and looked from me to Runolf. Beside the king, some of the ealdormen had begun to whisper, perhaps at my audacity for speaking to the king so forthrightly.

"Would it work?" Æthelred asked of Runolf.

The Norseman shrugged.

"Anything is possible," he said, and I had the urge to slap him. This was a delicate moment and not the time for his frequently uttered flippant comment. "My countrymen are great warriors," Runolf went on, his accent strange, but his Englisc clear enough. "I have told you before that they will take what is easily taken, like the fox with the hen, or the wolf with the sheep." The king glowered at the Norseman. I tensed, concerned that Runolf would snuff out the interest I had fanned. But I needn't have worried. "But a good shepherd has a brave dog to keep the wolves away," he continued. "And the men of Rygjafylki are no fools. Like the wolf, they will seek the easiest prey. If they see that you have ships as fast as theirs, and men willing to stand and fight, they will think twice about attacking your land. Like most men, they seek fortune and gold more than battle-fame. If you go to the king of my people and offer to trade silver, wool and woad in exchange for furs, iron and slaves, I think he would agree." He scratched at his thatch of beard and I nodded, pleased he had remembered the items we had discussed.

"Trade rather than raids, then?" said the king.

Runolf hesitated, perhaps confused by Æthelred's words. But after a few heartbeats, he gave a curt nod of his shaggy head.

"Anything is possible. I see no reason why he would not agree to such terms. Both kingdoms would be strengthened without more blood." Runolf grinned, his teeth bright in the dim light of the hall. "Besides, there are many other kingdoms ripe for raiding."

Æthelred stared at Runolf. The whispers from the seated men grew in volume. Runolf, seemingly oblivious to the effect his words had on the men, continued, enumerating the lands his people could savage instead of Northumbria.

"The islands of the north, the soft southern kingdoms of Britain, Hibernia, even Frankia." If the Norse truly considered attacking all of those kingdoms, the scope and casual nature of their ambition was staggering. At the mention of Cormac's homeland, Hibernia, I recalled my dead friend's tale of the murder of his family at the hands of Norse raiders, and his outrage at our trust in Runolf. Seeing the glint in Runolf's eye as he spoke of raiding, it was easy to picture him, axe in hand, leaping over the side of a sleek ship and rushing up the beach at the head of a pack of sea wolves. Did the men in the hall see him that way, I wondered? Could they imagine the man I had witnessed standing against his own kin and countrymen to protect two defenceless children at Lindisfarnae? How was one so accustomed to slaughter and rapine, capable of risking his life for the people of another land? I understand now, that like all men, Runolf was both light and darkness, good and evil. I am pleased that he considered me his friend and chose to show me the lighter side of his nature. Few survived an encounter with the darkness within Runolf.

The murmuring of the king's advisors had risen to a hubbub.

"Surely you are not considering what these men propose," shouted out one jowly man with grey whiskers and a bulbous nose. "Your forces are already spread too thinly across the marches of Pictland in the north, and Mercia in the south."

"It seems to me," replied the king, "that it would not prove too costly to at least see this plan put into motion. Just enough to pay some fisher folk to help with the shipbuilding, and of course, timber for the ship. They are not asking for warriors."

"We would need iron for rivets too," rumbled Runolf. "And a smith."

"You see, lord?" said the old man. "The cost is already mounting."

Æthelred waved a hand, as if these were trivial considerations. "Yes, yes. But these are mere details."

"We will need good rope too—" I silenced Runolf by gripping his arm. He looked down at me and I offered him a small shake of my head. Now was not the moment to list all that we would require.

"No vision this time?" enquired Daegmund. His voice, dripping with sarcasm, but accustomed to preaching before the faithful in the church of Saint Peter's, carried easily over the buzz of conversation.

The king turned to the priest.

"What are you prattling about, Daegmund?"

Even before the priest replied, I knew the meaning of his words. He questioned the truth behind the vision I had claimed to have had when last I had petitioned the king in this very hall. I had spoken of seeing Runolf scything down the king's enemies, a white dove flying over his head. It was perhaps this vision that had persuaded Æthelred not to kill Runolf. Daegmund had been forced to baptise the Norseman, but the priest had made no secret of disliking and distrusting him. And he had not liked the fact that I, a mere novice monk, had turned the king to my will over his.

"Why, lord king," scoffed Daegmund, "don't you remember young Hunlaf's God-sent dream of this heathen defending the minster?"

I glared at the priest and felt a stab of guilt, as I remembered embellishing what I had seen. Runolf growled deep in his throat, scowling and taking a step forward. Daegmund shuffled his chair back, as if expecting the Norseman to attack.

"But he is a heathen no longer," said the king, his tone jovial. "Isn't that right? You yourself baptised the man."

Undaunted, Daegmund tried a new tack.

"Neither, it would seem, is Hunlaf still a monk. Perhaps he has apostatised from the one true path."

"What are you saying, man?" asked Æthelred, his smile slipping.

"Young Hunlaf here, came before you in the summer a monk. Now he bears a sword. Perchance he has lost his faith and is now governed by more venal desires."

"Do you believe only monks and priests can have faith, Daegmund?" said the king, his tone as cold and sharp as broken ice. "For I am neither. Do you think I am no Christ follower?"

"No... no... of course not, my lord," stammered the priest. "That would be a foolish thing to believe."

"Foolish indeed to doubt one's king, I would say," snapped Æthelred. "Isn't that so?"

Daegmund swallowed, his throat bobbing, his sudden fear a reminder of the dangers of crossing the king. Æthelred fixed him with his gaze and did not seem inclined to look away.

"I meant no disrespect, lord king," said Daegmund at last,

in a small voice. His lips trembled and for a moment I thought the man might weep.

"Besides," said Æthelred, turning away from the priest, "why cast doubt on Hunlaf's vision? It was proven right. They slaughtered the Norsemen, just as he said they would. Besides, I find a man with a keen mind and a sharp sword of much more use than a priest or monk. The clergy are fine if I want to pray, but most problems can be solved with a blade and quick wit." He chuckled. "And silver, of course. Which brings us back to your request." The king halted then, turning to face Daegmund. "Unless, of course, His Divine Worship has any objections to me making a decision on this matter?"

Daegmund's face grew scarlet, but he shook his head.

"Of course not, lord," he managed in a strangled voice.

"Good," said the king, clapping his hands together. "Then it is my wish that Runolf Ragnarsson be given what he needs to build his ship, that he teaches men in the craft, men who are loyal to me. And once the ship is built and seaworthy, it is my desire that Hunlaf of Werceworthe form a crew from such men as would be able and willing to sail the vessel, and together with Hereward, man of Uhtric, Lord of Bebbanburg, they travel in my name to the king of this land whose name I cannot pronounce." Æthelred paused and there was a dutiful smattering of laughter. I noted that Daegmund did not join in. "And once in that land," the king continued, "he will agree a treaty of trade and mutual peace and benefit betwixt our two kingdoms."

The men around the king erupted in outrage at the sudden pronouncement. I turned to Hereward, who looked as shocked as everyone else by the king's decision. Runolf slapped me on the back, making me stagger.

"Remember," he said, "we need ropes, sails, pitch, iron. And tools, too." He was grinning. "There is much to do."

"Not now," I hissed. I could scarcely believe what had happened, but I was already tallying up things we would need and trying to plan how we would achieve our aims at Werceworthe.

"My lord king," a voice shouted over the tumult.

Gradually, the men fell silent and we all turned to face the speaker. It was a sour-faced man in a drab kirtle. Unlike the other men, this man had no finery. The cloth of his garments was dark and simple, and the clasp for his grey cloak was dull bronze, not the glistening gold of those worn by his fellow counsellors, even Daegmund the priest.

"Lord Mancas?" Æthelred spoke the name with a raised eyebrow. "You wish to speak?"

"Indeed, my lord," Mancas said, standing and fastidiously smoothing down the wool of his kirtle where it was wrinkled.

Æthelred nodded, giving him leave to address the hall.

"Thank you, my lord king. You are most wise in having chosen this course of action." Æthelred smiled at the man's obvious flattery. "The cost to the royal purse will be quite small, and the possible benefits great. And, as you have reminded us, Hunlaf and Runolf have already proven themselves trusty servants. However, whilst I do not believe Daegmund expressed himself as well as he might have, I too have some reservations about this plan."

The priest was staring intently at Mancas, his expression unreadable.

"Indeed?" said the king. "Please explain."

Mancas cleared his throat, holding up a slender hand to his mouth.

"As there is much at stake, it is my belief that you should appoint someone, someone who you trust, who is beyond reproach, to first oversee the preparations of this ship, to ensure that your generosity is not abused."

"And secondly?"

"Secondly," Mancas went on, "they should act as your ambassador to the king of this land across the North Sea. Such a delicate mission, must not be left in the hands of one as young as Hunlaf, quick-witted as he undoubtedly is."

"Hereward will be with us too," I said, hoping that this might stave off this new proposal. "He is Lord Uhtric's man."

"Yes, and a fine warrior he is, I am sure," replied Mancas. "But this is not a job for a warrior. It is a task for a leader, a wise man who can think quickly. Someone who is adept at sparring with words, not swords. And, while Hereward is a good man, loyal and true, it is not his lord of Bebbanburg, Uhtric, who will pay for this endeavour. It is our lord King Æthelred, and therefore it should be one of the king's own men who governs."

Æthelred was nodding, and my heart sank.

"You are wise indeed, Lord Mancas," he said. "Do you have a candidate for this most important of roles?"

Mancas picked at an invisible mote of dust on his sleeve.

"Indeed I do, my lord. My son, Gersine, would be perfect for the task. He possesses all of the traits required."

"Ah, but Mancas, Gersine is not much older than Hunlaf here."

"Yes, but—"

"Gersine is a good lad," the king said, still nodding, a broad smile on his lips, "and he may have inherited much from you in the way of intelligence, but there is certainly something that he cannot have attained at such a young age."

"What is that, lord king?"

"Your experience," replied Æthelred. "The experience that guides your judgement and wisdom that I so value and you have so eloquently reminded me of. No, your son will not do for this task."

"Who do you suggest then, my king?" asked Mancas, the confidence of his tone ebbing away.

"Why, the answer is obvious, is it not? You, Lord Mancas. You will oversee the ship's construction, and be my ambassador to the heathens across the sea."

Seven

"Get a good night's sleep," Hereward said, looking at each of us in turn in the warm glow of the fire, "for this rain does not look set to halt any time soon and we have far to travel on the morrow." Outside, the rain continued to fall without pause. Every so often, a gust of wind shook the building, rattling flakes of soot from the beams and forcing water under the eaves, to drip down the northernmost wall that was most exposed to the prevailing wind. We had been provided lodging in a small hall within the royal enclosure and, having secured the king's agreement to the plan, we were anxious to head back to Werceworthe. We had sent for Drosten and Gwawrddur, and they had arrived not long before, wet and bedraggled from hurrying through the rain-sodden streets of Eoforwic, but flushed and exuberant from having spent a large portion of the day drinking ale.

The two men shook out their cloaks, draping them over a bench to dry, and stretched out their feet to the fire. The stink of the street wafted from the drying filth that caked their shoes and spattered their leg wraps.

"We will have time for sleep later," said Runolf. "First we drink!"

Drosten belched and laughed.

"And eat," he said.

"Yes," Runolf said, "we need meat and ale. Or maybe fine mead. We must celebrate our victory." He turned to me with a grin. "Can your silvered tongue get us what we desire?"

I smiled. Then, when I realised he was serious, I stood up with a resigned sigh. I had been pleased that my words had persuaded the king, but it seemed there was a price to pay that came from being chosen as the speaker of the group.

"I'll see what I can do," I said, "but you'll regret it in the morning."

"The only thing I will regret is having wasted the day waiting for the king to see us when I could have been drinking with Gwawrddur and Drosten." Runolf chuckled. "I have much drinking to do to catch up. But it is a challenge I accept!"

"It is no race," said Gwawrddur.

"That is good," replied Runolf, his grin broadening. "For if it was, you would lose, and we all know how you hate losing."

I left them to their banter and moved to the door of the hall, grabbing my drying cloak from where it hung near the fire. I planned to go in search of a servant or thrall who could bring us provender and drink, but before I could pull on the door, it swung open. Cool air and splatters of rain buffeted me. Surprised, I stepped back, my hand dropping instinctively to the seax I wore on my belt.

There, in the torrential rain, stood Lord Mancas. Behind him, were three hooded figures.

"I took the liberty of bringing food and some good ale," Mancas said. "Come on. Out of the way, young man. The ale will get watered down from all this rain."

Bemused at the sudden appearance and the lord's commanding tone, I stood aside. Mancas entered the hall, followed by the cloaked men, who, it seemed, were servants. One carried a large joint of ham, along with a round of pungent cheese. The second bore a tray piled with trenchers of hard bread. The third man laboured under the weight of a tray, upon which were balanced several brimming jugs and a stack of wooden cups.

At the sight of the dark-garbed lord, whose sombre face seemed to wear a constant, disapproving scowl, all merriment ceased. Everyone turned to stare at the newcomer, their expressions ranging from Gwawrddur's apparent disinterest, to Runolf's open disdain. We had spoken little of Mancas and his new role, but Runolf had made it very clear he had no time for his kind.

"He speaks like a woman," he'd said, emulating the delicate manner in which Mancas had covered his mouth when coughing. "We need strong men to build the ship, not rich lords who seek to control us."

"We are all controlled by lords," I'd said. "Without them, we would not be able to build your ship. We came here for the king's support. He has given it to us. If taking this Mancas with us is part of the bargain, so be it. Strength alone will not get us very far."

It had taken me some time to find my place within this small band of warriors and I was not overjoyed at having Mancas' involvement forced upon us, perhaps unsettling the delicate balance. But I could see no way out of it. It seemed that when it came to matters of dealing with men of worth, I had become the mouth of the group, and in my pride I had enjoyed the attention and the chance to show my value beyond my skill with a sword, which admittedly was still lacking when compared to the others, all of whom had much more experience than I. With the presence of Lord Mancas, I could easily imagine my importance to the others would dwindle.

The servants placed the food and drink on the table at the side of the room. One of them began to slice the food, while another set out the cups and jugs.

"That was fast indeed, Hunlaf," shouted Drosten, his

voice loud with drink, his Pictish accent stronger than ever. "However did you get them to bring ale so quickly?" I wondered if he was so drunk that he truly believed I had been responsible for the sudden arrival of the refreshments. Drosten rose, swaying slightly, before tottering over to the board. He accepted a slice of ham and cheese on a trencher, then held out a cup to be filled by a servant. Drosten took a deep draught of the ale and with another appreciative belch, staggered back to his stool.

Mancas cleared his throat, stepping closer to the fire.

"I thought we could discuss plans while we ate," he said. "I hope that is acceptable."

Drosten laughed.

"If you bring ale and food, you can do what you like."

I was less thrilled than Drosten as Mancas sat upon the stool where I had been seated until moments before.

"Hereward," he said, "I have been doing some thinking."

It appeared Lord Mancas had decided who was his second-in-command. I supposed he was right in his appraisal. We had all looked to Hereward during the defence of the minster, and he was the natural leader of our small warband. And yet it still rankled me to be brushed aside so easily when the idea that had brought us here, and the words that had convinced the king to accept the proposal, were mine.

"Yes, lord?" Hereward replied, accepting a trencher and a cup of ale from one of the servants.

Mancas took a proffered cup and sipped diffidently. He did not take any food. A slender man, I cannot recall ever having known someone eat as infrequently and in such small quantities as Mancas.

"First, tell me what your plans were," he said.

Hereward glanced at me and I shrugged. Discarding my cloak once more, I picked up a stool from the corner of the hall and carried it over to the gathered men. The seat was wet where rain had dripped through the thatch, and I used my sleeve to wipe it before sitting. Runolf, mouth full of ham and bread, shuffled his own stool slightly to make room for me by his side. I offered him a thin smile of thanks.

"To speak the truth," said Hereward, "I am not sure there was much of a plan, beyond getting permission from the king and then returning to Werceworthe to begin building the ship. I was at Bebbanburg until a few days ago." His expression darkened, perhaps as he thought of what he had left behind. "This was Hunlaf's idea."

He turned to me, clearly inviting me to speak. I nodded my thanks.

"As Hereward says, we planned to go back to Werceworthe—"

"Yes, yes," said Mancas, cutting me off. "I heard all that. But it will not do."

"How so?" asked Hereward. My cheeks grew hot, at being so quickly dismissed by Mancas. There was a sudden damp breeze as the door was opened. I was dimly aware of the servants leaving the building, but nobody paid them any heed. The door banged shut behind them.

"You need many things, no?" the thin lord asked. For a moment I believed he was speaking to me, and I opened my mouth to respond. But, of course, he was addressing Runolf, who replied, speaking in his gravelly rumble around the food in his mouth.

"Aye," he said. "Timber, rivets, ropes, tar, a sail, tools." He counted off the items on his thick fingers. Mancas nodded. Whatever feeling of anger he'd had at having been pushed into this role instead of his son, he had quickly brushed it aside, applying himself to the task in hand. In this, he was a fine leader of men, I admitted to myself grudgingly. "And of course," Runolf paused to take a swig of ale, "we need men. And we must be close to the sea or a river."

"How many of those things do you have at the minster of Werceworthe?"

Runolf drank more ale while he pondered the question. I took the opportunity to speak into the brief moment of quiet.

"There is wood," I said, eager to have my voice heard, "and it is close to the mouth of the river Cocueda, of course."

Mancas looked at me, and under his scrutiny I felt suddenly young and stupid.

"So, it is as I suspected," he said with a slight frown. "You have little of what is needed."

"We would manage," I said, sounding like a sulking child even to my own ears. Annoyed at myself, I rose, overturning my stool in my haste. I did not pause to right it, but went to the table with the food, turning my back on the others so that they could not see the flush of embarrassment on my cheeks.

"Perhaps, perhaps," said Mancas, his tone placatory. "But the king has placed me in charge of this endeavour, and whilst I did not seek the position for myself, I can see that he was wise to appoint me." Nobody spoke. The only sounds in the hall were the men chewing and the murmur of the rain on the thatch. I did not turn around, instead I helped myself to a trencher of bread and placed some ham and a sliver of cheese atop it. As I reached out for a cup to fill with ale, Mancas spoke into the hush. "Like Werceworthe, my lands are on the banks of a river, near the sea. There is good timber forest there, and on the coast there are men, both bondsmen and free, but all loyal to me. They build and repair the ships of the fishermen and merchants who trade along the coast all the way from Pictland to the land of the South Saxons, and even Frankia, across the Narrow Sea. So you see, we have all that will be needed right there, all in one place."

"There are forges?" asked Runolf. "And smiths?"

I turned and saw that Runolf's eyes gleamed in the firelight.

He was finally daring to believe he would build his ship. I was sure he could already see it in his mind's eye.

"Of course," said Mancas. "We will surely need more iron, but I will see to that." Runolf was smiling and nodding. Mancas looked over to where I stood. "You will be at home there too, young Hunlaf."

I drank from my freshly poured ale and met his gaze over the rim of the cup.

"How so?" I asked, feigning indifference.

"There is a great minster adjacent to my land. Nay, two really. Two minsters under one abbot. And a fine stone church where we can pray for the success of our venture."

"Your lands are near Gyruum, then?" I asked, excited in spite of myself.

I knew the minster that he spoke of. Beda Venerabilis, whose writing and knowledge had travelled to all corners of Christendom, had been a member of the brethren there from his childhood until the Almighty welcomed him to His right hand some six decades later. Under Leofstan's tutelage, I had studied some of the texts written by the great man's assured hand. His *De arte metrica* helped me understand the finer points of Latin verse and *De temporum ratione* made me feel insignificant and slow of thought, such was its brilliance. It always amazed me to touch the vellum that the great man had held, to follow the tracery of the well-formed script that Beda's own quill had scratched onto the parchment.

"Yes," replied Mancas, his expression unchanging, but a lightness entering his tone at the mention of his land. "I have several hides of land south of the River Uuir, where it meets the North Sea. Across the river lie the twin minsters of Gyruum and Uuiremutha. It is there, at the mouth of the Uuir, where we shall build your ship."

Eight

And so we came to Uuiremutha, where the stone church, named like so many churches after Saint Peter, rose high on the north bank of the Uuir. The structure served as a constant reminder of the minster and the brethren I had left behind. Mancas' lands were south of Werceworthe, closer to Eoforwic, so we did not return to the minster we had defended against the Norse; the home I had known for years and had been helping to rebuild. We were all excited to see the place where we could see our plan come to fruition.

Runolf was pleased with what we found there. There were many huts built along the southern bank of the wide river. It was a small but prosperous settlement of fishermen and shipwrights. The winter months were usually a quiet time for the people there, short days and long nights when they would repair their boats and mend their nets, eating slowly through their stocks of salted and smoked mackerel and herring while the North Sea raged in the cold winds.

But after a few desultory grumbles, there were no serious complaints when Mancas called upon the men to follow Runolf's commands and help him to build a great ship. Mancas promised them silver if they could complete the task before midsummer, but as Runolf described the ship he planned to build, sometimes stumbling over words and turning to me to interpret to the listening villagers, I realised that it was not the desire for riches that would make them labour for long months, often in the biting chill of the winter. I saw the glint in the eyes of the weather-worn faces of the craftsmen as Runolf's strangely accented words painted a picture of the great ship in their minds. These were men who had the hunger to learn what Runolf could teach them. They had all heard of the Norse attacks further north, and some had seen the sleek craft the Norsemen sailed on the Whale Road and wished to learn the secrets of those dragon-prowed vessels. They understood what the knowledge might mean for the kingdom of Northumbria, but most of them merely wished to understand. I recognised in them that passion for learning. They looked at the lines of strakes that made up the walls of a ship in the same way that I thought of the words on the pages of a book. They were things of beauty, but they were also something to be deciphered, picked apart, and then, when understanding had been reached, replicated.

There was some initial reticence from a few of the carpenters. They looked at the giant Norseman, with his bristling beard and thick mane of hair, and perhaps saw a raider and a killer, rather than a shipwright. But as soon as the first timber was brought from the nearby woods, dragged behind a pair of oxen supplied by Mancas' steward, and Runolf began to split the wood, and then fashion the long beam that would become the keel, any scepticism there had been, vanished.

Runolf read the grain of wood the way I read ink on a page. He saw the lines of a ship and its beams and thwarts in his mind's eye as I saw the curls and lines of letters in my mind before I scratched them into vellum. He was a master of his craft, and all who watched him as he worked the wood, and measured out the plan of his ship, were left in no doubt of his skill. Within a few days of our arrival, the settlement was abuzz with activity. Smoke hazed over the river from the cook fires and the forge, where a smith and a couple of apprentices spent all day forging the rivets that would be needed. The sound of hammering was ever present, as the glowing iron was shaped and beaten on the anvils, and as wooden wedges were driven into the seemingly never-ending supply of logs that were brought from the forest to the south.

At the end of each day Runolf was exhausted. He was supervising every aspect of the construction; travelling to the oak forest before the dawn to select the correct trees to be felled, then overseeing the splitting and planing of the strakes, informing the smiths of the correct size and length of their rivets, and of course, actually shaping and joining the bones of the ship together. Once he had paced out the length and created the keel, with its upward curve at each end, we all marvelled at the size of the thing.

"It is a beast," said Hereward, awe in his voice. It was well over thirty long paces in length, and would be some seven paces broad in the belly. "This will be the longest ship ever built in all the kingdoms of Britain."

Runolf grinned.

"Anything is possible," he said. "But there is still much to do."

That was certainly true. Could such a massive craft be built by the men of Uuiremutha, who until then had constructed nothing larger than a coast-hugging merchant ceapscip? I could see the doubt on their faces, but Runolf seemed undeterred. And his skill and self-assurance buoyed the builders.

Mancas too was as good as his word. I still disliked the man, though I wonder now whether that was more to do with the fact he treated me as a youthful scribe, not much more than a boy with the skill to write, to be ignored at all other times when that skill was not needed. But there was no denying that he was a great organiser of both men and the materials needed to build the ship.

The day after our arrival, Mancas had brought parchment, quill and ink to the guest hall where he had housed us. I was surprised to find that he could read, but it seemed he considered writing lists of requirements beneath him, for he had placed the writing instruments on one of the tables in the small but well-appointed building that lay between his great hall and the riverside settlement, and beckoned me forward with a click of his fingers.

"Hunlaf," he said, "take down all of Runolf's instructions, that I might begin to act on them. Procuring some of the items he needs may take me some time."

I hesitated, a sudden anger washing through me at the man's tone, but Hereward nodded in my direction, his meaning clear. I swallowed back my angry retort and sat down at the table. The list had been long, but Mancas had seemed unperturbed and, when he had left, saying he would start putting things in motion to purchase what was needed, Runolf was smiling.

"You realise that by having us build the ship here," I said, "the silver from the king goes into Mancas' purse?"

"What do I care?" Runolf replied. "Most of what we need is here. This is a good place to build my ship."

I scowled, but my anger felt childish and petulant.

"It is of no matter to us," said Hereward, nodding in agreement with the Norseman. "The king's silver was never ours. So it should not be our concern. If Mancas can provide us with what we need, then I say we are lucky."

I nodded, knowing they were both right. And yet I could not shake the feeling of resentment that Mancas' involvement stirred within me. It was foolish, I knew. What I wanted most of all was to sail in search of Aelfwyn, and I should have welcomed anything that furthered that goal. Nevertheless, despite Mancas' obvious talents, and his pleasantness in all his dealings with us, the sight of his slender form and scowling face engendered a nebulous feeling of anxiety in me.

My confusion at my feelings towards Mancas was further compounded when I met his son, Gersine. Like his father, Gersine was thin, with a narrow nose and a face that seemed more comfortable scowling than smiling. He was perhaps a year or two my senior, but he had led a softer life, I imagined, so appeared the same age or even younger. When he was introduced to us on our first full day at Uuiremutha, riding into the settlement behind his father, I wanted to dislike Gersine. It was a drizzled day and the earth squelched underfoot. Gersine dismounted and held out his hand to me.

"You must be Hunlaf," he said, his eyes wide, his expression sombre. "I have heard much about you." Surprised at being addressed before any of the older men, I accepted his outstretched hand, clutching his forearm in the warrior grip. He beamed at me, grasping my arm tightly. "Is it true that you had a vision of the defeat of the Norsemen at Werceworthe?"

I sensed my face flushing. I did not wish to speak of visions. But Gersine was persistent. Whenever he came to the settlement, which was most days, he followed me, asking me about my experiences. He often joined my weapons training under the watchful eye of Gwawrddur, and while he did not possess Cormac's rage-fuelled speed and recklessness, Gersine was of noble birth, so had been taught to handle a blade since he was a child. He was a worthy adversary. I was glad of another young man to share my training sessions, and I enjoyed sparring with him, not least because I could best him more often than not.

The last of the leaves blew from the alders that grew along the Uuir, leaving the trees to claw at the slate-grey heavens with their spindly twig fingers, their dangling catkins trembling in the wind. As winter came to the land with its frost and snow and winds so cold that they seemed to flay the skin from our cheeks, I found myself looking forward to Gersine's visits. There was always work to do, so I was never idle, but when

Gersine decided to stay at his father's hall and not ride to the bank of the river where the bones of the ship were slowly taking shape, I grew sullen.

I enjoyed Gersine's company, but truth be told, his adulation of me, and his pandering to my ego, agreeable as it was, did nothing good for my character. Many times in my life, my pride has led me into trouble. Even now, the act of penning this annal is borne from a prideful desire to tell my story. But I am an old man now, with an old man's perspective on my life. I can look back at the path I have followed and see clearly now the moments where I wandered from righteousness. Those moments have been too frequent. In spite of my keen mind and love of knowledge, I have been very slow to learn certain lessons.

Peering back now, through the swirling mists of my memories, I can see that over those long winter days, as weeks turned to months, part of me came adrift, like a boat untethered from its moorings. Without the guiding influence of Leofstan and the other monks with whom I had lived those past years, I found it increasingly necessary to act the part of the warrior. I was strong and fast, and the men and women of Uuiremutha had never known me as a monk. I carried a sword and wore a byrnie, and was friend to the son of their lord, so I was a warrior in their eyes. I held my head high and strutted about the settlement of huts, hand on the hilt of my sword, as I had seen Gwawrddur do.

The men Mancas had instructed to work with Runolf lowered their gaze when I passed. They offered me deference and I saw something in their eyes, fear perhaps, or maybe admiration, and I enjoyed the sensation it brought me. At times, when Gersine had not come, or when he had already returned to his father's hall, I would think about Leofstan and what he would have said about my transformation. At such times, feeling ashamed, I would have one of the fishermen take me across the Uuir in one of their small skiffs. I would enter the cold gloom of the stone church and gaze up at the watery light of the winter sky oozing through the different coloured glass panes of the church windows, a thing of wonder indeed that the locals said had been created by Frankish craftsmen before living memory. Kneeling in the pools of light on the hard flagstones, my breath steaming in the air before me, I would pray silently and listen for the voice of God. I know the Almighty hears all, but He never spoke to me in that cold church.

Then, on one crisp winter day, the sound of the monks singing at None drifted to me on the still air, beckoning, reminding me who I had been until very recently. I trudged up the path to the minster itself, the frost-rimed grass crunching underfoot. By the time I reached the buildings, the singing of the liturgy had finished. A few tonsured monks hurried across the open ground, holding their habits tightly about their thin frames, anxious to be back inside. Crossing the vallum, the ditch that encircled the holy site, I strode towards the long building where most of the brothers were headed. I recognised it as the scriptorium and I could already imagine the books inside, the smell of the encaustum and the calf skin vellum. I had not written or even read anything since acting as Mancas' scribe on the day we arrived. At the thought of writing, my fingers twitched, longing to hold a quill. I had not realised how much I had missed it. Shapes began to form, unbidden in my mind; patterns and animals that I could draw around some of the large first letters on an ornately decorated page. It was as much the beauty of books, as the learning they held that sang to me, and I rushed towards the scriptorium like a sailor floundering in the surf might strive to reach an outcrop of rock.

Before I reached the sanctuary of the scriptorium, a stocky figure emerged, blocking my path. His bald pate was encircled by greying hair. Even though it was cropped short and his tonsure was well shaved, the man's hair gave the impression of being unruly and untamed. His cheeks and nose were broad and traced with veins. Around his neck hung a thick chain, from which dangled a large, golden crucifix, dotted with garnets like drops of blood. He offered a slight nod of the head, his gaze never leaving mine. He made the obeisance feel somehow defiant.

"Yes?" he said, his tone flat.

I had not expected this confrontational meeting. The song of the brethren had called to me from the church where I had been praying. I had thought I would be welcomed by my Christian brothers.

"My name is Hunlaf," I said. His expression did not change. "I was at Werceworthe. One of the brethren there, under Abbot Beonna."

The old monk sniffed.

"I know who you are," he said. "I am Fridwin, the mynsterfæder here."

There was a long pause. In the distance, I could hear the hammering from the smiths across the river. From the east came the hiss and sigh of the waves washing the beach. Behind the monk, the dark doorway of the scriptorium yawned. I could see nothing in the gloom, but imagined the bowed heads of the monks, all straining to hear the words being spoken just outside.

"I heard you reciting the prayers of None," I said, unsure how to proceed.

"I am glad your hearing is intact," said Fridwin, the slightest of smiles on his lips. "You have not lost that, along with your faith. God is good."

Met with the minster father's implacable demeanour, I had at first been unsure of myself. But his obvious disdain now kindled something within me, an anger that I had come to know lurked just beneath the surface.

"I had hoped to see some of the great tomes you have here," I said. "I have copied parts of Ceolfrith's pandect and Willibrord's calendar. My teacher, Brother Leofstan, told me you had a copy of Beda's *Historia ecclesiastica gentis Anglorum* within your library."

Fridwin sniffed again.

"Brother Leofstan is correct," he said, looking as if he had smelt something disgusting. "In that at least."

I nodded, making to step past him into the shadowed scriptorium. He moved to block my path.

"Alas, you cannot enter the scriptorium. The books are for the eyes of our brothers in Christ alone."

I stopped moving, as if Fridwin had slapped me across the face. I felt my rage building up inside me and I opened my mouth. I wanted to shout at him. Until a few months before I had been copying texts in the scriptorium at Werceworthe. But I could see from his expression that he knew this. A small, dark voice inside me whispered that I should punch the man. Who was he to deny me?

Perhaps Fridwin saw some of my conflict displayed on my features, for he took a step backwards.

"You are no longer one of our brethren, Hunlaf." He swallowed, maybe thinking of who I had become. What I was capable of. His eyes flicked down to take in the sword and seax on my belt. "If you wish to pray, might I suggest, Saint Peter's? There is a fine carving of Christ on the altar, and the coloured glass in the windows is truly a marvel. Many find the colours soothing as they pray for spiritual guidance."

I glowered at him, my fists clenched at my side. He had no idea of the sacrifices I had made. I had been forced to decide between the brethren and the blade. It had been clear to me that I needed to embrace the way of the sword if I was to protect those I loved; my family at Werceworthe. I did not regret my decision, but it was perhaps not until that moment, with the sneering Fridwin denying me access to the scriptorium, that I understood the true impact of my choice.

Saying nothing, I turned and walked back along the path, towards the river. The clanging sound of the smith's hammer reminded me of the warning bell of Werceworthe. As I walked, my leather shoes crunching the frosted blades of grass, my heartbeat roared in my ears, merging with the distant wave-sound of the beach and matching the rhythm of the smith's hammer and my steps.

Nine

The incident outside the scriptorium hardened my resolve to act in every way the warrior. If my former family rejected me, I would fully embrace my new kith, my sword-brothers. They understood me better than the monks of Uuiremutha, it seemed. In the evenings, as the winter winds buffeted the hall, Drosten, Hereward and Runolf would drink copious amounts of the ale and mead Mancas' steward delivered to us. Gwawrddur would sip from his cup, always drinking with restraint. Where I had previously drunk sparingly, I now drank as much as the seasoned warriors, laughing and riddling noisily. I would often end the night staggering out into the cold darkness to vomit. On more than one occasion I puked where I lay and the men would laugh at me in the morning, as I rose, groaning and bleary, stinking and sticky from the cold reminder of my excesses.

One morning, not long after Crístesmæsse, I awoke and staggered over to a bench, where I slumped down. I moaned, my head still spinning from too much ale. Gwawrddur came to sit beside me. He placed a bowl of porridge on the board before me and filled a cup with water from an earthenware jug.

The thought of eating sickened me and I pushed the bowl

away. My head was pounding, my stomach sour, and roiling like a stormy sea.

From the far end of the hall came snoring, despite it being well after sunrise. I glanced over at the half dozen cloak-wrapped shapes of the slumbering men. The previous afternoon, Hereward had returned from Bebbanburg with six warriors. Some of them I recognised from my first visit to the fortress and the journey to Eoforwic. There was Bealdwulf, a thickset man, and older than the rest. He was broad of chest, and his face scarred. Then there was Gamal, a sharp-faced man, who seemed to be perpetually sneering, and his friend, Ida, who rarely uttered more than a grunt, but was never far from Gamal's side. Oslaf was short, broad of girth and quick to smile, which gave him a soft aspect that was undoubtedly misleading. The last two warriors were Sygbald and Pendrad, who both had the look of formidable warriors, tall of stature, wide of shoulder, with great barrel chests. So alike were they that they might have been brothers, but where Sygbald was fair, so Pendrad was dark, with hair as black as a crow's wing.

All of them had all been members of Uhtric's hearth-guard, his most trusted warriors.

Uhtric was dead.

Word had reached us of his death just before the Crístesmæsse feast. As he'd predicted, he had not made it past midwinter. Hereward had made no comment about the tidings, but he had drunk himself into a stupor that night. Two days later, when the storm, which had been lashing the coast, abated, he had saddled up his tan mare and ridden north. That had been a fortnight before and we had begun to wonder if he would return.

When he came riding out of the dusk, an icy wind at his back, he was accompanied by the six warriors, all good fighting men, well-known to Hereward.

"We will need doughty men once that ship is finished,"

Hereward said, introducing the grim-faced warriors. His mood was still sombre, but he was pleased with himself, and clearly glad of the company of men he had known for many years. We too were gladdened by the arrival of the new recruits, and also by Hereward's return. We had drunk even more than normal to celebrate their arrival, and my memories of the night were a blur. I can only recall one other time in my life when I have been drunker, but that was still far off in my future, in the smoke-filled tent of a Kumyk leader who insisted we drink a potent concoction made from fermented mare's milk. After that night, on a far-off, sun-beaten, windswept plain, I awoke beside one of the leader's daughters and was led to believe that I had agreed to take her as my wife. But that is another tale. On this particular morning, my head felt as though it had been used to hammer rivets, and my stomach curdled at the sight and smell of food.

Gwawrddur nudged the bowl towards me.

"Eat," he said. "Drink."

I held my head in my hands for a time, before relenting and picking up the cup of water.

"I worry about you, Killer," Gwawrddur said, his voice quiet.

His use of the name he had coined infuriated me, but I was too weak and sickly to react. I took a small spoonful of the porridge.

"Why?" I asked when I was sure I would keep the porridge down.

"You have been through much these last months," he said. "You have learnt much about the sword. About life." He sighed. "And death. And about yourself."

I grunted and ate a bit more of the warm oatmeal. I could feel it settling my stomach and I welcomed the easing of the sensation that I might throw up at any moment.

"You have taught me well," I mumbled.

He shook his head.

"Do not forget yourself, Hunlaf. You do not need to become what you are not."

I stared at him. His words confused me. I remembered Fridwin at the scriptorium, turning me away. What was Gwawrddur telling me?

"I know who I am," I said, pushing myself up. I did not truly believe my own words, but I could not face talking to the Welshman further.

It was later that same day, with my head still throbbing and my thoughts in turmoil, that I first noticed Cwenswith. I had seen her before, of course. She was pretty and one of the few girls close to my age in the settlement, but I had never paid her much attention. Until then.

A while before, Runolf had seen Gersine and me loitering and had shouted at us to make ourselves useful. Not wishing to admit I could not keep up with the older men, despite my headache, I had hurried to do Runolf's bidding. Perhaps taking pity on me after the night's escapades, he told Gersine and I to carve as many trenails as we could. The shipwrights needed dozens, if not hundreds of the things, and it was something Runolf knew I was capable of, even in my sorry state. The dexterity that allowed me to scribe clearly formed letters on the page, also gave me the steady hand and good eye to make the wooden pegs that would serve to hold much of the ship's strakes and thwarts together.

Gersine and I sat together on stumps of timber, splitting small logs with a hand axe, then splitting those pieces again, until each log provided four of the trenails. After splitting, we used a sharp knife to pare away the wood, leaving one end thicker than the other and rounding the ends so that the mallets would not split the wood when the pegs were driven home. From the offcuts of the logs, we whittled the wooden wedges that would later be hammered into ridges cut into the thick ends of the trenails, thus expanding them and holding them in place. It was not the most strenuous of activities, for which I gave thanks to Runolf, but it demanded concentration.

It was when we paused, deciding to go over to the smith to sharpen our knives, that Gersine nudged me. The wind had blown the clouds away in the night and the sky was a brilliant blue. The low winter sun shone bright, but with little warmth. I was taciturn and had been poor company ever since Gersine rode up at mid-morning, tethering his dappled stallion beside one of the storage huts. I had grumbled constantly at him while we worked on the trenails, criticising his carving, picking up pegs he had finished and comparing them unfavourably against the example that Runolf had given us to copy. Now, perhaps wishing to deflect my bad mood away from him, Gersine pointed to where the sun gleamed from Cwenswith's golden locks.

It is strange how these things happen. Despite having seen her many times over the previous weeks, it was as if I saw her that morning for the first time. She glanced up from where she was carding wool in the sun and before she looked away demurely, some form of silent communication had passed between us.

Sensing it, Gersine laughed and slapped me on the back. I growled in anger and embarrassment and strode off to the smith. But that afternoon, as we worked, I could not stop thinking about her, and it was only a few days later that Cwenswith followed me into the storeroom.

I knew she was betrothed to Wistan, one of the young carpenters, but I was a warrior now and I would not be dissuaded from taking what I wanted, no matter the consequences. To begin with, we were careful, meeting in secret. But as our passion grew, I became increasingly flagrant.

When it became obvious to the others what was happening, Gwawrddur and Hereward both cautioned me, pulling me aside and telling me that there was only one way this would end: badly. But I was a young man and filled with the lusts of youth, and a smile and a wink from a pretty girl, and the promise of pleasure, was more than I could resist. Not that I wanted to. I persuaded myself that I loved her. It was as though a madness had taken over and I succumbed to the Devil's temptations of the flesh wholeheartedly.

I knew my friends were right, but I did not care. As the days grew longer and warmer, I made ever less effort to hide my encounters with Cwenswith. It was only a matter of time before Wistan would discover us together. And yet, despite the danger, or perhaps because of it and the thrill it brought, I did not stop. I convinced myself that this was how warriors behaved; bedding whom they pleased, when they wanted.

I have had many years to think about those months, and I believe now that I wanted Wistan to find us. I longed to be confronted, to face a foe I could fight against, rather than trying to grapple with the self-doubt and loss I felt at being cut off from my brothers in Christ and the life I had abandoned.

If that was so, I got what I wanted that early summer's day as I circled Wistan, sword and shield in hand. I had given him every chance to surrender, but he had refused. He was already wounded, but he was still a strong man. I could not risk him landing a lucky blow. The time had come to end this. Catching his clumsy attacks on my shield, I stabbed beneath his guard. I felt my blade make contact. I pushed hard and he grunted.

I sprang back, wary of a wild swing of his sword, but Wistan did not attack. His eyes were wide, and he stared at me for a heartbeat before looking down. I had meant to gut him, sinking my blade through the fat and muscle of his belly. And yet, although there was blood staining his kirtle, it was from my previous cut to his side. His midriff appeared whole. With the same shock on his features that I felt, Wistan gazed down at where my sword stroke should have pierced his flesh. I saw what had happened at the same instant that he understood.

He wore a thick leather belt about his waist. It was secured with a heavy bronze buckle. The metal of the buckle was scored and pitted where my sword had struck. He would be bruised, but his buckle had prevented my killing blow.

Our eyes met. We both knew that he should be dying. His face was pale and I hoped that he might end this now. He could not hope to stand against me and survive for much longer.

That was when the shouting started. All about us, the men and women who had gathered to watch the duel, were yelling and screaming. Some turned and ran towards their homes. Runolf and Hereward were bellowing orders, but I hardly heard them.

Wistan's gaze had shifted and now he looked over my shoulder. His eyes grew fearful and his mouth dropped open. For an instant I thought it was some kind of ruse, that he wanted me to turn my back on him. It was the only way he could possibly win the bout, I thought. But then I saw the horrified expression on Cwenswith's face, the terror on the features of Wistan's parents. None of the villagers were interested in our duel any more. All those who had not fled, were staring out to sea.

I realised that while we had been fighting, the black clouds that had been threatening on the horizon had grown, covering the sun and plunging the land into gloaming. The wind had picked up too, whipping at the marram grass and bending the alders that grew by the river.

The squall raged above us, and a spiteful rain began to fall. The suddenness of the storm and the twilit darkness seemed unearthly, as if God Himself was angry. I followed the gaze of Wistan and the others and I thought that perhaps that was indeed the case. For speeding over the wind-fretted waves came an enemy whom many had said were the wrath of the

Lord made flesh, sent to chastise us for the errors of our ways and the sins of our leaders.

If I had truly yearned for a physical foe to fight, it seemed the Almighty had granted my wish.

Surging towards us, listing with the power of the wind in their sails and throwing up great sheets of spray as they ploughed through the waves, came two Norse sea-serpents. Their prows bore the carved heads of dragons and behind the ravening maws of their prow-beasts, the bellies of the ships were filled with dozens of armed and armoured Norsemen.

Ten

"Don't just stand there," roared Hereward, snapping me out of my reverie. "Remember what we have practised."

I flicked a glance at Wistan. He was unmoving, his face pale.

"With me," I shouted at him. He seemed unable to pull his gaze away from the approaching Norsemen. I understood the fear that gripped him. The ships were as lithe as wyrms on the surf, and the ranks of Norse raiders leering from the deck far outnumbered us. "Wistan!" I barked. "Follow me."

At last he turned to look at me and I saw the reality of the situation dawning on him. Gersine was nearby and I grabbed his shoulder, turning him from where he too gawped at the ships.

Runolf and Hereward were bellowing orders, and, as if we had awoken from a dream at the same moment, we all started to move at once.

I tugged at Gersine's sleeve. "Come on."

We hurried along the river's edge to where we would make our stand.

Beyond the usual supplies of hemp nets and ropes, each of the storage huts now also housed shields, spears and the other trappings of war we had taken from the Norse at Werceworthe.

Skidding to a halt, I darted into the hut that held my byrnie, and Gersine's too. Lugging them out, I flung one of the iron-knit shirts to Gersine.

"Help him," I said to Wistan. For a heartbeat he did not move and then, without acknowledging me, he set to helping Mancas' son into the armour.

Dropping my shield and sword to the ground, I threw my own byrnie over my raised arms and head. Wriggling and jumping, I managed to get the iron-linked shirt partway on before it became stuck on my chest. I could not bend my arms enough to pull the shirt down, so was trapped with my hands in the air, my stomach exposed to the cold rain.

Looking beyond Gersine and Wistan, my mind reeled to see the ships growing ever closer. The wind howled now, a gale such as sweeps the coast in autumn or winter. There was a chill hatred in that wind. The waves, whipped up by the sudden storm, crashed on the beach, adding their roar to Runolf and Hereward's shouted orders. The Norse were coming on fast, driven by that bitter wind. The sight of them stirred up dark memories of death, fire and blood. The rain slashed into my face, spattered chill against my belly where my kirtle had risen up, caught by the byrnie that had me trapped. I began to panic, twisting and shaking in an effort to dislodge the iron shirt.

It would not budge. I was held tight, defenceless and ridiculous as the Norsemen sailed ever closer, as inexorable as wyrd.

Strong hands pulled at the hem of my byrnie, tugging it down and freeing my arms. It was Wistan, and for a moment I shuddered to think of my bare stomach facing him. He could have finished our quarrel there and then. But he was a good man. He had finished helping Gersine with his byrnie and, putting aside our differences, had turned to my aid. I nodded my thanks, unable to speak for the shame I felt. I had almost killed him only moments before. Blood seeped from the cut to his side and, if not for his belt buckle, he would now be dying.

With a last shake of my shoulders I shifted the position of my byrnie. There was no time to remove my belt and refasten it over the iron shirt. But at least I had armour, as did Gersine, the son of the Lord of Uuiremutha. The Norse were coming with nothing but death and destruction on their minds, and we would face them where Hereward had planned. Wistan, already bleeding and certainly no warrior, would stand before the Norse killers with nothing but a shield and spear, and the sword he had borrowed from Runolf.

Without a word, we each snatched up a spear from the stack in the store, and hurried off.

The men were amassing on the riverside in a protective line that would present as solid a defence as possible. Runolf and Hereward had decided where the shieldwall would be placed. There were few areas along the river mouth where ships could land. We would form a line at the lip of the riverbank, near where Runolf's ship was being built. Our shieldwall would defend the bones of the ship, and also provide enough time for the women and children to flee.

The air was full of chaos; shouts, the wind, the roar of the sea, and now a new sound was added to the cacophony: a clanging bell from far off. It came from across the water and, as we sprinted to our positions to join the others at the water's edge, I saw smoke against the dark sky. I could imagine the flames consuming the minster buildings, and my stomach churned at my recent memories. Gulls, buffeted by the wind, shrieked in the sky, like the cries of dying men. I wondered whether, rather than the birds' calls, I might perhaps be making out the sounds of the brethren being slaughtered to the north of the Uuir.

When we arrived at the designated place, the shieldwall was already formed. We slid in amongst the other men, gripping our shields and weapons tightly. Hereward was nearby. His face was grim, his jaw set, as he watched the approach of the

Norse ships. He glanced up at the louring sky. The rain seethed around us now, lashing us like icy whips.

"Do you think this is Heaven-sent?" Hereward asked.

I looked across the river at the pall of greasy smoke that rose from the direction of the minster.

"God controls the heavens and the seas," I replied, shuddering from the cold and the fear of facing the Norsemen in battle once more. "But I think Fridwin might regret his decision to put all his faith in the Lord against the men of the north."

Hereward frowned, but did not reply.

We had always known that the Norse might attack the minsters here. It was no real surprise to us to see the ships skimming across the waves out of the rising sun. We had seen their like attack lonely minsters twice just the year before with devastating effects. And Runolf had warned us of the plans of the Norsemen to continue working down the coast, snapping up the poorly defended, but wealthy holy sites. But we had not expected an attack so soon.

And yet, it seemed all the raiders had been waiting for was for the weather to break, for the seas to be calm enough for them to make the crossing safely. The loss of a handful of men and a couple of ships at Werceworthe was not enough to deter the call of the riches and thralls they hoped to snatch from the holy houses dotted along the coast of Northumbria.

But we were not defenceless monks. We were well-prepared for an attack. Ever since we had arrived, Hereward had spent much of his time creating defences and drilling the people in what to do if Norse ships should come. I had gone with him when he had crossed the river to speak to Fridwin and Ethelbald, the abbot of the minster at Gyruum.

"God will protect us," Fridwin had said.

The abbot had seemed uncertain, but he was a timid man and nothing we said could make him speak against the mynsterfæder of Uuiremutha. Of course, neither of them had witnessed the attacks at Lindisfarnae or Werceworthe.

"I am reminded of Didymos the Apostle," I said, my tone harsh. "He doubted Jesus had risen from the tomb until he had seen the marks of the nails, and placed his hands in the son of God's wounds. Pray that you do not live to see the dragon ships. That you do not face the wrath of the Norsemen, feel the bite of their blades, the heat from the flames of your scriptoria. I fear that once you have touched that wound, it will be too late for you to profess your belief in the danger we warn you of."

I regretted my words now. They had only angered the monks, turning them further against us and our offer of protection.

As we had returned, leaving the minster behind, Hereward had sighed.

"It is a good thing for us that they refused our aid," he said with a frown.

"How so?" I asked.

"There are nowhere near enough of us to defend even one of the minsters, let alone both of them, divided as they are and cut off from us by the Uuir. No, we will be hard pressed enough to defend ourselves, the ship, and Mancas' folk."

Hereward's pragmatic tone had angered me at the time. Despite the way that Fridwin had acted towards me personally, these were Christian monks who would be murdered and enslaved if the Norse came. But watching the two ships that sped towards the river mouth, I knew Hereward was right. Each ship held some thirty warriors or more. I looked along our ragged line. We numbered closer to a score of men, and most of them, not hardened fighters. But Hereward had drilled into us that we did not need to butcher all of an enemy to be victorious. All we needed to do was make ourselves a stronger opponent than could easily be vanquished. The brethren to the north were the sheep that attracted the wolves, we needed to make ourselves deadlier prey. Wolves would not seek out hounds, when there were lambs nearby.

"Remember, lads," Hereward shouted now, projecting his voice over the hiss of the rain and the rumble and crash of the waves. "Hold the line and listen for my commands. Many of us have stood in battle before and we will not be easily overcome by these Northern pirates." Around Hereward, the six Northumbrians who had come from Bebbanburg began clattering their weapons against their shield rims. Beyond them stood several pale-faced carpenters and fishermen, their resolve bolstered by the towering presence of Runolf with his huge axe on the flank, where we would be at risk of having the shieldwall turned. To my right, past Wistan, Gersine and a handful of other men, I spotted the burly smith. Beside him was Gwawrddur, his face impassive. His eyes watched the approaching Norsemen the way a hawk observes river rats. At the end of the line, the tattooed face of Drosten grinned back at me. The Pict seemed gleeful at the prospect of battle. Shaking my head, I turned back to Hereward.

"Hold the line and let them come to us," he yelled over the storm and the beating of spears and swords on shields. "Your families will be safe, so long as we do not falter. We have sent word to Mancas, and he will be riding here with his hearth-warriors with all haste. When they arrive, if we have left any of the Norse alive for them, you will see true slaughter. Now, hold firm, and with God's grace and stout hearts, we will send these Northern curs back into the sea."

All of the men were hammering their blades and spear-hafts against their shields now, sending out a thundering threnody of doom to the raiders who threatened us.

As if God Himself answered Hereward's words, a great gust of wind ripped leaves from the alders. One tree, its branches heavy with foliage, cracked and splintered, toppling over into the river. Such was the rage of the storm, we did not hear the splash the tree made as it collapsed into the Uuir. The ferocity of the tempest was unlike anything I had encountered before, and I wondered at Hereward's question about it being sent from heaven. The wind must surely have been directed by the Almighty, for as we watched, the foremost ship, barely a spear's throw from the riverbank, was caught in the gust that had broken the alder. The ship leaned precariously over for a heartbeat. Its wale skimmed the surface of the river. Men slid and fell on the deck, tumbling between the thwarts. An instant later, the men all along the shieldwall erupted with a great cheer. The ship had capsized, tumbling its men into the fast-flowing, muddy waters of the churning river mouth.

The ship's mast shattered. The sail, waterlogged and heavy, swallowed up several men who were battling against the water's pull. Caught now in the river's flow and the wind, the overturned ship began to turn. From where we looked, it seemed a slow movement, but a ship of that size is hugely heavy, its previously sleek lines now cumbersome, as it wallowed like a leviathan of the deep come up for air.

The second ship was in total disarray as the sailors rushed to try to avoid the inevitable. But it was too late. With a sickening crunching crack, the second ship struck the first, splintering strakes and thwarts. Carried forward with the power of the wind in its sail, the dragon prow rose up high into the rain-riven air. Men were crushed and broken beneath its keel as it drove onwards, slowing eventually as it climbed up the slope of the overturned ship's hull.

We had fallen silent now, watching the destruction of the two ships in awe. Moments before, the Norse raiders had believed they would slaughter us. Now, the astonishing power of the wind and the waves, surely guided by the hand of God, had destroyed their vessels, smashing them into so much kindling and flotsam.

With an echoing sound as loud as thunder, the upturned

hull of the capsized ship broke apart under the weight of the second wave-steed. The second ship dropped down into the water, sending up a great wave that washed the river's bank. The broken ship began to drift away, but the collision must have holed the second ship, for it too now listed terribly. The men aboard were in turmoil, like ants when their nest has been kicked. They heaved on ropes, shouting orders and desperately trying to save the ship. But, despite their efforts, the wind, tide and the invisible rupture beneath the waterline mercilessly pulled the ship down towards the riverbed.

Men in the churning water were floundering. Some found their footing and slowly waded ashore.

"Forward!" bellowed Hereward, breaking the spell that had fallen over us all at witnessing the destruction of the ships. "Do not let them get a footing on the beach. Kill them all!"

He ran forward, his comrades from Bebbanburg beside him. A heartbeat later we followed, running down the riverbank into the muddy shallows to begin the slaughter.

Eleven

The fear of the defenders quickly changed to rage as they understood that the Norsemen had been defeated by the elements. Hereward and his half dozen warriors reached the water's edge first, hacking down the spluttering, drenched Norsemen who had managed to claw their way safe of the wrecks. They staggered through the shallows only to find death on the Northumbrian blades.

Hot blood pumped into the brown waters of the river, staining them red. The sight of the blood seemed to ignite the flames of the villagers' anger that these strangers would dare to sail across the North Sea to kill them and enslave their wives and children.

Hereward kept his men close to the water's edge and he bellowed for the others to remain on the beach. But all was chaos and with screams of rage, I saw several of the armed craftsmen wading into the water, hacking with their axes and tools.

The second ship appeared to have run aground now. It was half submerged, leaning drunkenly to the side. The debris of the first ship spun slowly in the water, languidly colliding and scraping its way out towards the open sea. I could not tell how many men had already drowned, pulled down by their armour, or crushed beneath the wreckage, but there were still at least a couple of dozen Norsemen in the water, making their way towards us.

"To me!" shouted Hereward. "Form the line!" His voice held an edge of desperation. The villagers had long spears. If they remained on the shore, they could not lose against the Norse, who battled against the cold waters of the river. To meet them in the water was to remove our advantage, and in such conditions, the savage Norse would quickly seize the initiative. These were true killers, men who had risked all to reach our coast. They would not be so easily slain.

As I watched in dismay, a broad-shouldered Norseman, his plaited beard long and dark from the water, his teeth bared in a furious grimace, surged up to grasp the wrist of one of the fishermen who confronted him with a hand axe. Hammering his forehead into the fisherman's face, blood splattered, bright against the muddy water. The Norseman wrested the axe from the fisherman and without hesitation, smashed his skull. The fisherman sank into the water like a stone. The water bubbled dark with his blood, and then he was gone.

"Back! Back!" Hereward yelled. Another villager was struck down by one of the bedraggled raiders.

At last, the men's discipline began to return and they slowly retreated from the Norsemen who rose out of the river like sea monsters from a mead hall tale. Splashing through the water, pulling against the sucking mud, they came out of the river.

But one man did not heed Hereward's call.

A tall man, the waters lapping at his thighs, stood unmoving before the attacker who had killed the axe-wielding fisherman. In the defender's hands were a shield and spear. But inexperienced as he was, encumbered by the water and the mud, and without an iron-knit shirt for protection, the man could not hope to stand against the byrnie-clad warrior who was wading towards him.

"Father, no!"

The voice pulled my attention away from the water.

Wistan, his face pallid, sword and shield still in his hands, sprang forward and rushed into the water. The man who remained in the river was Eafa, his father. Like Wistan, Eafa was no warrior, but by God they were both brave men. I could not stand by and watch them slain.

With a roar of anger at having been forced to disobey Hereward, I ran after Wistan.

Sliding and slipping down the last of the beach, I hit the water, sending up sprays of surf. The water deepened rapidly, and cold mud clung to my feet, as if fists clutched my ankles. I imagined the corpses of the drowned Norse, groping for me, unseen beneath the murky water. I hurried forward as fast as I was able.

Wistan surged ahead of me, his first splashing steps in the river now changed to a slower wading gait as the water deepened. He shouted again, but Eafa did not turn. He was fully occupied fending off the bearded Norseman.

All around us, other Norsemen were coming ashore. Some were trying to make their way upriver in an attempt to avoid the waiting defenders and their sharp spears. But the current was too strong and the Norse could make no headway in that direction. Others allowed themselves to be swept downstream, away from the shieldwall prepared for slaughter on the beach, and towards the mouth of the Uuir. If they could not reach the wave-washed beaches of the coast, the deep sea awaited them. I doubted many would survive for long, but if they somehow made it to shore and escaped the immediate threat of Hereward and the spear-men, they would surely be found soon enough by Mancas and his hearth-warriors.

I was closing on Wistan, who had nearly reached his father, when a tall Norseman, caught in the water's pull, clattered into me, almost knocking me from my feet. I had been so intent on

Wistan and Eafa, my shield and sword held high above the water, that I had not spotted the floating man until he collided with me. He was young, with blond hair and bright blue eyes that were wide with fear. He had long, sinewy arms, strong from years of hard work and, maybe, sword-training. But he had no sword in his hand now. The Norseman wrapped one of his powerful arms around me and I staggered, struggling to remain upright with his sudden bulk pulling me down. For a heartbeat he held me close and I thought he must have been glad to have found someone to halt his journey down the river to an almost certain death by drowning.

Then I felt a pain in my midriff. Looking down I saw with a shock that he held a knife in his right hand. He pulled his fist back and once again delivered a powerful blow, higher this time, that drove the wind from my lungs. Without thought, I bellowed, and tried to hit him with my shield. But he was too close, embracing me tightly, and as near as a lover. I could not punch him with the shield boss, instead I was only able to deliver an ineffectual blow with the inside of the linden board.

Shrugging off the weak battering from my shield on his back, he again hammered his knife into my stomach. The only thing that saved me was the byrnie I wore. I had ring-shaped bruises for many days afterwards, but the byrnie turned the Norseman's blade, preventing him gutting me like a mackerel. But I knew iron links could be sundered. The man was strong and determined. Left unchecked, his knife would eventually break through my armour and pierce my flesh.

In desperation now, panic rising within me like bile, I twisted and writhed in his grasp. His next strike missed its mark, glancing against my side. He was too close to allow me to bring my sword's blade to bear, but I was not about to release my grip on the weapon. With a howl of pain and fury, I punched him in the face, my fist wrapped tightly around the sword's grip. The hilt and pommel smashed his lips and teeth, his blood shockingly red on the golden hair of his beard. A wave washed over us both, filling my mouth with cold water, making me choke and cough. The river had cleaned away the blood from his face. I hammered my sword hilt into his mouth again, sending a fresh spurt of blood over my fist and his chin. His grip weakened and I pummelled his face another couple of times before I was able to shove him away. His eyes were glazed now, his face streaked with gore from his broken mouth. I did not hesitate. As soon as he was at an arm's length from me, I slashed down with my blade, shattering his skull. He fell back, to float away, his pallid, blood-soaked face staring up at the storm clouds above us before his body tumbled over and was lost to the river.

My chest and stomach ached where the knife had gouged at my byrnie, but I was not seriously hurt. Shaking off the shock of the encounter, I cast about for more hidden adversaries. There was nobody near me now apart from Wistan, his father, and the Norseman he faced.

As I watched, Wistan reached his father. Eafa was cowering behind his shield and jabbing at his attacker's bearded face. The Norseman might be armed only with the hand axe that he had snatched from his first foe, but he was fast, and he was strong. Lashing out with his left hand, the warrior gripped the spear haft and twisted it away from him.

Eafa stumbled back, trying to avoid the sudden threat of the short axe. Losing his footing in the clinging mud, he sprawled, floundering and flailing in the water. The Norseman waded forward to deliver the killing blow against this carpenter who had dared defy him.

"No!" screamed Wistan, surging forward to protect his father.

Wistan was brave and his actions saved his father's life. The Norseman's axe clattered against his outstretched shield. But from where I was hurrying to join the fight, battling against the chill tug of the deep water, I could see that Wistan was over-extended. By defending his father, he had left his body open to attack. Any warrior could see this. Wistan was brave, but he was no warrior. The Norseman before him was a trained killer, and instantly shifted his focus from the older spear-man to the sword-wielding youth. Seeing how Wistan was off-balance and unprotected, the Norseman hacked down with the axe. The axe's blade bit deep into Wistan's chest and he threw both his arms wide in shock, as if he meant to embrace his attacker.

Before the Norseman could strike again, I shoved Wistan away with my shield. He splashed into his father, but I could not rip my gaze from the bearded man before me. Fresh blood dripped from his axe. Seeing me, he grinned, as if glad to have another adversary. All about us was a maelstrom of destruction, and this man was smiling.

I swallowed my fear, and bared my teeth, showing the Norseman that he faced a warrior now. I held my sword high, over the rim of my shield. It was stained red with the blood of his countryman.

"Ready for the hall of the slain?" I said in his native tongue. Runolf had often told me of the beliefs of his people, and how they thought they would be carried to Valhöll upon their deaths in battle.

The man's eyes widened at my words. But he quickly recovered. With a glance at the wreckage around us and the corpses bobbing in the churned water, the Norseman met my gaze and licked his lips.

"You think you are man enough to send me to Óðinn's hall?" He spat into the water. "We shall see."

I did not waste my energy on a reply. Lunging forward, I feinted at his face with my shield rim, then, as he swayed backwards, quick as a striking viper, I slashed my sword blade across his throat. I could not be certain, but it seemed to me that he made little effort to defend himself in those last moments. Blood spouted from his severed arteries, spraying into the water all around us and raining down hot on my face. Clutching the axe tightly in his hand, the man's grin seemed to widen as he fell back to be swallowed by the muddy river.

With Eafa's help, I dragged Wistan out of the water. His face was as grey as fish guts, and we left a trail of red in the water behind us. Throwing my shield and sword down onto the mud of the beach, I got my hands beneath his arms and pulled him free of the water. Gently, I lay him down. His face was close to mine and I felt his breath, hot and ragged against my cheek. As I rose and looked down into his face, I saw there were tears there, or perhaps it was rain or river water. I reached for his hand, clutching it tightly. He stared at me in horror.

"I am sorry," I said, though what I was apologising for, I could not say.

His hand was limp in mine. His eyes gazed, unblinking. I realised with a pang of pain in my chest as acute as if the Norseman's knife had pierced my heart, that I had failed. The shuddering warmth of Wistan's breath on my face had been his last.

Beside me, Eafa looked down at his dead son. The futility of it all hit me then and I rubbed a hand over my face. What makes a man a foe or a friend? I have oft thought of this over the long years. I have fought friends, and I have befriended enemies. That morning I had clashed blades with Wistan, then moments later we had stood together against the threat of the Norsemen. It felt like a kind of madness. Tears stung my eyes as I looked down at the corpse of the man I had failed to save in the end.

I do not recollect much of what happened after that. I was dimly aware of Mancas arriving with his hearth-warriors. They came at a gallop, dismounting on the run and adding their numbers to the shieldwall. Soon, all the Norsemen were dead, massacred by the grim-faced warriors and the villagers whose terror was replaced by fury. The mud of the beach was a quagmire of red-foamed puddles by the time they had finished, the cadavers of the raiders like so many fish washed ashore on the tide.

A shadow fell over me.

"Are you hurt, Hunlaf?"

Looking up, I squinted into the bright sunshine. The rain had stopped, the storm fleeing as quickly as it had appeared. The sun lanced down now in great beams from between the dark clouds. I searched the sky for a rainbow, a promise from God of better things to come, but I saw none.

"Hunlaf?" the voice said again.

I peered up at the shadowed face. A hand reached for me. After a moment's hesitation, I grasped it and allowed Gwawrddur to pull me to my feet.

I had not moved from Wistan's side and I looked about now as if awakening from a dream. My ribs and stomach ached from the Norseman's knife blows. I half-expected to see Eafa still staring down at his son's corpse, but he had gone. Further up the beach, I spied him with several other villagers heaving bodies into a great pile of the dead.

Gwawrddur followed my gaze and nodded.

"Eafa it seems has found a taste for slaying." He glanced down at Wistan and sighed. "Perhaps revenge is all that is left for a father whose son is killed."

I looked down at Wistan's pale face. He had been a good man, brave and true. I had convinced myself that God had chosen me to defend the minster at Werceworthe, that it was the Lord who fanned the fire of anger within me, making me a formidable adversary. But surely it was not the work of the Almighty that I should believe myself above other men. That I should strut about proudly with disregard for the very people

I sought to protect. I should have been a friend to Wistan, instead I had betrayed him. And now he was dead.

Gwawrddur must have seen some of my thoughts in the bleak expression on my face.

"You cannot take the blame for all that happens in this world, Killer," he said. I scowled at the use of that name, turning angrily to face the Welshman. Dark mud and drying blood streaked his cheeks and forehead. "Each man can only be responsible for his own actions."

"That is what I am afraid of," I said, the anger ebbing from me as quickly as it had come. I was horrified to see what I had become. I understood then, all at once in a rush of clarity, how I had acted over the previous months. Gwawrddur had tried to warn me.

He placed a hand on my shoulder.

"You think you have done wrong," he said. It was not a question, but I nodded. He sniffed. "So do better next time. It is all any man can do."

I stared into Wistan's dead eyes. Next time? I vowed then that I would never again behave as I had that winter. I would not lust for another man's woman, nor break the trust of allies. But of course, I was yet a young man, and it was pride itself to believe I could fight against the weakness of my nature without the help of Christ.

Gwawrddur squeezed my shoulder.

"Enough moping, my friend," said another voice. Turning, I saw Runolf walking towards us. His red beard jutted and his eyes shone. "Look about you." He indicated the length of beach with his huge axe. I noticed that he had not yet cleaned the blood from its blade. "We have been victorious and there is much to celebrate."

I took in the corpses littering the beach, the puddles of blood and the debris from the shattered ship snagged against sandbanks and reeds. The hulking corpse of the sunken ship still jutted from the brown water, waves lapping against its timbers and rigging. Beyond the wreck, across the Uuir, dark smoke still smudged the sky where the minster buildings burnt.

"I see little to be thankful for," I said, my tone bitter.

"Well, I don't know why you are so glum," Runolf said with a wolfish grin. "I am beginning to believe you truly are blessed."

"Blessed?" I asked, my voice rising with the anger simmering close to the surface. I looked about the death-strewn beach. The sound of women's wailing, and the smell of smoke drifted on the breeze. "How am I blessed?"

Runolf raised his hand to calm me.

"Maybe that is the wrong word, but it seems to me your Christ god truly wishes us to finish building my ship."

"He's your God too," I answered, without thinking.

Runolf ignored me, raising an eyebrow. No matter how many times I reminded him, Runolf refused to admit he had been baptised and had accepted Christ as his saviour.

"How so?" I asked.

"You recall there were two things that Mancas was struggling to provide us with?"

I stared at him, forcing myself to think beyond the traumatic events of that morning and remember recent conversations about the procurement of supplies. Gwawrddur began to smile, but still I was unsure of Runolf's meaning.

As a reminder, the Norseman nodded towards the wreckage of the ship that rested less than a spear's throw from the riverbank. My eyes widened as I finally understood. Mancas had been able to find almost everything we needed, but there were two things he had not yet been able to find, both crucial for us to be able to depart once the ship was complete.

"Ropes," I said. "And a sail."

Runolf grinned.

"You see?" he said, looking out to the wrecked ship.

"You think God sent the storm?" I asked. I could not deny that we now had ample rope and the ship's sail was still clearly visible lapping in the river's muddy current.

"Who can say?" he replied. "Anything is possible."

Twelve

By midday, the dark clouds had vanished. The sky was pale and bright, the sun warm. Gazing up at the heavens, watching the guillemots and gannets swirling and swooping, I could almost forget the sudden violence of that morning. I had shrugged off my byrnie and soaked kirtle and examined my pale flesh. The imprint of the iron rings marked my skin like flower petals, surrounded by the beginnings of bruises that would bloom over the next few days. The iron shirt would need to be oiled and cleaned. If it was left for too long it would tarnish and rust, so later that day, we had some of Lord Mancas' thralls roll them in barrels of dry sand and then rub the clean byrnies with lard. But on the beach that morning, I was too tired to do anything. My body ached. But a deeper pain gnawed at me.

I thought of Leofstan and the disappointment on his face after the bloody battle at Werceworthe, and for the first time, I think I understood him.

Along the beach, the women set about tending to the wounded and the dead, while the men stripped the armour and weapons from the corpses of the Norsemen. Runolf and Hereward shouted orders, hurrying to save what they could from the shattered hulk of the ship in the river. Dully, I listened to Lord Mancas' soft voice, so unlike that of Hereward and

Runolf, as he ordered his hearth-warriors to ride along the river to search for any survivors who might have made their way ashore.

While the riverside was bustling with activity all around me, I slumped on the wet mud, seemingly unnoticed, or perhaps ignored. For a long time, I could not rouse myself. I languished in self-pity, watching the birds in the sky and allowing my mind to drift with them, pushing aside all other thoughts.

At last, Gersine came to me, pulling me away from the solace of the wheeling birds and my attempts to forget what had happened and who I had become.

"I've brought you a dry kirtle," he said, sitting down beside me and handing me a bundle of cloth.

Shaking out the garment, I recognised it as one of his. It was a creamy colour, with patterned hems the blue of the sky threaded with red. Nodding my thanks to him, I pulled it over my head.

We sat in silence for a time. Far off, I could hear women's voices. I thought I could detect weeping amongst them. I focused on a group of gulls, bobbing on the water at the river's mouth. I did not wish to be reminded of the sorrow left behind after the battle. Some time before, men had carried Wistan away, and I felt ashamed that I had not offered to help them.

I had been staring at the sky for so long in a daze that I was almost shocked to see the partially submerged wreck of the ship in the river. It was a tangle of splintered spars and sundered strakes. Several men swarmed over the wreckage and I could make out Runolf, his red hair and beard, bright in the warm sunshine. A couple of the fishermen had moored a boat against the hulk, and men were handing them coils of rope and other items that they managed to retrieve.

Beyond the ship, smoke from the minster still hazed the horizon.

"I was terrified," said Gersine, his voice small.

I glanced at him. He stared out at the ship and the men working there. He did not meet my gaze.

"Anyone who says he is not frightened when facing armed foe-men, is a liar," I said. "Or mad."

"Which are you?"

I frowned.

"I never said I was not scared."

"But I saw you. You did not hesitate. And you killed two of them in the water. I've never seen the like." His tone embarrassed me. He was in awe of something that did not exist. It was true that the strange coolness I had first felt at Lindisfarnae had come over me, as it always did in battle, but that did not mean I was without emotion.

"I was as frightened as any man," I said.

"But the way you killed those men!" He sounded much younger than his years and his tone grated on me. "It was so easy for you."

"No!" I shouted, pushing myself to my feet. I could still see the smiling face of the dark-bearded man, and the split skull and frightened eyes of the first Norseman I had slain. Their faces would be added to the others that came to me in my dreams. "Killing is never easy."

He stood beside me in awkward silence. Neither of us looked at the other, instead watching Runolf directing the men on the ship who were cutting away the sail for the fishermen in the boat to begin pulling in its great sodden expanse to the beach.

"You two," called a voice, and we both turned, glad of the distraction from our conversation. It was Hereward. He was beckoning to us.

We trudged up the strand to where he waited.

"Don't forget that," he said, pointing back to the mud where my heaped byrnie lay. "I think it will be too late now, but you don't want to be without it, should things get lively."

I retrieved the shirt. It was still wet and very cold. The sun had not warmed it at all.

"Where are we going?" asked Gersine, sounding eager.

"Over there." Hereward pointed across the wide river where the smoke still rose like a feather above the land, as if God Himself were writing on the parchment of the earth.

One of the fishermen, a quiet man called Heca, who always chewed a stick of hazel, ferried us across. From the water we could see the other side of the ship. It was clear why it had sunk. There was a hole in its hull that yawned dark as a cave. Runolf waved to us, grinning broadly as he worked to hack free the steering board from its frame. I raised my hand in greeting, but could not bring myself to smile.

Disembarking quickly, we made our way inland. Passing the stone edifice of Saint Peter's, I thought of its coloured glass windows and the golden rood that stood atop its altar.

"If that wind hadn't driven the ships onto the southern shore," said Gwawrddur, "I doubt much of that glass would remain unbroken."

"Perhaps God protected Fridwin's minster after all," said Hereward. I followed his gaze and understood his words. The smoke on the horizon was from further afield, not from the monastery of Uuiremutha, but from the more northerly buildings at Gyruum.

The same sombre mood I had felt ever since the attack descended on the others as we walked northward along the track. Bees and other insects, oblivious to the woes of mankind, flitted and droned over the comfrey and clover that grew in the thick hedgerows beside the path.

"Where is everyone?" asked Bealdwulf, who had picked up a long gash to his cheek in the fighting.

We had reached the minster buildings, but there was no sign of movement.

"Hiding like womenfolk," said Gamal.

"What else were they to do?" I snapped, angered at his tone. "They are men of prayer, not warriors. They were surely praying for our deliverance, and we are alive, are we not?"

He raised his eyebrows at my outburst.

"What about the monks at Gyruum then?" he asked, nodding northward at the pall of smoke in the sky. "Are they not praying? Does God not listen to the brethren there? For I wager that smoke is not from burning bread."

There was no answer to that, and I felt my face flush. I could smell the acrid smoke on the breeze and imagined how the fire must be raging at Gyruum for us to see the black column rising from so far away. The scent of the smoke carried with it dark memories. I had witnessed the savagery at Lindisfarnae. I knew the truth; that no amount of prayers would protect against the wrath of the northern heathens.

And yet, a small voice whispered, did not God send the sudden storm that wrecked their ships? Without the squall we might well have been overrun.

"Hail! Fridwin!" shouted Hereward, as we crossed the vallum. "You have nothing to fear from us. We have slain the Norsemen."

We walked into the open ground between the buildings and looked about us. Some hens scratched at the earth on the far side of the enclosure. Just beyond the ditch that surrounded the monastery, several piglets grunted and squealed in their muddy pen.

"You are safe now," called out Hereward.

We stood still, unspeaking. The silence was heavy. I could almost taste the fear on the air, mingling with the smoke. And I sensed we were being watched from the shadowed doorways and windows.

Hereward must have felt it too, for he raised a hand for us to remain silent while we waited patiently.

Eventually, tentatively, as if he expected to be struck down at any moment, a scrawny, long-legged monk I had not met before stepped from the scriptorium. He blinked in the bright sunshine. His skin was very pale and the thick black circle of hair on his head stood out starkly, as if he wore a strange cap of beaver fur.

We all turned towards him as he came outside. The monk flinched.

"You are safe," repeated Hereward. Other monks began to step into the daylight. "Where is Fridwin?"

The tall monk shook his head, then, after a pause he spoke.

"He is not here." His voice croaked, as if he had forgotten how to speak. I recalled life as a monk and the long days of silence. I could easily imagine this bookish man scratching away at the vellum in the scriptorium, seldom uttering a sound. "My name is Benesing."

"Where is he?" asked Hereward gruffly.

The monk made the sign of the cross, and several of the other men did the same.

"He went to Gyruum, to speak to Abbot Ethelbald."

Hereward sighed, casting a glance at the smoke over the northern minster.

"Do you have healers here?"

Benesing inclined his head, as if embarrassed by the question.

"The Lord has blessed us with some skills in that regard," he said.

Hereward nodded curtly.

"There are some injured men across the river. Go and tend to them."

"We will," replied Benesing, seeming pleased to be told what to do. "Alfhun, Sibbi," he called out, "fetch clean linen, honey and birch bark."

Trusting the monks to help Mancas' folk, we carried on northward. We didn't speak much, each lost in his own thoughts. We were guided by the dark pillar of smoke and, as the smell of the fires grew stronger, so our mood soured. We had survived the attack, but the greasy smear of smoke in the sky above Gyruum told us all we needed to know about what we would find there.

The ships had only just departed when we arrived. We watched three dragon-ships, their oars rising and falling like great fluttering wings, slide out of the Tine and into the grey waters of the North Sea.

"If only we had come sooner," said Gersine, his voice trembling with passion. Out on the swell, one after the other, the ships' sails unfurled to catch the afternoon breeze.

Taking in the devastation of the monastery, Hereward shook his head.

"Thank the Almighty that we did not," he said, his voice hollow.

"But we could have fought," Gersine said. "We might have saved some of the brethren here."

Hereward shook his head and walked away from the young man.

The buildings still burnt. Their heat was strong on my face. Most of the roofs had fallen in, leaving jagged dark timbers reaching from the flames and smoke like desperate fingers clawing at the sky. Corpses littered the ground all the way from the river bank to the blazing minster buildings. Some bodies bobbed in the shallow waters of the Tine.

I closed my eyes, trying to shut out the horror, but the stench of burning meat stung my throat. There was no escape from that nightmare. The sights and smells brought back vividly my memories of the previous summer.

"We should have fought, shouldn't we?" asked Gersine.

I turned my back on him and stalked away, following Hereward into the hell of the minster's destruction. Out on the Whale Road, the Norse ships' sails billowed with wind, pulling the heathen raiders away from Northumbria and towards their homeland. I thought of Aelfwyn, her husband slain before her eyes, and then carried off as a thrall, and a sudden rage filled me.

"If God wills it," I said to Gersine, "we will meet those men on our travels and we will make them pay for what they have done."

Thirteen

"I don't know," Gamal said, shaking his head. "I still don't understand that abbot." He reached for a piece of bread, soaking up the remnants of the pottage in his bowl.

Hereward did not answer immediately. Lifting his cup, he drank deeply.

"I think any man would be angry to see his people killed," he said at last with a sigh. "To watch his home destroyed."

"Yes." Gamal's speech was muffled by the wad of bread and pottage he was chewing. "It was not a great day for the monks, that is for sure." Across the small hall, Ida snorted at his friend's understatement. "But," Gamal went on, "Fridwin was angry at us. At you, and the boy."

He waved a hand in my direction. I said nothing, but to be called a boy infuriated me. Does a boy fight with sword and shield? The instant I thought this, I pushed my anger aside. Perhaps my behaviour these past months warranted me being referred to as a child.

We were seated in the gloom of the small hall south of the Uuir, safe on Mancas' land once more. Well, as safe as one can ever be. Hereward and Mancas had both insisted that we set a watch over the ship and the neighbouring settlement. Three ships had left Gyruum and it was possible they might sail a short way down the coast to seek retribution when they found that the two ships that had headed for the Uuir did not return.

Runolf had shaken his head at the suggestion.

"The wolves do not seek out the shepherd's hound when they have bellies full of lamb. They have taken much from the minster to the north. They will return home now. There is no need to risk losing what they have."

Runolf's words had the ring of truth, but Hereward and Mancas were cautious. None could truly say what the Norse might do, so it made sense to set a guard. There was too much at stake. But I thought Runolf was right. He understood the way our foe thought. If he said they would not attack again, I trusted his judgement.

One thing was certain: the three ships that we had seen sailing into the North Sea out of the Tine had been laden with treasure. They had stripped the church at Gyruum of its gold and silver trappings, and as far as we could ascertain from the monks who remained, about a score of the younger men and half a dozen women were missing, most likely bound and taken as thralls. The Norsemen had even snatched some of the more valuable tomes from the scriptorium before putting the building to the torch. I wondered at that. They had seemed uninterested in the books at Lindisfarnae, but later we had discovered they had taken *The Treasure of Life*, or at least its ornate cover. Perhaps they had realised the value of the writing on the pages now, and not just the gold and gems that encrusted the leather that bound them.

Bealdwulf yawned expansively, then winced as the movement caused the scab on his cheek to split. We were all exhausted.

"A man will always blame those who bring him bad tidings. That is why Fridwin raged. It is the way of things." He shrugged, and sipped his ale.

"But we warned him this might happen," I said, recalling how the red-faced abbot had screamed at us, as the minster burnt and his brethren lay dead. "We offered our aid."

"Men seldom admit their own failings. It is ever thus. When a tiny child learns to take its first steps and then seeks to run, his mother will warn him that he will trip. And when he does and barks his knee, who does he blame? Himself? No, he screams at his mother. She told him what would happen, so it must be her fault."

I wondered whether Bealdwulf had children of his own. He was older than the rest of the men who had come from Bebbanburg. He was broad of chest, and his face was scarred and often dour, but he was thoughtful and had shown me nothing but kindness. During that long hot afternoon at Gyruum, he had helped Gersine and me with the hard work of digging graves for the fallen monks. I realised now with a start, that although I had known him for months, I knew next to nothing about the warrior. He reminded me of Drosten in that regard. Some men rarely speak of themselves. Such men are like oysters, clammed shut until, from time to time, they open up and offer a pearl from within their shell.

Bealdwulf had barely spoken all that afternoon. None of us had. We had put our heads down and pushed the wooden blades of our shovels into the sandy soil. The sun was hot on our necks and the heat from the dying fires warmed our cheeks. Soot, smoke and ash stung our eyes and caught in our throats. After Fridwin's outraged outburst, I wanted nothing more than to focus my energies on a practical task, away from the dazed, hollow-eyed faces of the men and women who had survived the attack. The stink of burning, and the sounds of lamentations from the survivors conjured up memories of Lindisfarnae and Werceworthe. How many more monasteries would be sacked? How many more innocents defiled, murdered or enslaved? I'd glanced at the smouldering remains of the scriptorium. How much more knowledge and learning would be destroyed?

"You should not have come here!" Fridwin had yelled at me, his soot-stained face streaked with tears.

"We come to offer our aid," Hereward had said, speaking in a soft, soothing tone. But his words did nothing to placate the abbot's fury.

"No!" he screamed, spittle flying from his mouth. "Look! Look at what they have done." His words caught in his throat as he sobbed. He spread his hands wide to encompass the terrible destruction of the minster. "You," he shouted suddenly, his voice as harsh and loud as a slap. He stared into my face and I was shocked to see genuine hatred there. "You brought this upon us. You turned your back on the Lord and now you reap what you sow."

The old abbot of Gyruum had tottered up to us then. Ethelbald's face was also smudged with dirt and soot, but rather than tears, his cheeks and forehead were streaked with blood from a deep gash in his head. He nodded sadly to us and unsteadily led Fridwin away.

I'd thought about Fridwin's words as we dug. Was I somehow to blame for what had occurred? Could it be, as Leofstan had feared, that *The Treasure of Life* had unleashed some strange evil upon the land? I knew then, as I know now, that my actions had led to the duel with Wistan. And, even though I had tried to save him in the end, if the Norse had not attacked that morning, I would have taken his life, harvesting the bitter fruits of the seeds of discontent that I had planted by my selfish actions.

Later in the afternoon, an elderly monk, his eyes vacant and sorrowful, brought us a skin of water. When we paused to drink and wipe the sweat from our brows, I glanced out at the sea, glad that the Norse ships were ever further from land. I felt a great relief when the last sail had disappeared over the rim of the earth. And, not for the first time, I questioned the wisdom of the plan that would see us sail a single ship across the Whale Road to a land of forests and mountains inhabited by such heathens as these men who would slaughter God-fearing people for silver and gold.

Still, it was my plan. I would reap what I had sown.

It had been dark when we had returned to Uuiremutha. The brethren and those lay people who remained at Gyruum had huddled into the few houses that had not been consumed by the flames. The women, thin-lipped and dark-eyed in grief, had set about preparing food. Ethelbald offered us a roof over our heads and such hospitality as he was able to give, but there was barely enough room for the inhabitants of Gyruum. And perhaps Hereward could sense the mood amongst us, for he declined. None of us wished to be there, surrounded by sorrow and mourning, so we had traipsed home as the sun touched the treetops of the forests in the west.

At the riverbank we had needed to call out several times before Heca shouted back over the water. Shortly afterwards, his boat had slid out of the darkness.

"I thought you were not going to return this night," he grumbled, as we clambered aboard. The boat rocked and Pendrad, the youngest of the warriors from Bebbanburg, cursed as his foot slipped into the water. Strong hands grabbed him, hauling him into the vessel.

"Well, here we are," Hereward said.

Heca tutted and, though I could not see his face in the night, I could imagine the hazel twig in his mouth twitching.

The shadowy form of the wreck loomed to our left as Heca and his boy poled the boat back to Uuiremutha. Nobody spoke.

As we disembarked, Heca whispered, "Was it bad, lord?" Like many of the fishermen, Heca called any man with a sword "lord".

There was a brief silence and I wondered whether anyone was going to answer him.

"Aye," said Hereward, his tone bleak, "it was bad."

It was shortly after we had left the river's edge to make our way back to the hall when we were stopped by one of Mancas' men who was on watch. Hereward had a brief conversation with him, before saying that Oslaf, Sygbald and Pendrad would join the men on guard as soon as they had eaten. The three warriors groaned, but did not argue.

The night was quiet and still, the only sounds the whisper of waves to the east, the rustle of the wind through the leaves of the oak trees that grew near the hall and the crunch of our weary feet on the track.

In the distance, I could see a thin light shining from beneath the door of the house Cwenswith shared with her father and three younger sisters. I had not seen her since that morning, but the thought of her, where once it would have excited me, now just filled me with sadness and regret. I saw then that I had never truly loved her. The moment I had stood before Wistan and heard her screeching calls for me to injure him, the image I'd had of her in my mind was shattered.

"You think the king will send us more men?" asked Ida, bringing me back from my memories and into the hall.

Mancas had sent a rider to Eoforwic with the news of the day's events.

"Anything is possible," replied Hereward, provoking a chuckle from some of the men at his use of Runolf's favourite phrase. "But I doubt it. Æthelred is not generous when it comes to such things."

"If nothing else," said Gwawrddur from where he was stretched out wrapped in his cloak, "the tidings of the attack and the sacking of the minster at Gyruum will further our cause."

"Yes, there should be no doubt now that we need to better

defend the coast." Hereward sipped his ale and nodded at me. "And a trade deal with these Norsemen, if such a thing is possible, would be preferable to these attacks."

For a time nobody spoke. It was late and the food, drink and the events of the day had all taken their toll. Ida and Gamal finished sharpening and cleaning their blades, both sliding their swords into their scabbards and setting them aside. Bealdwulf shook out his cloak and moved to a dark corner of the hall to sleep. Oslaf, Sygbald and Pendrad had gone some time before to join the watch, and I knew it would not be long before I would be called to do my duty. My eyelids were heavy. I needed sleep. Emptying my cup of ale, I rose from the bench, preparing to follow Bealdwulf to the shadows with my cloak and a blanket, when a sudden commotion outside halted my movements.

Shouts and clamouring came from the direction of the river.

Instantly, every man in the hall was alert. It had taken us a long time to relax after the stresses of the day, and those yells in the night dispelled what peace we had found in an eye-blink. Pulling byrnies from the greased sacks where they had been kept after cleaning, we shook them out and wriggled into them once more, ready for what the night held in store for us. Belts were strapped tightly, and swords loosened in their scabbards. With a clatter, we each fetched our shield from the pile near the entrance.

Hereward flung open the door of the hall. Far off, we could hear yelling. A bright light sprang up from a fire down by the beach, where our ship was being built. Was this another attack? Could it be that the Norse had returned to exact vengeance? My throat was dry as I followed Hereward and the others out into the cool air of the night.

I peered into the darkness. There was movement there, a figure silhouetted against the fire. It was running towards us. I placed my hand on my sword's grip, ready to draw the blade out.

"Oslaf?" Hereward called out, evidently recognising the man by his size and gait.

"The same," Oslaf panted. "I did not think you would wish to miss this."

"What has happened?" asked Hereward, his words clipped. "Another attack? Have they returned?"

"No," said Oslaf. The pale light from the rush lights in the hall spilt from the open door and illuminated his face. His eyes were wide, excited, and a half-smile played on his lips. "But there are more Norse bastards down there."

"What do you mean?"

"We captured two of the whoresons on the beach."

Fourteen

By the time we arrived at the water's edge, one of the Norsemen was already dead.

Someone had lit a large fire and for a fleeting moment I wondered at the wasted wood, until I remembered the wrecked ships. There was surely enough detritus for a bonfire. The flames leapt high into the night sky, and the heat on my face brought back to my mind the afternoon's toil at Gyruum. In the flickering light I could make out the inert form of a bearded man. He had been stripped. His pale skin was mottled with bruises and blood. His eyes were wide open. The flames' reflection danced in them, giving the impression of movement.

"That one tried to run," said Oslaf, nodding at the corpse. "He didn't get far."

Several men were gathered around the fire, their faces stern and sombre in the hot light of the flames.

We pushed our way through the crowd, until we were able to see what they were looking at. On the muddy earth, where that morning I had faced Wistan, knelt a thickset man. His hair and beard were fair and long. Blood trickled from his nose, but he appeared otherwise unhurt. To my surprise, I saw he was smiling, gazing up at the man looming over him.

It was Runolf. His bulk and red hair unmistakable, as was the massive battle axe at his side. His back was to me, but I could hear his voice and there was no warmth in his words.

"Do not grin at me, Torfi Sturlasson," Runolf growled. "We are not well met here."

The kneeling man licked his lips. His eyes darted to the naked man sprawled on the earth.

"I am doing better than Orm."

Runolf shook his head.

"Orm fought."

"And lost." Torfi shrugged. "What good is there in that?"

"Mayhap he is now dining with Óðinn in his corpse hall, for the All-father loves the brave warrior above all else."

"I am no coward," Torfi said, his gaze twitching nervously to take in the grim faces of the men staring down at him. "You know this."

Runolf sighed.

"It is true," he said, nodding. "I heard tell of your hólmgang with Sokkolf the Quiet. They say he shattered all of your shields and still you fought on."

"And I won." Torfi puffed out his chest, attempting a boastful pose that was hampered somewhat by being knelt in the mud.

"What are they speaking of," asked Sygbald from the gloom. Several of the others grumbled, adding their voices to the question. Runolf and Torfi were conversing in their native tongue and whilst it was possible for Englisc and Norse to understand each other using simple words and phrases, often with the aid of signs and gestures, I was the only Northumbrian there who understood the language of the Norsemen well.

"They are speaking of the man's bravery in combat," I said. "He won a great duel, it seems."

A growl of anger rippled through the gathered men, as if they were a pack of hounds, sniffing a hare on the wind.

"We care nothing for the man's battle-fame," said Hereward to Runolf. "What we need is information."

Runolf glanced over at Hereward and nodded.

"You sailed with Øybiorn, no?" Runolf asked.

I continued to interpret their words in a hushed commentary for the men listening.

"Aye," said Torfi. "Some skipper he was. He led us to one defeat after another and then wrecks his ship. The gods alone know why such a fool should gain so much wealth. To have his own ship and warband, but never know victory."

"He knew victory well enough," said Runolf, "when he was a young man. And Øybiorn was no fool."

"Tell that to Orm and all the others who died today."

"You cannot blame Øybiorn for the weather. That storm came from nowhere. None could have predicted it."

Torfi spat.

"Perhaps. His luck had changed of late, for sure. And I do blame him for leading us to defeats. The holy men of the White Christ are rich and soft, and yet still Øybiorn failed us."

"He was wise to turn away last year," Runolf said. Øybiorn had sailed his ship with Skorri to Werceworthe, but had left in search of easier prey after our first clash when we had killed several of the Norse.

Torfi's eyes narrowed. "Perhaps. But if we had stayed, things might not have gone so badly for Skorri."

Runolf shrugged.

"Anything is possible. But my brother and all those with him are now dead. It seems to me that Øybiorn gained you another year of life."

"I am not dead yet."

Runolf shook his head.

"You will never leave here with your life," he said. "These people will not allow it."

A log shifted in the fire, settling with a crack. Torfi flinched at the sound. A flurry of sparks flew into the dark sky to be lost in the stars that glimmered there. Once again, Torfi cast his gaze around, taking in the hard faces of the men surrounding him.

On hearing my translation of Runolf's pronouncement, the warriors, fishermen and craftsmen around the fire nodded and grumbled.

"You yet live," Torfi stated, staring up at Runolf.

"I do. But you are not me," he replied. Was there a hint of sadness in Runolf's tone? "But I can offer you something."

"What?" Torfi's tone was eager. He sensed a way out of this.

"If you tell me what I want," said Runolf, his voice as gravelly and dark as the beach where we had slaughtered Torfi's countrymen, "I will place a blade in your hand when the time comes." He paused, holding Torfi's gaze. "And I will make your death quick. I know you to be a brave man. I think Óðinn would want you at his table."

Torfi swallowed. For a long while he said nothing. The flames crackled and hissed. Despite the heat they gave off, I shivered in the darkness.

"There is no other way then?" asked Torfi.

I wondered whether it might not be better to keep this man alive. He could sail and fight, and we would need all the men we could find to crew the ship once it was complete. But Runolf shook his head.

Torfi sighed and lowered his head as if in prayer. After a time, he looked up once more. His eyes gleamed.

"Very well," he said. "But I curse Øybiorn for his bad luck. What would you know from me, Runolf Ragnarsson?"

Runolf leaned forward, his voice low, like the whisper of the waves off in the night.

"Tell me of Estrid."

A thin smile returned to Torfi's lips.

"Ah, it is always the womenfolk that drive us."

Runolf said nothing. I thought of Cwenswith and my cheeks grew hot in the darkness. I did not relay their words.

"What would you have me tell you?" Torfi asked.

"How does she fare?"

"If you are asking whether she has found a new husband, the answer is no. Though I doubt such a beauty will be alone for long."

Runolf growled and I noted his huge hand tightening on the haft of the great axe that rested on the earth at his side.

"Come now, Runolf," Torfi said. "You have asked me for tidings of her, and you know as well as I that a steading cannot be run by a woman alone." He hesitated, perhaps weighing up the impact of his next words. "After you left," Torfi went on, "Estrid took in with Skorri. You knew this, no?"

Runolf's shoulders tensed. He nodded, but did not speak. Torfi, seemingly satisfied that he would not be struck down for speaking, ploughed on.

"Since he failed to return at the end of last summer, Estrid has found it hard to work the land. As soon as the snows melted, she went about buying more thralls. Skorri left her a wealthy woman, so silver was no problem."

At the mention of thralls, Runolf flicked a glance at me. I was busy speaking their words in Englisc for the onlookers, but I nodded at him, willing him to enquire about Aelfwyn. All we had discovered the year before was that Aelfwyn had been bought by a wealthy landowner. A man Runolf knew, called Kolfinn.

"You know anything of the thralls bought by Kolfinn?" he asked.

Torfi seemed surprised by the question and sudden change in the direction of the interrogation.

"Kolfinn Refsson of Talgje?"

"The same."

"It is strange you should ask about old Kolfinn."

"How so?"

"Well, I was telling you about Estrid buying more slaves for the farmstead. She went into Hesby when the snows thawed and bought several strong men. She wasn't looking to buy any womenfolk, but Kolfinn made her an offer she could not refuse, so she took a pretty little thing off his hands."

My heart pounded with hope.

"Do you remember her name, this thrall?" I asked.

Torfi stared at me for a moment, his eyes narrowing.

"Do you think I recall the names of all the thralls taken in the raids last year? She was one of your folk. Skorri took her from the holy island to the north of here. I don't know her name, but no man would forget her face. Now there's a thrall to warm a man's bed during the cold winter months."

I snarled, and took a step forward. Torfi laughed.

"It seems Kolfinn had the same idea as me," he said, undaunted by my anger. "But his wife was not so happy with such a comely thrall in her husband's hall. It was she who made him sell her. Last I heard she was one of Estrid's household."

There could be no doubt. Surely this thrall he spoke of was Aelfwyn.

"Of course, I haven't heard anything lately from up the Boknafjorden. Not since the Ljósberari came with his fires, and his talk of demons and darkness." Torfi shuddered. Much of his face was in shadow, but the firelight picked out the fear in his eyes.

"Ljósberari?" asked Runolf. He sounded as confused as I was by this new name.

Torfi nodded, his expression sombre.

"It is a grave thing," he said. "They say he was a thrall—"

His words were cut off by a shrieking howl. Everyone turned to see where the sound came from. The men around me stumbled back, pushing and shoving. For a heartbeat, I was confused. My hand dropped to my sword. This must be another attack. Perhaps the Norse had sailed through the night and now, while we were distracted by Torfi speaking in the glare of the fire, they had crept up to us to mete out their revenge. But even as I thought this, so I saw there was only one man. Maybe another Norse survivor, come to rescue his comrade.

Firelight glinted from a sharp spear-point that the screaming man held aloft. The flames lit up his face as he rushed past me and I knew instantly that this was no rescue for Torfi. This was Death himself, come in the guise of a grieving father.

Eafa bellowed as he sprang forward, rushing between the gathered ranks of men around the fire. Torfi was still kneeling, his mouth open, eyes turned towards the sudden disturbance. Eafa's spear tip plunged into the Norseman's left eye, killing him instantly. Such was the force of the blow that the steel point burst through the back of Torfi's skull. The weight of the corpse tugged the spear haft from Eafa's hands and Torfi slumped onto his back, his legs twisted beneath him, arms wide as if welcoming an embrace. His fingers twitched for a few heartbeats, as if plucking at invisible threads. The spear haft quivered, and then was still, jutting towards the sky like the mast of a canted ship.

Eafa, chest heaving, looked down at the dead man. There was very little blood, I noticed, just a trickle beneath Torfi's pierced eye. Like a dark tear.

Runolf surged forward, pushing Eafa in the chest. Eafa, older and smaller than the tall axeman, staggered. He was caught by some of the onlookers.

"You should not have done that," said Runolf. In his hand he held his axe, as if it weighed no more than a twig. I wondered whether he was going to slay the man then, such was the fury on his face. Without thinking, I stepped forward, placing myself between Runolf and Eafa. Wistan had died to save his father, I would not allow the older man to be killed now.

I drew in a deep breath. If Runolf struck with his axe, I would die. I would not raise my sword against him, but even if I attempted to defend myself, I was no match for the Norse giant.

"Runolf, no," said Hereward, his voice firm, but low.

Runolf glowered at me. Then, with a shake of his shaggy head and a sigh, he turned away, looking down at Torfi's body.

"You should not have done that," he repeated. "I gave him my word."

"Those bastard Norsemen killed my boy," said Eafa, his words turning to sobs.

"This bastard Norseman likes to keep his word," said Runolf, but the ire was gone from his tone. I looked down at Torfi and felt my own pang of anger at Eafa. Torfi had known about Aelfwyn. What more could he have told us? But as his friends and neighbours led Eafa away, I let out a sigh. The man had lost his son. Who was I to question his actions?

Runolf placed a hand on my shoulder. I started at his touch, glancing into his bearded face. But there was no rage there now.

"It seems, young Hunlaf," he said, "that both of the women we seek – the treacherous whore and your innocent kinswoman – are at my brother's hall."

I shook my head, trying to make sense of this.

"Who is this Ljósberari, he spoke of?" I asked. Something about the name troubled me.

"I have no idea," said Runolf, frowning. Suddenly, he grinned. "But we will find out. Just as soon as we finish that ship." He gestured with his chin towards the shadowed shape of the ship. It was no longer just bones. Much of the hull was completed, and with the ropes and sail from the wrecks, it would only be a matter of weeks before we could sail.

The crowd dispersed. Some of the men were once again set to guard the beach and the approaches to the settlement. I had not slept, but slumber seemed far away now, so I took my turn on watch, glad of the tranquillity of the night. But as I stood at the river's mouth, staring out into the darkness of sea and sky, the only sound the wave-rush on the beach, the only light the cold moon and stars high above, I could not silence my thoughts.

Aelfwyn was part of Estrid's household. The thought of her, far off in a pagan land that I could barely imagine, filled me with anxiety. But it was not the thoughts of Aelfwyn that caused the cold fingers of dread to scratch down my spine.

A name echoed in my night-time thoughts. It hissed with the waves sighing on the shingle in the darkness.

Ljósberari. The light bearer. I had heard the name before, I was sure, but not in Norse.

Fifteen

"It really is a thing of beauty," I said, and I meant it.

The ship was finally finished. The day before, we had rolled it down to the water's edge, lowering it as carefully as possible into the waters of the Uuir. We had all strained at the ropes, and my palms bore the blisters from helping to hold the great bulk of the vessel. The ship was huge, as big as any ship I had ever seen, and when on land, I had wondered at its sheer size. How could such a massive thing, as large as a hall, and as heavy, float on water, skimming atop the waves of the Whale Road?

But as soon as it slid into the river with a splash, it was as if the ship had been born again, baptised to become a new thing. It had rocked and bobbed on the broad waters of the Uuir, and instantly, I believed anew that this ship that Runolf had built would carry us over the North Sea and beyond.

"It is," said Runolf, unable to keep the grin from his face. "It might be the finest ship I have ever built. Which is a feat indeed considering the men I had to work with." He laughed, taking the sting from his words. He slapped Wihtgar on the back. Wihtgar, a stocky man with wise eyes, smiled. He was a quiet one, but he had picked up Runolf's instructions effortlessly, and I knew that the Norseman valued him as a fine craftsman and someone worthy of taking on the new skills he had imparted.

Since the attack, some five weeks previously, both men had driven the builders harder than ever. On hearing about Estrid from Torfi, Runolf's desire to set sail burnt with a hot flame, and Wihtgar was keen to help him. Wihtgar had already begun the process of finding suitable lumber for a new ship, and I believed he relished the idea of building his own vessel without the help of his Norse mentor. I recognised the gleam in his eye. I used to feel the same sensation when presented with a fresh page of vellum. Wihtgar longed to test the limits of his knowledge and create something truly his.

Runolf and Wihtgar had come down to the moored ship to perform their final inspections before the feast. They had checked everything before, but they were both restless. The day was growing old, the shadows lengthening as the sun lowered into the west, but we were close to midsummer, so it would not be dark for some time yet. Everyone had been invited to a great feast at the small hall, and the smell of roasting pig was already thick in the warm air. Mancas had offered to host the celebration at his great hall, which was much larger and would easily cope with so many visitors, but we were all anxious not to be too far from the ship we had spent months building.

Despite Runolf having salvaged as much as possible from the sunken ship, its timber ribs still jutted from the river at low tide, a stark reminder of the attack and what can occur to a vessel when bad luck strikes.

We had seen no further sign of Norse invaders, but sometimes, far out to sea, we saw sails, and I wondered whether those might be ships bearing heathen raiders to some unsuspecting minster along the coast. We had seen no sails for days, but we were not prepared to leave the ship unprotected. And yet, after so many weeks of gruelling work, the prospect of the feast was alluring, and none of us wished to miss it in order to stand guard beside the river.

In the end, Hereward made us draw lots to see who would be on watch, while the rest gorged on roasted meat and smoked herring, drank Mancas' fine ale and mead, and told tales and riddles into the night. Counting out a stalk of hay for each man, Hereward ripped three in half. Then, he placed all of the stalks, long and short, in his fist so that only the ends could be seen. We each picked one.

I had been crestfallen to pull a short straw from Hereward's clenched hand. I knew the night would be long, and I did not relish the seemingly interminable darkness, alone with my thoughts, listening to the distant revelry coming from the hall.

I had been surprised when Drosten had reached over and exchanged his long stalk for my short one. The tattooed Pict had smiled.

"I don't mind watching over her," he said. "Just see that you bring me a flagon of ale."

"I will," I said, grinning.

"See that you bring my ale before you collapse. We all know you cannot handle your drink, Killer." I frowned at his use of Gwawrddur's name for me. But Drosten grinned and clapped me on the back and my anger quickly faded.

Now, with the golden light of the afternoon sun picking out all of the details of the ship's sleek lines, I saw that Drosten was already here. Hereward had said that the night guard could first eat at the hall, before coming down to the wharf at dusk. Neither of the other guards was there yet. But they did not have the affinity for the ship that Drosten had. He had discovered that his hands, gifted as they were for fighting, also possessed the ability to create beauty. When Runolf had seen how the Pict worked the wood, how he could sense the flow of the grain, working with it to split and shape the timbers needed for the ribs, thwarts and strakes, the Norseman had given Drosten a huge piece of oak to carve.

I had watched them whispering over the hunk of timber, drawing on it with a piece of chalk, measuring out lines, sketching curves. It was to become the prow beast for the ship. One night in our hall, Drosten told Runolf he was not capable of such a task. It was too much responsibility.

"This is your fear talking," Runolf said. "When you stand in battle, you are scared, no?"

Drosten shrugged. No man liked to be reminded of his fear.

"We are all scared," Runolf said. "We fear what might be, the unknown. But still we fight."

The other men nodded. Drosten shook his head.

"This is not the same," he said. "I am fighting nobody here. There is just the oak. And me."

Runolf nodded.

"And you must defeat both. The wood, that does not always wish to release its secrets, and your own fear, that will only make your hands tremble. Cut boldly. Reveal the beast within the timber. I have watched you shaping wood. You have a rare talent. You must not listen to your fear. Listen to me, for I say you can do this thing and I wish to see what your knife and chisel will bring forth."

From that moment, whenever he was not called upon to work on the ship itself, or to stand guard duty, Drosten spent all his waking time carving the prow. He would sometimes even miss the evening meal, working in one of the storage huts by the light of a tallow candle. One dark spring night, when the moon was new, I had slipped out of the hall to meet with Cwenswith. We saw the light from beneath the ill-fitting door of the store building. Creeping close, we peered through a crack, our faces close, Cwenswith's hair and breath maddeningly stroking my cheek, igniting my desire. Drosten was unaware of us. He was hunched over his work in deepest concentration, his brow wrinkled, his tongue protruding from his mouth as he meticulously carved a tricky shape. He had the appearance of a scribe surrounded by quills, ink and parchment, and yet all around Drosten were the curled feathers and shavings of wood that his knife lifted from the block. Cwenswith had sniggered at the burly warrior's intense expression, whispering disparagingly about his unswerving focus on the wood. Not wishing to interrupt the man at his work, I had led her away, angered by her demeaning words. I respected the fire of creativity that had been kindled within the Pict and I felt as though Cwenswith's jibes were directed at me. She saw only the sword-wearing warrior, who swaggered in a fine cloak, she knew nothing of who I had been. Of the man I truly was. By the time we had reached our own store room, I had made up my mind that I would not succumb to Cwenswith's charms until I had made her understand what drove men like Drosten. And me. That night I discovered how very weak a young man's resolve can be when confronted with the determined ministrations of a comely woman.

As the days grew relentlessly longer and warmer, Drosten's beast slowly took shape. His nervousness was palpable on the day that Runolf pronounced to us all that the prow was finished and that the following morning Drosten would unveil it for us all to see. I had never before seen the Pict so uneasy. Here was a man who could best most opponents with his fists. I had watched him take a beating from a man larger and stronger, only for Drosten to come surging back to drop his adversary with precise and powerful punches. I had seen him rushing to Gwawrddur's defence at Werceworthe, the Norse corpses piled before them. And yet now, at the prospect of having his friends bear witness to something he had created from his imagination, Drosten's kirtle was drenched in sweat and he could not stand still.

The following day was bright and there was an air of

excitement about the settlement. Runolf had covered the figurehead with a cloak. He grinned as we crowded around. The men put down their axes, adzes and augers. The goodwives set aside their spindles and their cooking spoons. Even the children ceased their incessant rushing about, to stand quietly and see what the surly Pict had been working on for so long.

"Drosten," called Runolf, "come here." Reluctantly, the Pict, his tattooed face adding to his scowling appearance, stepped forward. "Drosten is worried that we will not like what he has produced." Runolf swept us all with his gaze. "But I tell you now, he has nothing to fear. Unlike those who seek to fight against us when we sail in the ship bearing this beast upon its prow." His grin broadened, and Gersine, Gamal and Ida let out a small cheer at Runolf's bravado. The Norseman nodded at them, then waited for the men to quieten once more before continuing. "I have not wished to tell you the name of the ship we have built before now, but it has been in my mind for a long time. I wished to see Drosten's completed carving first, to see whether it would be a fitting beast for the name." Drosten looked at the ground. His tattoos stood out bold against the flush of his cheeks. Runolf put his arm around the man and chuckled at his discomfort. "But now that I have seen it," he said, "I find it is more than fit. It is the best thing I have ever seen, and there can be no doubt that it suits the ship, and the name."

He gripped the cloak in his huge fist, readying himself to pull it away. His other arm was wrapped about Drosten's neck, preventing him from fleeing and missing this moment.

"Behold," Runolf said, "the prow beast of *Brymsteda*."

He tugged the woollen cloth back to reveal the sculpture. I had seen glimpses of it during the process, but I was not prepared for the effect the final creation would have on me. I had thought Runolf's words to be said partly to please Drosten. But as I gazed at the carving, standing starkly against the pale blue sky, I understood that Runolf had merely spoken the truth. The carving was exquisite. And it was undoubtedly fit for the name he had given to the ship.

Brymsteda, the sea steed.

It was the head of a horse, ears flat and mane flowing, as if galloping. The hairs of the mane were interlocked and intertwined, carved in such a way as to appear alive with movement and yet also following a pattern of interlacing lines. The stallion's eyes were wide and piercing, surrounded by whorls and curls reminiscent of the tattoos upon Drosten's body. Its mouth was open, the patterned lips pulled back from the teeth, which were picked out in exacting detail. The animal's nostrils flared in fury, giving the beast a warlike aspect.

Everyone fell silent, in awe of the skill and artistry displayed. And then, as if agreed beforehand, we all began to clap and cheer at once. Drosten's cheeks were red behind his tattoos, but he grinned with relief and pleasure at the reception of his work.

It was only a few days later that the beast was lifted onto the prow of the ship. It was attached in such a way that it could be removed easily when needed.

"We do not wish to frighten away friendly spirits," Runolf had said, by way of explanation. I frowned and made the sign of the cross, but I said nothing. Despite being baptised, I knew he was no follower of Christ, not in his heart. He still believed that Þórr caused the storms that lashed the coast during the winter, that Freyr breathed life into the shoots of the plants in spring, and quickened the bellies of the womenfolk when they became pregnant. Whenever I could, I spoke to him of Jesus' teachings, but I sensed they never captured his attention in the same way as the tales of the grey-cloaked All-father, Óðinn, striding across the land with his two ravens, Huginn and Muninn.

Runolf seemed bored when Benesing came to bless the ship.

The Norse giant had stood on the deck with his hand proudly on the mane of the stallion's head, staring out toward the grey expanse of the sea. In his mind, I thought he was already sailing there.

Hereward had invited Fridwin, as the senior member of the brethren, to perform the rite, but the abbot sent Benesing instead. The toll on the minster at Gyruum had been terrible, and Benesing told us that Fridwin had not been himself since that day. I had not seen him since he had screamed at me, but he still allowed Benesing and some of the other monks to come to the settlement, where they tended to the wounds and ailments of the villagers. The monks were well-liked and I don't think any of us missed Fridwin's presence when we saw it was Benesing, accompanied by the younger Alfhun and Sibbi, that Heca ferried over the river for the blessing ceremony.

I liked Benesing, he was kind, and I would sometimes speak with him and the other monks when they visited, taking solace in being able to converse with men who had a shared background with me. On a couple of occasions I had followed them back over the Uuir when they had headed home to the monastery. At those times I persuaded them to pray with me in the church, and I was thankful to them for their communion.

"Harken, O Lord, to our supplications and bless," Benesing intoned in Latin, making the sign of the cross in the air, "by Thy holy right hand this ship and all who travel in it, as Thou hast vouchsafed to bless Noah's ark carried upon the waves of the flood."

Benesing was pleasant enough, but he was no orator. I understood the words he recited in Latin, as we stood beside the ship. And yet I was the only one there who did, apart from his fellow monks, and his tone droned as he prayed over *Brymsteda*.

"... send Thy holy Angel from heaven," he went on, "who may deliver and protect this boat from all dangers, with all who will be therein: and repelling all adversities, grant Thy servants a calm voyage and the always wished-for haven, let them carry out and rightly finish their business, and when the time comes again, call them back to their home with all joy. Amen."

Thankfully, just as the children started to fidget, the blessing was over.

The people drifted away, and Hereward thanked Benesing for coming.

I looked at the ship and saw Runolf standing alone, still at the prow. As I watched, he pulled a leather flask from beneath his kirtle. Unstopping it, he poured some liquid on *Brymsteda*'s strakes, prow and deck. He had his back to me, and the brisk breeze from the sea shook the alders, so I could not be certain, but I thought over the rustling of the leaves and the distant sigh of the sea, I could make out Runolf's rumbling tone.

Captivated, I clambered aboard the ship, making my way from its broad belly to the sleek rearing prow where Runolf stood. The ship was redolent of sap and the dark pine tar used to caulk every join. At the sound of my step, Runolf spun around. Seeing my eyes flick down to the flask in his hand, he hesitated, then held it out to me.

"Mead?" he said. "I was drinking to the ship." He took a deep breath through his nose and sighed. "Smell that? I love the smell of a new ship."

I accepted the leather bottle. Tugging out the stopper, I took a swig. It was good and sweet. Mancas' steward only supplied us with the best.

"What were you saying?" I asked.

"Just now?"

I nodded.

"I was naming the ship," he said, taking the flask back from me and drinking deeply.

"You already named it. A good name."

He looked into the distance, at the line where the sea met the sky.

"Yes, a good name," he said, "but an Englisc name all the same. It is good that it has been blessed by your Christ god."

"Your God too," I said, without thinking.

He smiled.

"I wanted it to be named according to the ways of my people, as my father and his father before him named all of their ships."

I noted the sadness in him then, and imagined how lonely he must have been. I missed Leofstan and the brethren who had been my family for years, but I was still in the kingdom where I had been born, surrounded by men and women who spoke and thought like me. And though I had left the monastery, I could still pray as I wished.

I placed my hand on Runolf's shoulder. I felt closer to him in that moment, than ever before.

"How did your father name his ships?" I asked. "What words are said?"

"They are not Christian words," he said, his voice low. "Not words from your god."

I did not correct him this time.

"Still, I would hear them, if you would speak them to me."

He nodded.

"It is well. We have both drunk of the mead and I have offered some to the ship." He extended his arm and poured a trickle of the liquid into the river. "And now I have offered some to the god of the ocean."

I held my breath. I felt that if I should breathe, somehow I would be giving part of my life to whatever pagan ritual was about to follow.

Runolf held my gaze for a time, and then spoke in his deep voice, not whispering now, but glad to be sharing these words with another.

"May Njörðr always fill the sail of *Brymsteda*," he intoned. "May its sails always grace the horizon and may its keel always kiss the sea."

Runolf drank again and made me take another sip of mead. And with that, it was over. The flask was almost empty now, and Runolf grinned as he drained the last drops. I wondered how Beonna, the old Abbot of Werceworthe would react if he knew what I had been part of. I told myself that to listen to these words did not make me a heathen.

"Is that it?" I asked.

"Yes!" said Runolf, making his way to the midships, where ropes were tied to the ship's standing knees. "One should never sail without an offering to Njörðr."

I looked out to where the timbers of the wrecked ship jutted from the murky river water.

"Do you think they forgot to make the offering?" I asked.

Runolf laughed.

"Anything is possible," he said, his voice booming. Before he jumped over the side, he turned to me. "Thank you, Hunlaf."

I nodded and watched him go ashore. Moments later he was bellowing at Wihtgar about rearranging the ballast stones to adjust how the ship sat in the water.

I wondered what would happen to Runolf if he never saw the truth of the Word of God. Would the Lord claim his soul as one who had been cleansed of his sins and accepted Him as his father, or would his continued belief in the pagan gods see him sent to Hell? I knew not the answer, though I feared the worst. I added this to the matters I would discuss with Leofstan, when next we met.

Now, in the golden afternoon light, I watched as Wihtgar and Runolf walked the length of *Brymsteda*. They pulled on ropes, checked the halliard block and examined the steerboard mounting.

"Everything in order?" I called out.

Runolf glanced over to see who had spoken. His features were pinched with the worry of the impending test of his work, but on seeing me standing beside Drosten, he grinned.

"Yes. We will not be lading her with food and supplies yet, but she is a good ship. She has been blessed and named, and," he nodded at Drosten, "she has a fine prow." Runolf looked out to the horizon where the sun gilded the dark clouds far out over the North Sea. "If the weather holds, and the wind is not too strong, she will do well tomorrow."

The plan was to take *Brymsteda* to sea, as much to test her new crew as her seaworthiness. The crew was going to be made up of warriors, fishermen and a few thralls. None, save the fishermen, had any experience manning a vessel and, despite our eagerness to depart, Runolf had been adamant for the need to train before heading across the Whale Road.

"You led us on land," he'd said to Hereward, "but out there, I will lead. The steed will obey our commands and carry us where we will, but it would be a foolish man who would gallop into the unknown without first learning to ride his horse."

"How long do you think we will need to learn the ropes and the ways of the ship?" asked Gwawrddur. The Welshman seemed uncharacteristically anxious at the prospect of setting sail. Perhaps we all were.

Runolf had shrugged.

"I cannot say how good you are as students." He smirked. "Can you tell me when Hunlaf will be able to fight well with a sword?"

"We cannot wait years before putting to sea, surely!" replied the Welshman, with a chuckle.

The men laughed, and I bit my lip. I was ever the brunt of their jokes, but I knew that it was a sign of their affection for me. To be ignored would be worse.

"A few days should be enough," Runolf said, scratching at something beneath the thatch of his red beard. "Those fishermen know their steerboard from their halliard. That will help." He thought for a moment. "Yes, with fair weather and some luck, we will be ready to sail for Rygjafylki in a fortnight."

"Good," replied Hereward, though this still seemed like a long time to wait before being able to go in search of Aelfwyn. "Let us pray for good weather then. But before that, let us feast."

Sixteen

"Where is my son?" Mancas asked.

I made a pretence of looking over the people who had spilt out of the small hall onto the open area of grass before its doors.

"I know not," I said. It was true that I did not know where Gersine was, but I had a good idea. I chose not to tell his father that I had seen him being led by the hand into the darkness by Cwenswith.

Mancas' features were partly shadowed, but illuminated enough by the fires that burnt in the great cooking pits, for me to see his frown.

"I mean to address the crew before they get too drunk to listen, and I would that Gersine were here to listen to my words."

"Would you like me to look for him?" I asked. I did not relish the thought of stumbling upon my friend and my erstwhile lover clinched in an embrace beneath a bush, or in one of the storage buildings down by the river. Perhaps they were even in the hut we used to frequent. Cwenswith had barely spoken to me since the day of the duel and the Norse attack, but she had made it very clear that she considered me to be somehow responsible for Wistan's death. It was unfair, I knew, but I could not blame her. I blamed myself too. And, even though I felt a small stab of jealousy at seeing her and Gersine slipping away together, I could not be angry at him for being drawn to her very evident appeal. While I cannot deny that I missed our night-time meetings, I did not yearn for Cwenswith. With the duel, her true character had been shown to me. Gersine was welcome to her, but that did not mean I would like to interrupt their tryst.

Mancas scanned the faces of the men and women who were close enough to the fires to be recognised. Many more could be seen milling about outside of the fire-glow, holding cups and trenchers of roast meat. There were yet more people inside the hall, but it was hot and stuffy inside. We had been lucky with the weather and the night was warm, so most of the revellers had made their way outside.

"No, thank you," said Mancas, shaking his head and taking the smallest nibble from the corner of a piece of bread. "He must be here somewhere. He will probably hear my words from wherever he is seated."

I nodded, doubting what Mancas said to be true.

The sound of singing came from within the hall. A strong, melodious voice lifted on a tune picked out on the plucked strings of a lyre. Mancas smiled.

"Beorn has started to sing. I must not delay too long now. Once the singing starts in earnest, it is hard to quieten the men."

The people hushed, listening to the words of the song. A few joined in with the familiar tune, humming, or lending their voices to the words. It was the sorrowful tale of Beobrand and Sunniva and, despite having heard it many times before, I found myself drawn into the story of love and loss by the talented singer. I had seen Beorn, one of Mancas' hearth-warriors, with a lyre under his arm when he arrived, but I had never heard him sing before. Many men played an instrument and could carry a tune, but few were as gifted as Beorn. He had a wonderful voice that carried out of the hall and into the darkness where it soared, conjuring images from the words and the melody in the minds of the listeners.

"I see you have formed a bond with my son," said Mancas. I felt a flash of anger at the interruption of Beorn's singing. No doubt Mancas had heard him sing the song before but I wished for nothing more than to be silent and listen.

"Yes, lord," I said, trying to hide my annoyance.

"Gersine will be coming with us," Mancas went on.

I nodded, but said nothing. Beorn was singing of Sunniva's sadness with heart-breaking passion and skill, but it seemed Mancas was not moved by the song, for he continued to speak.

"I expect you to watch over him," he said. "He is my heir and nothing must happen to him. This voyage was your idea, so I am counting on you to see that Gersine is safe."

That got my attention. With a sigh I resigned myself that I would not be able to enjoy the rest of the singer's lament.

"I will of course do my best to keep your son safe, lord," I said. "Gersine is my friend," I added. "But your men will guard him well enough, I am sure."

Mancas had told us that six of his hearth-warriors, including Beorn, with his powerful voice, would accompany us. I wondered whether Beorn would bring his lyre too.

"Hush, husband," said Aelfgyth, stepping up and taking Mancas' arm, "can you not see that Hunlaf wishes to listen to Beorn's singing? You will have time enough to speak of other matters when the song is over."

Mancas raised his eyebrows, but said nothing more for a time. Aelfgyth smiled at me. She was a matronly woman who seldom ventured out of the great hall. We had barely seen her since arriving at Uuiremutha in the autumn. But clearly she had decided she could not miss this evening's celebration.

We stood quietly, listening to the final lines of the song.

They told of the death of Sunniva and how Beobrand burnt for vengeance. I thought of Cwenswith, Wistan, Gersine, and the meaning of true love. Beorn held his last note longer than I would have imagined possible. There was such sorrow in his voice, such a depth of emotion, that I could scarcely reconcile it as belonging to the heavily muscled warrior, whose nose was twisted and misshapen from some long-ago brawl.

"You smile," said Aelfgyth, "and yet the song is sad. Did you not find it stirring?"

I squirmed.

"I did, my lady," I replied. "Beorn has a true talent. I was transported. I could imagine the love between Sunniva and Beobrand, and the anguish he felt at losing her."

"And yet you were smiling." Aelfgyth stared into my eyes.

"I was marvelling that God should give such a gift to..." My voice trailed off.

"To?" she asked, smiling now. I sensed she was teasing me. "Do you think it is strange that one who looks like Beorn should be able to create something of beauty?"

My cheeks grew hot.

"Something like that."

"So only beautiful people can create beauty?"

"No," I said. "I know that not to be the case."

"How so?"

"When I was at the minster at Werceworthe I put my pen to more than one page, and I was told by my betters that some of my illuminations were works of art. Beautiful even." I paused, raising my eyebrows and turning so the firelight caught my face, showing clearly my nose that was twisted from where a Norse warrior had broken it the year before. "And look at me."

She laughed. Mancas frowned. Stepping forward, he pulled away from Aelfgyth's grip on his arm.

"Listen, all of you," he shouted, raising his voice above the general hubbub that had descended on the people after Beorn's song had finished. "I would speak to you."

Someone in the darkness groaned and another laughed. Mancas tensed, but, raising a hand, he spoke with a light tone.

"Never fear. I will not keep you long from the ale and meat."

A cheer from inside the hall. More laughter.

"A year ago," Mancas said, his voice carrying easily in the still night air, "none of us could have imagined we would be here today. But if I have learnt anything in my life, it is that all you can be certain of is uncertainty itself. We could not have foreseen the dreadful assault on Lindisfarnae. We all heard of that attack, and we felt sorrow. But as is the way with all men, we did not think such a terrible thing could happen to us."

The audience was silent now, Mancas' sombre words dampening the mood. People had expected a celebration, not to be reminded of past horrors and the danger we faced in our future.

"But now we have seen some of these raiders with our own eyes. Their blood has mingled with that of our injured and fallen on the beach by the river. We saw the smoke in the sky from the burning of the minster at Gyruum. These are dark times, my friends, and it is at such times that heroes step forth into the light. A small band of brave warriors stood against the Norsemen when they attacked Werceworthe. Hereward's heroes defeated the Norse, and without their aid a few weeks ago, we would surely have suffered many more losses when the Northerners' ships came here."

I glanced about us. All faces, ruddy and shadowy in the light from the fire pits, were turned towards Mancas. From behind the hall, even the sounds of the playing children had ceased. They had been whooping and hollering since the feast began, but they seemed now to realise that the time for games was over.

"I know we are all glad that Hereward, Gwawrddur,

Hunlaf and Runolf were here when the Norse sought to land their ships. They have become our friends." I tensed at these words, picturing Wistan's pale face staring up at the sky when moments earlier I had attempted to gut him. Mancas, perhaps having similar thoughts, rushed on. "Many of you have even stood beside them in the shieldwall. And I thank them for their bravery and strength. But more than that, I wish to thank all of you. Every one of you has made sacrifices, and each of you, in your own way, has helped to build *Brymsteda*, whether splitting and planing timber, laying the strakes and hammering in rivets, or in other ways, such as feeding the men, or working longer at sea to make up for some of the fishermen being unavailable while they worked on the ship. You should all be proud. I know I am filled with pride to be your lord. I raise a cup to you and offer you this feast in your honour. In these dark times, you have stepped into the light, and I drink to you all."

Mancas raised his cup. There was a ripple of movement in the shadows as everyone did the same.

"To heroes in the darkness," he said.

I drank deeply, wondering what everyone else had made of Mancas' words. He was slender and unimposing, different from other powerful men I had met like Uhtric, who always seemed to fill any room he entered. And yet there could be no doubt that Mancas could hold a crowd's attention.

When everyone had drunk, he continued. There were no jeers or sounds of dissent now.

"It was Hereward who led the men at Werceworthe, just as he led us in defence of my lands. But it was Hunlaf here who saw what the future would bring." Mancas reached for my arm, pulling me forward to stand beside him. I was glad that the onlookers would not see me blush. "God spoke to him, and Hunlaf in turn spoke to the king. In his wisdom, Æthelred ordered a ship to be built, that we might travel to the lands of the Norsemen and broker a peace with them."

"Peace?" shouted Eafa, and I cringed. "Was it peace that Hunlaf brought when he fought with my son?"

"It was terrible, what happened to Wistan, but it was not Hunlaf who killed him." I winced, remembering my sword being deflected by Wistan's belt buckle. "Did Hunlaf not seek to avoid the fight with your son? It was an unfortunate matter, but young men will always be young men."

"Wistan will never grow old, that is for sure," Eafa said, his face haggard in the dim firelight. He took in a deep breath, in an attempt to calm himself. "It may not have been Hunlaf who killed him, but my boy is dead." I wondered whether Eafa knew how close I had come to slaying Wistan. "Wistan was slain by one of those heathen whoresons. What peace can we hope for from such people?"

"I understand, and share your anger," said Mancas, "but the Norse are no different from us. They seek shelter and food for their families, just like you or I. They are formidable fighters, with ships that can reach further than anything we have built." He flicked a glance at Runolf, who stood a head taller than everyone else. "Until now. God guided the king to spare Runolf's life, that he might aid us against these heathens. And he has done that. Do you deny the king's wisdom?"

Eafa glowered from the shadows, but said no more.

Mancas nodded, seemingly content that the matter had been set aside for now.

"Runolf has stood beside us in our fight," he said. "Is he not a man, like you? He has taught us how to build ships like those of his people. And now that the ship has been completed, we will face new challenges. We must first learn to sail *Brymsteda* and then, soon enough, we will head out onto the North Sea to voyage to..." Mancas turned to Runolf. "What is the name of your people's kingdom?"

"Rygjafylki," rumbled Runolf.

"Yes, there," said Mancas to scattered chuckles from the

audience. Some of the tension ebbed from the gathering, carried away on that nervous laughter.

"Along with Hereward and his heroes from Werceworthe, we will be joined by more warriors from Bebbanburg, strong, brave men one and all."

Mancas nodded to where Bealdwulf, Ida, Gamal, Oslaf and Sygbald lounged together near the hall's entrance. The last of their small band, Pendrad, was down by the river on guard duty with Drosten and the others who had drawn the short straws. Ida raised his cup in silent salute to Mancas.

Mancas smiled in acknowledgement.

"And my own hearth-warriors. Beorn, of the sweet voice—"

"And not so sweet face," shouted a man called Os, prompting more laughter and further easing some of the strain brought on by Eafa's outburst. One of Mancas' men, Os was round of face, but tall and slender of frame, and always seemed to be jesting and laughing. He struck me as a buffoon, but Mancas trusted him enough to have him travel with us as part of his retinue, and I had noted Os' spear was bloody after the fighting on the riverbank. His full name was Oswald, named after that most saintly of kings of Northumbria, but as there were two warriors with the same name in Mancas' warband, everyone called him Os.

"And Os," said Mancas, "of the not so quiet voice, will also travel with us." There were guffaws of laughter at this. "Oswald too, and Arcenbryht, Eadstan and Cumbra." I followed Mancas' gaze and saw his most trusted warriors standing at the doorway of the hall. They were all good men, but there was still little feeling of camaraderie between us. Each of the bands of warriors kept to themselves. I wondered whether that would change once we set sail.

"*Brymsteda* is a large ship," Mancas went on. "Larger than any built here before, and it could never have been completed without all of your hard work and sacrifice."

"And a wrecked Norse ship!" shouted Os. A few people chuckled. My gaze fell on Eafa. His face was sombre and unsmiling.

"It is true," said Mancas, "that the wreckage enabled us to equip *Brymsteda* with the rope and sail she needed much more quickly than would have otherwise been the case."

"And a lot cheaper too," bellowed Os.

"Yes, that too," replied Mancas, fixing Os with a stare that informed the warrior clearly that his interjections did not amuse his lord. The man sipped his ale and fell silent. "I thank the Almighty for the squall that shattered the Norse ships," continued Mancas. "It shows that God is on our side, but it is also a warning to us. The ship we have built, guided by the hand of a master shipwright," he inclined his head towards Runolf, "is big, and it will be fast and strong. But its crew will still be at the mercy of the weather and the waves. So all the men who have volunteered for this mission should never have their bravery questioned. I thank each and every one of them. The warriors I have already spoken of, but I must not forget the men who have offered to sail with us. Alf and his brother Garwig, and Mantat, Dunn, Scurfa and Snell have all accepted the challenge, and I know Runolf is pleased that there will be some men aboard with knowledge of the sea."

The small group of fishermen were seated close to one of the fire pits, and the glow from the embers showed their grins, as they laughed and joshed one another at having their names called out by their lord. The oldest of their number, Alf, was about twenty-five years of age, and each man was strong, with the brawny forearms that came from heaving on ropes and nets, and the ambling gait of someone who spends more time standing on a rocking deck than on immovable earth. Their eyes gleamed with excitement in the firelight. I supposed they saw this as an opportunity to become wealthy, for Runolf had agreed with Mancas that all freemen who sailed aboard

Brymsteda would receive a share of any treasure we acquired, whether through trade or conquest.

"And to complete the crew," Mancas said, "will be myself and my son." He cast about for Gersine, but did not find him in the crowd. "Who appears to have disappeared."

"He's polishing the prow beast," shouted a voice from the darkness. Several of the men laughed knowingly.

Mancas frowned, peering into the gloom, but evidently he could not see who had spoken. He did not mention anyone else, despite having told us just the previous day that half a dozen of his strongest thralls would man the oars and pull on ropes when needed. I glanced at the men who had been turning the hog on the spit all afternoon. They still stood beside the fires, their skin glistening with sweat and streaked with soot. They were broad shouldered and strong and I imagined they would be amongst the men who sailed with us. The thrall nearest me met my gaze and held it, his face impassive. He was dark-skinned, his beard black. His eyes burnt with a brilliant flame of defiance. I looked away before he did.

Mancas beckoned to Runolf. Reluctantly, the Norse giant stepped forward.

"Do you have any words?" asked Mancas. Runolf looked confused. "For the men who will sail with you tomorrow."

Runolf pulled himself up to his full height, towering above Mancas and me. Chin lifted and beard jutting, he surveyed the faces of the gathered throng.

"Mancas has done enough talking, I feel," he said. More than one man cheered. Most laughed. Mancas smiled and held up his hands. "I have little to say," continued the Norseman, his deep voice rolling over us. "All the men who will set sail on the morrow are brave. The sea is a dangerous bitch, but if you do what I say, we will be well. We could do with more men, but *Brymsteda* will sail well, even with fewer hands. Listen to me." He swept everyone with his gaze, his piercing eyes hidden in the shadows beneath his brows. "Obey me as you would your lord, even you, Lord Mancas." Runolf placed a meaty hand on the lord's slim shoulder. "When we are at sea, my word is law. Obey me, and together we will tame the bitch. Tomorrow we shall see how *Brymsteda* follows our commands, but now, drink!"

He held his cup aloft, and the night was filled with the sounds of merriment.

I threaded my way between the groups of people sitting on the grass and standing in chattering huddles. A light breeze picked up from the sea. The embers of the cooking fires were fanned into sputtering life again, the dancing flames lighting the expectant faces around them.

Eafa turned at my approach, his face set and severe. I moved away, slipping inside the hall. It was almost empty now, still and hot after the refreshing wind from the sea outside. I found what I was looking for at the back of the room. On the board were several earthenware pitchers of ale. The third one I picked up was full. Carrying it outside, I turned away from the throng of people, all talking now, following Mancas' and Runolf's speeches.

"Is that all for you?"

I halted at the voice. I had been looking over my shoulder, so had failed to see Gwawrddur. The Welshman stepped from the shadows beside the hall. His face was a pale blur in the darkness.

"Spare some for me?" he said, holding out a wooden cup. His voice, always musical, seemed to be somehow softer than usual, the words stretched like warm leather.

"Are you drunk?" I asked.

"Tonight is a celebration."

"And after all your talk of control."

He pushed his cup towards the pitcher in my hand. After a brief hesitation, I poured a little.

"This jug is for Drosten and the others on guard."

"Ah, yes, he took your duty and now you feel guilty. Such a soft heart, Killer." He drained the ale and held his cup out again.

I shook my head.

"You've had enough, and this is not mine to give. What did you think of Mancas' speech?" I asked, changing the subject.

"The man can talk, that's for certain. Perhaps we stand a chance after all that he will be able to strike a deal with the king of Ryg— Ryga—"

"Rygjafylki," I said.

"Easy for you to say."

We both laughed.

"Mancas has surprised me," I admitted. "If not for him, we would not have the ship ready so quickly. And I think the king chose him wisely. If anyone can convince the king of Rygjafylki," I pronounced the name slowly and clearly for Gwawrddur, as one speaks to a child learning to talk, "it will be Mancas."

"If we survive," mumbled Gwawrddur. He stared into his empty cup, as if he hoped more ale might have miraculously appeared there.

Slowly, a thought dawned on me.

"You are scared of sailing," I said.

He looked up, his eyes narrowed.

"I am scared of nothing."

I had seen Gwawrddur throw himself into a line of Norse warriors, his sword flashing faster than the eye could follow. He had shown no fear in the battle for Werceworthe, it was true.

"Scared of no man, perhaps," I said. "But I see it now. You are frightened of the sea."

"I am not frightened," he shouted. I stepped back, such was his sudden fury. He took a deep breath. "If you will give me no more of your ale," he said, his voice blurry and soft once more, "I will go in search of a more generous friend."

He stumbled away. I watched him go. We were soon to sail across the Whale Road, on a new ship to a land we had never been to before. Our only knowledge of the people came from Runolf, a few traders we might have crossed paths with over the years, and the recent attacks on the minsters along the coast of Northumbria. It was natural enough to be concerned for what the future held. But of all the men who would travel with us, Gwawrddur was the last I would have expected to be frightened of anything. He longed to pit himself against the best swordsmen in the world, but the sea was not something one could defeat by skill of arms. And no man can control that which might frighten him beyond all reason. I once knew a man who served Al-Ma'mun as the Keeper of Knowledge at the Bayt al-Ḥikmah, the Grand Library, of Madīnat as-Salām. He was terrified of beards, and was confined to one room in the Library, only interacting with young boys and hairless eunuchs. He could barely breathe if he ever needed to step outside his room and deal with a bearded scholar, or the caliph himself, who wore his beard thick and long. In comparison, Gwawrddur's fear of the sea was much more understandable.

I thought about Gwawrddur as I walked down the slight slope towards the cluster of houses and huts that lined the riverbank. The smell of roasting meat that had been so strong in the air, was faint now, wafted away from me by the sea breeze. The sounds of conversation and laughter became distant and subdued, but every now and then a shriek from the playing children, or a bark of laughter, splintered the night-calm. As I drew closer to the river, I could make out the whisper of the waves washing the beach off to my right. Light from the stars and moon glimmered on the dark expanse of the sea and I wondered what it would be like to be surrounded by water, with no land in sight. I shuddered at the thought. I offered up a prayer that God would smile on us. All would be well. Benesing had blessed the ship. The sea would not claim us.

And if the Almighty did not protect us, hopefully Njörðr would. I cursed my own stupidity and lack of faith. Perhaps I should cross the broad mouth of the river and go to the church. I should certainly pray before we sailed in the morning. The Lord Almighty would be displeased that my thoughts were tainted by such pagan nonsense. I transferred the jug to my left hand and made the sign of the cross with my right as I recited the paternoster under my breath.

Eager to be back at the hall, I hurried on, scanning the darkness for any sign of Drosten. Nothing. The night was dark, impenetrable apart from the dull gleam from cold, distant stars. I picked out the shadowy form of *Brymsteda*, black against the river's darkness. Its timbers creaked where it rubbed against the staithe we had built.

I walked on, casting my gaze about for anything that would alert me to Drosten's position. I did not wish to call out in the darkness, it felt somehow wrong to shout when all else was still and calm. I heard a whisper not far away, and I turned towards the sound. Again came the groaning of *Brymsteda*'s strakes.

Something was wrong. I felt a sudden chill, that reminded me of when I had plunged into the waters of the Uuir to aid Wistan and Eafa. The sounds of the ship were coming from further upriver, not from where *Brymsteda* was moored beside the wharf, but in the same direction as the whispered voice I'd heard. I held my breath and strained to listen. Perhaps I had been mistaken. I took a few tentative steps upriver, away from *Brymsteda*.

Silence.

Shaking my head at my own imagination, I turned back. Perhaps I should just call out for Drosten and the others. They would be pleased of the ale and then I could head back up to the merrymaking.

There it was again. The sound of wood against wood, followed by a hissed curse. There could be no mistaking it now. There was someone on a boat on the river. I could think of no reason for anyone to be out there at night unless there was mischief afoot. My memory filled with visions of Norse warriors sliding out of the dark on silent ships, seeking vengeance for the slaying of their brothers.

Dropping my hand to my belt, I realised with a start that I had left my sword back at the hall. All I had was my seax. But even if I'd had my sword, I would not be able to stand alone against an attack. I could remain silent no longer. The time to act was now.

Setting down the pitcher of ale, I pulled the seax from its scabbard and bellowed into the night.

"Alarm! Alarm! To me!"

Shouts came from further along the river mouth. I heard men running along the river towards my position. I hurried towards the river and where I judged the stealthy sounds to be coming from.

"To me! To me!" I shouted.

Light, bright in the gloom flooded the night behind me, sending my shadow out long on the earth. Without thought, I spun around. The light spilt from the open door of a storage hut. The very hut where so often I had met with Cwenswith. In the doorway, dark against the bright light of the candle within, was Gersine.

"Hunlaf?" Gersine said. "I can explain."

The cries of alarm were resounding in the darkness, as more voices responded to my shouts. Had I been mistaken? Had the sounds I'd heard come from Gersine and Cwenswith's lovemaking? I felt sick at the thought, then shoved it away. No. I knew what I had heard.

"We are under attack," I hissed to Gersine.

I turned back to peer into the darkness, my eyes tricking me with the after-images of my friend standing with his back to the light. I blinked. Was there movement there, out on the water? Stumbling forward, I made my way closer to the river. There could be no doubt, there was something out there. My stomach twisted at the thought that the Norse might have come upon us when most of the men were drunk at the hall.

I sensed Gersine's approach, but I did not turn.

"I have no weapon," he said.

As I am writing this tale many years later, I could have said that I had made a quip about Gersine using a different type of sword that night. That is how tales should be told, I know, with the hero laughing in the face of danger, with a witty retort always on his lips. But I am no hero and such is not the way of things when you believe death is coming for you out of the darkness. I made no joke that night, instead I said, "I only have my seax."

There were more shouts now, as the guards closed in on where we stood. Far away, I heard yelling. Then a horn sounded, long and plaintive and I knew that, drunk or not, the men of Uuiremutha would come to our aid. All we had to do was stand firm until they arrived.

Drosten came sprinting out of the dark, followed a heartbeat later by Pendrad.

"What is it?" asked Drosten, panting.

"Out there," I pointed. "There is a ship approaching."

"A ship you say?" He stared into the black night and pulled his sword from its scabbard.

"I am sure of it. I heard them speaking, and what sounded like oars in the tholes."

We all peered into the darkness. The faint light from the open door of the storage hut reflected on the river and a vessel slid into view. I held my breath, at once pleased that I had been right, and also horrified that we would need to face a shipload of Norsemen.

But then a voice came from the water, and everything changed.

"Hunlaf," the voice said. "Is that you?"

I closed my eyes and let out my pent-up breath. I knew that voice and, when I opened my eyes again, I could make sense of what was coming out of the gloom. It was not a dragon-prowed ship laden with armoured and armed Norsemen, it was a small rowing boat with what appeared to be two men aboard.

"Don't kill us," said the voice, and I groaned, already imagining the taunting I would receive for raising the alarm for this.

Seventeen

Brymsteda's prow rose up over the swell. Drosten's stallion figurehead seemed to survey the white-capped waves all about us, standing proud against the cloud-streaked sky, before plunging downward, as if galloping, into the trough between the waves. A great shower of spray, cold and salty, washed over those of us who stood at the bow of the ship.

I grasped the forestay to avoid stumbling and let out a cry of joy at the sensation of speed.

The day had dawned with a brisk wind that Runolf had deemed not too blustery for us to sail safely. All those who were to travel on the voyage were aboard, with the exception of Mancas who was going over final preparations for provisions for the trip with his steward.

Behind me, I heard the sounds of retching as someone puked. Whoever it was, they were not alone. Several of those aboard had succumbed to a terrible sickness. I wondered whether the food the night before had been bad.

"Grab that man!" bellowed Runolf from the steerboard at the stern.

Turning, I saw the sick man was leaning over the wale, his head almost skimming the water. The next wave we ploughed through might cause him to lose his footing and send him tumbling to a watery grave. There was nobody close to the man who would offer him aid. Everyone was occupied with ropes, or just as sick as him, or clinging to the rigging in fear of falling. I hurried back to the vomiting man, grabbed a damp wad of his coarse woollen habit and hauled him back from the edge.

"You did not come all this way just to drown, did you?" I asked.

Leofstan turned to face me, his legs unsteady. My old teacher's face was pallid as he wiped spittle from his mouth on the back of his hand. The keel trembled as we sliced into another wave. Leofstan staggered. I caught his arm, preventing him from falling.

"Perhaps the Lord is telling me something," he said. "I think I might be dying."

"You are not dying," I said. "Sit there, and if you must puke, do it into the ship. I wouldn't want to lose you to the sea before we have even set sail for Rygjafylki!"

"I hope you would not wish to lose me to the sea after we have set sail either," he moaned, forcing a thin smile. He slumped against the side of the ship and lowered his head in abject misery.

"Nobody is getting lost," I said.

I could still barely believe that the monk had travelled to Uuiremutha unannounced. When he had called out from the boat in the river the night before, I had been as surprised as I had been elated. I had missed Leofstan. I had realised over the winter that I had taken his guidance for granted, and the thought of being able to speak and pray with my old master once more, filled me with joy.

By the time we had secured the small rowing boat and Leofstan and the man he had travelled with had disembarked, most of the warriors from the hall had arrived. Some bore sputtering brands from the fire pits, and they came charging and roaring down the path, brandishing shields, swords and spears.

My cheeks had burnt as I told them there was no attack, that there were only two men, a monk and a fisherman, and they came not in search of vengeance and plunder, but of roasted pig meat, the scent of which had travelled over the Uuir.

I had worried that the men would once again make me the butt of their jests, but it had not been as bad as I had feared.

"Hunlaf is always at the centre of every battle," Ida had jeered. "But I am not sure we need a shieldwall against a monk and a peasant."

A few of the men had laughed, but most just seemed pleased that they were not called upon to fight while their stomachs sloshed with ale and food. They had trudged back up to the hall, and, after I had retrieved the jug of ale from where I had left it and given it to Drosten, I had followed them, leading Leofstan and his travel companion, whom he introduced as Eadmaer, up the path towards the renewed sounds of merriment and the inviting smells from the cook fires.

Leaving Leofstan, I made my way towards Runolf. The great sail was full, straining at the rigging. The mast creaked and I marvelled at the huge forces being placed upon the oak and the skill needed to shape the keel, strakes, ribs and thwarts so that the vessel would not splinter apart. *Brymsteda* flexed beneath my feet like a living creature and Runolf laughed with the pleasure of riding the waves once more. I had watched the Norseman fight with his massive axe, and believed him to be born to battle. But now, leaning on the steerboard and shouting orders to the crew of this ship that had been fashioned to his design, I thought that, deadly as he was, his true place was here, master of a beast-prowed wave-steed.

"It sails well, Hunlaf," he said to me as I drew close. "Even with this useless crew!" He laughed. It was only the afternoon of the first day of sailing, and to my mind things had not gone well. Runolf, though, seemed undeterred. "When you all know what you are about, *Brymsteda* will be as fast as any ship ever built."

In the midships, Ida doubled over and vomited, though there was little in his stomach for him to bring up now. He had been sick ever since we had rowed out of the mouth of the Uuir and hit the first waves. His face was a sickly greenish hue. I didn't much like Ida, but I worried at this sickness that had affected so many of the men aboard.

"We will not be able to sail, if all the men are sick," I said. "Do you think the pig was badly cooked?"

Runolf glanced at me, then seeing I was serious, he howled with laughter. For a time he could not speak, such was his mirth.

"Did you not eat last night?"

I nodded, annoyed that he made light of the men's malady.

"As did I," Runolf went on. "I ate and drank, and we are both well." He chuckled again at my expression, wiping tears of mirth from his cheeks. "Do not fret about the men. They are not truly ill."

"Tell that to Leofstan, Ida and the others."

"This is just the way of the sea. Some men take longer than others to grow used to the rolling of a deck. They will be better soon enough." He was not looking at me as he spoke. Instead, his gaze roved over the ship, the crew, the rigging, the sea around us, the sky. He missed nothing.

Runolf had assigned each of the fishermen a portion of the crew, a section of the ship, and certain tasks and roles for which they were responsible. In this way, the ship was broken into six sections. At the prow was the Foreship, under the command of Garwig. The front of the sail and keeping watch were their main duties. Next was Mantat's Tack crew, who were busy when sailing into the wind. The Midship crew, just before the mast, was in charge of the sail and much of its rigging. Behind the mast was the Drag crew. Under the stern eye of young Dunn they ensured the sail did not become fouled when sailing close to the wind. They also watched for water in the bilge. Following the Drag was the Aft crew, in which I had been placed. Scurfa was our leader, and our principal jobs, when not rowing, were to handle the braces and sheets, the ropes that controlled the angle of the huge sail. Finally, the stern-most crew was the Lifting, from where Runolf steered and skippered *Brymsteda*.

"You there, Alf," Runolf shouted now. "By Þórr's hammer, what is your man doing?"

Shortly before, with the wind picking up, Runolf had given them the order for the Midship crew to reef the sail. Their leader, Alf, and most of his men, apart from Ida, who was too busy spitting strings of bile into the sea, were following the command, as best they could. They were clumsily lowering the sail to perform the task of reefing it to make its expanse smaller. Alf had to correct his crew regularly, warning them to be careful when handling the ropes, and to be mindful of where they were standing so that a suddenly taut halliard or stay would not pin and crush an ill-placed foot or snap caught fingers. But it was not the men's slowness that had caught Runolf's attention.

One of Alf's sail crew was standing to the side, not helping the others with the hard work at hand. He was a slim man, with long dark hair tied at the nape of his neck. His beard was wispy. He stood with the effortless balance of a man used to being at sea and there was no indication of any sickness about him. His skin was dark and weathered, despite his youth. He must have been no more than twenty. I recognised him as Eadmaer, the man who had arrived with Leofstan.

I had not met the man before, but I had thought there was something familiar about him when Leofstan introduced us by the flickering light of the torches the men held aloft.

"This is Eadmaer," he'd said. "He has travelled all the way from Lindisfarnae. We met at Werceworthe, where he had stopped for shelter. He had heard you were soon to sail, you see. When I learnt he was heading south to join you, I seized my chance and accompanied him."

"Join us?" I asked, confused.

"Aye," said Eadmaer. "I know boats. Grew up on the sea."

"Well, we have need of all the good men we can get. If you have knowledge of sailing, all the better, for few of us do. But why have you travelled so far to seek to join the crew of *Brymsteda*?"

"Why, I seek the same as you," he said.

His words confused me. "And what is that?"

"Why, to find Aelfwyn, of course. And bring her home. It is what Eadwine would have wanted."

"Eadwine?" I knew the name, but there, in the darkness by the river, the sounds of the hunting horn and the warriors' shouts still fresh in my mind, I could not place it.

"Aelfwyn's husband," Leofstan said. I stared blankly at the monk, still unsure what any of this had to do with Eadmaer.

"Eadwine was my brother," Eadmaer said.

Now, I saw it was Eadmaer who stood by and watched others struggling with the ropes to shorten the sail.

"You there," roared Runolf, his voice easily carrying over the ship, "help Alf with the sail."

Eadmaer ignored Runolf. Other men rushed to help before Alf and his men lost control of the great spread of woollen sail in the stiffening wind. Mantat, Alf's brother, shouldered Eadmaer out of the way, and Scurfa joined him to help with reefing the sail. Eadmaer glowered, but did not move to help.

With Alf and Scurfa's aid, the sail was soon shortened and hauled aloft again. *Brymsteda* once more skimmed over the surf southward, towards the mouth of the Uuir. We had not travelled far from land, always keeping the coast in sight, but, much as I had enjoyed the thrum of the deck beneath my feet and the surging speed of the sleek *Brymsteda*, I looked forward to standing on dry earth once more.

"Hold her steady," growled Runolf, pulling me towards him with his prodigious strength.

"You want me to steer?" I asked, my voice rising in panic.

"Just hold her like this," Runolf said, placing my hands upon the steerboard's tiller, where his had been. I could feel the warmth of his touch on the smooth oak that we had salvaged from the wrecked ship. Fleetingly I thought of the other hands that had held that tiller over the years. Where had they guided its original ship? How many had been slain by the men carried aboard? But I did not dwell on such thoughts. The moment I held the steerboard, the pulse of the waves and the wood throbbed in my hands and it was all I could do to keep her steady. The rushing water tugged at the board, which felt like a living thing in my grasp.

Runolf did not wait to see whether I would manage, he leapt forward, bounding towards the mast. Men watched wide-eyed as the flame-haired giant strode down the deck. Eadmaer must have seen the shock in the men's faces, for at the last moment, he turned to see what they were looking at. Perhaps with a heartbeat's more warning he might have evaded Runolf, but as it was, the moment he turned, the Norseman's massive hand clutched about his throat.

Eadmaer's eyes bulged and he clawed at Runolf's forearm as the Norseman pushed him backward. His feet scrabbled at the deck for purchase, but did little to slow their progress towards the wale and the dark sea beyond.

It seemed as though Runolf would simply carry the smaller man straight over the edge of the ship without stopping. But at the last instant, his left hand lashed out and caught hold of a tight shroud. Using this to halt his forward momentum, Runolf stopped on the verge of plunging over the side. Eadmaer was leaning precariously over the water that rushed along the strakes. All that prevented him from falling was Runolf's formidable strength.

"Runolf, enough," snapped Hereward, striding towards them.

Runolf paid him no heed.

"Aboard *Brymsteda* I am king," he said, his voice loud and clear. "If you do not obey my command, men will die." He stared into Eadmaer's eyes. The young man's skin was sallow beneath his tan, his eyes white-rimmed with fear.

"Enough," repeated Hereward.

"Whether by accident or my hand," Runolf snarled, not loosening his grip on Eadmaer, "men will die. Do you understand me?"

Eadmaer tried to speak, but all he could muster was a croaking, gagging sound. Runolf held him for a moment longer, before pulling him back from the brink of the ship and throwing him down onto the deck.

"Do you all understand me?" he shouted, looking over the men. "There is no time for questions aboard a ship. And no space for men who do not obey orders."

Several nodded. Nobody spoke.

Hereward opened his mouth, but after a glance at Runolf's face, he thought better of it.

Leaving Eadmaer sprawled on the deck behind him, Runolf stalked back towards the stern and took the steerboard from me without a word.

For a time, there was silence aboard, the only sounds the hiss of the water beneath us, the groan and creak of the ship's timbers, and the sorrowful cries of the gulls that followed in our wake. I wondered at the force of Runolf's anger. Glancing at him, I saw that his face was pale, his eyes brimming with tears.

As we passed the broad mouth of the Tine on our right,

with the charred remnants of the minster at Gyruum to remind us of the importance of our mission, Runolf began to shout orders to the crew as if nothing had happened. The men leapt to do his bidding. I helped to unship the oars, ready for the final approach to the wharf at Uuiremutha and the now familiar cluster of huts and buildings there.

Glancing over to *Brymsteda*'s port side I noted that Eadmaer stood beside Alf, silently coiling a slack halliard with a sailor's easy skill. Perhaps sensing my gaze on him, he looked up. His hands never stopped working, but his face was clouded with a barely suppressed rage.

Eighteen

That night, the atmosphere was subdued in Uuiremutha.

Despite his moment of fury with Eadmaer, Runolf had leapt onto the newly built wharf with a grin for Wihtgar who was excited to hear how *Brymsteda* had performed. There was no doubt that the ship handled well and Runolf happily answered the carpenter's questions as we disembarked and secured the ship.

"The crew still have a lot to learn," Runolf rumbled, "but it is as good as any ship ever to sail." He made no mention of his clash with Eadmaer, but the men gave the Norseman a wide berth as they made their way ashore. Several of them, including Leofstan and Gwawrddur, were pale and weak from the terrible bout of sickness that had come over them, but it seemed that Runolf had been right, and they had not been poisoned by bad meat. They had not been long off the rocking deck of the ship before the colour returned to their cheeks and, where at midday they had imagined they would never eat again, or might even die, now, as the sun dipped over the land, they complained of their hunger after the long, tiring day.

Still, after the day of constant sickness for some, and the relentless nature of the work, hauling on ropes and heaving on the oars when the wind did not blow in the direction we needed, the prospect of setting out to sea the following day did not fill everyone with joy.

I had watched Runolf grinning and looking truly happy for the first time I could recall, and I knew he would gladly spend every moment of daylight out on *Brymsteda*. I too had felt the thrill of the speed and power of the ship. I had not suffered from the sickness that had so afflicted many, and even though my hands were blistered, and my back and shoulders ached from working the oars and pulling on the ropes, I started looking forward to the next morning as soon as I had finished eating the bowl of thick pottage and the fresh bread the womenfolk had made for our return.

The ways of the ship opened up in my mind like a new language. I longed to learn more of its syntax and grammar. How should a sail be adjusted so that the ship did not need to sail directly away from the wind? What was the secret to steering such a massive vessel by leaning or pulling on the steerboard. I recalled the thrumming of the tiller in my hands and hoped that Runolf would teach me all there was to know about steering a ship. I marvelled that such a long ship could be manoeuvred so well with nothing more than the small oaken rudder and the pull of the oars. In spite of the crew's general inexperience, while we were far enough out to sea to run no risk of collision, Runolf had taught us how to turn the vessel and how to row as one. We still had much to learn and we were not as quick to respond to his shouted commands as Runolf would like, and yet we had still managed to control the ship well enough after some practice. The banks of long oars did not yet rise and fall with the grace of a swan's wings, as I had witnessed on the Norse ships that attacked Lindisfarnae or Gyruum, but even so, we were able to steer her alongside the wharf we had built downriver from the dangerous jagged bones of the partially submerged ship that jutted from the murky water; a sombre reminder of what could happen to an unlucky vessel.

The sun had already touched the western horizon as I walked to the wharf and climbed aboard the moored *Brymsteda*. The riverside was calm and quiet. Most of the men were up at the hall, and the others had retired to their homes further upstream and inland. I had volunteered for guard duty. My body was aching and tired, but my head was filled with thoughts and concerns. I did not relish the idea of drinking ale with the rest of the men, but I knew it would be some time before they quietened enough for me to begin to contemplate finding sleep.

I reached up and ran my hand over the finely carved prow beast, tracing with my fingers the curls of the horse's mane, as I stared out to sea. A small flock of dunlin fluttered at the river's edge, lifting and circling in the air every time a wave washed their stretch of mud, before they landed again moments later, only to repeat the motion with the next wave. Out over the grey Whale Road, a pair of puffins darted straight and low over the surf.

"I thought I might find you here."

The voice startled me and I anticipated the criticism and comments about my lack of attentiveness while on watch. After the previous night's embarrassment, the taunting would be unrelenting.

Turning, I saw the voice belonged to Leofstan and I sighed with relief.

"Wondering what the future holds?" he asked.

I looked back out over the sea. The dunlin were still there, but the puffins had vanished.

"I can scarcely believe what Runolf has achieved," I said. "The ship is truly beautiful."

"Runolf is an extraordinary man," Leofstan said, stepping closer and reaching for a taut shroud, as if he expected the deck to move as violently as it had during the day. "But he is not the only one. He would never have done this without your help. Indeed, without you, he would have been dead these several months past."

It was true, I supposed, but I did not feel worthy to be compared with the Norseman.

"It does not bear thinking about what would have become of us all, if we had not stopped Uhtric from hanging Runolf."

Leofstan moved gingerly to stand beside me to watch the sea grow dark with the setting of the sun.

"It is madness to think of what might have been. There is only what was, what is now, and what will be. And we can only affect the last of those."

"What do you see in our future?" I asked.

"The only thing I am sure of is there will be more sickness for me. By all the saints, if I had known I would suffer on the sea so, I would not have come."

"Runolf says that the sickness will pass, in time."

"I pray that he is right. Many more days like today and I might be tempted to jump into the sea and take my chances swimming."

"You know how to swim?" I asked, surprised, as few men had that skill.

"I do not!"

Leofstan laughed and I joined in. It felt good. There had been a tension between us ever since the battle at Werceworthe.

We stood in silence for a time. I fancied I could just discern the dark shapes of seal heads bobbing out there in the deep water, but the swell rose and I lost them in the twilight.

"I have thought long and prayed much about what took place when..." Leofstan did not finish his thought, but I knew he was remembering that blood-soaked morning at Werceworthe where he had wielded a sword and slain Norsemen in the shieldwall alongside the other warriors.

I said nothing.

"I owe you an apology," he said at last.

"You owe me nothing, Leofstan," I said, shocked at his words. "If anything, I should say sorry to you."

"No, Hunlaf, we each choose our paths. Our actions are our own and ours alone. I took up a blade and fought for Werceworthe. And I killed when I had vowed never again to take a life." His voice was laden with sorrow and regret.

"I am sorry." I longed to hear of his past, of who he had been before becoming a monk. But I would not pry. It was his tale to tell, and if he chose to keep it from me, I must respect that, however difficult.

"You have nothing to be sorry for," he said with a sigh. "I know your choice was not an easy one. I was a poor friend to you. I was your teacher, and a teacher should offer support. Instead, I judged you." He scratched at his tonsured head. The hair above his ears was greying. "I blamed you for my own part in the fighting."

I knew he had resented being placed in a position where he had needed to kill, but to hear him speak the words, that he had blamed me, hurt more than I would have imagined.

I took a long breath. My left hand rested on the pommel of my scabbarded sword. Absently, I traced the familiar shape of the iron pommel, plain wooden grip and simple cross guard.

"You are right that this path has not been easy," I said. "There are days when I wonder at the decisions I have made."

"All men question themselves," said Leofstan. "At least, good men do."

"I am not so sure I am a good man." I searched the sea for sign of the seals, but they had gone now, if they had ever been there. "I have missed you," I said suddenly, not allowing myself to think too much before uttering the words that I knew to be true. "And I have missed your guidance."

Leofstan nodded, as if he expected me to say as much.

"You are a good man," he said. "But I will not always be

there to guide you." His words had the sound of a premonition, and I looked at him askance. Leofstan's face was in shadow, but his eyes gleamed with the last light of the day reflected from the North Sea. "God will always listen to your prayers, Hunlaf, even when I am gone. But," he finished with a smile, perhaps sensing that the tone of his words had shaken me, "I am with you now."

"Why *are* you here?" I asked. I was glad he had come to Uuiremutha, but it was unclear to me what his purpose was.

"I have thought much on *The Treasure of Life*." His tone grew sombre, darkening just as the world around us closed in with the dusk. "The words I read in its pages had great power."

"Aren't they just words?" I asked, recalling what he had said to me in the past.

"Yes, but knowledge and words have power. The more I prayed and pondered over the winter, the more I grew to believe that such a book is dangerous." He held up his hand to stop me from speaking, anticipating my protestations. "No, I still do not believe it should be destroyed. To burn a book, any book, is something I cannot countenance. But some learning is best kept away from those who are weak of mind. Or weak of faith.

"When Eadmaer arrived, saying he had heard of the ship being built here and how he meant to travel to Uuiremutha, I felt God calling me to accompany him."

"And Abbot Beonna allowed you to travel with him?"

"He did. Truth be told, I think he wished to be rid of me."

"Surely not. Beonna values you immensely."

"Perhaps, but I fear that ever since the fighting..." He scrubbed a hand over his bald pate. "I have not been myself."

His words worried me. I had always looked to Leofstan for direction. He was more knowledgeable than any other man I have ever met, with perhaps the exception of Alhwin, who I met in the court of Emperor Carolus, and Abu Jafar Yusuf ibn Sa'īd al-Zarqālluh, with whom I once spent several enlightening days in Al-Andalus. But neither of those men, learned as they undoubtedly were, could rival Leofstan for wisdom and a solid sense of wellbeing and faith in the Lord that came upon me in his presence. That is why his next words shook me so profoundly.

"I have questioned my faith these last months," he said, his voice not much more than a whisper. "When I broke the vow I had made to forswear violence, it was as if my very soul had come untethered. I fear it was adrift for some time, and as sick as my body was today."

"And now?" I asked.

"I have managed to claw my way back to shore, I think." He stared out at the gathering gloom for a long time, perhaps remembering the struggles he had faced. "I will never kill again," he said into the hushed evening air. "Even if that means others will die. I have made this sacred promise before God, and I will not – I cannot – break my word to Him again."

I nodded. But I knew not what to say, so remained silent. Leofstan seemed eager to unburden himself now, and he carried on speaking with earnest conviction.

"Beonna asked me why I wanted to come here," he said. "I told him I think this could be my penance for breaking my vow. For killing again." His breath caught in his throat at these words, but he pressed on. "I feel compelled to find *The Treasure of Life*. I cannot rid my thoughts of what I saw in its pages, and the more I have thought on its content, the more convinced I am that it is my sacred duty to find it and bring it back to Werceworthe, where it can be studied and kept safe."

"I too have spent a lot of time thinking about *The Treasure of Life*."

"Indeed? And what have you thought?"

"When the Norse attacked here," I said, not answering his question directly, "one of their number survived."

"Did you learn from him about the whereabouts of the book?" Leofstan's tone was excited. "Where is he now? I would speak with him."

"That will not be possible." He turned to look at me. Seeing the meaning of my words in my expression, he nodded and let out a sigh.

"What did he say about the book? Before..." he hesitated. "Before he went to meet his maker?"

"Nothing," I said. "But I remembered our conversations about the writings of the Mani. You told me that he did not believe that Jesus was the son of God, or that the Almighty had absolute power."

"That is true," he said, making the sign of the cross at such heresy. "Mani taught that every man and woman's soul is a battleground between the darkness and the light."

"Yes," I said, staring out at the sea that had become silently enshrouded in the cloak of the night as we had talked. "I remembered that, which is why the final words of the Norseman we captured remained with me."

"What did he say?"

"He spoke of someone he called Ljósberari, the bearer of light, and I remembered the title being used in the book. He mentioned fires, demons and darkness. And that this Ljósberari, whoever he is, had only recently come to the lands of Rygjafylki."

Leofstan let out a long breath.

"This can surely be no coincidence. My fears are come to pass. Could it be that this Ljósberari," he stumbled over the Norse name, "could it be that he has possession of *The Treasure of Life*?"

"I know not, but when I heard the name, I could think of no other explanation."

He placed a hand on my arm.

"Together, you and I will find out."

"So you will travel with us to Rygjafylki?" Although he had come to sea with us that day, he had not made his intentions about the voyage clear.

"If I survive the crossing, I will," he said with a thin smile. "I believed it was God's will before. Now I am more certain of it."

I shuddered as a cool wind blew in off the dark sea. I did not like Leofstan's repeated talk of dying, but I could not deny that I was overjoyed to have his thoughtful presence alongside me once more.

"But if we are truly going to ride the waves on this terrifying steed again on the morrow," he said, "I need some rest." He turned to go, then hesitated. "I have missed many of the offices of the day, so I should pray before I seek sleep. It must be past the time for Compline. Would you join me?"

"I would like that," I said, wondering if Leofstan, in his wise way, could see how much I craved the communion of the brethren I had left. "But I am on watch."

Leofstan clapped me on the back.

"Then we shall pray here. It will do me good to get used to reciting the offices on deck."

And so we knelt amidships, as if the ship was our chapel and the mast Christ's rood towering over us, and we prayed. But this was like no chapel I had worshipped in before. The oak of the deck was hard on my knees, the air pungent with tar and the lard and fish oil that had been lathered on the woollen sail. The night was alive with the sounds of water lapping against the keel, the breeze sighing through the rigging and rustling the alders along the bank, and every now and then, when the wind shifted, a snatch of singing reached us from the hall. And yet, despite the strangeness of our surroundings, I felt my body and mind relaxing as Leofstan and I went through the familiar liturgy and prayers of Compline.

When we had finished and Leofstan finally headed toward the hall, to be swallowed by the darkness, I stood guard over the ship that Runolf had built and I wondered at the meaning of it all.

If I was a warrior, should it feel so natural to kneel in prayer and take on the role of a monk once more?

Nineteen

My memories of the following days are jumbled, with each day much the same as the one before with little to distinguish it. Every morning we set sail aboard *Brymsteda*, where Runolf barked out orders and we did our best to obey them. Some days we sailed northward as far as Cocwaedesae, the small island where Anstan had given his life and warned us at Werceworthe of the coming of the Norsemen. Other days we travelled south, all the while staying well within sight of the coast. At the end of each gruelling day, we would return to Uuiremutha, our bodies aching and our heads swimming with what we had learnt. Once back on land we fell into the routine of guard duty, eating and drinking, and resting before the sun rose to usher in another day of hard labour aboard the ship.

The men often grumbled, but as the days passed, the sickness felt by some of the crew lessened, and with the improvement in their health, so their performance also improved. After a week, Runolf did not have to explain what he wanted us to do, and at his shouted commands, we would each jump to the task, knowing our place in the smooth running of the ship.

In the dawn light each morning I knelt with Leofstan beside the river and prayed. We did the same every evening, and I felt a calm serenity I had not experienced for months. I enjoyed the time we spent sailing and rowing, learning the ways of the ship. I asked Runolf to explain each aspect of the craft, and how it handled in as much detail as Leofstan would have expected of me if I had been studying some complex text of theology. Sometimes Runolf would growl and grumble at my incessant questions, but he never seemed to truly tire of talking about *Brymsteda* or the sea. His eyes sparkled with the sunlight that glittered blindingly off the waves, as he imparted his knowledge to me, and the wind made his shaggy red hair and beard dance about his face like flames.

Now that he could keep his food down for the whole day of sailing, Leofstan no longer spoke of death. This pleased me. And I was also glad that the rest of the men quickly took a liking to him. Leofstan was pleasant and softly spoken, and threw himself into the chores and tasks needed of the crew, never shirking his duty, even in those first days when he had to halt frequently to vomit. Such determination endeared him to the men who had not met the monk before. But there was something else that coloured their opinion of him. On more than one occasion I overheard them speaking of Leofstan in hushed awe, recounting how he had stood with the warriors at Werceworthe, bloody sword in hand, to fight against the Norse. I was sure that Leofstan would rather not be known for a deed that he found abhorrent, but no man can control what others say of him. I suspected Hereward had brought up Leofstan's bravery in battle, though he never admitted it. And yet, if it was him, perhaps he was right to do so, for it appeared that the addition of the calm monk, whom the men also knew as a formidable warrior, had an uplifting effect on the morale of our company.

The crew grew increasingly adept at handling the ship, and their demeanour improved along with their skill. Where there had been glum faces, groans and retching on that first memorable day aboard, now it was not uncommon to hear laughter, and even song, led by Beorn's powerful voice, echoing out over *Brymsteda*'s deck and the sea around the ship.

Those of us who had not sailed before grew in confidence. Some soon appeared to feel more at home aboard ship than on land, surprising even themselves. Drosten took to sailing as naturally as he had to carving. Even when *Brymsteda* yawed over in a strong wind, seeing men clinging to the wales and shrouds to keep their footing, Drosten would hurry along the deck with the uncanny balance of a cat.

"Are you sure your father was not a Norseman?" shouted Runolf to the Pict one day when Drosten had effortlessly run along the deck to snatch up a loose rope that had slipped from Cumbra's grasp.

"My father was Galanan," shouted Drosten, his tattoos accentuating his scowl at Runolf's comment. "I am no son of a Norseman."

Runolf laughed and held up his hands.

"I meant no offence, friend," he said. "But you walk the deck like one born aboard a wave-steed!"

Drosten glowered, still unsure if he, or his family, was being insulted.

"I don't know which I would be more upset about," said Os, loud enough for all to hear. "To be fathered by a Pict or a Norseman!"

Pendrad and Oswald laughed, but quickly fell silent as both Runolf and Drosten, the two most imposing warriors on board, turned their furious faces towards Os. The Northumbrian mumbled something about only jesting and found a knot in the rigging that he suddenly felt the need to check.

Only two members of the crew did not seem pleased with our progress. The first was Eadmaer.

Eadmaer performed his duties as ordered, but he was never quick about it and his face wore a perpetual frown. When Runolf was nearby, the fisherman from Lindisfarnae grew sullen and withdrawn, watching the tall Norseman from under his brows. He never spoke out against him, but it was clear to everyone that he resented Runolf and how he had made an example of him on our first voyage.

One evening, just after we had moored at the staithe and the men were making their way to the hall and their homes, I pulled Eadmaer to one side. As I tugged at his sleeve, he spun about and for a heartbeat, I thought he might strike me. When he saw it was me, he sighed and shook his head. Turning, he followed the others to trudge up to the hall.

"Wait," I called, but he did not slow. I hurried along and fell into step beside him. I had barely spoken to him since he had arrived, but I could see that his feelings of resentment would fester over time if they were not dealt with. "Runolf is a good man," I said. "You would do well to believe that."

"A good man?" he hissed, spinning to face me. "His kind killed my brother." His face was dark with hatred. "He almost killed me."

I shook my head.

"If Runolf had wanted to kill you, do you truly think we would be talking now?"

He held my gaze for a long moment.

"And you think that makes me feel better about him?" He spat into the nettles that grew beside the path. "That he did not throw me into the sea to drown? I must be blessed that he merely choked me before all the men." His rage simmered hot as a banked forge.

I had wondered about Runolf's reaction to Eadmaer on that first day, but when I had tried to broach the subject with him, he had merely repeated that when men did not obey a ship's skipper, they died. He would say no more on the matter.

"Perhaps it was wrong of him to treat you thus," I said.

"Perhaps?" Eadmaer said, chuckling without mirth. "I cannot believe that we are allowing that man to lead us. I pray that Aelfwyn is well and I can bring her back safely to her kin. I do not wish to spend any more time than needed with that pagan whoreson."

"He is a Christian," I said without conviction. "He was baptised at Eoforwic."

He laughed then, a jagged ugly sound, like the bark of an angry hound.

"Of course he is," he said. "And I am the King of Wessex." Turning on his heel, he left me watching after him, thinking of the trouble we were storing up by taking him with us to Rygjafylki. And yet I felt for the man. His brother had been slain, his friends and neighbours slaughtered, and his brother's wife stolen away. He was a brave man to travel here and to join us in the search for Aelfwyn. I said nothing of my fears to Hereward or any of the others. It was not for me to stand in the face of such courage.

There was one other who seemed unhappy. Gwawrddur's sickness abated, and he was strong and quick to learn, so the chores of the ship were no problem for him. And yet, even as the spirit aboard *Brymsteda* lifted with each passing day, so Gwawrddur's mood seemed to sour.

There was no time for our regular training with sword and shield, as each day was spent sailing. I wondered whether he would have been content to teach me as he had since we had first met the previous summer, if we'd had the time and not been too exhausted. For ever since I had spoken to him at the feast, he seldom addressed me and avoided my company.

Gwawrddur's distance saddened me, but my days were full, and my mind was swirling with the things I learnt each day and also worries about what the future would bring when we set sail for the land of Runolf's people. Every night I fell into a deep sleep, but when I caught a glimpse of Gwawrddur's tight-jawed expression, I wondered at his dark humour, and I missed the time we usually spent together as teacher and pupil.

My daily prayers with Leofstan went some way to fill that void, but it was not the same, and I feared I had irretrievably broken the bond of friendship that existed between the Welsh swordsman and me. One evening, when Leofstan and I had finished our Compline prayers and were walking up the gravelly path to the hall, I tentatively asked the monk what he thought was wrong with Gwawrddur.

"You confronted him with his fear of the sea, you say?" Leofstan asked.

As we drew close, the shadowed hall before us rang with the laughter, singing and riddling of the men. I halted, needing to have this conversation before we arrived and were swept up in the buoyant atmosphere of the gathering.

"I meant no harm by it," I said with a frown. "I was shocked that Gwawrddur was frightened of anything."

"Every man is afraid of something, Hunlaf, you should know this as well as anyone." I thought of my conversation with Gersine on the beach and nodded. "Warriors are proud men," Leofstan continued. "None prouder than Gwawrddur, I would say."

"His skill with a blade is beyond compare."

"And yet does he not seek to challenge himself? To find an adversary that will truly test him?"

"Yes, I think he hopes he might find such a worthy foe on our travels. That is partly why he will sail with us."

"Only partly?" Leofstan asked with a raised eyebrow.

"Mostly, perhaps," I acknowledged. "Who can say what truly drives a man like Gwawrddur?"

Leofstan started walking again and I followed after him.

"How do you think such a man as Gwawrddur would like the prospect of facing his fears?" he asked over his shoulder.

The answer seemed clear to me.

"Is that not what he lives for? To confront what scares him?"

Leofstan shrugged.

"To face other men, perhaps. He knows that with God's grace, his skill, bravery and maybe a little luck, he can defeat any enemy. But what of a foe that can never be conquered, no matter how strong and skilful Gwawrddur might be?"

I nodded slowly, finally understanding what my old mentor was saying.

"I imagine such a thing would not sit well with him," I said, glad of Leofstan's wisdom.

In the days that followed, as Runolf pushed us ever harder to test us and *Brymsteda* to the limits, I watched Gwawrddur become more taciturn and surly. I contemplated speaking to him of his fears, but in the end thought better of it. Some battles a man must face alone. Perhaps, I hoped, once we had crossed the North Sea, he would feel that he had conquered this particular adversary. There was certainly no doubt that he was brave. His face was ashen whenever we put to sea, and yet he did not complain and his movements were not sluggish or reserved. When called upon, he acted without delay. And yet all the while I could see that he was swallowing his terror of the deep, biting back the scream of horror that threatened to burst from his throat.

Despite Gwawrddur and Eadmaer being less than elated by the prospect of the upcoming voyage, the preparations proceeded with pace. Mancas and his steward had amassed provisions enough for several days. Barrels of smoked herring, salted hams, ale and water, were brought down to the river's edge by cart, and then loaded aboard. We also took gifts for the king of Rygjafylki and trade goods, items to show the quality of produce Northumbria could provide. There were bales of good wool cloth wrapped in oiled leather against the rain and sea, barrels of precious woad pigment and a finely carved coffer that contained exquisite silverware made by the best craftsmen in Eoforwic. By the time we had finished lading

Brymsteda, she sat low in the water and Runolf grumbled that she would no longer handle like a serpent atop the waves but more like a pig wallowing in mud.

Runolf's comment did nothing to allay whatever fears Gwawrddur had, and the Welshman scowled as we made our way aboard.

The night before, there had been another feast, and most of us had heavy heads from Mancas' ale and mead. But we were young men, and we shrugged off the after-effects of the drink as easily as cormorants dry their wings in the morning sun. If I drink more than a single glass of wine now, not that Abbot Criba would ever allow it, I awaken with a mouth as furred and sour as a gooseberry. Back then at Uuiremutha, I was young and had stayed up long into the night, singing and riddling with *Brymsteda*'s crew. It was only as I had lain wrapped in my blanket with the hall spinning and the sound of snoring and farting filling my ears, that I realised I had laughed and drunk with warriors and fishermen, who until recently had kept themselves to those they considered their own. In the two weeks since we had first sailed Runolf's ship, we had ceased to be small groups of people and, like the rods of iron that are beaten together into the blade of a sword, so the work of the ship had forged us into a crew.

Little did we know then, that our tempering had not even begun.

Everyone had come out to see us off and the wharf and riverbank was thronged with men, women and children. On the far bank, many of the brethren from the minster had also come to wish us well on our voyage. I saw Benesing and raised a hand to him. He waved back.

Gersine was also waving, and I followed his gaze to see Cwenswith, her golden hair blowing around her smiling face. The wind pressed her green dress against the curves of her body, and I felt a small stab of jealousy before I looked away.

The sun was bright in the sky, the southerly breeze brisk, but manageable. Just as it had been for the two weeks we had been sailing *Brymsteda*. Looking back now, I wonder if the clement weather had not lulled us all into a state of complacency. We had not been truly tested by the cruel sea. And when the clouds grew black, turning the day to night, and the wind swung about and howled from the north, fretting the waves and tearing at the sail and rigging, none of us was prepared.

Twenty

We made good progress on the first day, passing the Farnae Isles and Lindisfarnae by midday and then carrying on up the coast. I gazed at the white-streaked cliffs we passed, watching the throngs of seabirds on their craggy perches, gyring in the air, and dotting the waves. Gannets speared into the dark waters beneath the cliffs. Black-backed cormorants and shags dived under the surface to arise again some time later and further away than seemed possible. The southerly wind filled our sail and we rode north on the easy swell of a calm sea.

"We are finally on our way," Leofstan said, from beside me.

We were both part of the Aft crew, led by Scurfa. He was young, not much older than me, but he had spent his life in boats and at sea. He was quiet, with thoughtful eyes, and seemed able to sleep no matter the weather or the circumstance. But over the previous weeks, we had learnt to listen when he spoke, and Runolf trusted him to lead the small Aft crew. As well as Leofstan, Scurfa and myself, the Aft crew was completed by Sygbald, Gersine, and the swarthy-skinned, black-bearded thrall who had stared me down at the feast. His name was Ahmad.

Each of the six small crews had to spend every moment together. We slept, worked and ate with our crew. When aboard a ship, surrounded by the cold sea, with nothing between you and death but strakes of oak and the skill of your skipper, you learn to put your trust in your crew mates, and to give your all in return that they might trust you. You may become tired of their jokes, their snoring and, in the case of Sygbald, their belches and farts, but at any moment, you might rely on them to save your life, just as their life could be in your hands.

I have found that the bonds forged in battle and aboard a longship are similar. Trust and cooperation are everything, and the friendships woven at sea are stronger than the thickest rope.

I glanced away from the birds I had been watching. Leofstan was smiling, pleased that we were at last on the quest we had begun to think of close to a year before. He seemed more at ease than I had seen him before, certainly more than I would have thought possible just two weeks previously. He clung to the shroud a little more tightly than perhaps was necessary, his knuckles white, but he was upright and able to function.

For my part, and for the first time aboard, my innards rebelled, and I was frightened that I might disgrace myself and puke.

"I can scarcely believe we are going," I said, watching a flight of guillemots settling on the ledges of a huge rock that jutted out of the sea like a fist. Waves broke against its base, turning the dark blue of the water a foaming, boiling white.

Leofstan placed a hand on my shoulder.

"We will find her," he said.

I nodded, unsure. Since she had been taken, I had avoided thinking too much of what might have befallen Aelfwyn. But after speaking to Eadmaer I could not rid myself of thoughts of her being abused in all manner of ways. I was scared of who we might find, if indeed we were able to track Aelfwyn down. Despite learning from Torfi that she had been bought by Estrid, I did not dare to believe we would find her so easily.

We cleared a headland, leaving the towering rock and the cliffs behind. Sunlight glared from the sea, as if from burnished steel. I squinted, the blaze of light turning my mind to other concerns. To the strange name that Torfi had uttered just before his death.

"I pray that we do find her," I said, choosing not to mention my worries, or Ljósberari.

"With God's grace, we will find all that we seek," Leofstan said, patting my arm. His face was bright in the afternoon sun, his eyes narrowed to slits as he stared at the land sliding past us on the port side of the ship. I wondered if he too was thinking about Ljósberari. Whenever my mind turned to the name, I felt as though cold claws scratched along my spine. If I was uncertain about finding Aelfwyn, I felt an unnatural fear of coming face-to-face with the one known as the bearer of light. There had been a horror in Torfi's voice when he spoke of him, and such fear was hard to ignore.

For a time that afternoon, we were followed by several dolphins. They leapt and cavorted all around *Brymsteda*, flying high into the air over the steerboard's white-churned wake, and then seeming to race us, the wooden sea-steed pitted against the creatures of the surf. The dolphins would often rise close to the surface as they swam, their faces visible just beneath the waves, and I could not shake the impression that they were staring directly at me. The men whooped and shouted at the animals, jeering and cajoling them. The sleek denizens of the deep appeared to respond to the goading, for they effortlessly sped past us, showing us that our timber horse was no match for their lithe, shining sinew and muscle.

The dolphins, seemingly content with their demonstration of superiority, disappeared as quickly as they had arrived. Briefly, I caught a glimpse of them far out to sea, leaping above the waves, and then they were gone. The animals, with their intelligent eyes and smiling faces, had filled me with a sense of wellbeing and now that they had vanished, a strange feeling of loss washed over me.

As the sun was lowering in the sky, we put into a small, sheltered cove. The beach was in shadow from the raised land that encircled it. As we waded ashore, before darkness enveloped the world, I thought I saw faces looking down at us from the marram grass that grew thick in the dunes. I mentioned it to Runolf, who nodded.

"I saw them too," he said.

"We must set guards," said Mancas, his tone sharp with worry. "This is Pictish land." The lord was glad to be off *Brymsteda* for the night. He had spent less time than the rest of us aboard in the days prior to setting out, and it seemed to me, that even though he had not vomited, he had suffered from the constant motion of the waves. He had been lucky that we'd had a good wind behind us, I thought. The ship did not roll as much when making way with a following wind.

"They will not attack us at night," said Runolf. Mancas frowned. "But yes," Runolf continued, "set a watch."

The Drag crew, led by Dunn, found some driftwood, and Arcenbryht asked Mancas if they could light a fire. The Lord of Uuiremutha turned to Runolf for his opinion. The Norseman nodded.

"We will be gone with the dawn, long before any Picts come to bid us welcome."

"No singing," said Mancas. "The men of these lands are not our friends. Keep your eyes and ears open."

I did not share Runolf's optimism that we would be left alone. I was sure I could sense people gazing on me from the night. When it was my turn on watch, I stared out into the darkness, convinced that every rustling movement of the wind was a Pictish warrior stalking over the dunes, ready to cut my throat.

When I sensed movement close behind me, I spun around, dropping my hand to the hilt of my sword.

"Hunlaf, it is I," hissed a voice that I recognised as Gersine's.

The sound of his approach over the sand had been hidden by the whisper of the waves rolling up the beach and the breeze sighing through the grass.

"Be careful not to sneak up on me in future," I snarled, angry at my own nervousness.

I took a deep breath to calm myself, then made my way to where the men rested beside the fire above the high-tide line. A couple of the men were sitting shoulder-to-shoulder, conversing in whispers too quiet for me to make out their words. I tossed a log onto the embers. Sparks and new flames lit up their faces. One was Leofstan and I was surprised to see that the other was the bearded thrall, Ahmad. They both looked sombre and I imagined Leofstan, always keen to spread the word of God, must be preaching of Christ to the infidel. I toyed with the idea of joining them, but I was tired and the thought of trying to explain theology to an ignorant slave dissuaded me.

Wrapping myself in my cloak, I lay down near the embers. I listened to Ahmad and Leofstan's murmuring voices as they mingled with the sea-sigh and wind-whisper. My head was still full of images of tattooed warriors, and it took me a long time to find sleep.

I dreamt of flames that licked at the bare feet of naked corpses impaled on great stakes. In my nightmare, I tried to run away, but something held me back. When I turned to see what was restraining me, I saw Aelfwyn, her face streaked with blood. She grinned at me and her teeth were stained red.

I awoke to a grey dawn. My dream had left me uneasy and out of sorts, but it appeared Runolf had been right. There had been no sign of anyone all through the night. And yet I was not the only one who had slept badly. The men were short-tempered, snapping at one another like bickering children. We quickly ate some of the bread we had brought from Uuiremutha, washed down with a cup of ale. Nobody complained when Runolf gave the order to wade into the water to push *Brymsteda* out into the rising tide.

We continued up the coast, glad to be away from the beach and its nightmares. The wind swung into the west, and Runolf called out an order for us to adjust the sheets and braces. We were used to the tasks now, and in moments, we had shifted the sail's alignment to Scurfa's satisfaction. Runolf nodded, pleased with our rapid response.

All that morning *Brymsteda* slid northward on a favourable wind.

When the storm came, there was barely any time to ready ourselves.

"I do not like the look of those clouds," Runolf said, peering into the north-west.

The horizon was shrouded in black thunderheads where moments before the sun had lanced through breaks in the thick, but non-threatening clouds. Such was the speed in the change of the weather that I was reminded of the squall that sank the two Norse ships at Uuiremutha. We had told ourselves that tempest had been sent by the Almighty to protect us. On seeing the dark clouds growing, and the swell rising around us, I made the sign of the cross. Could it be that God had forsaken us?

"Lower the sail and take in three reefs," shouted Runolf.

The wind was already picking up and in the distance the wave-tops were white. We needed the sail to allow us to run from the storm, but Runolf could see that if he did not reduce the sail's size, the mast, and therefore the ship, would not survive the power of the coming storm.

Scurfa hollered to Alf, relaying the order. The Midship crew rushed to their work, all aware by now of the threat of the approaching storm. They performed their tasks well, lowering the yard and then setting about tying up the reefs of the huge sail. But no matter how quickly they worked, it still took time and as soon as the yard was across *Brymsteda*'s midship, jutting out either side over the water, the ship began to turn. There was nothing to do but wait for the operation to be completed, but the rocking motion was terrifying by the time they had finished.

Tall waves were rushing in from the north now. A huge wave broke over the wale, washing the deck and dousing us all in freezing water. Runolf cursed. Mancas leaned over the side to be rid of his morning meal as quickly and quietly as he could. Further down the ship, I saw Ida doing the same. My own stomach churned, as much with the fear of what would come, as the sickening rolling of the deck now that we were making no headway.

I looked over at Runolf. He was pale and muttering under his breath. I wondered if he was praying to his Norse god of the sea.

"Bail out that water," he roared, his words being torn from his lips by the rising wind.

As we had now swung around, the side of the ship was presented to the waves. As each wave struck, more water washed over the strakes, or was forced around the wooden plugs wedged in the oar holes.

Dunn and Mantat's crews began to furiously bail out water with buckets and their helmets. I watched as wave after wave surged towards us. If we could not make headway soon, one of those waves could sink us. At the realisation, I shuddered and felt bile rise in my throat. I spat. A driving rain, bitter and cold, began to lash us and I wondered what we had done to displease the Lord. Could it be because I had allowed Runolf to speak his pagan prayer? Was this a punishment for my lack of faith in the one true God?

It certainly seemed that Runolf's offering to Njörðr had had little effect on the Whale Road, for the sea churned about us, the sky darkened as if night had fallen, and the wind blew off the cliffs, pushing us further out to sea.

"Ready!" bellowed Alf.

"All hands," shouted Runolf. "Raise the yard."

Without hesitation, we dropped down to sit on the thwarts and sea chests, bracing our feet and gripping the halliard. Alf called out the pace, and together we heaved the heavy yard and reefed sail up the mast. As the sail rose, so the wind caught it, causing *Brymsteda* to yaw to port dangerously.

"Keep pulling," shouted Runolf, an edge of desperation I had never before heard in his voice. We needed that sail up so that we could catch the wind and sail before it, turning the stern towards the waves. *Brymsteda* would then cease the dangerous and stomach-twisting rolling, and would be able to surf the huge crests, instead of being buffeted by them. I knew that without pausing to reef the sail, the mast would surely have splintered, or the sail would have torn asunder, either possibility disastrous for us, but every moment the sail was not raised, the more likelihood we had of being swamped or capsized by one of the great waves towering above us.

The hemp rope was rough, wet and cold in my hands as I heaved with everyone else, leaning back as if I was pulling on one of *Brymsteda*'s long oars, and lending my strength to raise the yard. But something was wrong. It was getting harder to move the rope and men were shouting, their words lost over the rage of the storm. Looking up, I saw that somehow, perhaps while Alf's men had hurried with the reefing, one side of the sail had become tangled in a rope. It was snagged and would not drop to catch the wind.

Alf was shouting at his men and Runolf's voice rose above the storm and the men's fearful cries. He fought to remain calm, but I could hear the edge of panic there.

"Lower the yard and free that sail," Runolf shouted. "Now!"

We brought the yard back down and once again the ship rolled terribly, unstable and rocking with the long yard and heavy sail resting across her beam. The instant the yard was lowered, one of Alf's crew clambered up onto it and shimmied along to where the sail was snagged. The man clung on as the sea crashed against the ship, dousing him more than once in the waves. With a start, I recognised Gwawrddur, and recalled the conversation I'd had with Leofstan. Perhaps this was the Welshman's way of confronting his fear of the sea.

Whatever the reason for his actions, there could be no denying his bravery. He was far out over the dark waters now, clinging on with one hand and tugging at the ropes that were preventing the sail from being lowered correctly. Another man scrambled onto the yard behind Gwawrddur. It was Os, the jester, but he was serious now. The two men shouted at one another, but I could not make out their words from where I watched. Then I understood their plan. Alf handed Os a knife, which in turn he passed to Gwawrddur. Moments later, Gwawrddur had sawn through the rope, untangling the sail.

They would need to make sure the sail was reefed correctly before we hoisted it aloft, and I wondered if we could spare the time, such was the ferocity of the storm now. Gwawrddur raised his hand to return the knife to Os, and a small cheer erupted from the men watching. I added my voice to theirs, pleased to see Gwawrddur conquer his fear of the sea.

He looked aft as if he had heard me, and offered me a small smile. In that instant, the largest wave yet hit the steerboard side of the ship, rocking *Brymsteda* terribly and sending the port-side portion of the yard and sail under the water.

Icy cold water washed over the deck, soaking us all. For a hideous moment, it seemed that the ship might capsize. *Brymsteda* tottered on the brink of destruction, before finally righting itself. I let out a breath of relief.

And then my heart lurched as I saw that where there had been two men on the yard, now there was only one.

Gwawrddur had gone.

Twenty-One

Men yelled. Some pointed over the edge of the ship at where the sea had swallowed Gwawrddur. I scoured the waves for sign of him, but there was nothing but the dark water and the lighter flecks of foam. The rain lashed down on us, spiteful and chill. Far off to the north, thunder growled.

Beside me, Leofstan began to mutter a prayer. I was silent, but my eye was drawn to every movement of the water, each splash of a wave. The wind ripped at the surf, shredding the wave-tops. The sheeting rain limited my vision and for as far as I could see, the slate waters were a churning maelstrom. Desperately I searched for Gwawrddur. There was nothing but water. He had vanished as if he had never been. Closer now, thunder boomed, echoing across sky and sea.

The Midship section of the ship, near the mast, was a confusion of men, ropes, sail and the long yard. *Brymsteda* was rocking crazily again and at any moment, we might be sunk. As I watched, the slender figure of Eadmaer rushed forward. For a heartbeat, as the ship rolled to larboard, he stood, balanced on the port-side wale, and then, as *Brymsteda* began to right itself once more, he leapt, diving into the chaos of the waves. In an instant, he was gone, lost beneath the water just as Gwawrddur had been.

"The man's a fool!" shouted Runolf over the scream of the gale. "Get that reefed sail aloft!" The urgency in his voice was as sharp as the axe he wielded in battle, but the men needed no encouragement. Under Alf's command, the Midship crew – bolstered by his brother, Mantat, and Drosten, who came back from the Tack position to help – frantically worked at the ropes and the sodden sail. There was no time to mourn. They knew as well as all of us that without that sail, we would all soon join Gwawrddur and Eadmaer in the cold darkness beneath the waves.

The wind, rain and waves battered *Brymsteda*. Several more men vomited, some over the side, but most onto the deck, where the contents of their voided stomachs was quickly sluiced away by the spray and breaking waves.

My stomach turned as the ship yawed and rolled, and all the while I scanned the waters around us. I felt the first stabs of grief for the loss of Gwawrddur. I was not sure how I felt about Eadmaer. He was clearly a fool, as Runolf had said, for what man would throw his life away for another so recklessly? But if he was a fool, he was surely a brave one. And had I not also thrown myself into danger to protect others? I gripped the smooth, slick wood of the top strake tightly. Should I not have jumped after my friend? I dismissed my thoughts as truly mad. I could not swim, and even if I could, what good would it do if I simply followed Gwawrddur to his death at the bottom of the North Sea?

"Anything?" asked a voice behind me.

Turning, I saw it was Mancas, his face as pale as the foam on the waves.

I shook my head, continuing to scour the water.

Mancas said nothing more, but I sensed his fear. Apart from the frantic activity amidships, a stillness settled over the rest of the crew. Some clung on to the rigging, others peered over the port side, searching for the two men who had disappeared. A few men retched and spat. I saw more than one make the sign of the cross, but gone now were the shouts and cries, replaced by the muttered prayers and tense communication between the men working on the sail. The rest of us waited and prayed, and a dark mood of despondency and despair fell over us all.

"Ready!" shouted Alf, and with his cry, some of the tension ebbed from the crew.

"All hands!" bellowed Runolf. "Raise the yard!"

The men dropped to their positions, grasping the rope that would hoist the yard and the reefed sail up the mast. I was about to drop down onto my sea chest, ready to add my weight and strength to the task, when something tugged at my attention. There was something out there, visible for a moment only as it rose on the crest of a wave. A dark shape. A seal surely. We had seen some of the creatures shortly before the storm struck. Perhaps the inquisitive beasts, like dogs sniffing at a dying bull, had come to investigate the wallowing hulk of *Brymsteda* and its forlorn crew.

I wiped the salt spray and rain from my eyes to get a better look, but the seal, if that is what it had been, had vanished, and around us all I could see were waves once more.

Wait, there it was again. A movement, dark against the darkness of the water. A splash. A flash of pale skin. It couldn't be!

Most of the crew were already seated and, in time with Alf's calls, they heaved the yard aloft, the shortened sail falling freely now beneath it. As soon as the sail was raised, the wind caught it, billowing out the reefed expanse of wool. In moments we would be swinging away from the gusting gale, to race before the storm.

"A rope!" I yelled. The shape I had seen bobbing in the wind-tossed waves was no seal, it was Eadmaer and he dragged Gwawrddur behind him. "A rope, by Christ's bones!" I shouted again, panic in my voice. "They're out there!"

Snell, standing close to Runolf at the helm, was the fastest to react. He rushed over with a long coil of rope in his hands.

"There," I shouted over the bluster of the gale.

He peered into the gloom. Biting his lower lip, he gauged the distance. They were not close.

"Can you make the throw?" I asked. "Is the rope long enough?"

"It will have to be," he said, and let fly the rope with a great underarm throw. Holding one end, the other streaked out over the water, and splashed into the tumult of the waves someway short of Eadmaer and Gwawrddur. Quickly, Snell pulled the rope back in, coiling it expertly.

The sail was up now, and I could feel the ship responding beneath us, turning, becoming more stable by the moment. Soon *Brymsteda* would be skimming across the waves, borne on the power of the great wind. Even with the reefed sail, we would rapidly be carried away and there would be nothing Runolf or anyone else could do to slow us. We needed the sail to keep steady and afloat, but if Snell did not manage to reach Eadmaer and Gwawrddur with his next throw, they would be as lost as we had believed them to be moments before.

The crew were standing now, shouting encouragement at the men in the water, and urging Snell to throw true. He threw the rope a second time, and it snaked out towards the swimmer, but again fell short.

The watching crew groaned.

Quickly, but calmly, Snell reeled in the rope again, coiling it as it came.

"Come on," I muttered. "Come on!"

I don't know if Snell heard me, but a third time he sent the rope out towards the pair in the sea. Perhaps the ship, that was already turning and moving towards the south, had closed the gap slightly, or maybe Eadmaer's valiant efforts had brought them slightly nearer salvation, or mayhap Snell's throw was better. Maybe God listened to the prayers of those aboard. Whatever the cause, this time, just as *Brymsteda*'s sail caught the wind, pulling us forward with a surging motion, the wet rope slapped into Eadmaer's face. He grasped the hemp cord and a great cheer went up from all the men watching.

I grabbed the rope and helped Snell pull the two men through the water. Leofstan and the others of the Aft crew caught hold of the rope behind us, lending their hands to the work. By the time we had pulled Gwawrddur and Eadmaer over the side, bedraggled, chilled and pale as death, *Brymsteda* was already sailing smoothly again, stern to the storm. We rode up a large wave, sliding down the other side. The rain still fell and the wind gusted, but the keel now slipped through the water, holding the deck relatively stable. After the recent tossing and rolling, the ship now seemed almost as solid as being on firm earth. With the sail hoisted and the ship underway once more, it felt possible that disaster had been averted. Perhaps we would survive this sudden storm after all.

Eadmaer was coughing, retching and spitting. He had been in the water for a long time and was now shivering uncontrollably. I could scarcely believe he yet lived. Someone wrapped him in a blanket, pulling him to his feet.

Looking down at the water-washed deck, my stomach clenched. I recalled what Runolf had said when he had named *Brymsteda*. That Njörðr always needed an offering. I shuddered. It seemed that the offering of mead had not been enough to appease the pagan sea god. A sacrifice of a life was what he desired. For there, at my feet, sprawled Gwawrddur, pallid and unbreathing.

Twenty-Two

I stared down, aghast at Gwawrddur's pale face. His hair plastered his forehead and cheeks. His eyes were half open, white showing behind the parted lids. *Brymsteda*'s prow hit a wave and the ship trembled. I stumbled, but I could not drag my gaze away from the grey pallor of the dead Welshman.

"I can help him," said a heavily accented voice.

It was Ahmad.

"What can you do?" I asked. "He is dead."

Leofstan stared into Ahmad's face.

"I think I know how to help him," he said, his dark eyes earnest and unblinking. "But there is no time to waste."

For a few heartbeats the monk and the thrall gazed fixedly at each other. Then, mind made up, Leofstan turned to me.

"Out of the way, boy," he snapped.

I was so stunned by the shock of seeing Gwawrddur's sorry state and Ahmad's words that I did not move.

"We cannot tarry," the old monk snarled, shoving me hard. I staggered a couple of steps and dimly felt the hands of others supporting me, pulling me away to give Leofstan and Ahmad room. I looked about me in a daze, unsure what was happening.

Gwawrddur was dead!

I had known it when he vanished beneath the waves, but now, to see his face, his unmoving body, brought the reality to me as keenly as a knife blade beneath a shieldwall.

Runolf was shouting orders, and the crew hurried to obey. We were still not safe from the storm. The wind whistled through the rigging, filling the reefed sail, causing the mast to creak and groan worryingly on the keelson. But despite the activity all around me, I was only vaguely aware of Runolf's commands, and I did not move to respond. Scurfa shouted at me, demanding that I perform my duties in the Aft crew. I ignored him, and after a short time, he left me alone.

Nobody shouted at Ahmad to lend his hands to the sheets and braces. He was otherwise engaged, and I watched on in fascinated dread at what he was doing. As soon as I was out of the way, with Leofstan's help he flipped Gwawrddur over onto his belly and then began to rhythmically press on his back between the shoulder blades. Leaning his weight onto his palms, Ahmad pounded the Welshman's back over and again.

The ship hit another wave, slapping cold spray into my face. With the chill touch of the sea, it was as if I had awoken from a dream. The noises and movements of the ship and crew returned in a torrent, and I stared down at Ahmad, horrified at how he was battering my friend's corpse.

"He is dead," I said, my voice quiet, lost in the chaos of the ship.

Ahmad did not cease his movements. Leofstan watched on. I wondered what madness had seized him to allow Ahmad to so abuse Gwawrddur's body. Reaching out, I placed a hand on the monk's shoulder.

"Stop this," I said. "Gwawrddur is gone." My voice was stronger now, though I was dizzy with grief.

Leofstan shrugged me off. Ahmad continued his crazed pushing against Gwawrddur's back.

"He is not gone," the thrall hissed furiously. "He has just forgotten how to breathe."

I stretched out a hand again, but Leofstan, sensing that I meant to pull Ahmad away, stepped between us.

"If you must do something, Hunlaf," he yelled, his voice tight, "pray! Pray that God will remind Gwawrddur to draw air into his lungs once more. That He will not take him just yet."

I did not reply. Leofstan's tone was hoarse and rasping. I am ashamed to admit now that I thought him moon-touched to allow Ahmad to assail Gwawrddur so. I believed the sight of Gwawrddur's corpse had brought on a madness within him, as it had caused me to stare and gawp, unhearing and inactive. And yet Leofstan had long been my teacher in Christ. He had taught me the Scriptures, and led me in prayer more often than I could recall. And so, despite my misgivings and outrage at what Ahmad was doing, and almost without knowing I did so, I began to recite the paternoster.

My lips moved as I muttered the familiar prayer. On the deck at my feet, Ahmad continued to administer to Gwawrddur and I watched on, unsure how to stop this folly.

Over the years, I have often berated myself for my lack of faith, but never have I felt more humbled in the power of prayer and belief than in the moments that followed. As I finished the paternoster, stating as I had so many times before that God's was the power, the kingdom and the glory, so Gwawrddur began to move.

At first I was not sure what I was witnessing. Water from the waves and rain sluiced the deck, so when the Welshman vomited up the water he had swallowed, it mingled with that already slopping around him. A moment later though, it was clear enough. Gwawrddur spasmed, voiding a great gush of liquid, and began coughing. He was alive! I made the sign of the cross, still unable to believe what I was seeing. Ahmad pulled Gwawrddur onto his side. Leofstan called for a cloak or a blanket.

Gwawrddur was coughing uncontrollably now, spitting and puking, while Ahmad rubbed his back. I snatched my own blanket from my sea chest, marvelling for a moment that it was still dry to the touch, protected as it had been by the oak chest made with Wihtgar's craftsmanship. Leofstan took the blanket from me without comment, wrapping it about Gwawrddur.

"We need to get him warm," said Leofstan.

Now that Gwawrddur was breathing again, Ahmad rose and stood awkwardly to one side, unsure of himself. I could scarcely believe what I had witnessed and the black-bearded thrall seemed dazed.

The rain still lashed down from the dark clouds, and *Brymsteda* regularly ploughed through waves, dousing us all in salt spray. Scurfa shouted for help and, without a word, Ahmad moved to obey, joining the struggling Aft crew at the ropes.

"It will be some time before any of us can get dry and warm," called Runolf from where he stood at the helm. "We must run before this storm for a while yet. Get those wet clothes off him and wrap him up well. The sea's cold grip remains on a man for a long while after he has been plucked from the waves."

I helped Leofstan pull off Gwawrddur's sodden kirtle and breeches, finding another blanket and a damp cloak of Scurfa's to wrap him in. Gwawrddur was shivering uncontrollably now, but he looked into my eyes and thanked me, speaking through the chattering of his teeth.

"Don't thank me," I said. "It was Eadmaer who saved you." I glanced over at where Ahmad grappled with the rigging, his teeth bright as he grimaced with the effort. "And Ahmad," I added.

Mancas brought a small flask of mead and we poured some of the sweet liquid down Gwawrddur's throat. He struggled to swallow it at first, choking and coughing again. But when he managed to keep it down, it seemed to soothe and warm him, and his trembling subsided somewhat.

By this time the ship was sailing well again, and it appeared that any imminent danger had passed.

Mancas beckoned Eadmaer over. The fisherman had shed his wet tunic and he now wore an expensive looking kirtle with patterned edging. I recognised it as belonging to Arcenbryht, and I thought again of the strength of the bonds that are formed at sea. I could not imagine a warrior of Arcenbryht's status lending his good clothes to one as lowly as the fisherman from Lindisfarnae under normal circumstances.

"You did well," Lord Mancas said, pouring a cup of mead and offering it to Eadmaer. "What you did showed great courage."

"It showed great stupidity," shouted Runolf from his position at the steerboard.

Eadmaer drained the cup. He scowled at Runolf's words, but before he could reply, Mancas held up a hand.

"Perhaps it was foolhardy to leap into the sea," he said, "but there can be none here who can doubt that it was also brave. Would you not throw yourself into the fray to aid a comrade in peril, Runolf?" The Norseman glowered, but said nothing. "And it would seem that Eadmaer has a skill that many of us lack." Runolf raised a questioning eyebrow. "He can swim!" Mancas laughed and, though there was little of mirth in his words, several of the men joined in with gusto, seemingly anxious to feel laughter's release.

Gwawrddur's recovery buoyed the crew's spirits. One of our own had been plucked from certain death. This was surely a good omen. In spite of the sudden wrath of the storm that had threatened to engulf us, we told ourselves that God was on our side and had answered our prayers when Eadmaer hauled Gwawrddur out of the deep.

The strong winds carried us south and east, away from land and out into the deep waters of the North Sea. Runolf held on tightly to the thrumming tiller, as *Brymsteda* rode the waves. He was grim-faced and sombre, concerned perhaps that we were being carried so far from the path he had set for us. But, despite Runolf's tight-lipped worry, the mood aboard lightened from the doom-laden fear that had gripped us.

Now that the sails were set, there was little for us to do, so we concentrated on getting ourselves warm and fed. Scurfa handed out some dried ham and stale bread, and I chewed on it even though I had no appetite. We slid up onto the crest of a huge wave, and down the other side. Spray and surf splashed over the wale, drenching me and the bread in my hand. I bit off more, and chewed, grimacing at the taste of the sea.

"I find the salt gives it extra flavour," said Scurfa with a grin.

I smiled in return, feeling some of the terrible tension leaving me.

"And the water softens it enough to allow me to chew it too," I said.

Picking up some of the food, I carried it to Gwawrddur and Leofstan who sat together between two thwarts, their backs to the strakes. They were huddled close, covered by blankets and cloaks, Leofstan giving his warmth to the shivering Welshman. I crouched down beside them as they chewed the bread and ham. The sounds of the wind and waves were muffled here, and the gale didn't reach down into this hollow. The rain had mercifully stopped, and I wondered if that meant we were outrunning the clouds. But even down here, we were still very exposed, and from time to time spray spattered the deck around us. The voices of the crew were distant and muted, but there were new sounds here. The rush of water sliding along the strakes, causing the ship's timbers to flex and groan like a living, breathing thing.

"How do you fare?" I asked Gwawrddur.

He nodded, shivering as he chewed. Despite the dry blankets, and the relatively secluded position on the ship, without a fire, Gwawrddur would not find warmth. I wondered how long he could go on shivering so. His skin was the pale colour of a mackerel's belly.

I handed him the small leather flask of mead that Mancas had left with us to help warm the men who had been submerged. With shaking fingers, Gwawrddur took the flask, but he failed several attempts to unstopper it. His fingers fumbled at the neck of the vessel, clumsy, finding no purchase. Eventually, he raised it to his mouth and yanked out the stopper with his teeth. Taking a long draught of the mead, he smirked.

"I told you I was not frightened of the sea," he said, his voice jagged from the shaking that still had a hold of him. I thought of how he had climbed out along the yard to free the sail. I nodded.

"I should never have accused you of being frightened."

"Oh, I am frightened, sure enough," he replied, chuckling through his clicking teeth. "But not of the sea."

His words confused me.

"Then what are you scared of?"

"Drowning!" he said, and let out a barking laugh that quickly became a coughing fit.

Shaking my head, I picked my way past Gersine, Sygbald, Scurfa and Ahmad, whose dark skin was sallow from his exertions, and moved to where Runolf was leaning against the steerboard's tiller.

"How does he do?" he asked.

"He's not one to complain." I looked past the high stern. The world behind us was enveloped in darkness. There was no sign of land. White gulls swooped in the sky and dotted the waters of our wake. "He needs fire. I fear for him if he can't get warm soon."

Runolf grunted.

"He'll be getting no warmth for a while." He pushed his thick red hair out of his eyes. "But when the winds lessen, I will turn us back towards the coast."

I stared along the length of the ship. The dark sea rolled away to the grey horizon.

"Could we not just continue on east until we reach your homeland?"

Runolf laughed.

"No, Hunlaf. Rygjafylki is closer from the northern tip of Pictland. From there, with a favourable wind, it will still take us perhaps three days to cross the Whale Road. If we do not turn back, how long do you think Gwawrddur would last without any warmth? The nights are colder than you can imagine out here. No, we will head back to land." Runolf swept the crew with his gaze. "I fear it is not just Gwawrddur that needs time to recover from his ordeal."

I nodded. Runolf was right. We were all tired, wet and cold.

"Is it always like this?" I asked, thinking of the sudden changes in weather and fortunes. The shouts of terror as *Brymsteda* went from stable sea-stallion, slipping across the waves, to lurching, rolling hulk at risk of sinking.

"No," said Runolf, "it is not always like this."

I let out a breath, relieved.

Runolf snorted. "Sometimes it is much worse."

"Worse?" I said, wondering if he was trying to make me nervous.

"If you think that was frightening, wait until you are sailing in a storm."

"What was that then? Was that not a storm?"

"That was just a squall." He sniffed. "It was over in moments."

"So not a storm?" I asked, trying to keep my voice even. It

had felt like a very long time to me since we had been on calm waters.

"Look," Runolf gestured over his shoulder, "already you can see the sun peeking through the clouds back there." I glanced back into the west and saw that he was right. A beam of sunlight speared through the clouds now. To the north, a bright rainbow shone against the gloom. "You have never known fear," Runolf said, "until you have faced a true storm at sea." He sighed, looking into the distance with his ice blue eyes. "That is something you never forget. Wind and waves that last for days, and you can do nothing but run before it, trusting your ship, your skill, and praying that Njörðr accepts whatever sacrifice you may throw to him."

I shivered, and only partly from the cold. Neither of us spoke for some time. Beyond the reefed sail, gravid and billowing with the strong wind, I watched Drosten's prow-horse seeming to gallop across the waves.

"Do not look so glum," said Runolf suddenly with a grin. "I told you I was a great shipwright." He patted the strakes beside him. "*Brymsteda* has shown us all what it is capable of. It'll carry us safely."

A strong gust of wind caught the sail then, causing the ship to list to larboard and, as if in direct response to Runolf's prideful words, the tiller in his hands became suddenly loose. Runolf spat over the edge into the swirling sea, and cursed loudly. I know I should show no belief in superstitions, or in the power of pagan gods, but I have seen many times in my long life that it does not do to tempt fate. Hubris often brings about disaster. Some call it bad luck, others believe that the gods laugh at those who declare themselves above them. Perhaps in this case it was the Almighty Himself reminding us to trust in Him, and in Him alone. Whatever the cause, at the mention of Njörðr and Runolf's assertion of his longship's quality, the leather strap securing the rudder in place, tore asunder under the great stresses of the ship's passage through the turbulent waters at such great speed.

"Lower the sail," Runolf bellowed, and the relative calm aboard was shattered once more as the crew hurried to do the skipper's bidding.

Twenty-Three

It was very late when *Brymsteda* limped past the looming shadows of cliffs and into the protected waters of a sound on the isle of Orkneyjar. Everyone aboard was exhausted from battling the elements and the ship. The sun had dropped behind the western edge of the world a long time before, but this far north and so close to midsummer the sky was never truly dark.

After the tumult of the day, the thrashing of the waves, the lashing of the rain and wind, and the accidents and incidents that had beset the ship, it had come as a shock when the wind had dropped out of the air that afternoon. The sea had lost its ferocity, and the sail we had needed to reef, so as not to risk snapping the mast, now hung limp. With the wind unable to fill the sail, it fell to us to propel *Brymsteda* back towards land. We divided the crew into two shifts, one pulling on the long oars, while the other rested.

It was shortly after the fifth change of rowing crews when we reached Orkneyjar. I was at the oar, my back and arms screaming from the exertion, and all I wanted was to be able to let go of the oar's handle that had blistered my palms, to lie down and sleep. But I continued to heave on the oar, my muscles complaining with each movement, as my eyelids drooped. The ship was quiet. Oars knocked and grated in the oar holes. Once in a while Runolf called out for the men on one side or the other to halt their rowing or to speed up, aiding his steering of the vessel, which was especially helpful after the leather strap holding the rudder had broken. A few of the men grumbled and muttered, but as dusk had descended, so the crew had become subdued, like men rowing into a dream.

From time to time I'd glanced over at Gwawrddur. In the late afternoon, his shuddering had subsided. Now he slept, cocooned beneath a pile of blankets and cloaks. He had been excused his turn at the oars by Runolf. The Norseman had said nothing, but I could tell he was worried about the slender swordsman. I too was concerned for Gwawrddur. That afternoon, after the storm had blown itself out and the sun had pushed its way from behind the dark clouds, I had spoken to Leofstan in hushed whispers.

"When will the shivering stop?" I'd asked, nodding towards the Welshman, who still sat, his back against the strakes, swaddled in blankets and shaking. His eyes were closed, but I did not think he was asleep.

"Only God can answer that," Leofstan said, "but..." His voice faltered and he looked out at the brightening sky and sea to the north.

"But?"

"Gwawrddur was underwater for a long while." He stared at me fixedly, as if trying to say something without words. I frowned, unsure of his meaning. Leofstan sighed and went on. "Ahmad says that sometimes, when a man is rescued from the deep and reminded to breathe," he whispered, "his lungs can forget again."

"He might forget to breathe?" The thought horrified me.

"It happens," he replied, his expression doleful.

I swallowed down my fear at the idea.

"And he would just cease to breathe?"

Leofstan pulled me closer, lowering his voice yet further so that none should overhear.

"If it is to happen, water would once again fill his lungs. Drowning him, even on dry land."

I shook my head in an attempt to rid myself of the terrible image Leofstan had painted for me.

"Do you trust Ahmad's word on this?"

"Ahmad's knowledge brought Gwawrddur back. Why would I doubt him now?"

I looked over at the thrall, who was busy coiling a length of rope. I had no reason to distrust Ahmad beyond him being a slave and a foreigner.

"You think Gwawrddur might yet die?" I asked.

"That is in God's hands now. Pray for him." Leofstan patted my arm and offered me a small smile, perhaps noting my grim expression on hearing his words about what might come to pass. "The Almighty saw fit to bring him back to us, so I am sure it is in His plan that Gwawrddur live on." He smiled again, but his eyes looked uncertain, and so, for the rest of that long day, as I rowed I prayed under my breath, reciting the paternoster, and then the prayers of the monastic offices at their correct times, or as close as I could figure. I prayed that God would be merciful and spare Gwawrddur. I also beseeched the Lord that we would find the shelter Runolf had spoken of.

After the rudder had broken there had followed another spell of shouting and anxiety aboard as Runolf, Snell and Scurfa all worked as quickly as they were able to mend the damage. Without the steerboard, it became very difficult to guide the ship, and without that ability to steer, if another strong wind caught us out at sea, we would struggle to sail to safety. As they worked, *Brymsteda* again lost headway and once more began to twist and roll in the swell. The lift to morale that had come from getting the sail aloft and then from Gwawrddur's rescue began to dissipate, as the men started to question our chances of surviving yet another disaster.

Runolf, though, trusting in his seamanship and in the ship he had built, did not appear to be unduly concerned. It didn't take long for him, with the help of the two fishermen from Uuiremutha, to rig up a replacement for the leather strap using a length of rope.

"That will serve," he'd said, patting the tiller and offering the crew an infectious smile. "But not for long." The men had groaned. "Do not fret," Runolf had continued, "and don't complain. Save your strength, for you'll be needing it. To the oars. The wind is dying and we need to pull *Brymsteda* westward." At that, the moaning from the crew had intensified. But soon enough the wooden bungs had been removed from the oarlocks, and the long oars had been unshipped.

I had been in the first group of rowers and had grudgingly taken my place atop my sea chest, lending my strength to the task of pulling the ship back towards the safety of shore. When rowing a longship, your world shrinks. There is nothing save your oar, the oarsmen closest to you, the sky above, and your view of the stern of the ship. You become acutely aware of the grain of the wood on the oar's loom and handle, every rough edge. Each burst blister and every throbbing muscle grows in your mind until you can scarcely imagine anything else. You cannot see where you are heading. You must place your trust fully in the skipper. After a time, you fall into a dozing daze, where your body pulls at the wood in your hand, leaning back and breathing in unison with the rest of the oarsmen fore and aft. But before you reach that level of exhaustion, with nothing else to occupy your mind, your thoughts and worries flap inside your thought-cage like a flock of angry gulls behind a fishing boat. You swoop and pick at decisions you have made, like fish guts thrown into the surf. Your mind conjures up the faces of those you have wronged, reminds you of sins committed in the past, and offers you a fearful, gloom-laden glimpse into what the future might hold.

Such was the state of my mind, turning over all the things that had befallen me since that bloody dawn on Lindisfarnae, the men I had killed, and the friends I had lost. I saw Cormac, Cwenswith, relived my part in Wistan's death. I was thinking of the building of *Brymsteda*, and of this mad venture to go in search of Aelfwyn, when Drosten broke into my reverie. He placed a hand upon my shoulder as he passed, stepping carefully along the length of the ship as he made his way to the stern. Glad of the distraction from my over-full mind, I watched the Pict go, admiring the easy grace of the natural warrior and sailor. He halted beside Runolf and the two men began speaking. I would not have heard their words over the waves, the squeaking oars in the oarlocks, and the rhythmic grunting of the men as they leaned into the rowing, if Drosten had not raised his voice. The sharp sound of his anger caught me by surprise, startling me. A few of the oars clattered together as others missed their strokes, and I knew from the hush that fell over the crew that everyone was listening.

"I told you," snapped Drosten, his face growing red behind his tattoos, "I cannot return."

Runolf glanced past the Pict at the faces of the crew. Frowning, he spoke quietly enough that I could hear nothing save for the rumble of his voice.

Drosten shook his head.

"Why can we not continue across the sea?" he asked.

Again, I could not hear Runolf's response, but I imagined he told Drosten much the same as he had said to me. The Pict growled something and now it was Runolf whose temper frayed.

"It is out of my hands, man," he shouted, his voice booming. "We must seek repairs." He leaned against the tiller for a time without speaking. He stared over our heads as we rowed, gazing towards the coast, and the destination to which he was navigating. "Besides," he said at last, more quietly now, but loud enough for those of us in the Aft crew to hear, "we are not heading for Pictland. We are making for Orkneyjar. Have you been to the islands before?"

Drosten shook his head. The muscles and tendons of his neck and jaw bunched and stood out like ropes.

"See?" said Runolf, slapping Drosten on the shoulder. "You have nothing to worry about. We will meet a man I know there who will help us, and then we will be on our way. Besides, we will not stay long. We will be gone before anyone apart from my friend knows we are there."

Drosten's face was dark, his brow furrowed, as he stalked back along the deck to his position before the mast. If Runolf believed the man's fears assuaged by his words, I thought he was very mistaken.

Now, as we tiredly pulled *Brymsteda* between two headlands, Gersine, who was sitting across from me, his face a pale smudge in the gloom, spoke. I was surprised he found the strength to utter a sound. We had all ceased talking long since, before dusk had cloaked the world in shadows.

"Why doesn't he want to come here?" Gersine asked.

My mind was as tired as my body, and I looked at him vaguely.

"Who?" My voice croaked like the cry of a gull. I hawked and spat onto the deck before me.

"The Pict."

I recalled a conversation the summer before in a darkened hall. My body had ached then too from digging and preparing the defences of Werceworthe. I remembered Drosten's burr, his words uttered haltingly in the gloom.

"It's his story to tell," I replied. The truth was, I knew little about Drosten's past, save for the few words he had spoken that night. He had said that he had been accused of a crime he didn't commit. I wondered how many guilty men believed the same thing.

I thought Gersine, ever hungry for knowledge, might press me to say more, but he had been at the oar as long as I and his head began to nod over the loom, as if he had fallen asleep whilst still hauling the ship through the water.

Shortly after, Runolf called out a series of orders, which we executed with precision, despite our exhaustion. Soon we had shipped oars. A few heartbeats later, as *Brymsteda* continued to slide silently through the night-dark waters, I rocked backwards as the keel grated softly against a gravelly beach.

Catching my breath, I slumped over my oar. My breath came ragged, drawing the cool air of the darkness into my welcoming lungs. There was no sound apart from the movements of the men, and a distant sighing of waves lapping at the strand and against the strakes.

Around me, men were stirring from the thwarts and chests, rising and stretching. I glanced over at the dark shape of Gwawrddur. He was still, his face covered by the blankets. I felt a stab of panic as I recalled Leofstan's words. But I had prayed all through that long afternoon and should not have doubted the power of the Lord. As I watched, Leofstan bent to the Welshman, shaking him awake.

With relief washing through me, I stood and looked over the ship's side at our island destination.

Twenty-Four

There was nothing much to see from the ship. The sky was awash with a spray of stars, and the memory of the day still glowed on the horizon, as if the sun might alter its unrelenting progress and return before the dawn. *Brymsteda* was in shallow water on a nondescript beach of sand and shingle. The land was low and uniform for as far as I could see in the sun's pale afterglow. Not a single tree rose above the grass and bushes. The only shapes that drew my gaze were a large, low building positioned well away from the beach, and a couple of vessels, both smaller than *Brymsteda*, but of similar construction, that rested on the sand.

All around me the men were standing, coughing, grunting, whispering, as if to speak aloud in such stillness was a crime. Several of the crew clambered over the side, the splashes loud in the night.

"Secure the ship," called Runolf, striding forward as if he felt none of the weariness that afflicted the rest of us.

Without pause, Alf, Mantat and Garwig went about staking a line on the beach, that would hold the ship in place even if the rising tide should float the hull.

I rubbed my eyes, stretched and was about to climb over

the side, when a bright light flared in the darkness. Blinking, I peered into the gloom. A wide door had swung open in the large building. Shadows flickered before the glare of the opened door, as men hurried into the dark. Some of those men bore sputtering torches. From their light, I could see other, smaller buildings scattered around what appeared to be a central hall from which men were still spilling into the night. Torchlight gleamed from spear-points and shield bosses.

Hurrying back to my sea chest, I snatched up my sword, throwing the belt over my shoulder. Some of the other men were also lifting their weapons. Sygbald, I noticed, was wriggling into his byrnie. I did not think there was time for that.

With the sudden prospect of combat, my tiredness vanished. Scooping up my shield, I dropped over *Brymsteda*'s side, splashing into the cold water. It was deeper than I had anticipated, reaching up to my waist. I stumbled and might have fallen, if not for a steadying hand that pulled me upright by my kirtle.

Wading up to the gravelly beach, I turned to see Drosten beside me. His face was set and grim, all shadows and swirling tattoos. I nodded my thanks, but if he noticed, he ignored me. His eyes were intent on the night and the men pouring from the hall.

A voice called out from the dozen or so men who had formed up outside the hall. The words were loud, easily heard in the still night, even over the splashing and hurrying of the crew around me. I recognised the lilt and meter as belonging to the tongue of Drosten's people.

"So much for not being in Pictland," Drosten grumbled beside me.

I wondered if he would shout a reply to the voice, but Drosten clamped his mouth shut. I noted the glimmer of steel. The Pict clutched a wicked-looking knife at his side. All around me, the men were lining up, forming a rough shieldwall.

"Easy, boys," hissed Hereward's voice from the darkness. Then, louder, "I thought you said this was a friend of yours."

"Well," rumbled Runolf, who had somehow found himself amongst the men on the beach, "who can you say is truly your friend until it is put to the test?"

The men from the hall were striding down towards us now, the light from their torches illuminating their stern faces, broad round shields, helms, spears and swords.

"I would rather not have to face the test of your friendship now," said Hereward. "They do not look very welcoming."

The leader of the band called out again. This time I understood his words, as he spoke in the language of the Norse.

"Who comes to my lands in the dark, like thieves?" he shouted, his voice gruff and tinged with menace.

"Have you forgotten me, old friend?" shouted Runolf.

The men continued walking forward, their steel threatening in the flickering light, no smile on their faces. Around me, the crew of *Brymsteda* were handing out shields and weapons along the line. Silently, without fuss, we prepared to fight on that forlorn beach, under the summer-bright night sky. There were perhaps a score of men approaching us now. We outnumbered them, but if they were seasoned warriors, it would be a hard-fought confrontation, and there was no guarantee that we would prevail. Many of our number were fishermen and thralls. Strong and hard-working, but not well-versed in the art of bloodletting. I felt the growing pressure within me that precedes a fight. Muttering the paternoster, I drew my sword from its scabbard and raised my shield, adjusting my stance, ready for battle, as Gwawrddur had taught me.

With a shock, I saw the Welsh swordsman, face pallid, but shield and sword in hand, standing towards the end of the line. I marvelled at his strength. I had worried he might die and here he was ready to fight.

The men from the hall halted some thirty paces from us.

They stood there quietly, an impassive wall of wood and iron, where the sand and shingle of the beach met the straggling marram grass. A slight breeze blew in from the sea now, tugging at the flames from their torches, fluttering them like standards before a battle.

For a time there was silence in both ranks. At last, Runolf stepped forward, perhaps so that the torchlight would fall on his face. If he was known to these people, surely there could be no mistaking him with his flame-red beard and great height. I saw he held his great axe by his side, its massive blade touching the sand at his feet. Perhaps he was not so sure of the reception we would receive here after all.

"It is I, Runolf Ragnarsson," he said, his booming voice filling the night. "We do not come to cause trouble."

A man stepped forward from the group before us. He was tall, though he would still need to look up at Runolf. Taking a torch from one of the other men, he walked half a dozen paces across the sand. The torch lit his handsome features. Like Runolf, he had long hair and a full beard, but his black hair was plaited and oiled in the way of the Picts, his beard groomed and combed smooth. He scowled at Runolf, his hand resting on the pommel of the sword hanging at his side.

"And yet, trouble so often follows where you go, Runolf Ragnarsson." He shook his head and glowered. "You are either foolhardy or brave to come here after what you did."

I tensed, my grasp tightening on my sword's grip. I sensed the men around me shifting their feet, imperceptibly raising shields, holding weapons more firmly.

Head held high, Runolf walked forward. His axe was still at his side and I wondered whether it would soon be swinging in the darkness, showering the night with blood. It seemed Drosten was not the only one in danger from coming here.

"I have been called both a fool and brave in my time,"

Runolf said, halting a few steps in front of the dark-haired man.

They stared at each other for some time, the tension building. Then, without warning, the man with the torch made a lunge at Runolf. The red-headed giant flinched and I saw the head of the axe lift from the earth by a hand's breath. But the torchbearer halted and did not strike Runolf. Neither moved for a heartbeat, each sizing the other man up. Then, with a grin and loud laughter, they suddenly embraced. They slapped each other on the back, and I saw Runolf had let his axe fall to the ground.

I sighed, releasing pent-up breath I had not known I had been holding in.

Still grinning, Runolf turned to us.

"This is my friend, Tannskári. This is his hall."

Tannskári's white teeth gleamed in the light of his torch.

"You are all welcome," he said. "My friends will help you unload what you need."

"I have need of repairs for my ship," Runolf said.

Tannskári barely glanced at *Brymsteda* before leading Runolf away up the beach towards his hall and the warm light that spoke of shelter and rest.

"Let us talk of these things in the morning," I heard him say as they grew distant. "It is late, and I would sleep a while more before daybreak."

"You'll not be needing those," said a thickset man with thinning grey hair and a scar that ran into his white beard. He nodded at our shields and weapons. He had led the rest of Tannskári's men down to the water's edge, and even as he spoke, they were setting aside their spears and boards, evidently sure enough of their safety to stand unarmed before us. "My name is Ottar."

Hereward and Mancas stepped close and I realised they might well not have understood what had been said in the tongue of the Norse. I quickly explained Runolf and Tannskári's conversation and then introduced them to Ottar, who I assumed was Tannskári's steward.

"I think we should put down our weapons," I added, pointedly laying my shield on the sand and sheathing my sword.

Mancas nodded, and Hereward shouted out the order. As the crew lay down their spears and shields, so the knife-edge sharpness that had lingered on the beach, softened.

With the help of Ottar and Tannskári's men, the ship was soon secured. While the men were lifting their chests from the deck, Drosten came close to Hereward and whispered something. Hereward nodded.

"I'll have some food brought down to you," he said. "You men," he pointed at the six thralls who travelled with us, "you will stay aboard with Drosten to watch the ship and the cargo." Most of them nodded subserviently. Ahmad looked away, but not before I saw the scowl that played across his dark features at Hereward's order. I felt for him. He had saved Gwawrddur's life and deserved gratitude, but I was too exhausted to speak up for the thrall, so I followed the others away from *Brymsteda*.

"There is no need to set a guard," said Ottar. "Your ship will be safe here. You have my word."

Hereward shrugged.

"I thank you, but I would feel better if some of my people watched over it all the same."

Ottar looked from Hereward to Drosten, his expression unreadable.

"So be it," he said at last.

When we reached the hall, I was surprised to find its walls made of rough-hewn sandstone. Before then, I had only seen churches built of stone, and old crumbling ruins abandoned centuries before by the Romans. But those edifices had straight lines of shaped and chiselled rock. The walls of Tannskári's hall looked more akin to the drystone walls that some farmers used to pen in their livestock. In Northumbria, some men would use the stone as it was much longer-lasting and resilient than timber that would rot over time. Here, on this treeless island, I presumed there was no alternative to using the stone that could be pulled from the earth.

I pulled off my sword belt at the door and left it on the heap of other blades and axes that had already been placed into a huge, stout-looking chest. A stern-faced man waited close by, holding an imposing lock with which to secure the weapons. For the briefest of moments I worried that perhaps we were walking into a trap; unarmed and unprepared.

The roof was covered in turf, giving the building the look of something that had grown up from the earth, or, I thought with a shiver, like one of the burial mounds that dotted the land, home to the dead of the old people who came before us. Entering the hall I had to step down and I realised that the building was partly beneath the level of the land, further enhancing the sensation of stepping into a stone-lined tomb. I made the sign of the cross nervously. Moments later I cursed myself for a suspicious fool as I was embraced by the comforting smells and sounds of a home like any other. On the hearth stone, rather than wood, clods of what appeared to be sod smouldered. The smoke from the fire may have been strangely pungent, but dried cod fish and legs of ham hung from the rafters, and the hall was crowded with people. All around were the faces of men, women and children, staring expectantly at the visitors who had come in from the sea.

A round-faced woman with sombre eyes handed me a piece of dark bread and a cup of ale. I murmured my thanks and picked my way across the floor to where Leofstan and Gersine were sitting. Tannskári and Runolf were seated on stools at the far end of the building, already deep in conversation, their faces ruddy from the embers of the fire and the rush lights that flickered in small niches around the stone walls.

I chewed the bread. It was good, even if a bit stale. I swilled ale around my mouth, softening it. The drink was good too, and I could feel my body relaxing, the strain from the day's perils seeping from me as I drained the ale from the earthenware cup.

For a time there was movement and noise. Men came and went, and the women served each of the crew members with drink and bread.

Sighing, Gwawrddur came to where we were sitting, and lowered himself down beside us. He quickly finished the bread he'd been given and emptied his cup of ale.

"By God, I needed that," he said, smacking his lips. "Do you think there is more where that came from?" He handed me his cup.

Pushing myself wearily to my feet, I went to one of the women. She was young, with uncovered braided hair the colour of summer sun. She reminded me of Cwenswith but when I smiled at her, she would not look me in the eye. My gaze lingered on the white smoothness of her arm as she poured ale into my cup, and I felt my face grow hot. Muttering my thanks, I hurried back to my friends.

When I got there, Gwawrddur was stretched out and snoring.

"Do you think he will be well?" I whispered to Leofstan.

Leofstan shrugged.

"I would say your prayers have been answered. The Lord has other plans for Gwawrddur, I think."

The effect of the tribulations of the day washed over me then like the storm waves that had threatened to swamp *Brymsteda*. I emptied the cup of ale I had brought for Gwawrddur, and lay down beside him.

In moments, I was asleep. I dreamt I was lord of a great hall. Upon my knee sat a flaxen-haired beauty. She fed me choice cuts of succulent meat and poured me great horns of ale and mead.

Twenty-Five

I awoke to smells of cooking and the sounds of bustling womenfolk. Opening my eyes, I stretched. My shoulders and back ached from the long afternoon of rowing, but I felt more refreshed than I had in days. The dream of the beautiful girl still lingered in my mind, the way the taste of honey sits in your mouth long after you have finished a sweet oatcake.

The doors to the hall had been opened to the day and I was surprised to see bright sunshine streaming in, the shaft of light hazing the smoke-laden air of Tannskári's hall. With a start I realised that Leofstan and Gwawrddur had already risen. Their blankets were neatly folded where they had slept. Looking around, I saw that most of the hall was empty of the men who had crowded the floor during the night. The only one of the crew who had yet to awaken was Gersine, who still snored softly near me. I rose, folding my blanket as the others had done, and made my way towards the door.

The round-faced woman from the night before stepped away from the cauldron she was tending and moved to intercept me. In the stark light of the morning sun I saw her face was lined and weary, her mouth pinched in a serious scowl.

"I saved you some porridge," she said in Norse. "You looked

like you needed the sleep." Her lips did not smile, but her eyes glimmered with a warmth I had not noticed before.

She held a bowl and a wooden spoon in her hands, which I accepted.

"My thanks," I said, using the language of her people.

She nodded approvingly.

"There is ale and water over there."

She turned back to the pot. At a table nearby, women were busy cutting dried fish, onions and wild leek, while others kneaded bread dough.

I made my way outside, pausing to pour myself a cup of water from a clay jug near the door. I blinked in the bright sunshine, again shocked at how late I had slept. Down at the beach several figures were working on and around *Brymsteda*. Runolf's height, and his blaze of red hair and beard marked him even from this distance. I thought I recognised Mancas and Hereward too.

A small group of children were running on the sand. A couple of dogs barked and chased them. Fleetingly, I wondered where the rest of the crew was, but such questions could wait. Setting down my cup on the grass, I took a deep breath of the fresh air and stared out into the sound. A light breeze blew in over the glimmering water, carrying with it the tang of salt. Fulmars soared above the sheltered sea, and several kittiwakes dotted the waves. I was excited to spot a small flock of dappled, long-billed birds I did not recognise, and I stared at them as they probed the sands of the shallows, far enough away to feel safe from the men working on the ship and the shrieking children with their noisy dogs. The sun was high in the pale sky, and all trace of the storm and the black clouds had vanished like a bad dream.

With that thought came memories of my own dream and I smiled as I took a great spoonful of the porridge and shovelled it into my mouth. I was ravenous and savoured the warm oats as I chewed and swallowed. The porridge was good and wholesome, and I was thankful to the serious woman for saving some for me. Still, I would have preferred choice cuts of roasted meat, lovingly prepared and pushed into my hungry mouth by the soft fingers of the lovely girl in my dream. I felt the stirrings of desire as I recalled the images from my sleep. The young woman's plump softness had been perched on my knee, one hand popping food into my mouth, seeming to revel in me licking the juice from her fingertips, the other hand stroking my neck and caressing my hair.

I shuddered at the thrill of the memories, and wondered whether the dream might have been Devil-sent. I squirmed uncomfortably as my body responded to the recollection of the dream. It had been weeks since I had lain with Cwenswith and I had thought, since I had recommenced my daily prayers with Leofstan, that I was free of these temptations. I know now that a young man's mind is seldom far from the fascinations of the flesh; carnal desires I all too frequently succumbed to in my long life. I have oft prayed for forgiveness from the Lord for my transgressions, but I fear the memories of lust never fade and even now, old as I am, I sometimes sin anew in my dreams, or when certain scents send my mind tumbling back through the years to the memory of pliant embraces of women I knew long ago and far away.

Back then, standing in the warmth of the summer sun outside Tannskári's hall, I was painfully aware of my body's excitement. I longed to return to the dream, where the pretty young woman had lovingly caressed me, but I tried to shake off the temptation of dwelling on such lewd thoughts. More than anything, I thought, I needed a piss. I scooped more porridge into my mouth, anxious now to be done with the food so that I could find somewhere to relieve myself. If I could empty my bladder, perhaps then I would be rid of the uncomfortable sensation that stirred my manhood.

"You are hungry, I see," said a voice very close to me.

Turning, I saw with horror that the speaker was the young woman I had dreamt of. I felt my face redden and, in my desperation to swallow the food in my mouth, I choked. Coughing and spluttering, I sprayed glutinous lumps of oatmeal from my lips. With terrible embarrassment I felt her small hand against my back. The delicate hand that had excited me in my dreams, now slapping me to dislodge the food that was causing me such distress. When I was able to breathe, I accepted the cup that she had picked up from the ground. I sipped the water, gradually easing my coughing. I took the moment to compose myself and to watch her over the rim of the cup.

She was even more beautiful than I had remembered. Her eyes were a blue as pale as the sky, her plaited hair shining as brightly as burnished gold. She was younger than I had thought too, the shadows of the hall at night lending her age. I wondered how long it would be before she was married. With such beauty, it would surely not be difficult for her father to find her a husband. But perhaps here on this island, far to the north of Pictland, there were not many suitable men. For the briefest of moments, I wondered whether I could be a prospective match for her. I had not considered marriage before, but in that instant, my young heart fluttered like a butterfly caught in a stiff wind and the idea of marrying this girl of my dreams seemed very real to me.

"Are you Hunlaf?" she asked and I almost choked again, this time on the water. She knew my name! I nodded, not trusting myself to speak. "Good," she went on. "I have been sent for you."

"For me?" I cursed inwardly at the squeak in my voice.

She smiled, and her face lit up, even more radiant than before.

"Yes. The old Welshman wants you. The one with the strange name."

"Gwawrddur?"

"Yes," she said. "That's the one."

I was confused. My stomach rumbled and I decided I should not waste good food when I had the chance to eat. Picking up the bowl of porridge, I quickly spooned it into my mouth, chewing and swallowing carefully now.

"You certainly like my mother's cooking," said the girl, her eyes sparkling like the sun-licked waves.

"I didn't get much to eat yesterday," I replied, my mouth full. "I would eat anything now."

She laughed at that and I squirmed, thinking of how my words must have sounded to her.

"I did not mean..." I stuttered. "Your mother's porridge... It is fine porridge." I stopped talking and finished the oats, scraping the last remnants up with my finger and licking it clean. The action made me think of my dream and I felt my cheeks redden. I showed the girl the empty bowl, as if to prove my point about her mother's food.

She laughed again. Taking the bowl from me, she disappeared into the gloom of the hall. Moments later, she reappeared, her mother's voice following her.

"Thurid Tannskárisdottir, you get yourself back here and help with the cooking. The men will be hungry later and there is much to do."

The girl, whose name must have been Thurid, pulled a face and called over her shoulder, "I'll be back directly." Then, in a quieter voice she said to me, "Come on. If I stay here, I'll miss the fun." She reached for my hand and I thrilled at the touch. Just as she was leading me after her, away from the hall, Gersine stepped into the daylight, yawning and rubbing his eyes. In his hand he held a bowl, which I assumed held porridge.

"Where are you going?" Gersine asked in Englisc.

"I'm not sure," I replied, certain that I would go wherever Thurid decided to lead me.

"No time to waste," she said, and, grasping Gersine's empty hand, she pulled us both eastward away from the hall and her mother's calls for her.

Gersine shook off his sleepiness quickly in the presence of Thurid and I felt a stab of jealousy as we ran, all three of us hand-in-hand, around the back of the hall and up a low rise. Gersine had Cwenswith waiting for him back at Uuiremutha. When we were some way from the hall and could no longer hear the shouts from Thurid's mother, we slowed the pace. I was glad to stop running as my bladder was full to bursting. But I felt a keen sense of loss as Thurid let go of my hand. Gersine ate his porridge as we walked, emptying the bowl without choking, which needled me. Again he enquired where we were going. I asked Thurid.

"Your friend does not speak our tongue?"

"No," I replied, feeling an irrational pleasure that Gersine could not communicate easily with this lovely girl. "But I too would like to know where you are taking us."

"I've told you," she said, flicking her plaits over her shoulders. "The Welshman sent for you."

"Why?" I could think of no reason why Gwawrddur would have sent this girl in search of me.

"He says you are the fastest runner of the crew."

I frowned. It was true that I was fleet of foot and probably the fastest of the men aboard *Brymsteda*, but I was still uncertain as to why I had been summoned and why Thurid had come to get me.

"But why does that matter?"

"That is obvious, is it not?"

I felt stupid that the answer was not apparent to me.

"Did she say," asked Gersine, "that Gwawrddur called for you? That you are the fastest?"

I nodded, cursing that Gersine was quick-witted and had a keen ear. Most Englisc men could pick out the rudiments of the

Norse tongue. Gersine had paid attention to Runolf these past months and understood more than most.

"Is there to be a foot race then?" he asked.

"Yes," Thurid replied, beaming. She had clearly understood his Englisc words too, and my heart sank yet further. "A race. And other games. The men always set up trials when a ship comes in. There have been fewer ships of late."

I thought of the two ships that had sunk at Uuiremutha, and Skorri's ships that had been destroyed at Werceworthe. I wondered if their loss had affected Thurid and the people on this island. Had she had kin who had lost their life?

"Did I hear your mother say you are Tannskári's daughter?" I asked.

"Yes, I have two older brothers, and two younger ones, and three younger sisters. The younger ones were all born here on Orkneyjar."

"And you? Where were you born?"

"My older brothers and I were born back in Skeie, in Rygjafylki. But I was only little when we came here."

"And your father, does he go raiding with the other Norsemen?"

"He did go a-viking once, but now he stays home. We have all we need here. Father is friends with all those who travel the Whale Road. Ships stop here for supplies, repairs and to rest."

"And they pay," I said. It was not really a question.

"Yes, they pay," Thurid said, giving me a sidelong glance.

I looked back at the hall and the scattered buildings around the beach. Beyond it were the few boats we had seen when we had arrived the night before, and dwarfing them all, *Brymsteda*. The image conjured up memories of the minster at Lindisfarnae, the chapel, scriptorium, cells and other buildings huddled peacefully beside the sea, unaware of the violent foes that would soon sweep in on their longships, bringing death and destruction to the holy island. A sudden anger flared within me.

"You are few here," I said. "Undefended. Why don't men merely take what you have?"

Thurid looked at me sharply, perhaps imagining that the crew of *Brymsteda* posed a threat to her folk.

"We are not weaklings," she said, her tone clipped with pride and anger at the implication that Tannskári's people could not defend themselves. "My father has close to a score of men who would fight to protect what is ours. It would be no easy thing to take from us." I thought of the torch-bearing warriors in the night and nodded. "Besides," she went on, looking away from me and striding ahead, "it would be an unwise skipper who did not foresee a time he might again be in need of my father's aid. Better to know that Tannskári's hall is here for such a time as a ship needs a safe haven."

I pondered her words, silently berating myself for angering her. I hurried to keep up, Gersine close beside me. I could see our destination now. Several huge, weathered stones, as tall as a man, jutted from the ground, far apart around the rim of the rise, forming a large circular area surrounded by the ring of stones. A large group of people were gathered there.

"There you are," called Os. "We thought you'd got lost." He winked and glanced at Thurid lasciviously. "Though none of us would have blamed you for dallying for a time!" He laughed at his own quip and was joined by some of *Brymsteda*'s crew. None of Tannskári's folk laughed.

"Well, I did not get lost, as you can see," I said, angry that Os had so readily imagined my feelings towards Thurid. I was also surprised that the mood had changed so drastically from the night before when we had faced each other with weapons in our hands. Now it appeared that the Norsemen of this island and those who had sailed into the sound in the night were like old friends. There was the air of a festival day about them.

Most of the folk who thronged around the stones were men, I noticed. A large number of *Brymsteda*'s crew, those who were not needed on the ship, I assumed, and several of the men who had met us on the beach the night before. The children and dogs from the beach had followed us up the hill too, but as far as I could see, there were no women there, apart from Thurid.

A tall, dark-haired man with the round face of the woman in the hall and Tannskári's swagger, sauntered towards us. He eyed me for a moment and I sensed the challenge in his gaze.

"Thank you, sister," he said to Thurid. "Now you had best be back home to help the women with the cooking."

Thurid raised herself up to her full height, though that was still a full head shorter than her brother. She placed her hands on her hips and jutted her chin out. I do not believe I have ever seen a more beautiful woman, and I have been tempted by the saffron-scented harlots of al-Askar and once shared a bed with the Empress of Roma whom many have said was as captivating as Helena herself. But in all my days, no woman has shone so brilliantly as Thurid did that morning, standing defiantly between the stones, the cool breeze from the sea ruffling her skirts about her legs, tugging at the gold of her braids.

"I will do no such thing, brother," she said. Her blue eyes flashed with a cold fury and I was reminded again that hers were a warlike people. "I can help Mother and the women every other day, but today I would watch you men compete."

The tall man glowered at Thurid for a heartbeat, but he could not maintain his severe expression.

"Very well then," he said, laughing. "I know better than to fight with you, little sister. I need to save my strength for the trials. Perhaps you wish to join in too."

"Perhaps," she said.

He raised an eyebrow.

"I will not stop you, but I will tell Mother I tried to send you back. That is a fight you will have to face alone."

Thurid smiled then.

"Thank you," she said. Then, to me, "This is Toki, my eldest brother."

Toki looked me up and down and I imagined what he saw. A slender young man, with shaggy hair and the wispy thin beard of youth. Toki was taller, broader of shoulder, and more handsome. His beard was dark and thick, his eyes a darker blue than his sister's, colder and more distant.

"This is Hunlaf," Thurid said.

"The Welshman says you are quick," Toki said, and I could tell from his tone that he did not believe it.

"I can run," I said.

"We shall see."

It turned out that I was not going to run against Toki, but against his younger brother, Varin. Like Toki, Varin was tall and strong, but Varin was slimmer, and ever taller than his sibling. He was perhaps a year or two older than me and he smiled at me as we prepared to race.

"I have watched the lad and I believe you can best him," said Gwawrddur, taking my kirtle from me. I had stripped it off, and removed my shoes too, so that I could better grip on the scrubby grass. The Welshman seemed to have fully recovered from his ordeal and now, standing in the mid-morning sunshine, I could scarcely believe he had almost drowned the day before. "Just imagine your life depends on it," he said, "as it did at Werceworthe, and you will win."

I thought of the strange twists in my life that would soon see me racing a Norseman for entertainment, when less than a year before I had sprinted away from armed Norse who had almost certainly rested at this very place before sailing south to attack us. Those men were dead, some by my hand. It was hard to take in the changes in my life. I could barely recall the time before I had picked up a blade to fight. That Hunlaf seemed like a different person, a distant memory of someone else's dream.

"Your life might not depend on it," said Sygbald, from where he leaned against one of the standing stones, "but my silver does. So see that you do not lose."

"I need a piss," I muttered, acutely aware of the pressure in my bladder.

"Then go," said Gwawrddur. "Your adversary is ready."

I looked over to see Varin bending and stretching. Like me, he was stripped to the waist. His torso was pale and finely muscled, and on his right arm I was surprised to see blue lines of tattoos like Drosten's. I held up a hand and hurried out of the circle of stones. One of the dogs followed after me, and behind the hound came a young boy.

"Away with you," I snarled, but both boy and dog continued to follow me. "I need to piss."

"Me too," said the boy happily.

Sighing, I ignored him and carried on.

There was no shelter from the eyes of those at the stones, so after I had created some distance between us, I loosened my breeches. The relief I felt at finally emptying my bladder was tempered somewhat by the certitude that Thurid was watching me from the circle of stones. Beside me, the boy dropped his breeches and let out a stream of piss, narrowly missing the dog that came to sniff around us. I could not help smiling as the boy emulated my sigh of pleasure, grinning up at me.

"What's your name?" I asked him as we walked back to the stones.

"Lambi," he said with a wide smile, pleased that I had deigned to speak to him. He must have been no older than five or six years. "Varin will beat you. He never loses."

I frowned. The prospect of losing before Thurid dismayed

me. There was little sense in it, I knew, but I yearned to prove myself in some way to her.

"Fast is he?" I asked.

"Like the wind." He emulated Toki's swagger beside me, making me smile. The similarity was suddenly very apparent. "One day I will be faster though."

"Varin is your brother?"

Lambi nodded.

"Come on, Hunlaf," shouted Os. "I hope you run faster than you piss, or we are all going to lose our silver!" The men of *Brymsteda* laughed. A few groaned as they began to fear for their wagers. Watching Varin as he limbered up his shoulders and stretched his leg muscles, I could well imagine they might be nervous to have placed their faith in me. I was apprehensive too. These last weeks I had spent most of my days aboard ship and my arms were as strong as they had ever been from hauling on ropes and pulling the long oars. But I had done little in the way of running, and seeing Varin's long legs, I was not at all sure I could beat him.

Thurid was watching me, and I grinned at her, exuding a confidence I did not feel.

"Go on, Hunlaf!" shouted Gersine. His closeness to Thurid irked me, and in that instant I vowed I would win.

Everyone crowded within the open area surrounded by the stone sentinels. Only Varin and Toki stood outside the circle, beside the tallest of the stones.

"Good luck," said Lambi cheerfully, leading the dog into the throng. I saw that the other dogs were being restrained to prevent them from chasing and tripping us.

"When I give the command," said Toki, his voice loud enough to carry over all of those gathered, "you will run around the stones three times. If you enter the circle, you lose. The first man to complete the three circuits and take this rune-staff is the winner." He lifted a short length of wood that he held and inserted it in a crack of the rock so that it protruded at an angle. Standing this close to the stone I could see there were carvings on it, whorls and swirls and interlocking circles that reminded me of Drosten's tattoos and those on Varin's arm. I wondered how much of the stone had been shaped by men, whether the cleft that Toki had used to hold the staff was natural or had been carved there for just that purpose. The crowd of onlookers had fallen quiet now and the only sounds were the distant sigh of the waves and the occasional cry of the gulls high in the sky above us.

"Do you understand?" Toki asked in a quiet voice.

I nodded, wishing I had taken more time to prepare. I had stretched briefly, but Varin was jumping on the spot, shaking his arms. He was lithe, bouncing with pent-up energy.

"Ready?" Toki said.

I jumped a couple of times, raising my knees up high, emulating Varin. I rolled my head once, hearing my neck crackle with tension. I was certainly not as ready as Varin, but there was nothing for it now. I could feel the eyes of everyone on me. I dared not look away from the direction we were to run in, but I sensed Thurid's gaze on me. I nodded.

Varin dropped into a running stance. I copied him.

"Very well," shouted Toki. "May the gods smile on you both, and may the fastest man prevail!"

I was taken by surprise when Varin, clearly knowing this to be the signal to start, sprinted off. He was fast and I was already a few paces behind him when I started my own run. It was as Lambi had said. His older brother ran like the wind, his legs carrying him over the turf seemingly without effort.

The crowd erupted in a great roar of shouted encouragement for their runner of choice. The dogs barked and the children shrieked in excitement. The ground was cool and hard beneath my feet. The short grass whipped against my bare feet and ankles. I ignored everything save Varin's back. I needed to push hard to close the gap between us, but as Varin passed the staff for the first time, I was only an arm's length behind him. I realised then that being so close to him it was easier for me to keep up Varin's pace, as the taller man protected me from the wind of our passing. I allowed the cheering to wash over me and matched Varin stride for stride.

I could tell in that second lap around the circle that if we had raced side-by-side, I would not have stood a chance against Varin. But perhaps by slotting in behind him, and taking advantage of the shielding his body provided me, I would conserve just enough energy to be able to pass him before the end.

I thought I heard my name in the shouts as we passed the staff for the second time. Those who screamed for me to win sounded desperate to my ears, increasingly certain they were going to lose their bets. Varin risked a glance over his shoulder and I saw the edge of a smile on his face as he saw me behind him.

We were halfway round the circle for the final time and I remembered Gwawrddur's words. I recalled how the Norse had chased me through the forest. I felt again the bite of the hand axe that had struck my shoulder. I had been the faster runner then and I would not let this Norseman beat me now. With a roar, I surged forward, pushing myself to greater speed. For a few heartbeats I was beside Varin. I could hear his breath, rasping with each step. I had not needed to run through the wind, thus conserving enough energy to outstrip him now. With a savage grin, I powered forward and passed him. An instant later I caught the rune-staff in my hand, tearing it from its hole in the tall stone.

Such was my speed, that I lost my footing on the trampled grass. Toppling over, I tumbled across the grass, bruising my shoulder as I fell.

A shadow fell over me. Looking up I saw it was Toki, his hand outstretched. I allowed him to pull me to my feet.

"We have a winner!" he yelled, holding my hand aloft.

The onlookers clapped and cheered. I scanned their faces until I saw Thurid. She waved and grinned, and the day seemed to brighten.

"Well run," said Varin, slapping me on the back. "Clever," he continued, panting.

"You are the faster runner," I said, bending double and drawing in great lungfuls of the cool air that blew in from the North Sea.

Varin offered me a lopsided smirk. "The outcome of the contest would say otherwise."

"I had to use my head. I could not have beaten you otherwise."

He nodded his thanks, his expression doubtful. Perhaps Varin believed my words were false modesty, but I knew the truth in them. I watched as he made his way back to the crowd, where his friends and family gathered around, commiserating with him on his loss.

Twenty-Six

The rest of the day was spent in more trials. First there was a spear throwing contest. Almost everyone joined in and it took a long time for them all to take their turn. I was surprised when Thurid stood and took a spear from Toki. She tied up her skirts, to better be able to run, and I knew I was not alone in revelling in the sight of her bare slender legs as she sprinted forward and let her javelin fly. She did not win, but her throw travelled further than many, easily beating my own attempt that fell somewhere in the middle of the pack.

"That is why I should not be peeling onions with the womenfolk," she said, returning to sit near me in the shadow of one of the stones.

Both Gamal's and Gwawrddur's spears had landed close together, several spear lengths beyond most of the competitors. But the winning throw came from Toki's hand, much to the delight of the locals.

Next, someone produced wooden practice swords and shields. They laid a large cloak on the grass for size, then staked out a rope on the ground for the fighting space in the way of the hólmgang. Several of the men vied against each other. Many wagers were placed, as the fighters parried and feinted, skipping back and forth to avoid the wooden blades, which, even though not sharp, could still bruise.

One of Tannskári's people, an older man called Hroar, with a broad nose that looked like it had been broken more than once, handed me a water skin. I drank deeply, nodding my thanks.

"You do not bet on your man?" he asked.

Pendrad was sparring with a thickset young man with a fair, red-streaked beard. The two appeared quite evenly matched, but it looked to me that Pendrad was the more experienced fighter. His timing and footwork were better, and his extra height gave him the advantage of a longer reach. Still, I had little to wager, so did not take the risk.

"Maybe later," I said, feeling Leofstan's disapproving glare on me.

I ignored him, concentrating on the rest of the bout. As expected, Pendrad was the first to land the requisite three blows, only receiving one painful rap against his wrist for his trouble.

I was surprised when Gwawrddur stood and walked towards the hólmgang square in the centre of the standing stones.

"You are fully recovered?" asked Leofstan.

The Welshman shrugged.

"God alone knows the answer to that," he said. "But if not, better I should lose when the swords are oak, rather than steel." He grinned, and I was glad the darkness that had gripped him appeared to have lifted. "But of course," he held up his hands as if in apology, "I will not lose."

His confidence buoyed my own. I had never seen Gwawrddur lose a fight.

"I will wager on the Welshman," I said to Hroar.

Toki stepped over the rope to face Gwawrddur and Hroar chuckled, clearly believing the older Welshman would have no chance against Tannskári's eldest son.

"Very well," Hroar said. "But I have no silver." He looked down at my belt and the seax that hung from the scabbard there. My sword was still back at the hall, along with all our other weapons apart from knives. Pulling his own seax from its sheath, he handed it to me. "How about this? Your knife against mine." I tugged my seax free and gave it to him, but my eyes were fixed on the knife now in my hand. The iron of the blade looked solid enough, and when I ran my thumb across its edge, it was sharp, with no rolls or nicks, but it was the handle that had captivated me. It was the colour of thick cream and seemed to be made from bone. It was exquisitely carved with runes and figures all around the base where the grip met the blade.

"It is from the tusk of a hrosshvalr," Hroar said.

"A hrosshvalr?" The name was strange to me. "Part horse, part whale?" I could not imagine such a creature.

"Aye. They sometimes come to these shores. As common as sheep on some of the beaches further north. Huge beasts."

Looking at the knife's handle, intricately carved from a single tusk, I could barely fathom how large the owner of the tooth must have been. I could find no words to describe how I felt about the object in my hand. I had to possess that knife.

"A fool and his treasure are easily parted," said Leofstan, perhaps noting my expression as I gazed at the seax.

Thurid, who sat nearby, appeared to understand him, and smiled at the monk's words. Perhaps I was a fool, but the knife was a thing of beauty and I coveted it.

"The bet is agreed," I said and shook hands with Hroar.

We placed both knives on the grass before us, and it took a great effort to drag my gaze away from the ivory handle of Hroar's blade to watch the fight that would determine whether it would become mine. We had thought to remain seated, but the onlookers, sensing that this fight would be special, crowded forward, impeding our view.

Grumbling, Hroar picked up the seaxes, handing mine to me. Rising, we hurried forward as we heard the first clatter of oaken blade against willow board. Shouldering our way through the throng, I clutched Thurid's hand in mine, pulling her with me. Her fingers gripped me tightly, her palm was cool. Gersine was close by, but I noted Thurid had not reached for his hand, and my heart soared.

For a heartbeat I could think of nothing else save for Thurid's hand in mine, but then the two fighters closed together for the second time, and my focus narrowed to Gwawrddur and Toki, facing each other across the expanse of the roped off area, wooden swords striking and parrying with blurring speed.

I had been certain that Gwawrddur would prevail against a single foe, but in those first clashes, when each warrior probed the other's defences, testing the strength and skill of his opponent, I began to wonder. Toki was as fast as any swordsman I had ever seen. His stance was balanced, his footwork nimble and quick. Darting forward, he almost landed a blow. But Gwawrddur was also fast, and he managed to deflect the strike with the rim of his shield. Having drawn Toki's blade off line, without pause, the Welshman flicked out the tip of his sword in an effort to score a hit on the younger man's unprotected chest. With cat-like speed, Toki flung himself backwards, avoiding the blow by a finger's breadth. He almost stepped outside of the fighting area, which would have cost him a point, but with a force of will, he kept himself within the staked out boundary, teetering for a moment before righting himself. Gwawrddur could have pressed his advantage then, striking with his sword or pushing Toki backwards, but the Welshman stood his ground.

Toki nodded to him, acknowledging the other's forbearance.

They circled, both now wary of the other. Gwawrddur did not blink, his gaze never leaving Toki's eyes.

Without warning, the Norseman leapt forward. The crowd

gasped, as it seemed inevitable that the taller, younger man would connect with his wooden sword. But with an alarming apparent lack of effort, Gwawrddur closed to meet him, parrying the strike on his shield with a crack, then, with a sidestep and a twist of his body, his thick practice sword's blade smacked down into Toki's outstretched sword arm.

With a grunt, Toki's weapon fell from his grasp. Rubbing his wrist, he glowered at Gwawrddur. The Welshman's face was impassive. Toki must surely have been glad they were using wood, I thought. He stooped to retrieve his weapon, but Gwawrddur caught it under his foot and flicked it up towards the younger man. The Norseman caught it, but there was no thanks from him now. He swung the blade a few times in the air, testing the strength of his grip. I could see a change had come over him. Fury drained the colour from his face. And in that instant, the outcome of the fight was clear to me.

Thurid's grasp on my hand tightened, but I was barely aware now, as I was held transfixed to see such sword-skill on display.

Toki's attacks became increasingly savage. If his blows had struck Gwawrddur, they might have broken bones, such was their ferocity. But the Welshman was a master swordsman. He seemed to flow like water, avoiding every scything swipe, each vicious lunge.

It was over in a few heartbeats.

Choosing the perfect moment each time, when Toki was off-balance, or fully committed to an attack that did not connect, Gwawrddur would flick out his sword with the speed of a striking viper, touching his weapon's wooden blade first to Toki's throat, and then to his thigh. He did not strike with any force now, which alone showed great skill, but with each hit, the crowd sighed. Everyone watching knew that each of the three strikes would have been killing blows with iron blades.

After the third hit, it seemed that Toki would rush to attack again. He quivered before Gwawrddur, his face twisted in a snarl. Slowly, and surely only with a great effort, he let out a long breath and threw his sword down on the grass. Sighing and rubbing his bruised arm, he offered Gwawrddur his hand. The Welshman took it in the warrior grip, making the younger man wince at the pressure on his bruised forearm.

"You are a fine swordsman," said Gwawrddur in Englisc. "You are fast, brave and skilled."

Without thinking, I interpreted the words for Toki. It was important for him to hear what Gwawrddur had to say.

"And yet I never touched you," Toki replied, with me echoing his words for Gwawrddur. "If we had been using steel, I would be dead three times over."

"Ah, but we were not using steel, my friend," Gwawrddur said, patting him on the shoulder. "Learn from this. Do not let your anger get the better of you. Fight with a clear head. Draw your enemy to you, and respond. You have the makings of a great warrior, Toki Tannskárisson."

The sun had moved into the west by the time the sword fighting was over, and we began to think about food. But there was one more contest that the men of Orkneyjar were keen to hold.

Hroar handed over his fine knife to me after Gwawrddur's victory, but he frowned, clearly as shocked as the rest of Tannskári's folk at Toki's defeat. Now he stripped off his tunic to reveal a scarred, barrel-like chest.

"Perhaps we can wager again," he said. "I would win my knife back."

I thought he meant to face someone with the practice swords, as he stepped towards the roped off area. He looked old and slow, but there was no denying the slabs of muscle on his chest and arms that spoke of enormous strength. A fast warrior would be able to beat him with the wooden blades. I was quick with a sword, but I could imagine the crushing power of a blow if Hroar caught his opponent, so I shook my head. I had won a contest and did not wish to run the chance of being defeated in front of Thurid. Besides, I did not wish to risk losing the ivory-handled knife.

When Hroar reached the fighting area, another man stepped forward, producing long strips of cloth that he proceeded to wrap about Hroar's hands. I was glad I had fought the temptation to accept his challenge. I might have stood a chance with the wooden blades, but Hroar did not mean to use the practice swords. His weapons were his fists and I was sure I would have lost that fight against the burly warrior.

"Who will face me?" he called out while his hands were being bound.

"Where is Drosten?" shouted Os, standing and looking about the circle of stones theatrically, as if searching for someone. Noisy and outspoken when sober, Os' words were slurred and I realised that the group of men he sat with had found a skin of mead from somewhere.

I caught Leofstan's eye. We both remembered how Drosten had beaten a man much larger than Hroar in Eoforwic. I had never seen anyone fight better with his fists. But Drosten would not leave the ship, and he had been anxious ever since we had arrived here. While Tannskári's people were Norse, Orkneyjar was still part of Pictland, and Drosten had vowed never to return.

Os had heard tell of Drosten's prowess with his fists over the winter months and he now saw a chance to put those skills to the test.

"I would wager this silver amulet," he held up a gleaming hammer-shaped necklace that he had taken from one of the fallen Norsemen at Uuiremutha, "that Drosten could beat any of you."

"Who is this Drosten?" asked Hroar.

"A Pict," called out Os. "Fastest fists in the land. He would ugly you up even more. If such a thing were possible." He laughed at his own words, pointing at Hroar's squashed and twisted nose.

Hroar frowned, clearly understanding enough of Os' words to reply.

"I would fight this Pict."

A tension was growing in the afternoon air. I could sense that Os' drunken shouts were angering our hosts, and I was sure that Drosten would not be pleased to hear that his name had been bandied about.

"Fight me," shouted a new voice. I turned to see Bealdwulf push himself to his feet. He looked at me and shrugged, as if we had both had similar thoughts and he had decided to step in before matters got out of hand.

"What of the Pict?" called out Os.

Bealdwulf glowered at him.

"Sit down and be silent, Os," he said. "You have said enough." Os hesitated only a moment, before obeying the older man.

Pulling his kirtle over his head, Bealdwulf threw the garment down onto the grass and accepted the strips of cloth from the man beside the fighting square. He rolled his shoulders and neck a few times while his hands were bound tightly, then stepped past the rope and faced Hroar.

They were both strong men and neither was a stranger to combat, their bodies equally scarred with the memories of past battles. Bets were placed, and again Hroar called out to me to wager with him so that he could win back his seax. Again, I declined. I felt I owed it to Bealdwulf though to place a wager on him. I bet a small piece of hacksilver that he would win, not really caring if I lost it, as long as I kept Hroar's knife.

At a shout from the man who had bound their hands, the two men began to fight. At first they each showed some skill, stepping in close when needed, blocking and dodging to avoid the worst sting of the blows. But each man was soon bloody, the bindings on their fists soaked red. What prowess they had shown was now replaced with sheer brute strength and determination to win. They pummelled each other, blood splattering the closest spectators and streaming down the fighters' chests from gashes on their cheeks and eyebrows.

I could not believe how long the fighting went on, with both Hroar and Bealdwulf dealing countless blows that would have felled lesser men. In the end, there was no deciding strike that knocked one of the fighters from his feet. Instead, Bealdwulf held up his hands. Blinking, Hroar stepped back. With a groan, Bealdwulf lowered himself down onto one knee.

"You are the victor," he said, his teeth stained with blood. He spat a gobbet of red phlegm onto the grass.

The crowd let out a ragged cheer, some glad to win their bets, others feeling let down by the anticlimactic end to the bout.

Hroar heaved Bealdwulf to his feet and embraced him. They slapped each other's backs for a time, and then separated. Hroar accepted his winnings, and the praise of his friends and kin.

Bealdwulf staggered back to *Brymsteda*'s crew. Someone passed him a skin of mead. He took it clumsily in his wrapped fists, drinking deeply.

I marvelled that he could still stand after the beating he had taken.

"Are you hurt?" asked Leofstan.

I thought this a strange question. Bealdwulf's face was slick with blood. There was a deep gash above his left eye, and another cut on his left cheek. But to my surprise, the Northumbrian smiled.

"Do not fret, monk. I'll live."

"Then why end it?" I asked.

Bealdwulf's left eye was already swollen closed and he twisted his head to peer at me.

"That whoreson is as tough as old leather. He was never going to fall." He took another swig of mead. "And neither was I. And unless I'm mistaken that's Hereward, Runolf and Mancas coming up the hill."

I glanced over my shoulder. Sure enough, the three men, accompanied by Tannskári and several others, were almost at the standing stones.

"I still don't understand why you would stop the fight."

"Runolf said they would work until the steerboard was fixed, so they must have finished the work." Bealdwulf hawked and spat again. "And I am hungry."

"Hungry?"

"Yes," he said, and despite his bruised and bleeding face, he grinned. "Tannskári promised a feast when the work was done, and believe it or not, Hunlaf, I'd rather be eating, than getting punched in the face."

Twenty-Seven

True to Tannskári's word, that night we feasted. There was fresh bread, fish stew, a rich mutton pottage, soft cheese, dark smoky ham and freshly brewed ale that carried a hint of the sea air and red clover in its gruit. There was also strong, sweet mead in copious supply. Tannskári was a generous host and there was more than enough to go round, despite the vast number of mouths to feed.

Runolf was happy with the repairs and seemed confident that we could sail on the first tide in the morning. Lord Mancas was less pleased with the amount of silver Tannskári had demanded for his aid, but he had grudgingly paid the price, agreeing that we would also take on some extra provisions for no further charge. I did not know how much silver Mancas had been forced to pay, but judging from the boards that creaked beneath the weight of platters and jugs, I judged that Tannskári had come out the better for the deal.

With *Brymsteda*'s steerboard fixed and the ship's stores and water barrels replenished, there was a building excitement about the crew that we would soon put to sea once more. After the storm we had endured, there was some disquiet too, but the men were enjoying the food and drink, and the bustle of the hall before setting out again on our mission.

My legs ached from the race with Varin, and Bealdwulf's face was swollen and already darkening with bruises. But the trials and contests of the day had been a welcome diversion for most of the crew and, apart from some banter and light-hearted arguing over wagers, there had been no real conflict between the people of Orkneyjar and *Brymsteda*'s crew.

Glancing along the benches, to the far end, nearest the door, I saw Drosten, almost concealed in the shadows. There could be no better indication of the warming of relations between the crew and the Norsemen of the hall, than to see the Pict here, enjoying Tannskári's hospitality. When I had noticed the tattooed man entering the hall just before the feast had begun, I'd asked Runolf what had happened to change his mind.

Runolf had shrugged. Even though it had been early, he had already drained several mugs of ale. He looked tired, the hard work of the day and the stress of the previous day's sailing showing in the dark smudges beneath his eyes.

"It was Mancas' doing really," he said.

"How so?"

"You know how he is," he said, scratching beneath his shaggy beard. "He would not cease his pacing while we worked. Tannskári asked what ailed him. Lord Mancas told him." He smiled, emptying his cup and refilling it from the jug that rested on a small table just inside the door. "I do not always see eye-to-eye with the man, but I respect his honesty."

"What did he say?"

"That the men of Northumbria are at war with Causantín mac Fergusa, and this island is still part of Pictland, and therefore Causantín's land." He found a splinter in a finger on his left hand and gnawed at the skin. "Then he said that it had been Norsemen who had attacked the holy places of his people. I think that was why he was truly ill at ease."

I thought of my own concerns about the people of this treeless island, and nodded.

"But you are a Norseman," I said.

"Indeed I am. And it has been no easy thing for Mancas to trust me."

I sighed, thinking of Eadmaer, and how he still avoided Runolf, clearly uneasy in his presence.

"How did this lead to Drosten coming ashore?"

"Tannskári is a good speaker," replied Runolf. "He has the tongue of a skald. Men listen to him." He grinned and winked. "Women part their legs for him." I thought of Thurid then, and my face flushed.

"So what did he say?" I asked, moving the conversation on.

"First he spoke to Lord Mancas. He said there were no enemies here. 'This is my hall,' he said. 'Everyone is welcome here. In my house, we are all comrades. We are all servants of the sea.'"

"Those are strong words," I said. "Good words. But what of Drosten? What did he say to him."

"I know not what Tannskári said to him," Runolf shrugged again, taking another gulp of ale. "When he saw Drosten aboard, he asked if he was a thrall. When Mancas said he was not, Tannskári spoke to Drosten in his own tongue. They did not speak for long. I assume he said similar words to those he spoke to Mancas, for when we had finished the work, Drosten followed us ashore."

I was glad for Drosten. The nights were still cold this far north, and it had saddened me that he had stayed aboard *Brymsteda* the night before. Runolf said the crossing to Rygjafylki would take two or three days. We would all have enough of the chill winds out in the expanse of the sea, so we should make the most of the warmth, provender and comradeship offered to us now.

Looking about the smoky hall, I was once again struck by

how easily we were all getting along. The men of Northumbria managed to understand and make themselves understood, and as the night progressed, laughter was heard frequently in the hall. We might have spoken different tongues and worshipped different gods, but looking at the men and women seated at the benches in Tannskári's hall, there was nothing in their appearance to separate them. The men, both Norse and Northumbrian, drank too much and told tales of their exploits in ever louder voices. The women served mead, ale, and the food they had prepared, watching their menfolk with the familiar blend of affection and exasperation that I had seen on my mother's face. It was the expression of goodwives everywhere, loving, yet resigned to the foibles of their men. The children too were like all other children. They shrieked and rushed around the hall, playing with each other and teasing the growling dogs mercilessly until one of the men or women shouted at them.

Hearing about Mancas' fears, I knew I had not been alone in my trepidation of these people. But after the day of comradeship and now, as the noise, sights and smells of the feast wrapped about me like a welcoming cloak, my opinion began to shift, just as the wind changes direction in the sky. I had been fearful for the journey to Rygjafylki, but now, I began to believe the mission we had been sent on by King Æthelred might not be impossible after all. These people were no different from us. Surely it would not be so hard to convince them to trade with Northumbria in peace, just as Tannskári had traded with Mancas for repairs and supplies.

I was disappointed that Thurid was not allowed to sit by my side on the mead bench. She sat at the high table, close to her mother. Whenever I looked in her direction, she met my gaze with a small smile and I felt the Devil whispering in my mind that it would not be such a bad thing if I should slip away into the night with her, to kiss her full lips, and to feel more of her soft flesh than I had when she had held my hand that day.

The mead was strong and my fantasies became increasingly passionate as the feast grew old. When I noticed Thurid rising to retire, I decided to act upon my desires. My mind was filled with her. Her smile, the cool touch of her hand, the soft weight of her on my lap, her fingers slipping into my mouth as I licked them clean. My memories and dreams swirled together, curdling my thoughts like old milk. I could not rid myself of the attraction I was sure we both felt, so I pushed myself to my feet.

Leofstan placed his hand on my shoulder, pulling me back down onto the bench. The men all around us were laughing, listening to one of Beorn's bawdier songs. I had believed them all caught up in the tale, but it seemed that Leofstan was not so easily distracted. He had drunk only sparingly, and his eyes were bright and clear in the flame light as he held me firmly, preventing me from rising.

"Let me go," I said, my tone sharp.

"I will not," he replied, speaking quietly, close to my ear so that only I would hear him. "You cannot act on what you feel, Hunlaf. We are guests here."

I cursed silently. Had it been so obvious what I had intended?

"What do you mean?" I hissed. "Whatever you think, you are wrong."

Leofstan shook his head. He could hear the lie in my words. See it in my face.

"We both know that is not true," he replied, not releasing his hold on me. "These are not our people, Hunlaf. We will be gone in the morning."

Angry now, I shook off his hand and stood. Gwawrddur was suddenly there, blocking my path.

"Sit down, Hunlaf," he said. His tone brooked no defiance.

"I need to piss," I said, my drink-blurred brain searching for an excuse to be free of the two of them.

"And you will," he said. "Later." His voice was calm, but as firm as Leofstan's hand had been. "Now sit."

I stared into his eyes, unmoving.

"Why do you care what I do?"

"Think," he said, his tone instantly as sharp as a blade. "We have fought hard to be here. Would you throw all that away, all you have striven for? We have not yet reached our destination. Do you not wish to find Aelfwyn?"

His words dampened my ire. I sighed. Shaking my head, I let out a long breath, watching wistfully as Thurid, having bade her parents goodnight, slipped away behind the partition to her family's sleeping quarters.

"I meant no harm," I said, my voice sounding hollow to my own ears.

"I know, Hunlaf," Gwawrddur said softly. Gently, he pushed me back down onto the bench. The men had not noticed our brief confrontation, and Beorn's voice soared in the final verse of his song.

I made to pick up my mead, but Leofstan pulled it away, pushing a different cup before me. I tensed, but raised it to my lips and drank. Ale. I sniffed. Angry at both Leofstan and Gwawrddur, but angrier still at myself. I have ever been a fool for a pretty face and swaying hips, and there are many times my hot blood has got me into trouble. I begrudged them the intervention then, but deep down I knew they were right. No good could come of seeking Thurid out in the darkness. A few moments of pleasure would be little reward, if my actions shattered the peace and friendship we had found in Tannskári's hall.

The rest of the night was a blur. My head was muzzy from the mead, and I knew that in the morning light I would be glad that Leofstan had forbidden me from continuing to drink. For a time I had listened to Beorn's singing, and Ida's riddles, but I had not joined in with the merriment. Instead, I had sulked, thinking about what pleasures I might have shared with Thurid. Soon though, the exertions of the day's contests, the copious amounts of food, the mead and ale, and the laughter and companionship of the men, soothed me. Leofstan and Gwawrddur had been right, and yet, wickedly, I still hoped that the Devil might again send temptations to me in my dreams, even though I knew I could not succumb to them as I might have liked.

But of course, God delivered me from that temptation. Now that I had forsworn to act on my desire for Tannskári's daughter, when I wrapped myself in my cloak and stretched out beside the sputtering peat fire, my mind was devoid of the dreams that had hitherto so excited me.

Shouts woke me, dragging me suddenly from a deep, and disappointingly dreamless sleep. At first I thought that the cries were the expected orders from Runolf, rousing the crew and commanding us to head to the beach ready for the tide. But before I could sit up and rub the sleep from my eyes, new sounds, harsh and deadly, cut through my muddled thoughts, snapping me fully awake.

The unmistakable clash of blades rang out in the darkness. And the raised voices that echoed about the hall were not commands to awaken the crew for sailing on the rising tide.

These were screams of anger.

And shrieks of pain.

Twenty-Eight

The hall was in chaos. Someone leapt over me, almost tripping, as I started to rise. Blinking in the gloom, I peered about me, trying to make sense of the confusion. The doors of the hall were open and a wan grey light trickled in from outside. I stood. Others were jumping up all around. Gwawrddur was already on his feet. Leofstan too.

"What is happening?" I asked.

"I know not," said Leofstan.

"Nothing good," growled Gwawrddur.

Men were rushing past us, through the doors and into the early morning light outside.

"What is the meaning of this?" Runolf bellowed from outside, his huge voice echoing like thunder in the dawn.

A voice replied, but I could not make out words over the din in the hall.

Then came another voice. Loud and hard. The sound of its command cut through my confusion. I had learnt to obey that voice without question. It was Hereward, and he was calling the men of *Brymsteda*.

"To me! Shieldwall!"

"What is it?" asked Gersine, rising from his blankets nearby.

"Trouble," I said, grabbing him by his kirtle and dragging him to his feet. "Come on!"

I ran for the doors, glancing longingly as we passed at the great locked chest that was filled with the crew's weapons. The only way into it would be to break the padlock or to take the key from Tannskári. But there was no time for either course of action. We had left our shields and spears on board the ship and the only weapon I had was my seax. Dropping my hand to my belt, I felt the carved ivory handle of the seax I had won from Hroar. Without pause, I tugged it out of its scabbard and handed it to the dazed Gersine, who only had a small eating knife on his belt.

"Here," I said. "Better than nothing."

I had been worried that the door wards might have tried to hold us inside, but nobody hindered our passing. It appeared clear that treachery was afoot, but whatever was taking place, it did not seem to be well organised.

The sky and land were shrouded in thick cloud, the light flat and dull as ash. Distant sounds were muted in the sea fog that had come up in the night. The men gathered outside Tannskári's hall were not far away and their shouts were strident.

Close to the entrance of the hall, a line of men was forming around the towering presence of Runolf, his red hair acting like a beacon. Beside him stood Hereward, who continued to call the men to him. I still had no idea of what had caused this, but I knew Hereward well. So, without hesitation, I ran to join the line, taking my place beside Cumbra, whose eyes were bleary and his hair dishevelled from sleep. I scanned the group of men facing us some twenty paces away. I did not recognise them and I wondered if they had come by ship in the night. Then, shadowed and blurred by the mist, I picked out the looming shapes of horses cropping at the grass behind them. So they had ridden from elsewhere on Orkneyjar. I took in the details of their clothing, their plaid breeches, their oiled dark hair, and the tattoos that adorned their skin, and I remembered all too well Drosten's warnings and foreboding that this treeless island was still part of the land of his people. A people he had vowed never to return to.

There were about a score of the Picts. They were hard-faced and came dressed for war. Each had a shield, a short spear and several had swords scabbarded at their hips. Their leader wore a scaled shirt of iron that glistened in the mist like fish skin. On his head was a burnished helm, crested with the figure of a boar.

On the packed earth between our lines lay a figure. He wore Pictish garb and was unmoving. The dirt beneath him was stained dark.

I felt more men join the line beside me. With a glance, I saw it was Gersine and Gwawrddur. The Welshman held a small hand axe he must have picked up from somewhere within the hall. I was glad of his presence. We might be unarmoured, with no shields and only knives and hatchets, but there were many doughty warriors amongst our number. We would not easily be defeated.

And yet, strong and willing to fight as we might be, I could not envisage a way we could be free from this situation without great loss of life. As I watched, still trying to make sense of what was happening, a third group of men was forming up to our right, closer to the hall. This was Tannskári's kith and kin, and I recognised the faces of the men who now stood with shields and weapons in their hands as they had that first night on the beach. My mind reeled at their betrayal. The day before we had played games with these people, shared meat and drink with them, riddled and sung together long into the night. Now they greeted us with steel and iron.

Dogs barked, their snapping and yapping incessant and piercing. Men yelled at them, restraining them with rope leashes and cuffing them about their heads until they quietened.

"Release him," shouted Hereward, seeming to ignore Tannskári's people, instead addressing the leader of the Picts.

I wondered at his words and surveyed the line of sombre-faced Picts. With a twist in my gut, I saw who Hereward was referring to. Near the centre of the Pictish line, struggling against the strong hands that held him, was Drosten. He snarled, and as I watched he attempted to smash the back of his head into the man restraining him from behind. But Drosten's struggles were to no avail. One of the Picts punched him hard in the face, twisting his head sideways with the force of the blow. Blood trickled from Drosten's split lip as another man clutched tightly his braided hair, pulling his head back savagely, exposing the corded muscles and tendons of his throat. With a whisper in Drosten's ear, the man placed a vicious looking knife against the tattooed skin there. Drosten grew very still.

"Drosten mac Galanan will not be freed," said the Pictish leader in passable Englisc. "His name is known to all our people. And," he inclined his head towards Tannskári, "to our friends. Drosten has long been wanted for his crimes. He will be taken to stand before Causantín mac Fergusa for the charge of murder."

"Drosten is one of my crew," said Hereward, "and he will sail with us on the tide."

"No, *Saes*." The Pictish leader spat his people's name for the men from the south as if it were a curse. "He is a kin-slayer. Killer of Eithne, bride of the king's cousin, and he must pay." The Pict's words fell, heavy and final like stones piled atop a barrow. They had the heft of truth, but surely this could not be so. Drosten was a killer in battle, but this? To murder a woman, his kin? I could not believe it was so.

Drosten snarled some words in his tongue and sought to pull away from his captors. The man gripping his hair tugged and pressed the knife to his throat. A droplet of blood dribbled from the blade and Drosten ceased his struggling. His eyes burnt with a dreadful light in that grey morning.

The Pictish leader glared at Hereward. He made a show of slowly surveying the unarmed men to either side of the Northumbrian, then Tannskári's armed Norsemen, then, finally, he opened his arms. His mist-soaked coat of metal was slick and glistening, highlighting as effectively as any words the point he was making. We were outnumbered by armed opponents. If we fought, we would surely be slain.

"You are lucky, Saes, that Tannskári is your friend. He made me agree to let the rest of you sail free. I would happily gut the lot of you."

Hereward spat.

"Tannskári is no friend of mine. And we will not leave this island without Drosten."

Tannskári stepped forward. His eyes sparkled, despite the dull mist. His teeth were bright. Was he enjoying this?

"Come now, Hereward." He spoke slowly in his mother tongue, and I was certain that Hereward and the other men of Northumbria would understand most of his words. "I have agreed with Eddarrnonn here," Tannskári went on, "that you and your crew are free to go. You only need to leave Drosten here. He is but one man, and a murderer at that."

Runolf stepped forward menacingly.

"He is my shield-brother," he snarled, raising his great hands and clenching them into fists, as if gripping an unseen opponent. Tannskári swallowed and his smile faltered. Perhaps he was imagining those huge ship-builder's hands closing around his throat. "I would trust Drosten with my life," Runolf said, "as once I trusted you. It saddens me to see your word is worth less than spit in the wind. You are a nithing."

Tannskári shrugged, shaking his head sadly.

"Your words are like this mist. They do not hurt me." He waved a hand, taking in the hall and the buildings around it.

"But my hall is built on the land of the Picts. I cannot allow you to take Drosten with you. But have I not been fair to you?"

"Fair?" snapped a new voice. Lord Mancas, bare-footed, kirtle loose and unbelted, had stepped out of the hall. Some of the women and children were milling about there too, pale-faced and anxious. I saw with a shock, Thurid's golden hair. Her brother, Lambi, held her hand. His eyes were wide and staring as he took in the armed men. One of the hall's hounds, quiet now, but still tense, ears up and hackles raised, stood beside the boy. There was death in the air, and I could not imagine that this was how Tannskári had planned for this encounter to go. Surely, he did not wish for there to be fighting so close to his family. But however it had come to pass, we now faced a dilemma, with three bands of fighting men facing each other. The wrong move now would certainly bring death on its heels. The only uncertainty was who, and how many of us, would die. It seemed to me that if fighting erupted, however valiantly we might struggle, in the end *Brymsteda*'s crew would be slaughtered.

"Fair?" Mancas shouted again, his voice rising in anger. "You have taken my silver and now betray us." He was ever concerned with his silver, that man. The crew let out a rumbled growl, the fire of their anger fuelled by their lord's fury.

Tannskári sighed.

"Did I not repair your ship?" he said, speaking slowly as if to a child, or a simpleton. "Did I not provide you with food and water? I have kept my part of the bargain. But I cannot ignore my neighbour's request for this Drosten of yours. Surely you understand that, Lord Mancas. We are both practical men. Clearly," Tannskári said, with a scowl at Eddarrnonn, "it would have been easier for us all, if my neighbours had not come at dawn, and instead had waited, as I had asked of them. But here we are. There is nothing for it now. They keep Drosten, who, after all is one of their people, and you go on your way, your ship repaired. There need be no more blood shed here this morning."

"Oh, there will be more blood," said Runolf, and even from a distance I could feel the heat of his ire. His axe might be locked within the chest in the hall, but even unarmed, Runolf was huge and imposing. There could be no doubt that if the lines of enemies attacked, Runolf would send several foe-men to the afterlife, even if he was ultimately cut down. Looking at the grim faces to either side of me, I saw several others who would surely acquit themselves well in battle, sword or no sword. Bealdwulf, face dark and thunderous, and eyes swollen from the fight with Hroar, was flanked by the other men of Bebbanburg. Warriors all, they had fallen in line together, the habit of many years fighting side-by-side against the Picts in countless campaigns. Os, his features stern and free of all sign of levity, was shoulder-to-shoulder with Beorn. Around them were the rest of Lord Mancas' men. I had seen them all fight when the Norse ships attacked at Uuiremutha. None of them would be defeated easily. Beyond them, Eadmaer was thin-lipped and unmoving. But he was standing with us, which showed great bravery. I thought fleetingly of how he had leapt into the waves after Gwawrddur. His bravery could never be questioned after that. Scattered throughout the line were the other men who had been fishermen before sailing on *Brymsteda*. They looked frightened and uncertain, and, if it came to a fight, I feared they would fall quickly. But we were all members of the same crew, and their courage lifted my spirits.

Thinking back to that terrible moment all those years ago, the three forces arrayed before Tannskári's hall in the drizzle-damp wolf-grey morning, I wonder what my own face looked like. I imagine it was neither the stern mask of the hardened killer, nor the pallid, fearful face of the fishermen. I had chosen the life of a warrior and had killed men before, but confronted with the prospect of a clash that would almost certainly see us all slain, fear gripped me, turning my guts to water. Drosten's dark gaze met mine and I offered him a small nod. There was no way we could leave him to his fate at the hands of the Picts, and yet, to fight would spell our doom.

My mind raced, searching for a way out, anything that could free us from this stand-off. Leofstan had often told me that my keen mind was my greatest weapon, and on that grey morning on Orkneyjar, an audacious idea suddenly entered my thoughts.

Tannskári's intervention, with his smile and placatory words seemed only to have fanned the fire of the men's anger, and as the day grew ever lighter with the rising of the sun far out over the mist-wreathed sea to our backs, the mood amongst the crew seemed to shift.

"Know this, Tannskári," spat Runolf. "If I die this day, I will send you to the afterlife before me." I shivered, even though I was not the object of Runolf's fury.

Some of the other men, goaded by Runolf's words, shouted their own insults at the Norsemen and the Picts. They could see no way out of this and so were seeking to swell their nerve, to stoke the fires of their anger so that battle-fury and bravery might carry them to victory, or at least a worthy death. A cornered animal is dangerous, for it will attack even when its death is assured. Warriors are the same, and I could feel the pressure building around me as the men, convinced there was no escape from this predicament, readied themselves to rush at their foe.

The idea had come to me fully formed as sometimes happens with the best plans. Or the most foolhardy. It was risky and the thought of it filled me with dread. It might well not work, and when I pictured what I would have to do, I thought I might puke. I offered up a silent prayer for guidance and strength. There was no time to await the hand of God, and if I dwelt on what might be, I knew I would never act. And surely, if there was even the slightest chance that I could prevent the violence that threatened to soak the morning in blood, it was my duty to try.

Without warning, one of the dogs began barking again. In a streak of brown fur and snarling teeth, it burst from Tannskári's people and sped towards Runolf. What had prompted the sudden attack, I could not tell, but then I saw the small figure, running after the hound, shouting, reaching for the animal's leash. And in that instant, I knew this was the Lord's plan and I was his instrument. The decision had been taken for me.

Giving myself no time to think of the consequences, I rushed forward, running as fast as I was able. As the previous day's race had proven, I was quick, and, unexpected as my movement was, nobody sought to intercept me before I had covered the few paces towards my objective.

If I needed further indication that this was the Almighty's doing, the snarling dog did not launch itself at me. Instead, it shied out of my path, seemingly terrified by my approach. Just behind the hound came Lambi, and I grasped his tunic in my left hand. I hauled him towards me, vaguely aware of the dog's barking. To my horror, I saw that Thurid had come after her brother and had seized his other hand. For the briefest of moments her gaze met mine. I pulled her brother towards me, but she refused to relinquish her hold. With a roar, I jabbed my seax blade in Thurid's direction, then placed it against Lambi's throat, just as the Pict held his knife to Drosten's neck. Thurid's eyes widened in horror and she let go of her brother's hand. Suddenly released, I staggered backward, dragging the boy with me.

Tannskári, smile gone now from his smug face, moved towards me. His men surged forward, threatening with their spears. I saw Toki and Varin amongst those who advanced on me. Behind Thurid, Tannskári's kindly wife, who had saved me some porridge the morning before, looked on, her round face aghast.

"Do not move!" I shouted in Norse. Lambi whimpered and I shook him. "Silence."

"Hunlaf, no!" shouted Leofstan.

I ignored him. Everybody was looking at me now.

Tannskári pulled Thurid back, then, taking a step forward, he held up his hands.

"Let the boy go," he said.

"Only when our friend is safe," I replied, fighting against the tremor in my voice.

"His life is not mine to give you," said Tannskári, his voice soft, despite the tension I saw in his eyes.

"Then when the fighting starts, you will see Lambi's blood on the ground before anyone else dies." Lambi let out a small cry and I hated myself. But I had no other option, I told myself. The Lord had seen fit to provide me with this path. I had to take it. Thurid's eyes were filled with tears and she looked upon me as one seeing a monster. I did not flinch or soften my gaze. I knew that I would never harm the boy. I could never bring myself to kill an innocent in cold blood, but the only way that this might work was if everyone watching believed me capable of such a vicious murder.

I stared at Tannskári. He narrowed his eyes, appraising me. I wondered whether the older man could see through my act. Lambi struggled and I twisted the neck of his tunic in my fist, making him cry out. Whatever Tannskári might suspect, he could not risk me killing his son, so, after several heartbeats of inaction, he turned to Eddarrnonn.

They spoke in quick, angry words in the language of the Picts. The exchange did not last long. Nobody else moved. The dog was silent now, its leash held in Thurid's trembling hand. Tannskári turned back to me, his expression desolate.

"Eddarrnonn says they have come here for Drosten, and

they will not leave empty handed. Please," he pleaded, "let my boy go. You have my word that my men will not cause you or *Brymsteda*'s crew any harm."

I heard the terror in the man's voice. I kept my face stern.

"Do not do this," said Runolf, lending his voice to Tannskári's pleas. I flicked a glance at my friend and saw a new anger there. I recalled how he had fought his own people in defence of children on Lindisfarnae, and how he had entered the hut at Werceworthe to rescue Wulfwaru's son, when the babe had been held hostage. "Let the boy go," Runolf said, his face a disappointed scowl. "You are a better man than this."

I wanted to tell him that he was right, that I would never harm the child, but I could not speak out. Swallowing my own disgust at my actions, I turned back to Tannskári.

"If they refuse to leave empty handed, offer them the silver Lord Mancas paid you. Either we leave with Drosten, or we stay and fight for him."

"You would all be slain."

"That may be so, but Lambi will be the first to die. And many more will follow before the bloodletting is over. Your treachery has failed, and there is only one path out of this now that sees your people safe."

He glowered at me and I could see in his eyes that if he had the chance, he would kill me. Whatever happened, I would never be able to come back to this place. Not while Tannskári lived. But first we needed to leave the island alive.

Approaching Eddarrnonn now, Tannskári spoke for some time. He gesticulated and his voice took on a distraught, desperate tone. The rest of us stood watching one another, fearful of what might happen next, unwilling to let down our guard.

Lambi was crying now, his body shaking against me, his tears wet against the hand that held the knife to his throat. In my long life, I have done many things that, when looking back with an old man's eyes, ashame me. But of all those dark, shameful memories, few induce more self-loathing than when I remember how that boy wept believing I would cut his throat if his father could not convince the dour Pict to part with his prisoner.

After a time, Tannskári turned back to me and nodded tersely.

"It is agreed," he said. "They will give you Drosten in exchange for my son."

Hereward and Runolf whispered briefly. Mancas had joined them too. He glanced in my direction and I thought I saw disapproval on his features. A breeze had picked up and the sun was burning away the sea fret now, the day hazy and light, where it had been gloomy and damp.

I let out a sigh.

"All will be well," I whispered to Lambi. God had answered my prayers and we would all live.

The boy turned his tear-streaked face towards me. His eyes burnt with the same hatred I had seen in his father.

"May you be fucked by a goat, you nithing," he said. Despite my shock at the words coming from one so young, I could not blame him for the sentiment.

Twenty-Nine

I leaned over *Brymsteda*'s side and watched the water rush past the ship's sleek strakes. The fog of the early morning had cleared and the sun was bright in the sky, gleaming from the waves ahead of us so brightly that I needed to squint against the glare.

Fulmars soared behind us and our wake was stippled with gulls, terns and kittiwakes. Beyond them, in the distance and hazed by the last remnants of morning mist, I could just make out the cliffs of Orkneyjar.

I let out a long breath, finally able to acknowledge that we had safely escaped from the island. There had been no time to rest before now.

As soon as Tannskári had agreed to my terms, Runolf had shouted at the men to make *Brymsteda* ready to sail. All around me, the crew had rushed to and from the hall, collecting their gear, and loading the last of the supplies we had been promised. Some of the door wardens had carried the chest with the weapons down to the beach, where they had unlocked it and seen the swords and axes passed onto *Brymsteda*.

All the while, Tannskári and his people glowered at me. I could not release Lambi until the dangerous time when the two hostages would be exchanged, and as the morning brightened and the mist blew away, I found myself becoming increasingly dejected. The boy's hatred for me was mirrored in the lours of his kin. I risked a single look at Thurid. She stared back at me with such utter disdain and loathing, I gasped as if from a physical pain. I did not look at her again. But perhaps even more so than the look I received from Thurid, it was the dark rage that emanated from Runolf, and the disappointed shake of the head from Leofstan that most upset me.

Did they not understand that I had rescued us all? I had prayed and this was God's answer to my request for deliverance. Surely they must know I would never have harmed the boy. And yet, Runolf barely paid me heed, and I knew that he was furious with me. So angry was he that for the first time I understood how his enemies must feel when faced with the giant's wrath in battle.

When everyone was aboard *Brymsteda*, and it had been pushed down the beach until its keel cleared the sand, I had walked a short distance up the beach, accompanied by Gwawrddur and Hereward, Lambi at my side. I no longer held my knife to his throat, but I gripped his arm tightly to prevent him from running away before Drosten was freed. I had not gone this far only to lose in the last instant. While the ship was laded and the crew clambered aboard, I asked myself repeatedly what I would do if the Picts, or Tannskári, attempted to betray us. I would not hurt Lambi, I told myself. But could I be so sure if it came to that? In the heat of a confrontation, might I not lash out and follow through with my threats?

I prayed there would be no treachery to put me to the test.

By the Lord's grace, the exchange of prisoners passed without problems. Few words were said and, with a nod, Eddarrnonn's men shoved Drosten towards us at the same moment I let go of Lambi's arm and the boy sprinted across the beach to his waiting mother's arms.

We had hurried to the ship. Tannskári's voice had echoed after us.

"If we cross paths again," he screamed, "I will kill you."

Nobody answered him. Perhaps he addressed all of us, but I felt his words were directed at me alone and I felt vulnerable and exposed as I turned my back to him to wade through the shallow waves. Reaching up, I grasped thankfully the helping hands of my crew mates and clambered over the side.

A few of the men clapped me on the back, congratulating me for my quick thinking. I was glad of their praise, and welcomed the thought that perhaps I was not loathed by all aboard the ship. A shouted command from Runolf silenced the men, and I was left to my brooding and in doubt of the skipper's opinion of me.

We manned the oars for a time, heaving the ship out into the sound. Even though I could not see over the strakes from where I sat on my sea chest, I imagined Tannskári's folk glaring at *Brymsteda*, spitting hatred and curses after us, as the ship grew distant and small.

I prayed silently for a time, but even the solace of prayer seemed unattainable to me. So for a long while, as I pulled on the loom of the oar, I relived the events of the last days, plunging myself ever further towards despair as I questioned what manner of man I had become.

Finally, Runolf had called for the oars to be shipped and the sail raised. We slipped out of the thinning mist, past the looming rocks and cliffs and onto the open sea. The wind filled the sail, and with a gentle creaking of the mast and a satisfying flexing of the strakes beneath us, the longship cut a straight line through the surf eastward.

"If this wind keeps up," I heard Runolf say to Mancas, "we will see the shore of my homeland in two days."

With the good wind, and the sail set, we could all begin to relax. Each section's small crew set about breaking their fast, and the scent of smoke drifted over the ship as small fires were lit in earthenware pots made for the purpose. I had no task, so I stood at the port side of the ship, my back towards Runolf and the rest of the men who thought me somehow tainted by my actions.

A hand touched my shoulder, startling me from my reverie. Turning, I saw it was Scurfa. He offered me a cup of water. I took it with a grunt of thanks, and drank.

"You did well," the sailor said. Then, after an awkward pause, he went on. "If not for you, we might all be dead. Drosten, for sure."

I grimaced and looked back at the sea, sky and birds. If only the lives of men were as simple as those of gulls. I snorted at my own thought. Were our lives really any more complex? Hadn't my dreams been filled with carnal fantasies of Thurid. Perhaps animals too dreamt of coupling in their quest to find a mate. I glanced to where Ahmad was hunched over, quietly preparing porridge. He didn't look up, seemingly lost in thought, his lips moving silently as he stirred the water and oats in a bowl atop the firepot. I pondered that so much of our existence echoed that of beasts. Animals sought food, and did what they must to survive. Had I not merely done the same? We had survived because of what I had done. How could that be wrong? But if what I had done was right, why did my heart hurt so?

Ahmad came to me then with a small bowl of the porridge. I accepted it, dipping the wooden spoon into the gloopy mixture and tasting it. It was hot and I was sure it would fill me, but it tasted like mud. And yet I was hungry and, like any animal, my body needed sustenance to keep strong, so I ate.

"I have not thanked you," I said, as Ahmad turned away.

He stiffened.

"You do not need to thank me for your food," he said. "I am a thrall."

His words were bitter, and I wondered briefly at his past and the manner of man he was.

"I did not mean for the food," I replied, the oats congealing in my mouth. "But for that too you have my gratitude. Gwawrddur lives because of you. I thank you for that."

"What good are your thanks to me?" he asked, not waiting for an answer before he moved back to the firepot.

Leofstan joined me while I ate the rest of the porridge.

"Why so glum?" he asked.

I swallowed more of the mealy paste and stared out over the sparkling waters to the north. There was nothing on the horizon. *Brymsteda* sailed alone in a world of water.

"I was wondering what separates us from animals," I said at last.

Leofstan surprised me by smiling.

"And there is the Hunlaf I know," he said. "And to think I was worrying about you."

"Why would you worry for me?"

"When I see a friend in anguish, I cannot help but be concerned." He scratched at the stubble of his tonsured head. "Perhaps that is what separates us from the beasts."

I swallowed the last of the porridge. It clogged in my throat.

"Is it not that we commit sin?" I asked. "We hurt one another when it is not necessary to do so. Animals only kill to eat."

"It is true that men and women can choose to go against the teachings of the Lord. They can stray from the path of righteousness." Leofstan hesitated, looking at me askance. "Do you think that is what you have done? Strayed from the path?"

I sighed, but said nothing.

"You are but a man, Hunlaf. Like any other. You must fight against the temptations that are laid before you. But with prayer, and God's grace, you will prevail. If you are worried about your part in what happened this morning, I did not see a man giving in to the Devil."

"You did not?" I grasped at his words like a floundering man, desperately hoping that they might pull me from the sea of my despair.

"No," Leofstan said. "I saw a man using the sharp mind the Lord gave him to save his friends and avoid bloodshed. Though I have to admit," he turned to me and raised an eyebrow, "for a time you surprised even me, and I know you better than most. I see now that you had to convince us all, and you played your part well. Though you are perhaps a little too good at dissimulating for my liking." His smile broadened, and he patted me on the shoulder.

Behind Leofstan, on the far side of the ship, Runolf stood at the steerboard, his red hair swirling in the brisk breeze. He stared fixedly along the length of the ship. I was sure he had noticed me looking at him, but he determinedly ignored me, refusing to meet my gaze.

"Do not be concerned for what other men think of you," Leofstan said, perhaps imagining the direction of my thoughts. "You alone must live with your actions. And if you are at peace with yourself and God, then others' opinions are of no import."

"Thank you," I said. His words gladdened me and I felt some of the weight lifting from me. But I could not shake the doubt that lingered in my mind. Was it only what others thought of me that scratched at my soul? Or was it perhaps that I doubted my own motives? "How did you know that Ahmad could save Gwawrddur?" I asked, shifting the conversation away from me.

"I did not. But I am old enough to know that others have skills and knowledge I do not possess."

"But he is a thrall."

"He is a man," Leofstan replied, his voice taking on a cold

edge. "Like you and me. Ahmad may not be free, but his mind is unfettered. Remember, Aelfwyn is also a thrall somewhere out there." He waved a hand eastward over the sea. "She is no less than she was before her capture."

I pondered his words, but before I could answer, he stepped back, making way for Drosten, who had walked along the deck from his place in the Tack crew before the mast.

"Now," Leofstan said, "it looks as though another wishes to speak to you." He moved away, leaving me with Drosten.

The Pict positioned himself beside me, gripping the top strake in his broad hands and staring out over the waves. The water hissed and sighed along the ship. The sail luffed briefly, as the wind shifted, before filling again with a fresh gust. I hoped that did not spell a change in the wind's direction. With a sidelong glance, I noticed the scars on Drosten's knuckles, pale, taut and shiny against the tanned skin of his hands. His tattoos curled about his wrists like shackles.

"I said we should not come here," he said, speaking without looking at me. "I knew something like this would happen."

Drosten seldom spoke of himself, and I could see that to do so pained him. But after the events of the morning, I felt I deserved an explanation. Perhaps he felt the same way.

"I don't think any of us could imagine your name would be so well-known," I said. "Pictland is a big place."

"My infamy is also large."

"So it would seem." I fell silent, thinking about Leofstan's words and all that had been revealed that morning in the mist. "Did you do the things they accuse you of?" I blurted out, not allowing myself long enough to think too deeply about the question, for fear I would not dare to ask it.

Drosten tensed beside me and for the first time he turned to look into my eyes. His expression was blank, but his eyes held a darkness I thought I might understand.

"Would it matter to you if I had?"

His answer shook me. I had expected him to deny the claims. This man had stood with me against the Norse when they came to Werceworthe. He had fought as hard as any there, risking his life for people he barely knew. He was sullen and surly, but I had never seen him do anything that would make me doubt his intentions. I recalled Leofstan's words and shook my head.

"No. Your past is between you and God. When you stood with us at Werceworthe, a bond was forged that cannot be so easily broken."

Drosten let out a long breath and stared once more out to sea. Far off, I saw a sudden spray of water jetting into the sky. Men cried out, pointing to the spot where many birds circled, darting into the water. I wondered what I was witnessing, then, a moment later, a leviathan's glistening mouth, seemingly as large as *Brymsteda*, broke the surface, surging out of the deep. The creature rolled, its massive, knobbly head disappearing once more beneath the waves, the arch of its great back and the short fin there visible for a time, then, at last, towering over the dark water, the wing-like flukes of a tail, stark and dripping and as wide as the sail that billowed before our mast. The tail stood there, dark against the sky for a heartbeat, and then it was gone, vanished beneath the waves once more, leaving only foam and the dotted sea birds to mark its passage.

I had never seen anything like it before. The power of such a huge creature was unimaginable, and to think of it even now swimming in the darkness beneath the flimsy keel of the ship made me tremble. That God had chosen this precise moment to have one of His most monstrous creatures appear before us could surely not be chance. All along the ship, men were flocking to the port side, peering at the churned sea in the distance, where the gulls and kittiwakes flitted and flapped in the water in search of any debris left by the whale's passing.

The strakes before me dipped perceptibly closer to the seething water and Runolf shouted at the men to move back from the edge. I made the sign of the cross, humbled at what I had witnessed and praying that God did not see fit to send the whale to splinter *Brymsteda*'s hull, to send me and the other sinners aboard to our dooms.

"I am no murderer," Drosten said, his voice quiet and meant only for me to hear. The rest of the crew was abuzz with the sighting of the great fish and nobody was paying attention to us. "But it is true that the bride of the king's cousin died because of me."

I said nothing, waiting for him to continue to unburden himself from a memory that clearly weighed heavily upon him.

"Eithne was so full of life," he said at last, his voice not much more than a sigh. "I could barely believe it when I learnt of her death. That they should accuse me of her murder..." He gripped the oak of the top strake so tightly that his scarred knuckles showed white. "That they should accuse me, who only wanted her to be happy." He fell silent, staring into the distance, through time and into the past. I thought of the great whale and wondered what other horrors dwelt out of sight beneath us, the way bad memories lurk hidden in a man's mind.

"We had been friends since childhood, Eithne and I," Drosten said, a wistful smile in his tone as he remembered his youthful friendship. "I had known she would be married to one more important than I, for she came from the line of Queen Aoibheann. But we played together as children and later, as we grew, we often rode across the land, hunting boar and stag." Now that Drosten had finally opened the door to his dark past, the words tumbled out of him, as if he couldn't stop them coming out into the light. "As I grew strong and joined the warriors on raids, Eithne's mother was frightened that her daughter would allow herself to be sullied by one as lowly as me, from a family of no worth." He sniffed, and shook his head. "But Eithne and I were never more than friends. We each knew what was expected of us, but that didn't change that we loved each other in our way. In the way of brothers and sisters, I suppose. And like a brother, I hated to see her sad. Maelchon is a brute, and it was soon after they were wed, that I noticed the change in her."

Drosten let out a breath, and rubbed a hand over his face as if he could rid himself of his memories. But he had gone too far down this path to turn back now.

"I am no fool. I know that not all women warm to the man with whom they are forced to share their bed, but this was more than that. Eithne became withdrawn. The light went out of her. She never laughed any more. It saddened me to see my friend vanish over those weeks and months."

He hawked and spat. In the distance, another plume rose above the water where the whale breached the surface once again. The men whistled and shouted, and my eye was drawn to the movement. I still marvelled at the size of the creature, but my fear had gone now. Drosten didn't seem to notice the commotion of the massive monster of the deep. His thoughts were far away.

"One day, she came to me," he said, speaking so softly now that I had to lean in close to hear him over the noise of the crew. "She was distraught. I had never seen her like that before. She was always quiet, but I knew that thoughts were running far beneath that still surface. Like a deep lake." He frowned. "Not that day. She wept openly. When she finally calmed down, she told me what had upset her so." He paused, staring out at the sea. Taking a deep breath, he said, "She had overheard her husband planning to have me murdered."

"He was jealous?"

"Aye." Drosten nodded. "The bastard was jealous of the friendship I had with Eithne. But more than that, he planned something worse than my death."

"He meant to hurt her too?" I asked, enthralled by Drosten's tale and at the same time wishing he would stop talking, for I knew no good would come at the end of this story.

"You are getting ahead of events," Drosten said, with a scowl. "Maelchon was plotting to slay the king and then, after killing me, he would name me the king's murderer. Thus, he would be free from suspicion and he would be rid of me at the same time."

"What happened?"

"I was but a warrior, with little of worth. Eithne gave me a precious necklace that her husband had given to her as part of her morning gift. She wanted me to have it, that I would be able to pay my way during my exile." He peered back at the haze beyond our wake, as if the images from his past were there, just out of sight. "She told me to flee, far away, where Maelchon could not find me. And like a fool and a coward, I listened to her. By Christ's blood, I did not know I would never see her again."

"But you lived. That was what she wanted."

He turned to me then, his face twisted in anger and his eyes ablaze.

"Don't you see?" he said, his voice suddenly loud enough for all to hear. "If Eithne had not come to me, if she had not overheard her husband and sought to protect me, I would be dead and..." He hammered his fist down onto the sheer strake. "And she would live." He took a deep breath, calming himself. "Oftentimes," he went on, his anger under control once more, "I have wished that were so. Death would have been a better fate than the life I have lived these past years."

"You cannot hold yourself responsible for the actions of others," I said, offering Leofstan's advice to Drosten. "Not Eithne's, nor her husband's." But when I spoke such words, my voice echoed in my ears, hollow and shallow, lacking the sage wisdom of my teacher. I don't know what the Pict thought of my counsel, for he did not acknowledge my words.

"Much later," he went on, "I heard that she had been found murdered in her bedchamber." I glanced at his face and saw the haggard lines of grief, as he relived anew hearing the tidings of her death. I remembered how I had felt when I had believed Aelfwyn was dead. How bereft and raw. I wished to reach out and comfort him, but I held my hands still, gripping the sheer strake. Drosten was a proud man and I did not know how he would respond to a gentle touch of friendship.

"I can only assume," he said, lost in the past and oblivious of my thoughts, "that Maelchon found out she had overheard his plotting. He quickly spread the word that I had been her lover. Everyone knew we had been close, so it was an easy lie to believe. I had been seen with her the morning of her death, so, when Maelchon found the necklace missing, everyone was certain I had stolen it before killing her. That day, my name became known as that of a thief and a murderer. It will never be safe for me to set foot in the land of my father again. And all the while, that whoreson, Maelchon, yet lives."

He hawked and spat.

"I am sorry," I said.

"Aye, so am I. Still, it is not all bad, Hunlaf." A certain levity had entered his tone I did not think I had ever heard before. It was as though by recounting his sorry tale, some of its sorrow had been lifted from him.

"How so?"

"I may be a man in exile, far from kith and kin, but I have friends that I know will risk all for me." Without warning he gripped my shoulder, surprising me. "Many men cannot say the same. I will never forget today, Hunlaf."

"Nor will I," I said, watching him walk away, lithely stepping over thwarts and chests, as he made his way back to his position before the mast.

I looked over at Runolf. He ignored me still, but I thought about Leofstan's words. I could not change what Runolf felt.

His anger saddened me, and I hoped that in time he would speak to me again, that we might be friends. But I clung to the fact that we were sailing once more and, whether Runolf approved or not, at the very least Drosten was alive because of me.

The Pict's tale had saddened me, but I was warmed by the trust he had shown in me by recounting the sorrow that followed him everywhere. He was right, few men possessed such friendships, and I counted myself blessed that no matter the dangers that surrounded me, I knew I would not face them alone.

I watched as the whale surfaced again and I offered up a prayer that the Almighty would see us safely to our destination. My mind was clearer now, and the words of the paternoster followed, soothing my thoughts and my soul.

Whether God listened to my prayers that day, I cannot say. But He chose not to send His leviathan to smash *Brymsteda* to kindling, and the wind continued to blow us steadily eastward, towards the land of Rygjafylki.

If I had known then our grim destiny of heartache and death, I might have been tempted to ask Runolf to turn the ship about. But the future is never known to any man, so we sailed on, across easy seas with the wind at our backs, unaware of the darkness that awaited us.

Thirty

The good weather held and as the sun fell to the horizon behind us, there was no land to be seen in any direction. The sea in our wake was aflame with the last rays of the sunset as we readied ourselves for our first night at sea.

Runolf had still not spoken to me, but the mood aboard had lifted during the afternoon. After the perils we had faced in the dawn mist on Orkneyjar, we were enjoying the peace of the open sea. We saw no sails, the newly repaired rudder was holding well, and the wind continued to send us unerringly towards our destination.

It was close to midsummer. The days were long, and even though it was never truly dark this far north, it was as cold as winter after the sun had set and there was nothing but the chill sea all around. We slept as best we could and when the sun rose once more, it seemed as if Runolf had not moved. He still stood at the steerboard, his face lit with the brilliant glow of the dawn, and wreathed in the flames of his red hair and beard.

That second day was much like the first, and we fell into the routines of life aboard the ship. All that long day, we saw no other ship, and the scarcity of birds told us we were far from any land. The wind continued to blow from the west and, though clouds formed far away in front of us to the east, there was no imminent threat of rain. For that we were thankful. The night had been bitterly cold, and a rime of frost had formed on the stays and exposed timbers. The thought of trying to shelter from the chill at night, while also wet from rain filled us all with dread.

But as the sky burnt red behind us for the second sunset, there were still only a smattering of clouds in the east and Scurfa said he thought it would be dry again.

"Perhaps we will see some rain tomorrow," he said ominously, sniffing the air.

I crossed myself.

"As long as we see no more storms," I said, "I will count myself blessed."

"I doubt we'll see a squall like that this side of autumn," he said, but then added with a shrug, "but God alone can be sure of that."

The second dawn at sea was not as bright as the first. Just as Scurfa had predicted, there were dark clouds over the eastern horizon, and the sun struggled to shine its light through the sheets of rain that smudged the sky beneath them. The wind picked up, but it was still manageable with adjustments to the sail and rigging. We were all sailors now and there were no mistakes. We quickly and efficiently obeyed Runolf's orders.

Since dawn I had noticed an increase in the number of sea birds in the water, and at midday we had another indication we were close to land. A light rain had begun to fall, closing the sea in around us in a drizzled shroud. Men were huddled under cloaks in a vain effort to remain dry. Gersine and Sygbald played tafl, cursing whenever the keel struck a wave with enough force to shake the pieces from the smooth wooden board. Visibility was much reduced, and we seemed to be sailing into a never-ending ocean.

Garwig's shouted warning snapped us all out of our lethargy.

"Sail!" he bellowed. "Sail to port!"

Runolf immediately yelled out orders for the sheets to be adjusted, as he hauled on the tiller.

Moments later, a small fishing vessel, perhaps a quarter of the length of *Brymsteda*, slid by. Five faces stared up at us from the bark. Before the bobbing ship was lost to view in the smirr of rain, Runolf called out to them.

"From where do you hail?"

The oldest of the fishermen called back a name that meant nothing to me.

"My thanks to you," replied Runolf, who clearly recognised the place mentioned, for a sudden urgency entered his movements. He had barely slept, apart from short dozes during the daytime when he trusted Snell with the steerboard, and I could not imagine where he found his energy. But he laughed now as he pushed the rudder, and called out fresh commands to adjust the sheets once more.

"The gods have smiled on us," he said. I remained silent, not deeming the time right to remind him of his baptism. In fact, the further from Britain we sailed, the more pagan Runolf seemed to become. "Before sunset," he went on, "we should be at my brother's steading. Hunlaf," he shouted out to me, a grin on his face, his anger apparently forgotten. "Ready yourself to see your cousin again. I think your meeting with Aelfwyn will be warmer than mine with Estrid." Despite the dark implication in his words, he seemed buoyant of spirit. Soon after, the rain stopped and the clouds parted, so that soaring peaks could be seen to the north of us. Islands dotted the waters of the vast sound, or fjord, we were entering, and as well as the shadows of mountains to the north, lower, craggy tree-thick slopes rose to the south.

Runolf's excitement to be close to his home was palpable, and infectious. We were nearing our destination and had made a crossing that few men of Britain had carried out.

Lord Mancas seemed less thrilled than the rest of us. He looked in awe at the dark lands around us, perhaps as well as taking in the gravity of what we had achieved, noting the scale and enormity of the land.

"Do not forget, Runolf," he said. "We are to travel to the hall of the king of this land that we may seek an audience. I am tasked with brokering an agreement of trade with him. This is of the utmost import, and for what *Brymsteda* was built."

Runolf looked down at the slender Northumbrian noble for a long while without speaking. Mancas squared his shoulders and met his gaze valiantly. It was not easy to look into those cool eyes. They spoke of the death of countless enemies and, after a time, Mancas cleared his throat and turned away.

"I will not forget my ship's purpose," said Runolf. Mancas stiffened slightly, but said nothing. "But remember, Lord Mancas, that while we are at sea, it is I who is in command. And I say we go first to my brother's steading. Besides," his expression softened and he grinned, "the king could be at any of his halls. Once we have put in at Sørbø, we can learn of his whereabouts."

Without waiting for a response from Mancas, Runolf called down *Brymsteda*'s length to Garwig at the Foreship.

"Take down the stallion. We do not want to frighten the spirits of the land." I noted how Leofstan made the sign of the cross at Runolf's openly pagan words.

"What about the people?" asked Os, with a smile. "Can we frighten them?"

"Your face might work better than the prow beast for that, Os," said Runolf. "But apart from my wife, I think it best not to scare the people of my homeland. And I think Estrid will be afeared enough to see me coming home without our beast prow or your face to frighten her."

But as we sailed around the headland of the island on which Skorri's steading was situated, sliding into the cool, sheltered shade on the eastern side of the land, we all grew silent and the mood aboard soured like old milk left in the sun.

Runolf's face became set in hard lines and his smile was replaced with a scowl. Apart from the handful of small fishing boats we had seen that afternoon, it seemed there would be no risk of Os' face, Runolf's anger, or *Brymsteda*'s stallion prow frightening anyone. For where Runolf expected to find his brother's prosperous farm, now run by his estranged wife, as we slipped through the shallow water towards the timber jetty and the shallow beach beyond, all that greeted us was a wasteland of destruction.

The great hall, which judging from its length, must have been an imposing structure, was now a charred husk, blackened timbers jutting from the ground like bones. Around the hall lay the remains of several other buildings, all black and crumbling.

No smoke lingered to haze the air. No dogs barked as *Brymsteda*'s side kissed the wharf and Garwig and Snell jumped ashore with ropes to secure the ship.

Nothing stirred in the settlement. It was as silent as a tomb.

Runolf's face was aghast as he stared about him, no doubt wondering what had happened here. I too looked at the barren remnants of the steading. Whatever had occurred, it had ended in ruin and nothing living now stirred. Tears welled in my eyes and I cuffed them away.

Both Runolf and I had thought to find the women we were searching for, and yet it seemed we had instead sailed into a place of the dead.

Thirty-One

We stumbled from the ship, conversing in muted whispers, as if we did not wish to disturb the spirits of the land or the ghosts of those who had surely died here.

"What happened to everyone?" asked Eadmaer, voicing the question that was on everybody's mind.

Nobody answered him.

Runolf walked silently up the grassy slope towards the burnt buildings. I followed, but many of the crew stayed close to *Brymsteda*, perhaps not wishing to walk on this foreign soil that was so obviously stained with blood. We had all heard tell of hall burnings, where people are locked in their hall at night and the building is set alight. Men with spears and swords would wait outside, not allowing any of those trapped within to escape the conflagration. Was that what had happened here?

As we reached what was left of the great hall, I closed my eyes. The air held the tang of old soot and ash, and I wondered how long ago this atrocity had occurred. I prayed silently for the souls of those who must have lost their lives. Was that the metallic scent of blood I could smell, or did I merely imagine it?

"Where are the dead?" asked Eadmaer, startling me. I did not know he had followed us. Glancing about me, I saw that Lord Mancas and his warriors had also come into the remains of the steading. Gersine too stood nearby, face pale and eyes wide. Drosten, Leofstan and Gwawrddur were also with us, grim-faced and alert. I remembered Drosten's words to me about friendship and I nodded to him. I did not need to speak.

Looking away from the faces of my companions, I peered about the wreckage of tangled beams and splintered pillars. I could imagine the screams of pain and fear of those trapped inside when the fires started to rage. Had Aelfwyn been in the hall? Had I travelled all this way just to find her dead, slain before I could save her? Was I too late? But Eadmaer was right. If the hall and the other buildings had been filled with people, where were their bones? Surely some would remain. If dozens of people had lost their lives here, would we not see the sightless eyes of skulls staring at us from the debris, long thigh bones sticking starkly pale from the mounds of ash?

I reached down and touched one of the blackened beams. It was cracked and charred, and my fingers came away soot-smudged. But the timber was cold and damp. I noticed then that fronds of nettles and bindweed were poking through the rubble in places, entwining in the ruins; verdant life pushing through the darkness of death to the light above. This place had been destroyed and abandoned days, or even weeks before. And, free of man's interference, the land had begun to claim the settlement for its own, to smother the buildings and obliterate all memory of those who had lived here. I wondered how long it would be before there was no sign that anyone had ever dwelt in this place? A generation? Two?

We passed what might have once been a smithy and fleetingly I wondered whether the fire might have started by accident, a stray ember borne on the wind from the forge. I dismissed the thought a heartbeat later. The buildings were far apart. It was inconceivable that sparks would have sowed the seeds of the blaze across all of them. No, this was a deliberate act of destruction.

We followed Runolf in silence as he stared about him bleakly.

We walked slowly past a timber trough. It lapped with water, reflecting the sky and the large building behind it. This structure was only partially burnt, with a section of its golden thatch roof miraculously intact. A stable perhaps, I thought. Peering into the shadows beneath the jutting timbers and thatch, I saw again that there was no sign of bones, not even of horses or livestock.

"You think Aelfwyn might yet live?" Eadmaer said. I wished he would be silent.

I could not imagine how my cousin could have survived what had taken place here, and yet I did not wish to confront my thoughts head on. Nor did I wish to talk to Eadmaer about her possible fate. I thought of the conversation with Drosten on the ship, and how to speak of his loss had unburdened him. But for years Drosten had held his grief close, speaking of it to nobody. I would not speak of Aelfwyn yet. Until I found her, or heard tidings of her fate, she was to me alive, somewhere in this land, and I chose to ignore the likelihood of her death.

Runolf did not speak as he walked through the wreckage of the buildings. Even Eadmaer fell mercifully silent. None of us knew how to respond to his questions. I certainly did not wish to be forced to think of the answers.

Together, sombre and tense, we walked in a morose hush through the settlement, until we came to a rise crowned with a copse of elm. Looking back the way we'd come, I saw we were some way from the *Brymsteda* now. I could make out that the crew were setting up camp on the beach there. Every now and then a snatch of their conversation reached us, but there was none of the laughter and jeering that was normal when many men were gathered together.

The stillness of the settlement was almost absolute. The only sounds were those of our breathing, our footfalls rustling through the long grass, the breeze sighing through the leaves of the elms on the hill and, as Runolf halted, the trickling burble of a stream that ran over rocks to where the path crossed it on a small timber bridge. The bridge was well-maintained, and its straight timbers and solidity were somehow shocking after the almost total destruction we had witnessed throughout the steading.

Runolf knelt close to the stream. I halted a few paces behind him, not wishing to disturb the man in his grief, and yet also wishing to reach out to him, to show him that he was not alone. We had come to this place together, to face whatever we may find, however dark. I too grieved, though neither of us truly knew what had occurred there.

Runolf sniffed and I saw the object of his gaze. A tiny cairn of standing rocks nestled in the grass near the stream. Just like the bridge, the pile of rocks was incongruous and unsettling, a stark reminder of the life of those who had inhabited this place.

With a grunt, Runolf pushed himself to his feet.

"Children leave butter for the elves here," he said, his tone desolate.

"Children?" I said.

Runolf turned to look at me. He blinked, as if he was only then aware of my presence. He took in the others who had followed him, and sighed.

"It has always been thus," he said. "I used to come here with Skorri and our sisters." He shook his head at the memory. "We'd leave gifts for the elves. To bring good fortune to the farm. To make sure enough lambs would survive the spring. That a sickly cow's milk would not sour. Once," he said, smiling unexpectedly at some distant recollection, "I left an amber necklace here and asked that my favourite horse, a white mare, would survive bearing her foal. Something was wrong and she had lain down. It looked like she would succumb. When my mother found out what I had done, she was furious. I got such a beating, and she sent me all the way up here in the dark for the necklace."

He snorted and looked about him at the towering oak and beech trees, perhaps remembering how the buildings had been back then when he was a boy. Until then, I had not realised that this steading was where he had grown up; his family's land. I tried to imagine what it would feel like for me to return home to Ubbanford, only to find nobody living there, and all the buildings consumed by fire. Again, I wanted to reach out to Runolf, but I fought the urge. He would not welcome it, and I could not bear the thought that he might push me away.

"I was terrified," he said, looking down at the cairn. "By the light of the moon, every tree looked like a creature of the forest, a tröll, or worse." He shivered at the ghost of his childhood fear. "The branches whispered and owls called in the darkness. When I could not find the necklace where I had left it, I didn't know what to do. In the end, I returned to the hall empty handed and got another beating. My father knew I was frightened of the dark and did not believe I had come up here, so he dragged me here again, but this time he carried a torch. I was still scared, but with the light, and my father beside me, the night seemed smaller somehow."

"Did you find the necklace?" I asked.

"No. And Father beat me again. He said I was a fool, that one of the villagers must have taken it. Or perhaps he thought I had kept it for myself. Thinking back on it now, Father was probably right. Maybe Skorri took it, for he knew what I had done. But the next day, the mare birthed a healthy colt, and I was certain that the elves had accepted my gift and fulfilled my wish. I was sore from all the beatings, but it was a price worth paying. I had not thought of that time for many years."

Runolf let out a long breath and turned to face me. There was something in his eye that made me wary. Without thinking, I took a step back.

"I did not like what you did back at Orkneyjar," Runolf said. "You are a better man than that, Hunlaf."

I swallowed. I had known this was coming, but I didn't expect then, in that place.

"I would never have harmed the boy," I said. "You know that."

"Do I?" Runolf scratched at his beard. "Did he? We make war on men, Hunlaf, not children. We tread the same path now, you and I. Who knows for how long? But while we walk together, you will not threaten or hurt a child."

I wanted to protest, to shout my innocence. I had done nothing wrong. I had saved Drosten and spared us all from bloodshed. But under Runolf's disapproving glower, my arguments melted away, and I simply nodded.

"I would not have harmed him," I repeated. "And I will never harm or threaten a child again. I am sorry."

He stared at me for a long time, as if weighing my words against his worth for me. It seemed he found my words had merit, for eventually he stepped close and slapped me on the back. So prodigious was his strength, that I staggered.

"Good," he said. "Being angry with you was tiring. Friends again?"

He held out his huge hand. I took his arm in the warrior grip, forearm to forearm.

"Always," I said, feeling relief washing through me.

"It is well," Runolf said, squeezing my arm. "I know not what has happened here, but I fear I will need all the friends I can get soon enough."

I was glad of his words. Now that we had moved out of the

tumbled remains of the steading buildings, and with Runolf once more speaking to me, some of the tension had lifted from us. But even so, many questions still assailed my mind.

Runolf teased open the small leather pouch he wore at his belt, and pulled out a sliver of hacksilver. With a shrug and a lopsided smile at me, he stooped and placed the metal on the cairn.

"Perhaps the elves will bring me luck once more," he said, rising again to his full height. Squaring his shoulders, as if with this act he had made a decision, he stared for a while northward, out over the waters of the island-dotted fjord. The sun was low now, the shadows dark. Clouds still brooded, heavy and dark, but the rain yet held off. In the distance we could see the shadows of mountains across the water.

Eadmaer stepped forward, taking a breath, but Runolf silenced him with a raised hand before he could utter a sound.

"I swear on Óðinn's one eye, if you ask once more what has happened here, Eadmaer, you will not live to find out."

Eadmaer opened his mouth, and for an instant I wondered whether he would be foolish enough to blurt out the angry retort I could see bubbling in his mind. Then, after a brief silent struggle, he clamped his mouth shut and turned away.

Lord Mancas cleared his throat. He had remained silent all the while, respectfully waiting for Runolf to speak. But now that the Norseman had broken his silence, it seemed the Lord of Uuiremutha could remain quiet no longer.

"The man is not wrong to wonder what happened here," he said. "I am sorry for your loss, Runolf. To find your home in such a state is a bitter draught to swallow. Perhaps..." He hesitated. "Perhaps we will never know what happened here," he forged on, "but maybe the king will know. We must not forget the mission our lord King Æthelred has sent us on."

Runolf growled.

"I do not forget my oath or my duty," he said. "But there is a way to discover the fate of my people. It is getting late, and we must camp now, but in the morning we will take *Brymsteda* along the island to the land of Oddløg. He is a good man, and has always been a friend to me. Yes," he said, as if perhaps seeking to convince himself, "Oddløg will know what took place here."

"Remember," said Mancas, his tone harsh, "that it is I who leads this mission. You said it yourself, on land, my word should be obeyed."

"But maybe not on my land, eh?" said Runolf with a sigh. "Perhaps tomorrow I will obey your word, Mancas. But not today."

Fury flashed over Mancas' features. He was not used to being dismissed so summarily. Like Eadmaer before him, he seemed about to respond, and then thought better of it. He had lost face, it was true, and yet most of the crew were back at the ship. He swallowed his anger and said no more. If he had questioned Runolf further, I do not know what might have happened. After that fleeting moment of warmth he had shown me, a cold hard anger had settled upon Runolf, making me wonder whether he had an inkling of who the perpetrator of the destruction might be.

What Runolf thought about it was unclear, for he had already turned away and was striding back down the hill along the path that would take him through the burnt husks of the buildings and to *Brymsteda* and the crew waiting by the beach.

Mancas looked after him and sighed. I avoided his gaze, sure that he would rather not share the moment with me. We were just about to follow Runolf when there came a sudden commotion from the trees. Arcenbryht and Beorn had gone into the thicket to relieve themselves and a sudden shouting startled us all.

"Go and see what is happening," snapped Mancas, perhaps glad to be issuing an order he knew would be followed.

Oswald and Cumbra drew their swords and hurried towards the trees. But before they could reach them, Beorn and Arcenbryht came into the dying light of the day pulling an elderly man between them.

The man was wizened, with wisps of white hair straggling from beneath his cap. His clothes were grimy and old. He was unarmed, and cowered, visibly scared of the warriors.

"Ask him his name," said Mancas, not needing to specify that his order was aimed at me.

I asked him in the tongue of the Norse and the old man sucked his teeth and peered at me as though I was far away, even though I was only a few paces from him.

"You are not from these parts, are you?" he said.

He had surely been observing us for some time, and must have heard us talking in Englisc. Perhaps he had even watched us arrive on *Brymsteda*. I didn't feel that such an obvious question deserved an answer, so I shook my head and repeated my question to him.

"My name is—"

Before he could finish, Runolf shouted out in his booming voice, "Audun, can it be you? Can you truly be alive, when everyone else is dead?"

Runolf had come running back up the hill at the sound of the man's arrival and now stood beside me once more, a look of amazement on his features.

The old man squinted at the sound of this new voice. Then a broad smile cracked his wrinkled face.

"Runolf Ragnarsson, is that you?" He chuckled, a phlegmy, liquid sound. "If you are surprised to see me with life, I am more so to see you breathing before me, unless my old eyes deceive me."

"Your eyes were never that sharp, old man," said Runolf, returning Audun's grin. "But your ears and your mind are as keen as ever, it seems to me. Now tell me," he said, his voice suddenly serious. "What happened here? Who did this thing? Who destroyed my father's farm?"

Audun shook off the hands of the men who held him and walked with a surprisingly firm step towards Runolf. Reaching up, he gently patted Runolf's meaty arm.

"It is a dark tale I must tell," he said, his expression sombre. "One filled with horror and sorrow. I will tell you what I witnessed, and who did this thing."

Thirty-Two

I picked up a log and threw it onto the blaze. Sparks and embers flew from the fire, drifting up into the starless sky. The flames lit our faces, warming them, but the clouds had closed in at nightfall, hiding any light that might have come from the night sky.

I rubbed my hand against my breeches, smudging soot on the wool. The timbers that the thralls had collected came from the remains of the buildings and many bore the reminder of their first burning. If Runolf cared that his kin's homes were being used as fuel, he said nothing. He had spoken little since we had met Audun on the hill.

The old man had been keen to tell his tale immediately, but Runolf had held up his hand, silencing him.

"It will soon be dark," he'd said. "Let us build..." He'd hesitated a moment, looking down at the destruction of his past life. He swallowed. "Let us build a fire, and make camp. Then you can tell us everything."

With that, he had strode away down the hill between the burnt bones of the buildings. We had traipsed behind, none of us daring to speak to him.

"The men will need meat after your voyage," Audun said, watching Runolf's back. "I am a goatherd," he went on. "I still have a few beasts over the hill. If I hurry, I can bring one, and we can have it roasting before dark."

I explained to Mancas, who frowned.

"Can we trust him?" he whispered to me.

Runolf was some way off, but his hearing must have been sharp, or perhaps he merely imagined what we had stopped to discuss.

"You can trust Audun," he called, without halting or turning back.

Mancas shrugged, but he was a cautious man and still sent Beorn and Arcenbryht with the old man to fetch one of his goats.

True to Audun's word, the three men returned soon after, and before the fire had burnt down to embers. Audun, with practised efficiency, sliced the animal's throat, and Scurfa, ever practical, caught the blood in a bowl. The sun had set by then, and the blood seemed almost black in the gloom. The animal struggled briefly in the old man's grasp as its life pumped from it. The instant it was dead, without pause, Audun flipped the dead goat onto its back and with his sharp knife set about gutting it. I looked away from the glistening offal that slipped steaming from the carcass, and turned to Runolf. His face was dark and set in a scowl. I wondered if he too was thinking of the men and women, his friends and family, who had died here. I could not forget the memories of the slaughter on Lindisfarnae. I had saved Aelfwyn from death then, but now, I could not shake the feeling that it had all been for nought, that we had arrived here too late.

Scurfa mixed the blood he'd collected with oats and later placed the bowl in the coals, where it cooked into a thick, meaty, black pudding that gave us another meal the following day. He then skewered the goat's kidneys, liver and heart onto sticks and handed them to others to be held over the fire. Arcenbryht, Beorn and Audun spitted the freshly gutted and skinned beast and lifted it to hang over the flames between two tripods of spears that Mantat and Alf had fashioned.

The smell of roasting meat filled the air, and I wondered at the beasts the scent might attract. Though surely we were too many, and our fire too bright for us to be troubled by wolves or bears.

With the onset of night, the land had grown calm and muted. The men, still subdued, whispered and murmured from the shadows. Hereward set guards. Like the rest of us, he was on edge and wary of what enemies might be out there in the vast land of mountains, water and trees that surrounded us.

While the goat was cooking, nobody spoke to Runolf. In turn, he said nothing. Audun busied himself with turning the spitted goat. He seemed content not to talk, but to wait for Runolf. Questions boiled up within me, rising to the surface like scum on a broth. I was desperate to speak, but Leofstan, knowing me well and sensing my mood, placed a hand on my shoulder and shook his head. So I waited until the meat was sliced from the goat and everyone had been given a piece.

Eventually, I could hold in my questions no longer.

"I would hear your tale now, Audun," I said, my voice loud in the flame-flickered darkness. Many ruddy faces turned to me in the gloom. I cleared my throat and voiced the thought that burnt hottest within me. "I believe I had kin here, and I must know what became of her."

Audun did not reply straight away. He turned to Runolf, who was slumped on the shingle of the beach, head lowered. At the sound of my words, the giant warrior looked up, first at me, then at the old goatherd. Runolf's eyes gleamed like coals in the firelight. He nodded his assent, and Audun settled down on his haunches. He held out his cup to be refilled with some of the mead we had brought from Orkneyjar, and commenced his story.

All was silent now, as the men leaned in to listen to the old man. I knew they would not understand all of his words, but I thought they would glean the gist of his tale, and I had not the strength to act as interpreter. That night I listened for tidings of Aelfwyn and what horrors had befallen the folk who had dwelt there. I could think of nothing else.

"They came at night," Audun said, his voice rasping like a door being pushed open after it has been long-closed. "Nobody had heard tell of Ljósberari then. Now people talk of little else, but this was one of the first halls to be attacked by that monster and his horde of devils."

"Devils?" I said.

Runolf growled, glowering at me over the fire, his face all shadows and flame-red beard. After making us wait so long for this tale, he seemed intent now on hearing it without interruption.

"Well, they howled like devils," Audun went on, "or creatures from Niflheimr."

"Niflheimr? The dark place?" The word was strange to me.

"The world of mists," he said. "It is indeed a dark place, where one of Yggdrasill's great roots is buried. Now, do you wish to hear what I have to say, or are you going to continue to interrupt me like a child?"

I sat back, my face hot from the rebuke. On another occasion, such a comment would have provoked much jibing from the other men, but not this night. Nobody made a sound as we all waited for Audun to continue.

"Come on, old man," rumbled Runolf from the darkness. "Tell your tale and be done with it. Hunlaf will speak no more till you are finished."

Audun bit his lip and nodded.

"I heard Ljósberari's people wailing from all the way up on the pasture," he said. "I don't scare easily, as Runolf will tell you." The big man grunted. "But that sound filled me with dread. There has been no bear or wolf on this island for many a year, but the cries of Ljósberari's people sounded more like those of forest creatures than coming from the mouths of men. And the things they did to the folk..."

He fell silent for a time, and nobody pressed him to continue now. We could all sense that he needed the time to rally his strength before going on to describe what he had seen. I felt a fleeting relief on hearing there were no wild beasts to trouble us on the island, but in the darkness, it was easy to imagine worse things than bears and wolves. And Audun had seen them. He drank from his cup and sighed. Outside of the firelight's glow, I could hear Os doing his best to translate the goatherd's words for the other listeners.

"I am not proud to say it," the old man went on at last, "but when the fires began, I hid in the trees. Up by the cairn. I was too scared to creep any closer, may Óðinn curse me for a coward." He stared into the fire and shook his head, lost in the visions of that night, with its flames and screams. "There were perhaps a dozen of them. Not many really, but enough that I knew there was nothing I could do. Perhaps when I was a young man... I might have..." He fell silent again, his haggard face betraying that he was remembering his youth, perhaps thinking that even when he had been hale and young, he would have remained in the shadows of the elms on the hill.

"There were so few?" asked Runolf.

Audun's focus snapped back to the present. He met Runolf's burning gaze. The warrior's eyes shimmered in the fire-heat.

"Aye, dróttinn minn." Audun bobbed his head obsequiously. Runolf frowned at being referred to as the old man's lord. "There were no fighting men here, you see," Audun said. "Not after Skorri took his ships a-viking. They never returned..." He chewed at the skin around his thumbnail, unable now to look into Runolf's eyes. "But you knew that, didn't you, dróttinn minn?"

"I knew that."

"They say there are many more in Ljósberari's band now," Audun said, moving away from the part Runolf had played in Skorri's disappearance. "A veritable host. But back then, in the spring, it was just him and a handful of whoresons. And that evil Frankish bastard, Chlotar."

"Who is this Ljósberari?" I asked. "And how do his numbers swell, if he slays all those he attacks?"

"He is a thrall. Taken from the south, they say, though I know nothing about that. And as to how his numbers grow. That is simple. He does not slay everyone in the halls he burns."

"Why?" asked Runolf, seizing on the possibility that some of his people might yet live; that his wife might not have been killed. "Why does he spare some?"

Audun dropped his gaze, once again staring into the fire's coruscating embers.

"I know not the reasons for the things he does. By all accounts he believes he is some sort of god. I understand none of that. But what I do know is that he kills all the adults in the halls and steadings he puts to the flame."

"Women too?" asked Runolf, his voice small and hollow.

Audun lifted his cup to his lips. Finding it empty, he let out a long breath, clearly seeing no way to delay imparting his tidings.

"Women too," he said, not meeting Runolf's eyes.

Runolf drew in a ragged breath. For so long he had awaited the moment when he could confront Estrid with her betrayal and now he found that, like his brother and so many others, she was dead. Audun's words hung in the air. I felt as though a strong man had wrapped his arms about my chest and was crushing the breath from me. Aelfwyn must be dead too. We knew she had been bought by Estrid, and now, after surviving that blood-soaked morning at Lindisfarnae, and finding her way into the household of a woman who I had prayed might have treated her with some kindness, to learn she had been killed along with everyone else, was a harsh blow indeed. I could not breathe. The fire's light blurred and swam before me, as my eyes filled with tears. The crackle of the wood and the wash of the waves on the beach receded, as if I had plunged my head underwater. The world became muted and dark. I feared I would swoon.

Then Runolf broke the silence.

"If he kills all the men and women," he said, "is his host made up of children?"

"Ah, there are children with them, that is certain. They say Ljósberari believes he is purifying the darkness with the fires of light, that children have not had enough time to have the battle within themselves. They must be given time to allow their light to overcome the dark within them." He spat into the fire. "Or some such madness."

"And yet you speak as though this Ljósberari has destroyed halls all over Rygjafylki. How could he do this with a band of children?"

"No, you misunderstand me, dróttinn minn," Audun said. His voice came to me as if from far away. "He kills all the free men and women. The thralls he allows to go free. They join him."

His words pierced my grief-stricken mind, and it was as though a spell had been broken. I drew in a shuddering breath. Sounds rushed back, and I rubbed the tears away from my cheeks. Leofstan placed a hand on my shoulder and, ashamed of my weakness, I shook him off.

Could it be that Aelfwyn yet lived? Dare I hope that God had listened to my prayers for her?

"Tell me of this Chlotar, the Frank," Runolf said.

"He is a thrall, like Ljósberari. I only saw him in the distance, but there can be no doubt it was him, from the stories I have heard since."

"Stories?"

"Of his cruelty. All true, I would say, after what I saw..." He faltered, as if only then realising that to continue on this path would lead him to describe the atrocities he had witnessed.

"What did you see him do?" asked Runolf.

Audun held out his cup with a shaking hand. Gwawrddur took the flask of mead and filled the old man's cup. The goatherd drank, holding the vessel with both hands to avoid spilling the precious sweet liquid. He took a deep breath, like a man preparing against the agony of having a broken limb reset, or a wound sealed with a red-hot blade.

"He said those to whom they show the mercy of the light were not worthy to see its glory." He bit his lip, then forged ahead. "So he put out their eyes." He winced, as if uttering the words had caused him pain. "I can still hear their screams in the night."

Runolf grew very still. Though he did not stand, he seemed to grow in stature in the gloom.

"This Chlotar did this to my wife?"

Audun could not speak now, but his eyes were answer enough.

"But the children and the thralls were spared?" I asked, grasping for some sliver of chance.

Audun nodded.

"Revna?" said Runolf, his voice questioning and desolate. I stared at him over the fire, wondering at his meaning.

Audun clearly understood, for he drew in a deep breath and met Runolf's angry gaze.

"They took her."

"You are sure?"

Audun hesitated.

"As sure as I can be, dróttinn minn. She was not amongst the dead."

I looked from one man to the other, trying to make sense of this exchange. After a moment, Runolf turned to face me. His eyes gleamed like gems in the dark.

"Revna is my daughter, Hunlaf," he said.

"Your daughter?"

Runolf sighed, and where his anger had seemed to make him grow, now his shoulders slumped.

"Yes," he said. "My daughter."

My head was filled with questions, but I snapped my mouth shut. Young and foolish as I was, I could see that Runolf was in no mood to speak to me now.

He shifted his dark gaze to Audun once more.

"You saw to the dead?" Runolf asked.

"There was— That is—" stammered Audun, his face a mask of tortured memories. "I buried them all," he said in the end. "Where your father and grandsire rest."

Runolf rose.

"For that, you have my thanks," he said, and, picking up his great axe, he stalked off into the night. Nobody followed.

With Runolf's leaving, the mood around the fire lightened somewhat, and the men began to chatter quietly about what they had heard. Leofstan tugged at my sleeve. I could see the glow of discovery in his eyes, that sharp focus that seized him when he opened the pages of a new book, or unearthed a nugget of truth from the Scriptures, or an ancient tome of philosophy. He clearly wanted to speak to me about this Ljósberari, but I waved him away. Such conversations could wait for later. The news that Runolf had a daughter, and that she had been taken by Ljósberari, lit up my thoughts like a beacon. There were questions I would ask of Runolf later, but first, I must speak with the one who had seen the destruction here.

Taking the mead from Gwawrddur, I sat beside Audun and poured some into his cup.

He pulled his gaze from the embers and grunted his thanks. The old man smelt strong, the tang of his goats intermingled with sour sweat, soot, the metallic hint of blood and the sickly scent of honey.

"Do you think Aelfwyn yet lives?" I asked, grasping at the hope Audun might provide. "Like Runolf's daughter?"

His eyes took a long time to focus on me, dulled by drink and lost in the blackest of memories.

"Aelfwyn?" he asked.

"My kinswoman. A thrall. She would have come here some months back. I believe Estrid bought her from..." I hesitated, searching my memory for the name. At last it came to me. "Kolfinn Refsson."

"Ah, yes. I remember now," Audun said, nodding. "A pretty little thing." I was anxious for him to reply to my question, and yet scared of what he might say. "I know not if she lives, young man. Many died that night." My heart sank. Perhaps seeing the grief on my features, he placed a hand on my shoulder. "But I can tell you that I do not remember her amongst those I tended to after Ljósberari and his fiends left."

I felt light-headed with the relief of hope rekindled.

"You are certain?"

He frowned, his brow furrowed and craggy, like a crumbling cliff.

"I told you, boy," he said, an edge of anger entering his tone, "I know not if she lives. I buried many. And Ljósberari's nithings left little for me to tend to, after they had done." He shivered. "I do not recall your kinswoman, but I have done my best to forget what I saw the day after Ljósberari came."

"I am sorry." I remembered the stench of burning and decay at Werceworthe, the bloated corpses, oozing with ichor. "I understand."

And I did. There could be no certainty, but Aelfwyn might still live! I clung to that thought, pushing darker possibilities aside. I wanted to shout for the joy of it, but I thought of Runolf out there in the night, surrounded by the charred remains of his childhood home, certain of his wife's fate. This last year had been hard for him, far from his homeland, abandoned by his kin and surrounded by Englisc who neither understood him or his people. To return, only to find death and destruction was devastating.

And yet, if what Audun said was true, Runolf's daughter lived. A daughter he had never spoken of to me. But Runolf rarely talked of himself, or his past.

I thought back to the battle at Werceworthe and Runolf's duel with Skorri. The moment they had faced each other in battle had been the instant I had learnt they were brothers. Runolf never spoke of that fight, or of what drove his terrible enmity with Skorri, and I had learnt not to ask. But Audun had known them both since they were boys, and, much like Leofstan, I have always had an insatiable appetite for knowledge and I could sense I might find answers to my questions that night.

I poured more mead. There were only a few drops left, but Audun smiled appreciatively. He appeared to have forgiven my previous pushing, so I decided to direct the conversation in a different direction.

"You have known Runolf since he was a boy?" I asked.

"Yes. I served his father before Skorri was jarl."

"Runolf is a good man," I said.

Audun nodded and narrowed his eyes, perhaps wondering where this was leading.

"And Skorri was a good jarl, truth be told," he said, then looked at me askance. "Were you there, at the end?"

"I was," I said, and he leaned forward. "They fought like gods. Blow after blow of axe and sword until their shields were tatters."

Audun's eyes gleamed in the firelight, imagining the great clash between such powerful warrior brothers.

"I would wager it was a fight worthy of a skald's saga," he said, sucking his teeth. "I would have liked to have been there." He removed his cap and scrubbed at the wispy hair beneath.

"How did Runolf slay Skorri in the end? Did he use some trickery? He always was a clever one. Strong too, of course, like his father, and Skorri. But truth be told, I would have placed my silver on Skorri winning in a fight to the death."

"Runolf did not kill him in the end," I said, taking pride in my part in Skorri's death. One day soon, I will stand before the Almighty's throne and face His judgement for my sins. I should repent for all of them, and they are many. There are things I have done for which I am sorry and I have oft prayed for forgiveness. And yet, even now, with death near, I cannot deny that I am proud to have helped slay that bastard, Skorri.

Audun frowned, and the rebellious part of me wanted to tell him how a woman had sent hunting arrows unerringly into the jarl's flesh, before I had severed his sword hand. But I wanted Audun to tell me of Runolf's past with Skorri, and so I omitted those details.

"Cormac, a Hibernian and shield-brother to Runolf, threw himself on Skorri. If not for him, Skorri would surely have prevailed. Your jarl even took the Hibernian with him to the afterlife."

Audun chuckled.

"A good death and a worthy shield-thrall to serve Skorri in Valhöll."

I bunched my hands into fists at my side as a wave of anger washed through me. Cormac had been my friend and Skorri had dealt him a slaying blow with a disdainful sneer. Still, Cormac had taken the Norseman with him in the end, rather than the way I had chosen to portray events for Audun's sake. I knew the truth of it, what did it matter what this old goatherd believed?

"What I don't understand is what made them hate each other so," I said.

Audun rubbed at his beard and set his empty cup on the sand. I tossed another log on the fire, sending a fresh smattering of sparks into the night sky.

"I always found it sad how things ended between them."

"What happened?"

Audun stretched out his tattered shoes to the fire, leaning back and groaning as his neck clicked.

"They always fought," he said. "You have brothers?"

I nodded. "One."

"Then you understand. It is that way with boys."

I thought of how my older brother, Beornnoth, used to infuriate me, and how we would wrestle and brawl at every opportunity. During our childhood we always seemed to be angry at each other, but I would be hard pressed to say what upset us so.

The log I had just placed on the fire hissed and popped. Audun watched a single glowing ember waft upward before winking out in the night high above us.

"But they grew," he said, "and each seemed happy enough with their lot. Several years ago now, their father, Ragnar, became sick. He weakened and wasted away quickly as some men do." He sighed. "He passed away one Jól, and Skorri became jarl. He took Ragnar's lands, as had always been expected. Many would think it would be then that the two brothers would truly begin to battle each other. That Runolf would be jealous of his brother's wealth. But Runolf was content with his smaller hall, building his ships."

"So what started their feud? I do not believe I have seen two men who hated each other more."

Audun puffed out his cheeks and held out his hands, palms up.

"Who can truly say? Some would say it was Osvif's death that sparked it."

"Runolf's son?" I had heard Runolf mention the name during his final battle with Skorri.

"Yes, a good lad. Tall like his father, but pretty like his mother."

"Estrid?"

"She was a beauty." He stopped speaking to wipe at his cheeks. I had not noticed him start to weep, but tears were flowing freely down his lined face. I looked away, adding more wood to the fire, to avoid shaming him. He sniffed and I glanced at him. He had regained his composure. "A beauty indeed," he went on. "And a fine woman. I have never seen finer. If you ask me, the wedge between the brothers was Estrid, and Osvif's death was the final hit of the mallet that split the log."

"How did he die?"

"Drowned." He let out a long breath, then sniffed. "Runolf took the boy to sea. They were attacked by Danes from Alabur. In the fighting, Osvif fell overboard. The sailors said that Runolf dived in after him, swimming far and long under the water. Time and again he went in search of his boy, until the men aboard feared that Runolf too would drown. But the boy's body was never found. Njörðr took him. The ways of the gods cannot be questioned, but Runolf blamed himself. And Estrid blamed him too. Said he should never have taken one so young to sea. Perhaps she was right. Runolf never got over it. He lost himself in his ships, splitting timber and shaping strakes. He seldom went back to the house, instead sleeping with the boats he built. And none built finer." He looked over at the shadowy shape of *Brymsteda*. "You have seen how he becomes when he is building."

I grunted. I had seen how the construction had consumed him, filling each moment of every day.

"He built many ships after Osvif's death. Nobody was

surprised when Estrid moved her household here after Skorri returned without Runolf. She always looked like the wife of a jarl, truth be told. Now, is there any more of this mead? Or ale, perhaps?"

Audun cast his gaze about for more drink. I rose and fetched him some water. He grimaced at the taste, expecting something stronger.

"I have dwelt much on sad tales this night," he said, stifling a yawn. "I am tired now, and would not linger longer on such darkness. I will sleep here with you men, then on the morrow I will return to my goats. Where will you go?"

Lord Mancas, who was evidently listening from the shadows close to the fire, offered his reply to Audun's question.

"Tell him we must travel to speak with his king."

I spoke the words in Norse, and Audun frowned.

"King Hjorleif?" he said. "They say he never stops swiving. Fucked his last wife to death, so they say." He laughed suddenly, the sound shockingly loud in the still of the night. "Still, I dare say we all would, if we could. What do you want with old Hjorleif Hjorsson, who men call the Fornicator?"

"What is the man saying?" asked Mancas.

"He is asking what we want with his king," I said, choosing to ignore the other things Audun had said.

"Tell him we must strike a trade agreement between Rygjafylki and the kingdom of Northumbria. Tell him it is of the utmost importance that we meet with the king."

I began to speak and Mancas caught my shoulder, halting me.

"And ask him where the king is."

I asked him all those things, and Audun waved his hands airily, encompassing at once everywhere and nowhere.

"He has many halls. He will be at one of them. Ploughing his latest wife, I'd wager." He cackled again.

"He doesn't know where King Hjorleif is," I said. Mancas

frowned, perhaps guessing at the meaning of some of the man's words.

"Well, wherever he is, we must find him soon. We will set sail again on the morrow. We must fulfil our mission." He peered into the gloom, maybe for sign of Runolf. "We should never have come here."

Thirty-Three

A little drizzle fell in the short night, soaking our cloaks and blankets and making sleep hard to find and difficult to cling to. I was already awake when Gersine shook my shoulder to rouse me for my watch.

Groaning, I pushed myself up, feeling as if I had not slept at all. The beach was littered with slumbering men around the glowing coals of the fire. Several more had decided to sleep aboard *Brymsteda*. I realised I was able to make out details of the shingled beach, and of the ship down by the wharf, the tall mast, furled sail and dripping rigging. Looking inland, I could already clearly see the charred timbers of the hall and the burnt buildings, even the swaying leaves of the elms on the hill. I felt as though I had only just closed my eyes, and now it was already dawn. The days are long and darkness fleeting so close to midsummer in Rygjafylki. The sky was clear now, the clouds and rain having blown over in the brief night.

I went down to the water's edge and watched the sun rise over the expanse of the great fjord. All around were mountains and islands. Gulls dotted the pale sky and I narrowed my eyes at the brilliant sunlight and sea glare. I breathed in deeply of the cool, early morning air. Standing with my back to the destruction of the settlement, all I saw was a peaceful, rich land of water, mountains and trees. If I thought about it too long, my imaginings of the anguish of the people who had died here threatened to overwhelm me. I recalled Runolf's pain as he'd heard about Estrid, and I thought of the terrible sorrow he must have felt at losing his son. To learn that his daughter, Revna, had been taken by this crazed thrall, must have tormented him. As far as I knew, she was his only remaining kin, and I was sure Runolf would never rest until he had freed her, or died in the attempt. He must have spent the night torturing himself with worry for what she was having to endure. I recalled walking through the burnt remains of the settlement the previous afternoon. Runolf's face had been set into a hard mask and I could only imagine the blackness of his thoughts as he took in the destruction, and thought of his family and friends' suffering.

Aelfwyn's face came to me then, as I stared into the rising sun, but I did not wish to open the doors of my mind to thoughts of her. I was not as strong as Runolf. I had hoped for so long that I would be able to rescue her, and now I found that she was gone, perhaps dead, or maybe in the thrall of this murderous Ljósberari. The thought of it was too much to bear.

Pushing Aelfwyn out of my mind with a great effort, I cleared my thoughts and began to mutter the words of Prime, the first office, quietly to myself. I would praise the Lord for our safe arrival in these strange lands. With His grace, Aelfwyn would be safe and I would find her, however impossible that might seem as I shivered in the cold wind blowing in from the sun-sparkled sea. The familiar Latin liturgy soothed my mind, and my tiredness slipped away, like melting snow. I wondered if the brethren at Werceworthe, Lindisfarnae and Uuiremutha were even at that moment reciting the same prayers?

A footfall made me turn. Leofstan was standing there, his

lined face flushed in the morning light, his eyes filled with the fire of the sun.

"Can I join you?" he asked.

I inclined my head, pleased to have his company.

Together we prayed and recited the office of Prime, keeping our voices low, so as not to disturb those who still slept. All the while, I scoured the horizon, not forgetting that I was on guard duty. Nothing but seabirds moved out on the sparkling waves.

When we had finished praying, we stood in silence for a time. The smell of smoke drifted to us as the wind shifted. On the beach behind us, the men were stirring. Someone had placed some tinder and the remaining logs on the fire, prodding the embers to life.

"He must have the book," said Leofstan, without warning.

I did not ask to whom he was referring.

"It truly has such power?" I asked. "Just words, you said. Besides, even if this thrall has *The Treasure of Life*, merely to possess it would mean nothing, surely. You cannot believe it has power beyond the words on its pages. And what thrall knows how to read?"

Leofstan shook his head.

"I know not the answers to these questions. But you feel it too, do you not? The book we seek, this man has it. I am sure of it. The name he goes by, this talk of the battle between light and darkness within each of us. These are from the teachings of Mani."

"If so, the teachings have unleashed a great evil."

"Which is why we must retrieve that book. It cannot be allowed to remain in the possession of this Ljósberari."

I glanced back at the shattered remnants of Skorri's hall.

"If he indeed possesses it, I do not think he will give it up easily."

"No. I think you are right." Leofstan scratched at the

stubble that had grown on his shaved pate. "But if Aelfwyn yet lives, she might be with him too. It seems to me that each of the paths we follow lead after Ljósberari and his horde of thralls. God has led us both here."

I frowned at the mention of Aelfwyn. Leofstan knew that she was perhaps the one thing that held more sway with me than my yearning for knowledge, learning and discovery. I too wanted to find the book, but I had misgivings. And I wondered if it had a grip on Leofstan that perhaps even he was unaware of. Did he merely wish to study its contents? If the horrors that had been brought upon this land were a result of reading *The Treasure of Life*, perhaps its vellum pages should be consigned to one of Ljósberari's purifying fires.

"If Ljósberari has somehow read the book and it has twisted his mind until he burns men and women alive; has their eyes plucked out," I spat the words with a vicious savagery, "merely removing the tome from him will not stop the slaughter. More blood will flow before we are able to find the book. Or Aelfwyn."

To gain what Leofstan sought, I could see no way that didn't end in killing. Though the Almighty alone knew how we would find Ljósberari. He could be anywhere in this vast land. Though judging from the destruction he left in his wake, it might not be so hard to follow his trail.

Leofstan nodded, his expression grave.

"I fear you are right, Hunlaf."

"And yet," I snapped, suddenly furious, "it will not be your sword that does the killing, will it? You say you despise violence. That you will never lift a sword again, and yet you are willing to send others to kill for what you want."

Leofstan was taken aback. He recoiled, as if I had struck him. I immediately regretted my harsh words, but before either of us could speak, raised voices from the camp drew our attention.

"And I say you will do my bidding," shouted Lord Mancas.

He addressed Runolf, who towered over him. The giant Norseman's hair and beard glowed like molten gold in the bright morning sunshine.

"We will sail when I say we are ready," replied Runolf, raising himself up to his considerable height. In his meaty fist he held his war axe. He must have returned to the beach at sunrise and I wondered if he had spent the night where Audun had buried his wife.

I had felt Mancas' frustration building over the last day and night, but this was not the moment for him to attempt to exert control over Runolf. Not now, when he was consumed with grief and regrets. Men were rising to their feet, sensing danger in the smoky air. Tempers would be short, and as with dry tinder, any small spark could start a fire. We were one crew when all pulling at the oars and tending to the rigging, but the individual factions would quickly remember their divided loyalties if a fight started.

Leofstan and I hurried back towards Runolf and Mancas, who both stood defiantly glowering at the other.

"Let us not forget that we are all friends here," said Leofstan. "We will break our fast and then pray for guidance."

Neither man acknowledged the monk. Already, I could see two groups forming on either side of the fire. To my left was Lord Mancas. Behind him was Gersine, his oath-sworn hearth-warriors and a couple of the Uuiremutha fishermen. On the right, behind Runolf's bulk was Hereward, Gwawrddur, Drosten and the warriors from Bebbanburg. There was a darkness that hung over the destroyed settlement. We had all felt it since we had first arrived. A brooding gloom as if the murder and torture that had been committed there had left a shadow; as if the screams of the dying still echoed in the air. I wondered again at the power of the book. Could it be cursed? Was it possible that Ljósberari carried it with him and that its presence here had somehow tainted this place? Was the sudden violence in the air the curse of *The Treasure of Life*?

"This is madness," I said. "We are all tired. Let us eat and talk."

They ignored me, as they had ignored Leofstan. I cast about for something that might distract them from this dangerous path. There was nothing on the beach, or in the ruins of the steading, so I glanced over at the ship. Perhaps the need to prepare *Brymsteda* to set sail would be enough to drag them back from the brink of this nonsensical conflict.

And then I saw it. It was far out on the waves of the fjord, so distant that I squinted against the glare for a heartbeat before I could be certain.

"A ship!" I shouted, and my tone at last cut through the tension that had wrapped around the men.

"Where?" asked Runolf, stepping towards me and shielding his eyes with his hand. I pointed and a moment later, he patted me on the back.

Hereward barked orders at the men, and Mancas joined him, clearly realising that this was no time for division. The warriors hurried to find their byrnies, shrugging them over their heads and wriggling, with arms stretched to the skies, until the heavy iron-knit shirts fell to their waists. They cinched their byrnies with sword belts. Men ran to the ship to retrieve shields and spears.

I snatched up my sword, remembering that my own byrnie was in my sea chest. I was about to sprint after the others to *Brymsteda* to fetch it, when I noticed Runolf sitting on his haunches by the fire. He had cut a piece of the blood pudding that Scurfa had prepared, and was warming it on the end of a stick.

"You do not seem overly concerned by the arrival of that ship," I said. I peered out to sea. The ship was noticeably closer already, its red sail billowing and full. It was still a long way off, but to my young eyes it looked to be a longship of a similar size to *Brymsteda*. As I watched I noted the glint of the sun on burnished metal from the throng of men aboard.

"I know when I have lost an argument," said Runolf. "There is no need for me to fight with Lord Mancas any more."

"But what of that ship?" I was confused by his sudden change of mood. "Is it not a war vessel? It looks to me to carry many men."

"That," he said, taking a bite of the sizzling black pudding and blowing with his mouth wide open as it scalded his tongue, "is Eldgrim, King Hjorleif's warmaster." Runolf took another nibble of the pudding, and, finding it now to be a temperature that he could manage, he popped the whole piece in his mouth. "It seems," he said, speaking around the mouthful of blood and oats, "that we will be seeing the king before we do anything else, just as you wished, Mancas."

Lord Mancas frowned, perhaps thinking that Runolf was making fun of him. He shaded his eyes and stared out to the water.

"But the ship is yet far away," he said. "How can you see the master from here?"

"I cannot." Runolf chuckled, and cut himself another chunk of the pudding.

"Then how can you be certain of who it bears?"

"That ship is *Grágás*. And it is owned by Eldgrim. And I should know: I built it."

Thirty-Four

Runolf had been right about the ship that rode the waves into Skorri's steading. Eldgrim was tall, but slender, his fair beard long and turning to silver. He was a sombre man, with eyes the grey of a winter's sky. He greeted Runolf warmly enough, but without a smile.

"We have been watching the Boknafjorden," he said, when Runolf asked how he had come to the island so soon after our arrival.

Runolf scowled.

"What do you watch for?"

Eldgrim brushed aside the question.

"I am sure King Hjorleif would welcome your presence at his hall in Jaðarr. You have been away a long time." He frowned as he took in the crew, our ship, and the burnt buildings. His gaze lingered for a time on Drosten's hard face, with his swirling tattoos and dark, oiled hair. "And you bring strangers to our shores. The king would meet any emissary from foreign lands."

Eldgrim's ship, *Grágás*, which meant Grey Goose, was almost as long as *Brymsteda*, with the same sleek lines. It's prow was plain, and I wondered what beast rode there when it sailed to war. But even though it was in friendly waters, it was filled with stern-looking warriors, with byrnies, axes, spears and shields. The implication was clear to us all. This was not an invitation we could refuse.

After the introductions had been made, Eldgrim insisted that Lord Mancas and Gersine, as men of noble birth who spoke with the voice of the king of Northumbria, sail with him in *Grágás*. We were to follow behind in *Brymsteda*. Mancas agreed without complaint, but again, the implicit threat was obvious: if we caused any trouble, Lord Mancas and his son would pay the price. Eldgrim allowed Arcenbryht, Os and Beorn to accompany their master, but if there was violence, there would be little the three of them could do to protect their lord against dozens of warrior Norsemen.

We sailed close to *Grágás*, winding our way first east along the coast of the large island that Runolf said was called Rennisøy. Then we swung to the south, threading between many smaller islands whose names I have forgotten. The weather was good and the spirits of the crew had lifted.

Hereward even laughed about how the mood was lighter without Lord Mancas aboard. Some of the men chuckled, but Oswald, Eadstan, Cumbra and Beorn glowered. I quickly changed the subject, anxious not to bring back the rift that had threatened to emerge between us. We were heading to meet the king of this mighty realm, and we could not afford to be divided.

"Is it true what Audun said about the king?" I asked Runolf.

"I have only met the man once, and that was years ago." He adjusted the steerboard and called out for the sail to be trimmed. I should have been at my post to help the Aft crew with the sheets. They were already short a man without Gersine, but Scurfa looked to have it in hand, so I stayed near Runolf, keen to hear what he might say about the king of Rygjafylki. Satisfied that *Brymsteda*'s course was correct, Runolf turned his attention back to me. "He is a huge man," he said, "as fat as a hrosshvalr. It is said he rarely stops eating, and when he does, it is to bed every woman who crosses his path."

Towards the end of the long summer day we entered a lengthy sound that narrowed the further south we travelled. To our left the land rose in tall tree-lined slopes. To the right, the hills were lower. We saw people on both shores and many boats on the water, mostly small fishing vessels and squat cargo ships, laden with goods. The halls we passed were intact, smoke drifting from their golden thatched roofs, livestock plump in their pens and crops green in the fertile fields that surrounded them. This was a prosperous land, and the water, sheltered from the open sea, felt safe and welcoming.

We arrived at our destination as the sun was low in the west. The shadows were long, but the last rays of the setting sun made the shingled roof of the great hall gleam. The hall was grand indeed, longer and taller than any building I had seen before in my young life. Inside, it reminded me of the halls at Eoforwic and Bebbanburg, with its carved columns, large hearth fire, and the boards and benches laid out for the guests. The walls were adorned with trophies, both of hunting and war. There were several skulls too. One, that seemed to be a type of deer, had huge antlers, as broad as a man is tall. There were also smaller, yet somehow even more impressive trophies: a boar skull with vicious, yellow tusks, and a hefty skull with finger-long fangs, that I surmised must have belonged to a proud bear. Hanging from the beams and pillars were splintered shields, torn and stained banners and bent, notched and shattered weapons, which I presumed had been taken from fallen enemies.

The inside of the hall was impressive enough, but the outside was like nothing I had seen before. The long roof rose in the centre, seeming to invoke the form of a great, overturned longship, with the keel being the spine of the roof. Along the length of the hall the walls were bolstered with stout pillars that angled up to meet the shingled curvature of the roof. Where they met the earth on either side of the building I could not shake the image of so many oars dipping into the sea.

A feast had already been prepared, and the rich smells of roasting mutton, frying fish and richly spiced stews wafted all the way down to the wharf as we disembarked and followed Eldgrim and his warriors to the hall. At first I wondered how the king's steward could have known of our coming, for surely such a lavish spread must have been prepared in our honour. But there was no way that our arrival could have been foreseen. This quantity and amount of food was the norm for our host. I marvelled at such a thing, but on seeing him, I could barely imagine the quantities of food a man would need to consume to maintain such a massive girth.

I have never seen a fatter man than King Hjorleif Hjorsson. He was famed for his lust, gaining him the epithet of "Fornicator", but it seemed that his other appetites were just as insatiable. His oaken chair seemed built for a giant. It was twice as broad as even a large man would need. It would dwarf Runolf, but King Hjorleif's broad thighs rubbed against the arms that were carved into sinuous lines of interlocking shapes and what looked like snarling wolves' heads.

The sight of the king sickened me, as he shovelled food into his mouth, all the while speaking, hardly pausing for breath, spattering specks of meat and sauce across the stained linen tablecloth.

King Hjorleif was in an ebullient mood. He welcomed us to his hall, and the crew of *Brymsteda*, tired after a long day of sailing, thankfully seated themselves at the benches, and set about devouring the food and drink laid out there. There was bread made from finely milled rye, roasted mutton, salty cod and haddock and several thick, flavoursome pottages. For a time little could be heard but the chewing of the grateful, hungry men.

I looked longingly at the provender as Mancas commanded me to interpret for him. He had the thralls from *Brymsteda* bring in the gifts we had carried from Northumbria.

There was a great bolt of good woollen cloth and one of the barrels of woad, and the coffer that held the silverware sent by Æthelred. A finely wrought goblet seemed to catch Hjorleif's eye, for he ordered it to be removed from the casket and placed on his table within reach of his fat hands and from time to time he would caress it.

"These are gifts of goodwill from Æthelred, King of the great kingdom of Northumbria, far across the sea to the west," Mancas said, through me.

Hjorleif nodded and smiled, but became quickly distracted as a new dish of pigeons stuffed with berries was carried in by a young woman who was too slow, or too frightened to escape the king's grasp. He snagged her dress, coiling its wool in his fist and yanking her towards him. Propping her on his meaty lap, he stroked and squeezed her flesh as he spoke to Mancas. The girl's eyes were wide and I squirmed when the king's greasy hand slid up under her skirts and she tensed, seeming to plead with me with her gaze. Of course, there was nothing I could do for her, and I shuddered to think of the horrors that awaited the poor slave should the king decide to take her to his bed. From what Audun had said, his women did not last long. To judge from the size of him, I imagined that some might simply be unable to draw breath when pinned beneath his vast bulk.

Lord Mancas wished to continue the formal talks about opening up trade between our two kingdoms, but Hjorleif waved his hand, indicating that we should be seated and eat.

"An alliance between our two mighty and rich kingdoms would profit your majesty greatly," I said, translating Mancas' words.

"And you would like to see an end to my people coming a-viking on your shores, no doubt." Hjorleif chuckled.

Mancas smiled obsequiously.

"Such endeavours are dangerous and costly, lord king. Many men die on both sides. Would it not be better for goods to travel freely across the Whale Road between our lands. The crossing is perilous enough, as I can attest to, without needing to take things by force."

Hjorleif shrugged, sending an obscene ripple over his voluminous breasts.

"I have many men. They like to seek battle-fame and fortune and wealth. If they die, it costs me nothing."

"Think of the ships and men lost in the last year alone," said Mancas, his tone measured and thoughtful. "Those men were your subjects. If they had come in peace, they would have returned here with goods. As your sworn men, they would have no doubt given you a share of their wealth. So their deaths cost you silver." I sensed a dangerous shift in Hjorleif's mood then, the way the air feels different before the first roll of thunder in a storm. There was a pressure in the room, building and growing. King Hjorleif continued to fondle the slave girl with one hand, pushing dripping slices of pigeon breast between his slavering lips with the other and smiling at Mancas' words, but I could feel the storm's approach.

Lord Mancas' next words were like the first crackle of lightning, ripping out of a darkening sky.

"Besides, I have seen the destruction on Rennisøy," he said. "We have been told the tales of the rebel slave and his marauding band. Can you truly spare more men to be lost on the shores of Northumbria when they are being slain here by this Ljósberari?"

"Ljósberari is a devil," Hjorleif bellowed. "A madman! He must be killed!" Spittle and crumbs sprayed from the king's quivering lips. His jowls shook with his passion, and the slender thrall girl perched on his ample lap looked in danger of slipping off his knee. As if reminded of the girl's existence, he clutched her to his wobbling chest, his pudgy hand grasping her small breast. For the briefest instant she looked terrified, but she made no sound to give away her feelings, and when the king looked at her face, she quickly offered him a smile. I could see there was no warmth in her expression, merely masked fear, but the king did not seem to notice, or care. Hjorleif held on tightly to the girl, perhaps fearing that she would escape while he was distracted with his anger. But his fumblings at her young flesh were half-hearted now, overshadowed by the rage that saw his cheeks shake, his eyes bulge and food spray from his fleshy lips.

Lord Mancas, his face a mask of courtesy and respect for the king of Rygjafylki, nodded and sipped at the blood-red wine that was a testament to the far-reaching trade links already in place with this northern kingdom.

"Ljósberari!" spluttered Hjorleif. "How that name haunts me! He comes with the moon and slaughters my people, like a night beast from the skalds' sagas." His eyes narrowed, almost vanishing within folds of fat. "Now I see a way that you can aid me," he shouted, gripped by a new fervour.

"Speak, lord king," said Mancas, eager to turn the talk in a more productive direction. "I am your servant."

I interpreted his words and Hjorleif laughed.

"Good!" he shrieked, planting a slobbery kiss on the lips of the trapped slave. She recoiled, but he seemed not to notice. "Now I see that Óðinn in his wisdom has guided you to my hall. You will kill this Ljósberari for me. Yes, that is what you will do."

Lord Mancas grew pale.

"My lord king, we are of course your servants, but we come in the spirit of alliance and trade. Not to fight your enemies."

As I repeated his words in the tongue of the Norse, Hjorleif's face darkened.

"If we are to be allies, then my enemies are your enemies."

"My lord king—"

Hjorleif did not allow Mancas to speak.

"Ljósberari and his horde of rebellious thralls have burnt farms and villages all along the edge of the Boknafjorden," he said, his voice harder than I would have believed possible for one with such soft flesh. "He has led them inland and up the Lågen, killing as they go. Nowhere is safe." He held up his finger, as if to demand silence, though Mancas had already closed his mouth, deciding wisely not to interrupt the king. "And, you may ask yourself why I, King Hjorleif Hjorsson, the mighty and great ruler of Rygjafylki, do not send warriors to slay this Ljósberari and his pack of crazed dogs. Well, you may ask, and I will answer you that I have done so! I sent my own brother to lead a warband to slay the whoreson." He reached a shaking hand to a fine glass goblet. The flesh of his bare arms quivered as he raised the glass to his lips and drained its contents. So dainty was the glass and so brawny his hand, I was surprised the goblet did not shatter. "By Óðinn," he went on, "my own brother. Hjalti was a good man, and a strong leader of men. But this bastard Ljósberari is more cunning than a fox. Eldgrim found Hjalti's corpse, charred and burnt like so much roasted meat." He licked his lips at the words, and bile filled my mouth at the thought that his brother's cooked flesh might make Hjorleif hungry. "The only thing not burnt was his head, so that I might recognise it. The man is a monster." He slammed his fist into the board, overturning the silver goblet we had brought. "He had put out my brother's eyes," he said, his voice wheezing now as he was almost overcome with emotion. "Ripped them from his head."

"Why not send Eldgrim, or others after him?" I asked, not waiting for Mancas to reply. "You no doubt have many more jarls with strong warbands on your land."

Hjorleif stuttered to a halt, blinking at my audacity.

"On my lands, young man," he said, "yes." He levelled his gaze at me and I thought I knew how the thrall girl must have felt, or how a vole must feel when staring into the eyes of an owl. I wondered then at the man's voracious lusts and appetites, and suppressed a shiver. Did his sins not stop at gluttony and lust for women? "And now you reach the heart of the matter," he said, holding me in his stare. "You see, Ljósberari is no longer on my lands. He has taken his villainous band of savages up the Lågen and into Hǫrðaland, the realm of Kaun Solvason." He let out a long breath, seeming to gain control of himself again after his zeal. "Now, it was not so long ago that I was at war with Kaun Solvason. I married my daughter to his son that we might have peace. I will not break that peace by leading my warriors into Hǫrðaland. No, he will use whatever he can over me. He already uses the presence of Ljósberari in his land to charge me more silver for the iron ore he ships to me. By Óðinn, if I know that man, he is probably in league with Ljósberari himself. Nothing would surprise me about him. Gods, how he must have laughed when he heard of Hjalti's death. Kaun always hated him. Well, I will be laughing soon," Hjorleif said, sliding his huge hand up the young thrall's back and gripping her neck so that I feared he would choke her in a salacious show of passionate rage. But he did not strangle the girl. Instead, he pulled her face to his and kissed her deeply. "Yes, I will be laughing," he said with a chuckle, "and you will have your trade agreement, Lord Mancas. Just as soon as you have played your part."

"Speak my words exactly," whispered Mancas to me, the tension clear in his tone after I had interpreted the king's speech to him. "Lord king," Mancas went on, loud and formal, "as I have already said, we are your humble servants. However, we are here to discuss trade—"

I never got the chance to translate more of Mancas' words, for Runolf stood up and called out in his booming voice.

"We will go, lord King Hjorleif. We will kill this beast, Ljósberari, for you."

Mancas scowled, understanding the meaning of Runolf's proclamation.

Hjorleif paid the Northumbrian lord no heed.

"Good!" the king said, picking up a slice of a fatty blood-sausage and pushing it into his mouth. "Bring me his head, that I may pluck out his eyes, as he did to my brother!"

Runolf bowed.

"It will be done," he said. "We will load up *Brymsteda* and sail in the morning, my king."

"Oh no," replied Hjorleif, shaking his head so that his jowls gibbered and shook. "Eldgrim will take you on his fine vessel, *Grágás*. No," he held up a hand to ward off Runolf's protests, "such a large ship as yours cannot travel where Ljósberari has taken his band of brigands. And I cannot be seen to be sending a warband into my neighbour's lands. Lord Mancas will remain here as my guest, of course. And I will ensure that your ship is kept safe on my wharf. You will take no more than a dozen men with you north."

Runolf's face betrayed his anger at these words.

"So few? But if we go aboard *Grágás*, we could take many more. We have heard that Ljósberari has a veritable horde of followers."

"Then you must choose your companions wisely, Runolf Ragnarsson, and tread with caution. You will not be taking *Grágás* beyond the Sandsfjorden. My warmaster will take you to Sand. There you will be given a vessel small enough to carry you upriver. There will be no room for more than a dozen of you. When I have Ljósberari's head in my hands, you may take your ship and sail back to this king of Northumbria, informing him that we can begin trade."

Thirty-Five

The journey north took us the best part of three days. For much of that time, there was little wind, and the crew of *Grágás* manned their long oars, pulling us with practised discipline smoothly past tree-capped islands and rocky crags. Everywhere I looked was water, sky and verdant mountain slopes. The days were long and the huge fjord we traversed seemed as endless as the pale sky, with its wisps of gossamer cloud.

Runolf grumbled at the lack of wind, complaining that we were making slow progress. But when Eldgrim replied that he would be glad for him to take his turn at an oar, Runolf glowered and muttered that he would row no ship but his own. On that first long day, he forbade us from helping with the rowing too. The only one of us brave enough to defy him was Gersine. His father may have been held as a hostage in all but name at Hjorleif's hall, but Gersine was as enthusiastic and excited as ever.

I had neglected him since we had left Orkneyjar. I had been jealous that Thurid had shown him any attention, and then I was ashamed of my behaviour. I thought he might challenge me on my coldness towards him, and perhaps my actions with Thurid and Lambi, and so I had kept my distance.

But on the trip northward towards the settlement of Sand, we rekindled our friendship.

On the first night, we put in to a rocky cove on an island called Hidle and Gersine sat beside me and handed me a cup of ale that one of Eldgrim's warriors had given him. The Norsemen all seemed to like Gersine, despite the barrier of their languages. He was eager to please and uncomplaining and, on that first windless day, he had been the only one of our band to sit at a bench and take to an oar.

"Do you think he is as bad as they say, this Ljósberari?" Gersine asked. "Does he really put out people's eyes? Do you think he truly burns them?" He sounded almost excited by the prospect. I knew it was more nervous tension than a lust for blood, but still it rankled.

"You saw the buildings at Skorri's steading," I said, staring out at the near-dark of the summer night. "You heard Audun, and the king. I see no reason for them to lie. But I know not what would cause a man to be so evil." I chose not to mention the book that Leofstan and I sought. "But evil exists. Temptation and wickedness are all about us. We must pray to remain strong and not to succumb as so many do." I thought of Hjorleif and his debauched lust. Was it possible that any man could become so depraved? I recalled how Cwenswith had filled my thoughts, my dreams of passion with Thurid. What separated me from a man like Hjorleif? I took a gulp of the ale. "The Devil must have a hold on the man they call Ljósberari."

"And it is our task to slay him," said Gersine. "Like in the saga of Beowulf and Grendel."

I thought of the story of the great warrior who rids the land of the terrifying beast, Grendel, that had been preying on the Danes. For some time I could not get out of my mind the image of Grendel's mother. Grendel must have been the hero of her tale, and to her, Beowulf the monster. Surely there could be no doubt here who was the villain and who the hero. Ljósberari was killing and destroying with impunity. And yet a splinter of doubt at the king's motives in sending us north needled me and every now and again I would worry at the scratching thought.

After the initial tensions that come of meeting strangers, we had laughed and told tales with *Grágás*' crew. At first, the men relied on my language skills to communicate, and I was exhausted by the time I lay down to sleep. But judging from the amount of speaking, laughter and shouted wagers over dice that echoed around the still island and across the sighing waters of the fjord, the men managed to communicate well enough without my help.

When, by midday on the second day we saw there was no sign of a breeze, most of our party offered to relieve the rowers. We all remembered the back-breaking work of rowing into the sound at Orkneyjar, and now that we had eaten and drunk with these men on Hidle, we felt a duty to help.

The only ones who stubbornly refused to lend a hand to the looms were Runolf and Eadmaer. It had taken some time for Runolf to choose the eleven men to accompany us on this mission, and Mancas and he had argued about it long into the night, their hissed voices loud in the hush of Hjorleif's hall.

Lord Mancas had been furious with Runolf for agreeing to the king's demands without any negotiation. The Northumbrian had kept his anger in check while the king was present, but as soon as Hjorleif had retired for the night, waddling behind the hangings at the rear of the hall, dragging the terrified thrall with him, Mancas had rounded on the huge Norseman.

"How dare you speak for the king of Northumbria?" he said, keeping his voice low, for fear that his words would be overheard and relayed to Hjorleif. Even when releasing his rage, he kept a leash on his emotions. I had never seen him fight and I wondered if he was a good swordsman. A lack of emotion was a skill Gwawrddur praised.

"I spoke for nobody but myself," replied Runolf, taking a sip of the fine ale Hjorleif's steward provided. "I will force no man to come with me. It will be dangerous, no doubt, but there are many more than a dozen brave men amongst our crew."

Runolf was right, of course, and several of those left behind were disappointed. Some, I am sure, were pleased to remain in the comfort of the king's hall, though as I heard Hjorleif's grunting and the thrall girl's whimpering cries in the night, I wanted nothing more than to be far from the place. I could do nothing for the poor girls the king selected to satiate his hungers, but if Aelfwyn was still alive, I could still help her. The sounds of the king's rutting made me wonder what horrors Aelfwyn had suffered at the hands of her masters. Was she even now being abused by Ljósberari and his host of murderous thralls?

One of those who did not seem to mind being left behind was Scurfa. Runolf had selected him as a safe pair of hands that he could depend on no matter the vessel we would be called upon to sail or row. But Eadmaer had pushed to the front of the men who had gathered in the light of the rising sun down by the wharf where both *Brymsteda* and *Grágás* were moored.

"Aelfwyn is my kin," he'd said. "I have travelled all the way from Lindisfarnae, and I will not be left behind if there is a chance she yet lives."

Runolf had stared at him for a long while. Turning to Scurfa, who was already prepared to come with us, he whispered something, and the sailor shrugged and nodded.

"Very well, Eadmaer," Runolf said. "You come in Scurfa's stead. But you will obey my orders, or you will not be returning with us."

We all remembered his rage at Eadmaer on that first day of sailing all those weeks before. No further threat was needed. Eadmaer nodded tersely and, scowling, clambered aboard *Grágás*.

"Who knows if any of us will return?" said Os, who was one of Lord Mancas' hearth-warriors who would travel north. Nobody laughed at his poorly timed jest. Along with Gersine, the other of Mancas' men was Beorn. I wondered whether he would have any opportunity to sing and play his lyre. Perhaps he could recount the tale of Beowulf, or maybe he would spin the tale of our search for Ljósberari into a new song.

From the men who had come from Bebbanburg, Bealdwulf and Sygbald joined the company. Hereward's place had never been in question. Both Runolf and Mancas respected his leadership and his battle-skill.

The rest of the survivors of the battle of Werceworthe were all deemed worthy of embarking on the perilous journey, and not one of us would have countenanced being left behind. I was glad we would have Gwawrddur's sword, and Drosten's stalwart strength, and I was equally pleased to see Leofstan also climbing aboard *Grágás*. Despite my misgivings, I would welcome his counsel, and being able to pray with the old monk would certainly ease my worries. Though I cannot deny I was surprised he had been called by Runolf for such a dangerous mission.

When we were underway, the banks of oars sweeping like rippling wings, dipping into the dark water as *Grágás* slid northward, leaving Hjorleif's huge hall dwindling in the distance, I joined Leofstan at the prow.

"You are shocked to see me," he said, staring out at the tree-covered slopes of the craggy land to starboard.

"We will be needing swords where we are going," I replied. "Not prayers."

"Prayers are always welcome."

I nodded, chastened by his reply.

"Of course. But we will not take Ljósberari's head without fighting. If there are as many thralls around him as we have been told, I am not sure any of us will return." The thought filled me with a cold fear, but I pushed it away. I had chosen the life of a warrior. Fear was something I must live with.

"All the more reason for prayer, it seems to me," he replied with a smile.

His evasive answers irked me.

"I do not believe Runolf would agree with that. He believes we make our own wyrd, with guile and the strength of our steel."

I noticed with a start that he wore a leather belt from which hung a scabbarded sword. Following my gaze, Leofstan shrugged.

"A loan from Gamal," he said. "A God-fearing man."

"I don't believe Runolf fears God."

"Perhaps not. But he remembered well how I had stood firm at Werceworthe. I may not be young, but Runolf values my wisdom and the experience of my years. And I have shown him I am no coward who flees before an enemy."

"I know you are no craven," I said. But something in his words nagged at me. No, something he had not said. The anger I had felt at Leofstan back on the beach of Rennisøy returned as I understood.

"You didn't tell him you would never lift a sword again," I hissed, "did you?"

Leofstan then did something I could not recall him ever doing before. He glanced about him furtively, as one does when scared of being found out. When they have committed a crime.

Or lied.

"I did not lie," he whispered, but his eyes told me the truth of it.

"Perhaps not with your words. But choosing to omit the truth is the same as lying surely."

He made the sign of the cross over his chest.

"No," he said, his tone earnest. "I would not lie. But I must find *The Treasure of Life*. Ljósberari has it. I am sure of it."

"Runolf won't like it when he finds out," I said, feeling a wave of sadness at discovering the monk's deceit.

"If he chooses to believe I will fight, that is his concern, not mine."

"Your words dishonour you. Runolf will not see it that way. You know this. And do you think God would agree with your distinction of what is, and what is not, a sin?"

Leofstan turned away from me, but I could see the flush of shame on his cheeks.

"Do you not see?" I asked, keeping my voice low. "The book is corrupting you. Even though you read from its pages nearly a year ago."

"I only seek it so that it can do no more evil. You saw the burnt hall. You have heard the tales of the horrors committed by this Ljósberari. He must be stopped, and the book must be kept safe."

"Or perhaps destroyed."

"I never thought I would hear you say such a thing, Hunlaf. I believed books were sacred to you."

His words needled me into fresh bitterness.

"And I believed that truth was sacred to you," I spat over the side of the ship. "I pray that your actions do not lead to any of us dying. Runolf will be counting on your sword." Turning away, I spoke more loudly over my shoulder as I left Leofstan at the prow. "We all will."

I spent little time with Leofstan on the voyage across Boknafjorden after that. He knelt and recited the holy offices during the lengthy days, and I would listen from a distance, mouthing the words I knew so well. But I could not bring myself to join him. He had become lessened in my young eyes. If I had seen him with the eyes of the old man I am now, I might have spoken more with him during that peaceful journey over the rippling sea between the fir-clad peaks and forested isles of Rygjafylki. I would have prayed with him for strength and guidance, for the Almighty knows I would need both soon enough.

I should have seen that Leofstan was a man struggling with his decisions, but instead, I turned my back on him, believing that our relationship could only be that of teacher and student, not understanding that no matter someone's years, they might still reach out their hand for help. In this, Coenric is much wiser than I was at his age. I am many years older than Leofstan was, but Coenric is always quick to offer his help, both spiritual, when he joins me in prayer, and physical, when he nurses me to health and prepares my writing implements and ink, so that I may concentrate on remembering the events of many years past and scribing them onto vellum. And that is just what I must do now. My mind has been wandering again, and there is still much to tell before the tale can be done with Rygjafylki and Ljósberari.

I regret it now, but the path of a man's life is often paved with regrets that cannot be lifted or altered. Instead of recognising Leofstan's need, and spending time with him, I sought out the company of Gersine and the other warriors. We jested, riddled, sang tales, ate and drank all of the ale that Eldgrim had seen fit to carry aboard. In that way, taking my turn on the oars when called upon, we made our way north, and, at the end of the third day, when the sun had dipped behind the hills that now rose in the west, *Grágás* rowed into the settlement of Sand.

Thirty-Six

The settlement of Sand was a desultory collection of dilapidated huts and storerooms huddling on the northern bank of the mouth of the Lågen. There were numerous vessels moored to the weathered wharf, but none came close in size to *Grágás*.

"That's where you are heading," said Skialg, one of Eldgrim's men, nodding towards the broad river mouth. The water was deep and dark and the river carved its way inland between steep tree-covered rocky slopes. The river looked wide enough for *Grágás* or *Brymsteda* to travel on.

"How far are we going?" I asked. Skialg shrugged.

I stared eastward, but the river's course was lost to view as it veered sharply behind a rocky outcrop. The setting sun glinted on the water for a moment, and then we were beyond the river mouth and turning towards Sand.

Eldgrim shouted across the water, announcing our arrival. Shortly afterwards, faces appeared in doorways and soon, when they saw the size of the ship that approached, and the obvious wealth of its owner, the locals hurried to make room for *Grágás*. Men shouted and rushed about. Several boats were moved and moored alongside other neighbouring vessels. I marvelled as men paddled out of our way on long thin boats that seemed to be nothing more than hollowed out logs.

Others, though larger, were still flimsy affairs that looked as if they were sewn together with birch bark.

It took some time for the green-streaked wharf to be made ready. But once there was space, the local men eagerly caught the thrown lines and pulled *Grágás* alongside the creaking timber structure. When we were safely moored, we clambered ashore and I looked out over the sun-gilded waters of the fjord we had followed to reach Sand. For the last day we had rowed between high mountains, as the sea cut far into the land.

"It is beautiful, is it not?" Runolf asked.

I nodded, barely able to put into words how I felt when observing the vast expanses of water and the towering mountain peaks.

"I can scarcely believe the size of this kingdom," I said at last, frowning because the words did not do justice to my feelings.

"Mountains do not make a man rich," Runolf said. "I have seen no land more beautiful, but this is a hard land, and it is difficult for a man to bring enough oats and rye from the soil to feed his family." He scratched at his red beard, his blue eyes seeing into the past. "The winters are bitter," he said after a time. "The snow lies as deep as a man is tall."

I stared about me, trying in vain to picture the forested mountains clad in such deep snow, the waters of the fjord dark with the cold, and the sky leaden and grey instead of aflame with the setting sun of summer.

Raised voices distracted me and I dragged my gaze back to the wharf. The crew of the ship were milling about there. Some had begun to unload *Grágás*, while local men shouted at them. It seemed they had not been aware of our visit, and Eldgrim needed to bellow that he was the king's warmaster and we had been sent by King Hjorleif Hjorsson himself, before the people of Sand would calm down.

They may not have known we were coming, but word of our arrival travelled fast, and it was not long before we were escorted to the largest building in Sand. This was the hall of Olvir, the Jarl of Sand, and he pretended well enough to be pleased to welcome us to his home.

Jarl Olvir was a slender man of perhaps forty years. He had long, plaited fair hair and a thick beard. His eyes were pinched with the hardships of long, harsh winters, and his hall was lacking in any ostentation. There were no trophies here. No rich tapestries or war gear from fallen enemies. Here there was plain, soot-stained timber and dirty rushes on the floor that looked as though they should have been changed weeks before. Olvir's skinny wife and children were silent, watching us with round, dark-rimmed eyes.

"How long will you stay?" he asked, soon after we had been seated. That this was his first question said much about the man's priorities. He had ordered food to be served, and each of us was given a small bowl of fish stew, and a mouthful of gritty, dark bread. The stew was more water than fish, but it was warm, and I had sympathy for the servants and thralls who needed to feed so many men with no warning.

"Not long," replied Eldgrim, stirring his stew with a wooden spoon and looking into it, as if searching for something solid. "And we do not come as beggars. We bring provisions to share with you. And these men are here to render a great service to you and the whole of the realm."

"Indeed?" Olvir raised an eyebrow. The mention of provisions had gone some way to alleviating his suspicion of us newcomers, but he was clearly still wary.

As we had trudged up from the wharf, I had been aware of the looks from the villagers. Several of us were obviously strangers in these lands and Olvir's folk had whispered and openly pointed at Drosten's tattoos. Children had laughed and shouted at us, pulling at our cloaks and asking for trinkets, but the men of Sand had scowled, watching us pass as if we were foe-men.

"And what service will these men provide me?" Olvir asked, sipping from a large horn that was decorated with silver. The sumptuous drinking vessel was out of place in the drab surroundings of the hall.

"The king has sent them to seek out Ljósberari," Eldgrim replied.

At the mention of the name, one of the thralls dropped a tray of empty cups with a terrible clatter. Luckily, they were turned wood and so did not break, but the elderly woman who had served me my stew earlier with trembling hands, dropped to her knees and began to hurriedly stack the cups again.

Olvir glowered at her.

"That name is not uttered in this hall, warmaster," he said.

"It is a name that with luck will be scrubbed from the memories of the land, soon enough."

"I pray to Óðinn you are right," replied Olvir, his face hard and pale in the firelight. "He passed this way some months back. Burnt poor Vigfus' place. They would have burnt more, but I took my men out to meet him."

Earlier, Gersine had pointed out a blackened husk of a building close to the river mouth. Its charred beams were jutted and jumbled like a shattered rib cage. There was no telling what the building had been before it had been consumed by flames. Fires were not rare, of course. Men dropped rush lights, or a spark blows from a bonfire, or even badly stored hay can burst into flame with no warning. But, while the burnt building might have been from an accident, both Gersine and I had suspected this was the work of Ljósberari. It seemed we were right.

"You fought them?" I asked. "How many fighting men does he have?"

Both Eldgrim and Olvir looked at me sharply.

"Yes, we fought that whoreson and his band of thrall dogs," Olvir said. "They were many, but who can say their true number? It was dark, but my men are brave and strong." He waved a hand at the eight warriors who sat at the benches closest to their jarl. "We made the shieldwall," Olvir went on, "and killed a couple of the bastards before they fled into the night." He sat up straight, boastful and proud of his exploits and of his hearth-warriors. "One moment they were there, with their howling, like Valkyrjur screaming for the souls of the slain, then they had vanished. The idiot thralls follow Ljósberari." He spat into the rushes on the floor, as if saying the name had filled his mouth with bile. "Even now, after what he did to Vigfus and his family, still some have slipped away in the dark these past weeks. To join him, no doubt. He fills their heads with madness. It is not right that a man should fear a knife to his throat from a slave. They should all be killed, if you ask me. That would be a lesson others would heed."

The thrall woman finished collecting the cups and bustled away. I wondered if she thought of dragging a knife across Olvir's throat.

"We will kill Ljósberari," said Runolf, his voice rumbling like thunder in the dingy hall. "What happens to his followers is not our concern."

"You will have to reach him first," said Olvir. "The last boat to come down from the mountains with iron ore and pelts was over a month ago, and the boatman said Ljósberari was all the way up the river, north of the Suldalsvatnet, in the kingdom of Kaun Solvason."

"I have heard the same," said Eldgrim. "That is why we need a boat, and a guide, to carry the strangers to where Ljósberari lurks."

Olvir was incredulous.

"You mean only to send a dozen men? I thought you would lead all the men from your ship inland. The journey would be difficult, but you might have stood a chance. But twelve men…" He puffed out his cheeks and shook his head in disbelief.

"The king has faith in the abilities of these men," Eldgrim said. "And you yourself have told us that Ljósberari is in Hǫrðaland, the kingdom of Kaun Solvason. King Hjorleif cannot be seen to be sending a force into his neighbour's lands. But he wants him dead more than anyone. Ljósberari and Chlotar, the bastard Frank who travels with him, killed Hjorleif's brother, Hjalti, and must pay the price. Now, do not be concerned as to our plans. All we need from you is a boat and a guide."

"Get us there," growled Runolf, "and Ljósberari and his Frankish cur will soon discover that a dozen men will be plenty."

"It will be difficult to find a man willing to lead these easterners," said Olvir. "What payment do you offer?"

Eldgrim frowned.

"You need no payment for doing your duty to your king."

"But no man will wish to place himself at such risk. To travel upriver, into the realm of Ljósberari…" Olvir faltered, looking at us and knowing that at least Runolf and I understood his words. "It will spell almost certain death," he said at last, seeing no way to avoid the harsh truth.

"Then be convincing, Olvir," snapped Eldgrim, his voice sharp with menace. "Or you will find out how persuasive I can be."

Olvir swallowed and looked away. He conversed in hushed whispers with one of his men for some time. Eventually, after much shaking of heads and heated debate, his man slipped out into the night.

"Skamkel has gone to fetch your guide," Olvir said. He smiled, but his voice was uncertain. "Now, tell me of the world to the south. How fares the king? And you," he turned to me. "You are not from these lands. Tell me of your home."

And so I spent much of the rest of the night talking, while

the remainder of the men drank and ate of the meagre fare on the boards. There was something about Olvir's demeanour that set me on edge, but he was an inquisitive listener, and he probed me with many questions about Northumbria and, when he heard about our voyage north, he asked me details of Orkneyjar. He knew of Tannskári and seemed to have met him once, long before.

"I am surprised that scoundrel yet lives," he said, before draining the ale from his great drinking horn. I was intrigued, but Olvir said no more about Tannskári. And I did not dare ask him.

Despite the ale and the warmth from the fire, the atmosphere in the hall was cool and tense. I felt like a man treading his way along a narrow path across treacherous marshland. Olvir and his men listened intently to every word I uttered, but their expressions and cold eyes told me they were judging me, and would pounce at any moment if I misspoke.

When at last the conversation died and men wrapped themselves in their cloaks to sleep, I slumped onto the rushes, uncaring that they were neither dry nor fresh. Within moments I was asleep. My dreams were shot through with flames and blood, and I awoke, unrested, with a start, to find the hall alive with sound and movement. Servants and thralls were setting the boards with food and drink and I was surprised at the change in Olvir's generosity.

"It seems our host is generous with other men's wealth," said Gwawrddur in a low voice.

I looked at him questioningly.

"That cheese and ham come from *Grágás*' stores," he explained.

I had told the Welshman and the others what had been said the previous evening, and the mood of the company was subdued. Only Gwawrddur seemed unconcerned by the danger of our mission, instead relishing the challenge.

We had not long finished breaking our fast when Skamkel, the man Olvir had spoken to the previous night, approached us.

"Come," he said, "your guide awaits you."

Thirty-Seven

"I wouldn't use this boat to transport dung," said Runolf, his voice loud. He walked the length of the boat, shaking his head. When he reached the stern, he hawked and spat into the sea that lapped at the wooden pilings of the staithe.

"Neither would I," said Ingvar, the man who was to be our guide. Ingvar was a short man, slim of build, with the leathered and lined face of someone who spends their life at sea, or on the river. "And I would rather not use it to carry a dozen fools to their deaths, but the good Jarl Olvir has given me this chance to clear old debts." He scowled, clearly unhappy to have been forced into this position. "I have no say in the matter," he continued, "any more than you do. Or did you in fact choose to end your life at the hands of Ljósberari?"

"It will be my hands doing the killing," snarled Runolf. As soon as he had laid eyes on Ingvar's boat, he had appeared to have taken a dislike of the man, as if the boat reflected poorly on its owner.

The vessel was some eight paces in length, broad in the beam and, though clearly much smaller, to my untrained eye, it had similar lines to *Grágás* and *Brymsteda*. There were tholes for six pairs of oars, and I could see that with the twelve of us aboard, along with the boat's skipper, it would be cramped. I was glad we were to travel on a river and not out to sea, for there would be no room to sleep aboard.

"How old is it?" asked Runolf with a sneer. Bending down, he scratched at the birch bark that covered the hull. Sheets of the bark were sewn with roots or sinews of some kind, covering the timber planks. In places the bark was flaking and there were streaks of dark tar sealing along the seams, or where it had torn.

As quick as a darting fish, Ingvar slapped Runolf's hand away.

"Old enough not to have to put up with your insults," he said.

Runolf's face darkened and I thought for a moment there would be violence. In spite of Runolf's huge bulk looming over him, Ingvar did not flinch. At his side, and equally uncowed, Ingvar's small dog, a scruffy brown and white thing that was no larger than a cat, barked at the threatening giant.

"Hush, Ulf," Ingvar said after the men's staring had lasted long enough to become awkward. To my surprise, the dog stopped its noise. "It may not look like much, but *Gullbringa* will carry us wherever we need to go."

"*Gullbringa*?" Runolf said. The name meant "Gold bringer" and the idea appeared to amuse Runolf, who suddenly laughed. "*Skítrbringa*, more like."

Ingvar sighed and turned away from Runolf.

"Your friend is rude," he said to me. I shrugged. I could not deny it. "Apart from the rude lump," Ingvar went on, "you are all foreigners?"

I nodded. He sighed.

"And you are the only one who can speak properly?" He shook his head in disbelief at his bad luck. "By the gods, this is going to be a long trip."

"We'll manage," said Hereward, his Norse clear enough. "Thank you for guiding us, Ingvar Styrsson." Like several of the men, Hereward had learnt to make himself understood in Norse and follow simple conversations.

Ingvar let out a barking laugh. He bowed in acknowledgement of Hereward's formal thanks.

"Load your things," he snapped, speaking to Hereward now and ignoring Runolf. "The sooner we leave, the sooner we can all be killed." He laughed again without humour. He watched as Drosten passed a bundled blanket and a small sack to Eadmaer, who had jumped nimbly aboard *Gullbringa*. Ingvar nodded, seeing in Eadmaer's easy movements a fellow sailor.

Waiting on the wharf behind Drosten stood Bealdwulf, Sygbald, Os and Beorn, each carrying their byrnie, shield, spear, helm and sword. They were unsmiling and grim, their faces and arms scarred from past fights. "Whatever happens upriver," Ingvar said quietly, as if to himself, "I would not like to be standing in Ljósberari's shoes."

It didn't take long for us to stow our things on *Gullbringa*, but it was still some time before we could leave. Ingvar inspected each item of our baggage, throwing back onto the wharf anything he deemed not to be essential. The men grumbled. Os swore when Ingvar insisted on tossing his spare clothes. The skipper threw Os' sack to one of the young boys on the wharf, who fumbled his catch, dropping it into the sea.

"By Christ," Os yelled. "Save it, save it!"

Gwawrddur quickly snatched up one of the company's long spears and snagged the sodden sack before it disappeared into the deep.

"He'll be throwing us overboard soon," Os raged.

Ingvar must have understood his meaning, for he laughed.

"Do not tempt me," he said. "You boys are strong, but we are heading upriver and that means rowing against the flow of the water. When you have been rowing all day, you will be glad of whatever weight we can shift now. And the less weight we have aboard, the easier it will be to carry *Gullbringa*."

"You mean to carry the boat?" I asked. "Doesn't the river do that?" I grinned, believing that Ingvar must be joking.

But there was not the hint of a smile on his features. He shook his head and spoke to me as if I were a fool or a child.

"There are long stretches where the river is deep and wide, but when we reach shallows, or rocks, where the water is white and raging, there is nothing for it but to go ashore and carry the boat."

"He says we are going to have to carry the boat," I said, hoping for laughter from the men. Instead I was met with stony expressions and groans.

"Anything you can do without," said Hereward, "leave it with Eldgrim. We'll collect it when we return."

If we return, I mused, and wondered how many of the others had the same thought.

There was a final flurry of objects being thrown to Eldgrim's crew on the wharf.

"We will return here in a fortnight," Eldgrim said. "If you are successful, we will bear you back to Hjorleif's hall."

"You will not wait here?" asked Runolf.

Eldgrim raised an eyebrow and glanced over at where Olvir watched on, surrounded by his warriors.

"Would you?"

Runolf snorted.

"See you in a couple of weeks then," he said.

"Good luck."

Strong hands shoved us away from the wharf and out into the deep waters of the fjord. Ingvar called out for the men to unship their oars and nodded with grudging approval as they followed his command promptly and without fuss.

"Pull," he said, and all six oars dipped into the water together.

Eldgrim raised his hand to us, as did several of his men. The children of Sand shouted after us, but Olvir and the men and women of the settlement watched our departure with something like sorrow on their faces.

We slid out onto the water, rocking gently as the waves hit *Gullbringa*'s hull. I glanced over at Runolf. His jaw was set, his eyes hard. I sensed he was unhappy to be on this small craft. All those long months of toil building *Brymsteda* to only now have our fate resting on the timbers and peeling birch bark of an old sexæringr, as he had called it: a six-oared boat, skippered by a stranger.

And yet, as the warm sun rose high above us, glinting off the waters of the river mouth while Ingvar turned *Gullbringa*'s prow eastward, I had a strange sensation of belonging. Runolf was gazing away from me, but his hand rested on the haft of his great axe. Beside him, Drosten nodded at me, and I recalled our conversation after Orkneyjar. Hereward, serious as ever with the mantle of leadership that once again had fallen on his shoulders, looked all about us, as if expecting Ljósberari and his thrall brigands to leap out of the trees along the river at any moment.

Gwawrddur had a small smile on his lips, as if he alone had the answer to a riddle nobody else had even heard. Leofstan made the sign of Christ's rood in the air and recited the paternoster under his breath. I joined him in the prayer, lending my voice quietly to his. Looking up in surprise, he offered me a thin smile. He still wore the borrowed sword at his side and I wondered whether he would wield it when the time to fight came, as it surely would.

But for that moment, as Eadmaer, Gersine, Bealdwulf, Beorn, Sygbald and Os hauled on the oars, leaning back as one to heave us into the river's current, I pushed aside my misgivings of Leofstan's intentions. I allowed myself to smile and enjoy the feeling I knew would be all too fleeting. The

Almighty alone knew what would befall us in the days ahead, and had I known then what was to transpire, I might have told Ingvar to turn around, but in that instant I was content. I was surrounded by men I trusted, men who had fought beside me in battle. I sometimes still missed the brethren of the minster, but these warriors were my family now. My brethren of the sword.

And surely God, in His omniscient wisdom, had pushed us towards this destiny, like streams flowing together to create a river. Runolf sought his daughter and vengeance. Leofstan was in search of *The Treasure of Life*. I too felt the call of the powerful tome, but more than that, like Eadmaer, I was desperate to find Aelfwyn, if she yet lived. Drosten was perhaps looking for a way to expiate the darkness from his past, or maybe he was resigned to having to flee from it forever. Gwawrddur hunted for his next adversary, and the other men of Northumbria hoped that success would bring them battle-fame and wealth. For surely if we could rid this land of Ljósberari, trade between our kingdoms would open up and King Æthelred would not forget those who had made such a thing possible.

Despite everything that had led us to this point, as the oars bit into the fast-flowing waters of the Lågen, I could not shake the feeling that rather than departing Sand, we had somehow arrived, and this moment had been my destination all along. The culmination of the last months brought us to the mouth of this broad river, a river that led silently and inexorably towards our wyrd.

And towards death in a night of flames.

Thirty-Eight

My strange sense of wellbeing was shattered soon after we had left Sand and the fjord behind. The rowing was hardest just after the Lågen's mouth, where the river was compressed between rocky walls. The water surged and roiled in powerful waves that formed over hidden rocks.

"Pull, you maggots!" shouted Ingvar. "Pull!"

The men at the oars heaved, and sweat streamed from their faces, mingling with the cold spray that shot up from the prow where it sliced into the standing waves. There was a moment of panic, where we gripped *Gullbringa*'s sides and I was certain that the boat would be capsized, tumbling us into the churning river.

But the rowers were strong and Ingvar knew the river well. He guided us into a channel of smoother water and as suddenly as it had come, so the turbulence was behind us and we were in water that was as flat as burnished silver.

"That is the worst of it for a while," Ingvar said, wiping water from his face. "But keep up your rowing. The water here looks still, but it still flows fast, and," he dipped his hand into the water, seeming to forget that we had all just been doused in spray, "it is cold. It comes down from the far mountains where there is always snow, even in the summer. But we should be able to relax for a while now. Like a serpent, the Lågen shows her teeth at her mouth, but she is quiet from now on."

As if his words had taunted the spirit of the river, the Lågen quickly reminded us never to be complacent of her power. Something beneath the water's surface snagged Sygbald's oar and he was suddenly thrown backwards off his thwart as the loom smashed into his chest.

All was chaos for a time.

Ingvar screamed orders, making himself understood with gestures and shouts. Ulf barked incessantly. Sygbald released his grip on his oar and it began to slide into the water. With the speed that made him so deadly with a blade, Gwawrddur sprang forward, catching the tip of the loom before it was lost.

Drosten caught Sygbald, pulling him back to make room for Gwawrddur, who clambered onto the empty thwart. *Gullbringa* rocked alarmingly and there was much shouting. All of the men at the oars had stopped rowing in shock, and both Ingvar and Runolf yelled for them to start pulling again. The boat was rapidly sliding towards the brown surge of the standing wave. If we did not maintain our position upriver of it, we would need to once again negotiate that treacherous water. Perhaps it was that thought that made the men snap their focus away from pale-faced Sygbald and start to row once more. Their motion was ragged at first, oar blades clattering together as their strokes were snarled. But quickly, they found their rhythm once more and we began to pull away from the rapids.

As we passed the place where Sygbald had been flung off his thwart, a trunk of a tree broke the surface, rolling over in the seemingly placid water to show branches and roots, before tumbling away out of sight once more. It reminded me of the whale we had seen and how it had shown the flukes of its tail before vanishing into the deep.

"How do you fare?" I asked Sygbald. His face was pallid, his skin dotted with sweat and splashed water.

"I will be well soon enough," he replied, through clenched teeth. "When I have caught my breath."

We rowed on into the afternoon, and we found that what Ingvar had said was true. The waters of the Lågen were calm and the current not so strong as to make rowing difficult. The sun was hot on the back of my neck as I took my turn at the oars. The river meandered generally towards the north-east. The southerly banks were thickly forested and steeper than the north, but in the bright sunshine of the afternoon we could clearly make out the peaks of mountains ahead of us.

The trees were noisy with the chatter of sparrows and finches, and from time to time the hammering of a woodpecker rang out. At one point we saw a herd of red deer down by the river's edge, lapping at the water. The stag stared at us proudly as we slid by, his antlers broad and soaring above his thoughtful-looking face. But we saw no other boats and no people.

"There should be log boats and skiffs on the river every day," said Ingvar. "There are barely any since Ljósberari has settled north of Suldalsvatnet. Those boats that have made their way down to Sand have told tales to turn your hair white. Their skippers are either desperate or brave."

I wondered which Ingvar was, and how exactly Olvir had compelled him to lead us towards Ljósberari.

"And yet Ljósberari has let some boats through?" I asked.

Ingvar pulled gently on *Gullbringa*'s tiller, his left hand resting on Ulf's sleeping form where the dog was curled on his lap.

"They say he is mad," he said, "but I don't think a madman would be so canny, do you?"

"Canny?"

"He charges a tithe of the value of the goods that pass his lands. He must be amassing as much treasure as the dragon Fáfnir, though what a priest needs with silver, I do not know."

When the shadows lay long on the ground, Ingvar pointed mutely to the northern shore. I was at an oar and the sun shone in my eyes, making me sweat and squint as I rowed, looking towards our wake. So it was with initial relief at turning away from the bright, hot sky, that I looked in the direction Ingvar was signalling.

My relief was short-lived. We slid past the burnt buildings of a small settlement. We watched in sombre silence, the only sound the creaking of the oars in the thole pins. A wooden jetty projected into the river, but there was no sign of any boats moored to its timbers. And no evidence of life, apart from a huge raven that stared at us with beady black eyes from its perch atop a twisted tree trunk.

Stooping its head, it pecked casually with its shiny black beak at the limb it was sat upon. I realised with a hideous sinking in my stomach that the bird was not resting upon any tree, but rather the charred remains of a man or woman that had been somehow held upright against a stake. The body was misshapen and twisted, unlike any form of human flesh and bone. The ground around the shrunken and wizened corpse was blackened and covered in ash. As my eyes became accustomed to what they saw, I made out the curve of the skull, the head a cadaverous, skinless husk now. I wondered whether the Frank, Chlotar, had put out their eyes before the fire set their clothes alight, before their hair shrivelled away and the fat of their body erupted in flames, filling the air with the stench of roasting meat.

My mouth filled with bile.

Ingvar spat into the river and touched the iron of the hammer amulet he wore around his neck.

"Did you know them?" I asked, unable to pull my gaze away from the grisly sight, in spite of the sickness that welled up inside me at imagining how they had suffered.

"I knew them," Ingvar said, spitting again and looking away.

"We should tend to them," said Runolf. His blue eyes seemed to burn with the light from the lowering sun.

"Perhaps," replied Ingvar, his tone sad. "But not today. There are those who say that Ljósberari's victims cannot be touched. That they are cursed and must be left as a warning."

Runolf sniffed, but I noticed he spat into the river and made the sign to ward off evil with his left hand.

"And you believe them?" he asked.

Ingvar shrugged.

"Perhaps," he said, his hand creeping up to touch the hammer pendant again. "If we were to stop to tend to the corpses of all the men and women Ljósberari has burnt, we would not reach him this side of Jól. They have been food for the ravens for weeks, a few more days won't hurt them. If you still want to tend to the dead after you have slain Ljósberari, then I will help you." Ulf whimpered, looking at where the raven still worried at the burnt corpse. Ingvar stroked the dog's head. "Of course, for that we'll have to still be alive."

I did not interpret Ingvar's words, but from the grim expressions on the faces of the others, there was no need.

"There are so many dead?" I asked.

"Aye," replied Ingvar. Something had changed since we had passed the burnt body, and our guide seemed more ready to speak to us. Perhaps he understood fully now that this journey had only two possible outcomes, and his luck was entwined with ours. Or perhaps he just wanted to speak so that his mind did not dwell on the death of his friends. "Ljósberari was bold by the time he reached Sand," he said. "His band of thralls and children had been steering clear of larger settlements before that. Olvir may be a fool, but he is no craven, and he takes his oath to his people seriously. When he led his warriors to meet Ljósberari the night they did for Vigfus and his folk, I think it was the first serious fight the light bringer had faced."

"Hjalti, the king's brother, led a force against him," I said.

Ingvar raised an eyebrow.

"I know nothing of that," replied Ingvar, "but if true, the king's brother did not best him. Whatever the reason, at Sand, they turned tail quick enough." He frowned, remembering the days and nights that followed. "But after that defeat, no small farm was passed without being put to the flame."

We rowed on in silence through clouds of midges and flies that swarmed above the water. The land to both sides of the river was steeper now, rising up to craggy peaks. With the sun low in the sky *Gullbringa* entered deep shadow when we rounded a northerly bend. It was colder here and I shivered. We passed the remains of another burnt building, this time a smaller hut, with no wharf. I offered up a silent prayer of thanks to the Lord that there was no visible reminder of the atrocities that had been committed there.

Nobody spoke, but Runolf pulled on his oar so hard that the boat began to veer to one side. Given his comments aboard *Grágás* and his disparaging remarks about *Gullbringa*, I had been surprised when Runolf had offered to row, but when it had been Sygbald's turn to row again, Runolf had taken his place without comment or complaint.

Sygbald remained pale, and by common consent it had been agreed that he would row no more that day.

"We will reach Suldalsvatnet in the morning," Ingvar said. "We will camp here tonight." He steered us towards a small island. The Lågen was wide here, and the island lay a spear's throw off the southern bank. "Tomorrow we will cross the great lake and with luck, we will reach the mouth of the northern river that will lead us to Ljósberari by the end of the day."

Gullbringa's keel scraped on the pebbles of the island's beach. Eadmaer jumped ashore, taking a line with him and securing it to a willow. There were several willow trees and alders on the island, offering shelter and firewood, but it was small enough that we could be certain we were alone. There was a circle of rocks surrounding old ashes from past fires. The sight reminded me of the charred corpse we had passed, and I shuddered.

Ingvar climbed ashore, and threw his rolled blanket down near the fire pit.

"In normal times, on a summer's day like today, I would often find other boatmen camping here." He watched Ulf as the dog leapt ashore, scurried over to the rocks and cocked his leg. "Fetch some dry wood," Ingvar said to me, nodding at the trees. I wondered how it was that once again, as soon as I was with a group of men, it became my job to collect firewood. I was thankful there were no horses to water, for that would surely have fallen to me too. I remember now that I longed for the time when I would not be the youngest in any group. Oh, the folly of youth, to wish those years away.

"Come and help me," I called to Gersine, certain that he would join me without complaint.

We had just entered the shade beneath the canopy of the alders, and had only picked up a handful of twigs, when the shouts from the beach drew our attention.

Hurrying back, we ran down to where *Gullbringa* rested in the shallows. Most of the men were on the beach, but Leofstan, Gwawrddur and Sygbald were aboard the boat.

"What is it?" I called out.

"It is Sygbald," shouted Leofstan, a scary edge of fear in his voice.

"Is he sick?" I had seen how pale and quiet he had been that afternoon, but we had all been subdued after we had witnessed the burnt buildings and Ljósberari's victim.

Leofstan looked me straight in the eye and did something that he had never done before while surrounded by these men. He spoke in Latin, and the only reason for him doing so could be so that the others would not understand him.

"I fear Sygbald is dying," he said.

Thirty-Nine

There had been little point in Leofstan hiding his words by speaking in Latin. It quickly became apparent to us all that Sygbald was very ill. He could barely stand, such was the pain in his chest and shoulder, and when at last we helped him to disembark from *Gullbringa*, he coughed uncontrollably after only the few short paces to where we were going to build a fire. Leofstan and Gwawrddur lowered him gently down onto the shingle, and the old monk exchanged a look with me that needed no further words, in Latin or otherwise.

"How bad is it?" whispered Hereward, pulling Leofstan and me aside, and out of Sygbald's hearing.

"I had thought it just bruising," said Leofstan, flicking a nervous glance back at Sygbald, who was propped up on some of the baggage. "How he managed not to cry out throughout the day is beyond me."

"He is a strong man," said Hereward. "And brave."

"Well, his bravery may well bring his death," hissed Leofstan.

"So bad?" Hereward's words caught in his throat.

"I fear his lung may be pierced."

"Pierced? How? We have not been in battle."

"The oar must have struck him with more force than we at

first believed. I cannot be certain, but I believe his rib may have cracked and ruptured his lung."

Hereward rubbed a hand over his face.

"Will he live?"

Leofstan made the sign of Christ's cross. His concern was clear on his features.

"Sygbald's life is in God's hands. There is nothing I can do for him. But I am sure of one thing."

"What?" Hereward's face was red in the last light of the sun.

"He cannot go on. Without rest he will surely die. No matter how much we pray for him, he cannot walk any distance, let alone row or fight."

Behind us, Drosten was kneeling near Sygbald. He had kindled a fire and was feeding twigs into the first hungry flames.

For a time nobody spoke. Then Hereward sighed.

"It will be dark soon," he said. "Let us see what the morning brings."

Darkness came late, as it did so close to midsummer in this northern land, but when it finally arrived, it fell quickly, as if God Himself had wrapped a shroud over the sky. Before the darkness had enveloped us, I had gone back to helping Gersine collect the firewood. We barely spoke. He asked me briefly about Sygbald. I shook my head. My expression must have been bleak, for Gersine, ever happy to talk, fell silent.

We ate some of the dark bread and dried haddock we had brought with us from Sand, the firelight flickering in the gloom, making the shadows of the trees dance. The men spoke in whispers, as if they thought they might be overheard. The fire was warm, the night pleasant. On another night perhaps we would have laughed at Os' riddles. Beorn might have sung. But we were subdued and worried. It seemed that the river itself had become an enemy, impeding our progress. I prayed silently for Sygbald, and I am sure that more than one of the warriors thought of our mission and wondered whether this Ljósberari, who thralls followed as if he were a god, might command some arcane power over the land itself, turning it against us.

Hereward had wanted to wait till the morning to make a decision, but it was Sygbald who broke the hush.

"You can leave me on this island," he said, his voice clear until he was racked by a fit of coughing. Leofstan hurried to his side and offered him water. Sygbald took a sip. His cough subsided and he held up a hand to silence Hereward, who had started to speak. "Do not say I will be well enough in the morning." Sygbald's breath wheezed in his throat now and he grunted with the effort of speaking. He shook his head. Hereward made to reply, but Sygbald cut him off. "Don't. I am too tired to argue with you, but I know the truth. I can feel it, in here." He pointed at the left side of his chest, but I noted that he did not touch it. "I am no use to you like this. Leave me some food and firewood, and I will await your return."

"We can carry you back to Sand," said Bealdwulf. The two were close friends. The older warrior's features were etched with worry.

"No," said Sygbald. "I will not delay you. Each day that goes by, God knows what horrors this Ljósberari is inflicting on the folk of this land. And if Hunlaf's cousin yet lives and Runolf's daughter is with them, I would not want to think of their suffering at the hands of that monster and his murderous thralls any longer because of me."

"I thank you for that," said Eadmaer from the far side of the fire. Runolf scowled, but said nothing.

"Then it is decided," said Sygbald, his voice determined. "You must continue without me."

We fell silent again. Out in the darkness a night creature shrieked. I shivered at the sound, wondering what unseen dangers lurked in the mountains and forests that surrounded us.

"Even if we are successful in our quest," said Ingvar, breaking the hush, "it will be several days before we return." He had clearly understood most of what was said, but I interpreted his words for the others now to make sure their meaning was not confused. "And if we do not come back…" he went on, but did not finish his thought. He did not need to. If we were slain, Sygbald's only chance of survival if we left him here would be to be rescued by one of the log boats that came down from the mountains with iron ore.

"I will take my chances," Sygbald said. "I have faith that you will conquer this madman. After all, you have God on your side," he nodded at Leofstan, who looked embarrassed. "And you have Killer, here." He tried to smile at me, to show he meant no harm in the use of the name Gwawrddur had given me, but a sudden coughing gripped him. When he stopped coughing, he leaned against Leofstan, breathing shallowly. He looked ready to swoon.

I spoke his words for Ingvar, leaving out the jibe at me.

"You have more faith in your god than I have in mine," Ingvar said, shaking his head. He threw a piece of dry driftwood onto the fire in a shower of sparks. "But perhaps we do not have to leave him here."

"How so?" I asked, voicing the question for us all.

"There might be another way."

Forty

None of us had been willing to accept Ingvar's suggestion that night. I had listened, making the sign of the cross as I interpreted his words for the others. On hearing his plan, Hereward had shaken his head. Leofstan had frowned, crossing himself just as I had. The others had whispered and hissed, spitting into the fire and muttering their clear disapproval.

Even Sygbald had said he would prefer to remain on this island and trust we would return, or that a passing boat might pass by and rescue him.

But as the sun rose, dew glistening like jewels on the grass and leaves of the willows by the river, the decision was taken for us. Sygbald's condition had worsened in the night, and in the cold grey light of dawn, his skin had taken on a pallid blue tint, the colour of fish scales.

Or death.

He was in great pain and could barely shuffle to the boat. Os and Bealdwulf walked either side of him, and they had to lift him into *Gullbringa*.

"It is near?" Hereward asked Ingvar.

"We will reach there before mid-morning," the old boatman replied. His face was haggard, as if he had not slept. Or perhaps he was having second thoughts about the plan he had put forward. But there was no turning back now. Sygbald would never make it back to Sand, he would surely not survive the rest of the journey ahead of us, and, if left alone on the island, we were all certain he would die from his injury before we returned.

Sygbald, it seemed, saw the wisdom in Ingvar's plan, or perhaps he was in too much pain to protest further. He sat at the stern of the boat, wrapped in a blanket, his face pale, his lips blue. None of us spoke. We pulled on the oars with a focused determination, leaving the island behind us.

The sun rose into the clear sky, warming the back of my neck as I rowed. The river widened. The forested slopes at either side climbed ever steeper until, not long after we had set out, we passed between two towering rocky cliffs. Trees and scrub clung to ledges and clefts in the rock face, and I gazed up in awe of the straight lines of fissures and seams in the rock that were marked by the foliage growing along the otherwise barren rock. These stone sentinels seemed to stand guard at the entrance to the lake of Suldalsvatnet, for beyond them the water opened up into a vast expanse, as wide as some of the fjords we had traversed on our way to Sand.

"Not long now," said Ingvar.

We heaved on the oars with renewed energy, and as the distance to the lake's shores grew on either side of us, so the going became easier. Gone was the pull of the current against us, and now the peeling, birch bark-covered sexæringr skimmed across the still surface of Suldalsvatnet. The feeling of the open water, the cloudless sky and our easy passage would normally have been enough to buoy our spirits, but none of us could escape the sight of Sygbald's pallid features. He was unmoving for the most part, the only sign that he yet lived, the occasional cough. But even the coughing, that the night before had shaken his whole body, was now weak and feeble.

I prayed that God would spare Sygbald, but I fretted that He would not look with favour on what Ingvar had suggested.

I saw the same concern when I glanced at Leofstan. Still, there was nothing for it now, so we continued to row as Ingvar steered us ever northward.

"There it is," Ingvar said, his tone a mixture of relief and anxiety. We had only been on the lake for a short while and I craned my neck around to look at our destination. It was an island, larger than the one we had camped on, but still tiny in the middle of such a body of water. At first I struggled to make out the small, wooded piece of land, for beyond it lofted a jutting mound of forested rock that thrust like a fist into the lake. It was a thin trail of smoke that drew my eye down to the island that Ingvar was pointing at. The feather of smoke was from a small fire, not a conflagration, so it seemed the skipper had been right and the inhabitant of this island had not been slain by Ljósberari and his host of thralls.

"What's that?" I asked, pointing.

Ingvar squinted. On the water to the north of the island, were two dark shapes.

"Looks like a couple of log boats," Ingvar said. "Perhaps they are heading towards Sand with ore."

But as we drew near to the island, it was clear that the log boats were heading away from us, travelling north in the direction of our quest.

"They didn't pass us on the river," Ingvar said, scowling and distractedly stroking Ulf's ears. "And nobody has headed upriver for weeks."

"They might be Ljósberari's men," said Runolf. "Could we catch them?"

Ingvar thought for a moment.

"Perhaps," he said at last, "but they are far off, and it would be a long hard row, if they do not wish to be caught. And I am not sure your friend would survive the race."

Runolf looked over at Sygbald. The injured man lay with eyes closed, his pale skin sheened with sweat. Runolf nodded.

"Let us see what this woman has to say. Perhaps she can tell us who is in those boats."

Ingvar nodded, his expression doubtful. Soon we had pulled *Gullbringa* up onto a small beach, not unlike the one where we had spent the night. It too was shadowed by willows and alders, but where the island we had slept on had been uninhabited, the ring of stones around the ash of old fires the only mark that anyone had been there before us, this island bore evidence of people's passing everywhere I looked.

Colourful strips of cloth hung from many of the trees' lower branches, and I could make out small straw figures, and carved figurines dangling from the limbs. The trinkets were thickest where a path led into the darkness beneath the canopy of the wood. Two posts stood at the entrance to the forest path. They were the height of a man and atop each was the skull of a horse.

I crossed myself.

"We should not have come here," I said. "We cannot trust one who places her faith in magic."

Some of the others copied me, also making the sign of the cross.

"If anyone can heal your friend," said Ingvar, "it is Gudrun."

"But at what cost?" I muttered.

"You will have enough silver to pay her, I am sure," he said.

I did not reply. I had not been talking of precious metals or wealth.

"I will watch the boat," said Eadmaer, after he had helped Bealdwulf lift Sygbald down from *Gullbringa*. Eadmaer was almost as pale as Sygbald, his eyes constantly roving across the trees, the rattling tokens hanging from their branches, and the sightless sockets of the horse skulls. I could not blame him for being afraid. I felt the scratch of fear down my spine as I thought about walking between those skulls and into the gloom under the trees. I'd had the same sensation when I had first spoken to Leofstan about *The Treasure of Life*, and again when Audun had told us of Ljósberari and how he had burnt those he believed had lost their battle with darkness.

Runolf turned to the men gathered on the beach. All of us had armed ourselves, as if we planned to fight. The heft of my iron byrnie on my shoulders and the weight of my shield in my left hand gave me a welcome sense of protection, even though I knew that iron rings and willow boards could not protect our souls from corruption.

"Beorn. Os," Runolf said, perhaps thinking of the two boats we had seen to the north. "Stay with Eadmaer. If anyone approaches, let us know, and we'll come running."

Neither of the warriors complained at being left behind. Beorn nodded at Sygbald, who was held upright between Bealdwulf and Drosten.

"Good luck," he said.

Sygbald gritted his teeth and nodded grimly.

"Come on," he said. "Let's go, if we are going."

It was cool under the trees, despite the warmth of the sun. The air was thick with the scent of loam and rotting vegetation. I sniffed and picked out the tang of woodsmoke too. It reminded me of the charred corpse of the day before. None of us spoke as we walked slowly along the muddy path that led into the gloom.

The silence was broken by a sudden croaking cry. We were all startled. Hereward and Ingvar, who walked at the head of the group, both took a step backward, colliding with Runolf, who swore. A raven flapped across our path, its broad black wings fanning the loamy air into our faces.

"By all the saints," said Hereward, making the sign of the cross, and spitting to ward off evil.

"It is only a bird," growled Runolf, pushing Hereward away from him.

"It is not only a bird," said a woman's voice.

None of us moved.

In the centre of the path stood a tall woman. How she had come to be there, I could not say. There had been nobody there a moment before, of that I was certain. She was a handsome woman, with a high forehead and full lips. Her plaited hair was white, and fell in a sinuous rope over her shoulder and between the curve of her breasts. Her eyes were the strangest hue and unlike anything I had seen before or since. They were the palest blue, but tinged with pink, as if they had been soaked in blood. They seemed almost to glow in the shadows beneath the trees. And, as if the colour was not enough to unnerve us, her eyes never ceased to move, flicking and swirling about as if unable to focus on any one thing for more than a heartbeat. Her gaze swept over all of us and none, without pause.

I could not say how old she was. The curves of her slender body, the smoothness of her face, and the firmness of her voice gave the impression of a young woman, but the whiteness of her hair told a different tale, and Ingvar had spoken of her as someone who had been known to him since his youth.

Ingvar was the first of us to recover his voice.

"Gudrun, Lady of the lake," he said, bowing low. In the short time I had known him, he had shown deference to nobody, and his obeisance further disquieted me. "We bring you an injured man, and ask that you might heal him."

"It has been a long time since last you visited me, Ingvar Styrsson," the woman said. Her voice was haughty, but soft, and just as with her body, it seemed ageless. "It saddens me that men only remember me when they are in need." She fixed Ingvar with her unearthly stare and he quailed before her.

"Can you help our comrade, or not?" said Runolf, stepping forward.

Gudrun stared up at the giant axeman.

"I know you," she said.

"I have never been here before," Runolf replied, scowling.

"And I would recall having met you." His voice was firm, and I admired his bravery, for there was a power emanating from the woman that could not be denied. Ingvar had not been able to meet her gaze for more than a few heartbeats, but Runolf squared his shoulders and did not flinch as she transfixed him with her pink-tinged icy glare.

"That you would," she said, with a chuckle. The sound of it was like splinters of ice tumbling down a frozen cataract. "But perhaps I have seen you nonetheless. Mayhap in my dreams."

Runolf frowned.

"Enough of your games, völva," he said, using the Norse word for seeress or witch. "Our friend cannot stand here talking of your dreams. Can you help him?"

Gudrun smiled.

"You have your father's anger, I see," she said.

"What do you know of my father?" Runolf growled.

"Nothing that you do not already know, Runolf."

It was Runolf's turn to be afraid now, his brash bravery dissolving like snow in spring.

"How do you know my name, völva," he said.

"I know many things. You would do well to remember that. There is power in names, and respect too, so I would have you use mine."

Runolf stared at her. For a time he did not speak, then Sygbald began coughing, shattering the spell that had fallen between the witch and the warrior.

"Very well, Gudrun," Runolf said. "Ingvar here said you were the only chance we had of healing our friend. Will you tend to his injury?" She stared at him as if he were an errant child. "Please," he finished.

The raven croaked somewhere in the forest. It sounded like laughter. I shivered. Leofstan made the sign of the cross.

"Your nailed god is no use to you here," Gudrun said to him. He must have understood her, for he grew pale.

Gudrun stepped close to Sygbald. The men around him pulled back from her, as if to touch her would burn them. Drosten and Bealdwulf, who were supporting the injured man, tensed, but they did not move.

With slender white fingers Gudrun probed gently at Sygbald's chest. He winced, unable to stop himself from crying out.

"I will help your friend," she said. "His rib is broken. And it has damaged one of his lungs." She closed her eyes and inhaled of the forest air, as if sniffing for something. "He might yet die, but I will do my best to save him. Follow me."

Gone now was the air of mystery she had cultivated since her sudden appearance on the path. In its place was an abrupt pragmatism. Clapping her hands, she flicked her braid over her shoulder and, sweeping past us, she strode along the path. For a moment, we watched her white hair swishing across her back.

The raven cried again and I thought for a moment that I spotted its black shape flapping between the trees, following Gudrun as she walked.

Sygbald coughed and whimpered with the pain.

"Come on," said Runolf, his voice cracking. "You heard her."

Half-carrying Sygbald, Drosten and Bealdwulf set off after Gudrun. The rest of us fell into step behind them. None of us dared speak as we walked in silence towards the lair of the witch.

Forty-One

Gudrun led us to a small hut. It was in a glade, surrounded by soaring aspens. The trees were so densely thronged around the building that light from the sun would only reach the hut at midday. When we arrived, the sun was at its zenith and the moss-covered shingles of the hut's roof seemed to glow in the bright daylight. Smoke oozed from a small hole in the roof. The day was so still that the smoke drifted and hung about the roof, giving the impression that it was steam emanating from the sun-warmed moss that draped the timber tiles and eaves.

Gudrun's hair flashed brilliant in the sunlight. The heat of the sun felt good on my face after the shadows of the forest, but Gudrun did not linger there. She hurried across the clearing and entered the building. It was dark inside and I glanced toward Hereward and Runolf, nervous of approaching in case unseen enemies lay in wait for us.

Runolf understood my hesitation, but shoved past me impatiently.

"We are here now," he said. "If you fear her magic, do not enter. But how many warriors could that shack hold?" He did not wait for an answer, but he was right. The hut was too small for even all of us to enter. "Not enough to stop me, that's for certain," growled Runolf, answering his own question and stooping beneath the sagging timber lintel. He disappeared inside. There was no sudden crash of fighting, so, taking a deep breath, I offered a silent prayer to the Lord for protection, made the sign of the cross, and entered the hut after him.

It was warm inside and pungent scents assailed my nostrils. My eyes took some time to adjust after the bright sunlight. When I began to see clearly in the gloom, my breath caught in my throat. Skulls adorned every surface of the building. They dangled from the beams, rested on boards, or were balanced in niches. I shuddered and scanned the bones for signs of human remains, but I saw none. They were of all manner of God's creatures, from the tiniest vole on a table, to what looked like a wolf skull, nestled on the ground beside the hearth. But the skulls that drew my attention most were flimsy things, with beaks and great gaping eye sockets. I have always been interested in birds, and loved to spend days walking the coast and fields of Northumbria, observing them and listening to their calls. It is one of the small pleasures I can still enjoy, even now, as my bones ache with age. I can sit and look out from the window of my cell and watch the moorhens, coots and ducks down by the river. There, in Gudrun's hut, as I grew accustomed to the dark, I became distracted for a time with those skulls. Most I had never seen before and I tried to imagine which one belonged to which species. Was that a kestrel, with its dainty arched beak? That must surely be a curlew, with the curving bill. That one was a puffin, there could be no doubt. The distinctive beak was faded in death, but the colours were still visible.

"You like my friends, I see?" Gudrun said, her sharp tone cutting through my fixation. She stirred something thick and glutinous that simmered in a small pot hanging over the fire. "You are not like the others, are you?" Frowning, I stared at her. Had she somehow seen through the thin veil of the warrior I wore. Was it so clear that I was a monk in a warrior's clothing?

"Never mind the boy," said Runolf. I bridled at his dismissive description of me, but I was glad that Gudrun's sunset gaze of blue and pink shifted away from me. "What about Sygbald?"

"Yes, yes. Bring him inside and lay him on the bed, there." She indicated a narrow pallet enclosed in a box of carved wood. Like everything else within Gudrun's home, runes covered it, etched deep into the wood. Runolf stared at the bed and I wondered if he could decipher the meaning of the angular letters.

I went to the door and called for Bealdwulf and Drosten to help Sygbald inside. While he shuffled into the hut, Gudrun busied herself pulling pots and pouches from nooks and shelves that dotted the walls. She plucked leaves of woundwort, vervain and betony from where they dangled from the rafters. When Sygbald was on the bed, pale-faced and panting shallowly, she shooed us outside.

"You cannot all crowd in here. Leave me now to do my work."

Bealdwulf hesitated by the door.

"I will do my best for your comrade," she said, her voice softening. "But I need space and no distractions."

I told Bealdwulf what she had said, and again, she looked at me, seemingly intrigued by my control of two languages.

"Tell her to make sure he lives," Bealdwulf said, not daring to look directly into her strange, otherworldly eyes.

I translated, and she nodded, curtly.

"I will do my best. You have my word. But your friend's life hangs by a thread. If the gods should choose to cut it, there is nothing I can do. No mortal has such power."

With that, she closed the hut's door behind us and left us blinking in the sunlight.

Gersine wandered off into the woods. I thought he had gone for a piss, but when he returned, he carried an armful of dry wood. He shrugged.

"We will be glad of it, if we are here when night falls."

Hereward nodded his approval.

The rest of us had slumped down on the grass, enjoying the warmth of the sun, and trying not to think what might be happening inside the hut. Gudrun was singing, and from time to time, snatches of her song, lilting and strange, reached us. I could not make out the words, but the sound made me shiver, as if a cold wind had blown through the glade.

"Do you think she has the power to heal Sygbald?" I asked Leofstan, keeping my voice low. Some of the others conversed quietly, but there was something about this place, or Sygbald's precarious predicament, that made us all feel we could not speak normally. It felt as if to make a loud noise might disrupt whatever spell Gudrun was weaving inside. I shuddered at the thought.

"I know not what power she possesses," Leofstan said. "But listening to her words, she said his life was in the hands of her pagan gods. That to me would imply she has no real power. No more than any man or woman. Pray for Sygbald, for you and I both know her gods can do nothing to help him."

"Then why have we come here? Why leave Sygbald inside with her?"

Leofstan looked up, watching the highest leaves of the aspens tremble in the light breeze. No wind reached us beneath the trees.

"The mind has a power of its own," he said. "If Sygbald believes Gudrun has the ability to heal him, he will more likely be cured."

I was aghast.

"You put great store in the power of Sygbald's mind."

"Ah, but I have faith in the Almighty, young Hunlaf. And do not forget that He guided Ahmad's hand to save Gwawrddur." Leofstan fixed me with a disapproving glare that reminded me of when I had studied my Latin declensions under his tutelage back at Werceworthe.

"Is it God's will that has brought us here?" I asked.

"Surely everything is God's will," he replied, scratching at the grey stubble that had grown on his shaved pate. "The Lord is all-knowing and all-powerful. Gudrun may be a witch, a seeress, a völva, as Runolf described her, but anyone can be the instrument of the Lord. Ahmad. Even you." He raised an eyebrow knowingly.

"That was different," I said, thinking of how God had led me to pick up a blade and fight. Before that moment I had been a monk, praying, singing, studying and writing all day. That single decision had changed my life forever. Surely the hand of God had been responsible. The alternative – that it had been a mere whim on my part, an instant of rage that had seen me snatch up a weapon – was unthinkable.

"Is it really so different?" Leofstan said. "For the Almighty, anything and everything is possible. Even using a cunning woman as His hand to heal one of His faithful. When I looked inside the hut, did I not see vervain and betony?"

I nodded.

"And that bitter smell was fennel, if I am not mistaken," he went on. "These are all things I would have used to treat Sygbald if I'd had them to hand. Alas, we had no such herbs, so apart from binding his chest to prevent the ribs from moving, there was nothing more I could do."

A raven croaked at the edge of the glade. The same big brute we had first seen in the forest, I thought. The harsh sound of its cry startled a flock of wood pigeons that must have been roosting on the far side of the hut's roof, for several of the grey birds flapped up into the sky with a great flutter, flashing their white wing feathers. They circled, dark against the pale blue of the cloudless sky, before flying northward and out of sight behind the trees, no doubt to settle somewhere more peaceful. The raven called again and I looked up. It was perched on the gnarled branch of an ash. The black creature was staring at me, and I wondered whether its skull would decorate Gudrun's hut one day.

"I do not believe Gudrun has magic that will heal our friend," Leofstan said, his voice barely more than a whisper, so that only I would hear. "But I do believe she has knowledge of healing and that God has brought us here that she might apply her skills to Sygbald."

By the time the sun was lowering in the west, we had all fallen into a doze. The glade was in shade now, and the warmth had quickly fled, so Hereward shook himself awake and went about lighting a fire.

He struck a spark with a small flint he carried in a pouch filled with shavings and strips of hoof fungus. It would have been easier to fetch a burning brand from Gudrun's hearth, but none of us wanted to venture into her home, or to distract her while she worked on Sygbald. Luckily, we were sheltered in the glade, and the tinder was dry. In moments, Hereward had a smoking ember caught in a piece of birch bark. To this he added some dry grass, wrapping it in a ball around the glowing tinder and blowing into it gently. Smoke billowed from the grass and an instant later, a flame appeared. Hereward added some twigs from the wood that Gersine had collected and soon we had a warming blaze.

We were staring into the flames, each lost to his own thoughts when Gudrun startled us all.

"Am I welcome at your fire?" she said.

Ulf started barking, its sharp yapping cries sending the raven flapping away. Gwawrddur half-rose, his hand already drawing his sword from its scabbard. Gudrun laughed, holding out her hands to show she was not armed. Not one of us had heard or seen her approach.

Ingvar hushed his dog.

"You are of course, well come, lady," he said, a strange quiver in his voice.

She laughed again at that. Then, smoothing her linen dress, she lowered herself down to sit beside him. Ingvar watched her all the while, his eyes filled with some unspoken emotion.

"How does Sygbald fare?" Runolf asked.

"He is sleeping," she replied. Her voice had the same timeless quality I had noticed earlier, but it was softened with weariness now. "He will sleep long, and, if he awakens, he will still need many days of rest."

"You are not sure he will awaken?"

"Nothing is sure in Miðgarðr," she said. "I have told you, his life is in the hands of Frigg and Eir. Not mine." For a time it seemed she would say no more on the subject, but then she relented. "Your friend is strong. With luck, he will live. I have done all I can, and it should be enough. Now, go see him, if you would like, but disturb nothing in my home."

Runolf rose. Bealdwulf stood too, and they made their way towards the hut.

"When you have checked on Sygbald," Gudrun called to them, "pick up the pot that is over the hearth, and the bowls and spoons I left there too." At Runolf's frown, she sighed. "I would not have my guests go hungry."

They brought back the pot and the bowls, setting them down before Gudrun.

"Sygbald seems well enough," said Bealdwulf to us all. "He is asleep, but there is more colour in his cheeks, it seems to me."

Gudrun nodded, clearly unsurprised by this declaration.

"I have worked quite enough today," she said. "Serve the food yourselves. I have no ale, but the water of the lake is fresh. Send someone down to fetch water and bring back your other men too. I would not have them want for food. Your boat will be safe on the beach."

Hereward understood most of her words and I interpreted the rest. He bit his lip.

"No, I will not leave the boat unguarded," he said at last. "It is our only way off this island. Gersine, Hunlaf, take some food down to Eadmaer, Os and Beorn. And bring back water."

I sighed, catching Gersine's eye. But where I was angered at once again having been given the job of a servant, or a boy, Gersine grinned and seemed happy to help.

"Help me get this byrnie off then," I said. "If I am to carry water like a thrall, no need to be burdened like a warrior." In this, Gersine appeared to agree with me, and we both shrugged off our heavy iron-ring shirts.

Ladling pottage into three bowls, I took one, leaving the others for Gersine. We picked up Gudrun's water skins from where they hung on a peg by her door, and strode off into the shadows of the wood.

I hurried, not wishing to miss any of the conversation back at the fire in the glade. Gudrun both frightened and intrigued me, and I would hear what she had to say.

The three men on the beach were pleased to hear that Sygbald had been tended to and that his prospects were as good as could be hoped for. But when they heard that the pottage had been made by the seeress, they pushed the bowls away. The food smelt delicious, but Eadmaer voiced all their fears when he said, "She might mean to poison us, or pass us a sleeping draught in the stew, so that she can slay us in the night."

His words unnerved us, so we filled the water skins and ran back along the path.

"You think we can trust her?" asked Gersine, a heavy water skin slapping against his back as he kept pace with me. I was glad I had removed my byrnie. Our kirtles were wet with sweat and the water that leaked from the skins.

I was out of breath from running, so said nothing, but my mind dwelt on Eadmaer's words. When we ran into the clearing, I half-expected to find all of our companions slumbering, having succumbed to some herb in the pottage, or worse, to lie dead, eyes open but unseeing, slain by the poison Gudrun had undoubtedly stirred into the food.

I halted abruptly on seeing them all alive and well, still seated on the grass around the fire. Gersine almost collided with me. Gwawrddur looked up at me with a thin smile, as if he knew why we had come running.

Gudrun too appeared to understand, for she laughed.

"Never fear, young ones," she said. "I too have eaten from the stew. I would never serve guests with food I would not partake of myself."

Ingvar grinned, as if amused by our fears.

"Is that what we are then?" I asked, suddenly angry. "Guests? What of those who came before us?"

"Many men have been guests of mine," Gudrun said, her gaze steady now when it had been constantly moving before. "Is that not so, Ingvar?"

The grin slipped from the old boatman's face. He picked up his empty bowl and poked around in it with his spoon, as if hoping more food would appear.

"I speak of those who were here today," I said, not caring for whatever secrets lay between the seeress and the boatman. "The men we saw leaving in two log boats heading north."

She drew in a long breath and nodded.

"As you no doubt suspect, they were followers of Ljósberari. I have no cause to deny it."

"So," I said, my voice rising with the excitement of wresting the truth from Gudrun, "you are in league with him."

A hush had descended around the fire now, all of the men absorbed in our exchange.

"No," Gudrun said, shaking her head. "I am not allied with Ljósberari. He has strong magic. But his gods are not mine."

"And yet he sends his men here to you?"

"I do not believe they came at his behest."

"So why did they come?"

Gudrun offered me a smile. Once again, her eyes would not stop moving, her gaze roaming around the clearing. The sweat cooled on my skin and a chill stillness wrapped about me. I wanted to tremble, but held my body in check. I would not show any weakness.

"Why they came here does not concern you, boy," she said and I stiffened. "Men come to me for all manner of reasons. You have brought a friend for healing. Others come for potions that will revive or cure a loved one. Some come to heal themselves." Her constantly moving eyes settled on Ingvar for a heartbeat, and he squirmed.

"Ljósberari's people come to you for healing?"

"Amongst other things."

"What other things?"

"That is between them, their gods, and me."

"You will not tell me?" Something in her tone infuriated me.

"No," she replied simply.

She was taunting me with her answers. Goading me. What did she hope to achieve by it? I could feel my anger at being thwarted building within me. My hand fell to my sword's hilt. By Christ's blood, I would make the witch answer me. Leofstan grasped my shoulder, holding me back.

"She has done us no harm, Hunlaf," he said, his voice quiet and soothing. As one might talk to an animal. Or to a petulant child. Realising how I must appear to the older men surrounding me, I took a deep breath, calming myself.

"If you are not with Ljósberari," I said, when I had gained control of my anger, "why has he not killed you?"

"I think he meant to," she said, "when he first passed by this island."

"But he did not." I heard the foolishness of my words and felt my face redden. To cover my embarrassment I dropped to my haunches, picked up a piece of wood and prodded the fire.

"No, Hunlaf," Gudrun replied, with a smile, "he did not kill me. I am no ghost." Her use of my name both frightened and excited me. There was power in names, she had said.

"Why did he not slay you?" asked Runolf. "You are neither a thrall nor a child."

Gudrun sat up straight, smoothing her white linen dress. Where she pulled the fabric down, it clung to her breasts. I was too busy staring at her chest to take in what the others were doing, but I would wager a fortune that every man there was looking in the same direction as me in that moment.

"No, Runolf," she murmured, "I am no child. And I am a slave to no man."

Runolf cleared his throat.

"And yet you still live."

"Hunlaf is not the only observant one, I see," she said. "Yes, I still live. Though my life was not assured when Ljósberari first came here. He was happy to let his people have their fun. His Frank, Chlotar, was eager to..." She hesitated, her body tensing as she recalled Ljósberari's Frankish henchman. "To teach me the ways of Mani."

Leofstan's grip on my shoulder tightened at the mention of the author of *The Treasure of Life*.

"We have heard of this Chlotar," said Runolf, his voice rumbling like a distant rockfall. "I will end his teaching days soon. You have my oath on that."

"Be careful," she said. "He is dangerous, that one."

"So am I." Runolf spat into the fire. "But if Chlotar was so keen to torment you, as he has so many others," Runolf's huge muscles bunched in his arms as he clenched his fists, "how is it that you can still look upon us with your strange eyes, völva?"

Gudrun snorted in amusement at Runolf's blunt words.

"I convinced Ljósberari to spare me."

"How?" I asked.

"First, I spoke to him, but I doubt that would have ever been enough. He has a mind as sharp as a blade, and knowledge as deep as the sea. I have never felt my intellect to be any less than a man's. But in the presence of Ljósberari, I felt as a child sitting at the feet of a teacher. You know that feeling, do you not?"

I flushed, angry again at her jibes, but I did not respond to her teasing.

"How did you convince him to let you live then?"

Gudrun grew still. She stared into the flames and for the first time I saw her for what she truly was. Not the statuesque beauty, the white-haired, pink-eyed seeress, but the woman, alone and vulnerable on her small island home, surrounded by men of war. To stand before us with only her wits as defence was as brave as anything I had witnessed. My anger at her vanished like smoke on the wind. What right did we have to question what she had done to survive? I imagined her on this very spot, encircled by the howling fiends that Audun had described, facing Ljósberari and the bloodthirsty Frank, Chlotar, whose name struck fear into all who mentioned it. It was clear that Gudrun was not one to scare easily, but in the vision of my mind's eye, she must have been terrified.

"Ljósberari had ignored my pleas," she said, her voice quick and curt, as if she wanted to rush through the telling and not to dwell on those memories. "His people had lit a fire, and they were ready to burn me, as they had so many before." She faltered in the telling for a moment. With a shiver, she forced herself to continue. "It was only when that bastard, Chlotar, set upon me that things changed. Perhaps I should be thankful to him for that. Ljósberari had been sure that like all his victims, I must have the darkness burnt from me. I was certain then that I would die. The children wailed and screamed, the men and women howled like beasts. Then the Frank ripped off my dress." She raised her shoulders, proud of this memory at least. "I stood before Ljósberari naked, and with the power of Frigg,

I willed myself not to show my fear to him, or to that monster, Chlotar, and the slavering thralls baying like hounds scenting a hart. If I was to die, I would die with my pride. I would not weep and beg. I stood tall, and stared at Ljósberari."

"And he spared you?" I asked, lost in her tale and uncaring now of the stupidity of my question.

"He saw for the first time the whiteness of my skin and hair. The colour of my eyes. These eyes and this hair, that so unsettle men, saved my life. For he believed I was touched by the light. He called off his Frank and the howling hounds then."

"Are you?" I asked.

"Am I what?"

"Touched by the light?" I could think of no better explanation for the hue of her skin, hair and eyes. I have never seen anyone else with skin and hair so pale, and her eyes were not natural.

Gudrun laughed at that, and it was as if with her laughter, we were able to breathe again.

"Ljósberari's light and darkness reside within us all." She shrugged. "Or perhaps in none of us. Mostly, I would say they dwell within him." She let out a long sigh and stared into the flames. "I believe the battle he sees in others is really his own."

Forty-Two

We slept around the campfire in the clearing before Gudrun's hut. When darkness fell, the seeress slipped away. I lay awake for a time thinking of her story, and imagining Aelfwyn and Revna amongst the onlookers to Gudrun's torment. How many people had they seen tortured and murdered? Even if they yet lived, would they still be the young women we were searching for? I pondered too Gudrun's strength. She was clearly intelligent and knowledgeable, but I wondered at the life she had led. The solitude she must feel here. Had she once lived in a village, surrounded by kin? Had she been driven away because of her pallor and pink eyes?

As the sunset turned the sky in the west as red as blood, Runolf had sought to pay Gudrun, pulling some silver from his pouch. She had shaken her head.

"If you return, you can repay me with the skull of that bastard, Chlotar."

"I thought the animals in your hut were your friends," he had replied.

"I will make an exception for him," she said, her smile cold.

I did not see her again before we left.

We awoke with the dawn and made our way through the trees down to *Gullbringa*. Pushing the boat out into the lake, we began rowing northward on the placid water. Thin wisps of mist lay softly on the still surface around us. The sky was clear but for the beginnings of white clouds rolling slowly over the peaks in the east and north. The sun hazed the mountain tops, setting them afire with the early morning light.

"We should not have left Sygbald there," said Eadmaer.

"She is tending to his injury," replied Leofstan.

"Is she?" Eadmaer snapped. "She is a witch. She cannot be trusted."

Eadmaer had not seen Gudrun, but he had listened intently to our description of her, and heard the awe in our voices. He had been nervous at the prospect of visiting her island when Ingvar had put forward the suggestion. Having spent the night there, his fears seemed to have coalesced into something harder and more brittle.

"She is a woman," said Leofstan, "nothing more."

"What of her eyes?" he asked. "Bealdwulf says her eyes are like those of a rat."

"Do you judge people on the colour of their eyes, Eadmaer?" asked Leofstan. "Are mine a colour that you trust? Gudrun no more chose the hue of her eyes and hair than did you, or anyone."

Eadmaer had no answer to that. For a while we pulled on the oars in silence.

"Her kind should be slain," said Eadmaer into the hush.

"Her kind?" said Leofstan. "What kind is that? Women? Or only those with eyes you don't like?"

"Witches," hissed Eadmaer.

Leofstan shook his head sadly.

"Men will all too often seek to kill that which they do not understand. Was our Lord Jesu not nailed to a tree by men? Does not Ljósberari murder those he believes to be unworthy?"

"It's not the same," said Eadmaer, but his voice had lost its strength and he sounded petty now, like a child who has been told he cannot have another oatcake. "It's not the same," he repeated, looking about for support, but finding none.

We rowed on, making good time on the smooth waters of Suldalsvatnet. I wondered how Sygbald fared. But despite my worry for him, I could not help thinking that perhaps he had been lucky to suffer the accident when he did. For now he rested in the hut of the imposing seeress, while we hauled on the oars' looms, pulling *Gullbringa* over the flat waters of the lake, heading towards fire and death. For what other fate could await us in Ljósberari's realm?

We stopped only briefly to change rowers and to eat some of the dried fish that we had brought from Sand. It was late in the afternoon when we reached the mouth of the river that Ingvar said would take us north. We would be travelling into the lands of Kaun Solvason, King Hjorleif's difficult neighbour, but Ingvar told us that upriver aways, whether Hǫrðaland or Rygjafylki, Ljósberari held total sway.

We had followed the lake as it twisted north and east, eventually reaching the northernmost shore, which was bounded to the east, north and south by steep, tree-clad mountains. The river disgorged its waters into the northern part of the lake.

"The going will be more difficult after this," said Ingvar. "The river winds its way into the mountains and much of our passage will not be easy." Staring up at the rocky slopes to the north, I could barely imagine how we planned to travel further, but Ingvar had brought us this far.

A small settlement stood on the eastern bank of the river mouth, and Ingvar steered us towards it.

"We will rest here tonight and set off upriver at dawn."

Dusk was still a long way off, but none of us complained as we rowed up to one of the wooden wharfs that thrust out into the lake. As Eadmaer jumped from the bow, taking a rope with him to secure *Gullbringa*, it became clear that this settlement had not escaped Ljósberari's wrath. The buildings had been torched, and along the river's edge stood several stakes, each supporting the charred corpse of an unfortunate man or woman. There were a dozen in all.

"I will not sleep here," said Eadmaer.

Runolf spat into the water, but did not argue. Ingvar made the sign to ward off evil and touched the amulet at his neck.

"These were good people," he said, his gaze sweeping over the blackened bodies. "Last I heard, they yet lived. Gods." He turned away. He beckoned for Eadmaer to return to the boat, and with a whispered command, we rowed back out onto the lake. "We will rest elsewhere," said Ingvar.

Nobody spoke as he steered us to the tree-lined shore to the west of the river. We tethered the boat to the lowest branch of a tall fir and clambered ashore.

"Can we risk a fire?" Hereward asked Ingvar.

"Do what you will," replied the boatman. "We will all be dead soon anyway, so we might as well be warm tonight."

"Hush your bleating," said Runolf. "Fear is an unbeatable foe once you let it get a hold."

"I am no warrior," replied Ingvar. "I am not brave, like you."

"Then be silent," Runolf snarled.

Hereward lit a small fire and set a watch. In the night I listened to the sounds of the forest and wondered what horrors awaited us. The more I thought of the burnt bodies, Gudrun's tale, Audun's fear when he had spoken of Ljósberari and his host of fiends, so the darkness seemed to grow deeper and colder, wrapping itself around me like a shroud. My terror grew, so that when Gersine touched my shoulder to take my place, I let out a small cry.

"It is just me, Hunlaf," he whispered.

I took a long breath, my heart hammering. I patted him on the arm and lay down beside the fire, thinking of what Runolf had said. I must not allow fear to get a grip on me. But as I lay there, a light breeze rustling the leaves above us, the shriek of an owl startled me fully awake once more, and I wondered if it was not already too late.

I awoke to half-remembered nightmares of fire and screams. I had been in the clearing on Gudrun's isle. Men and women were being consumed by bonfires all around. In the centre of the glade, shadowed, faceless men leered at the pale, naked body of the seeress as she stood defiantly awaiting her death. When I looked at her face in the dream, I was shocked to see not the pink eyes and white hair of the witch, but the freckle-cheeked, guileless features of Aelfwyn.

The forest was alive with birdsong and the murmur of insects. Warm sunlight lanced between the trunks of the trees. That summer morning seemed far removed from the twisted corpses of the people of the village at the mouth of the river. And yet, as we rounded the headland and entered the river, there they stood, stark and horrifying in the bright light.

With dour expressions, we turned away from the dead, pulling with renewed vigour at the oars. The river flowed fast here and we immediately understood Ingvar's warning of the day before. The mountains climbed up steeply, and everywhere we looked the slopes were covered in densely packed trees. As we hauled *Gullbringa* laboriously upriver, we repeatedly passed from bright sunshine into shadow, but never for long enough to cool us. Dense swarms of insects whirred in the patches of sunlight, making us curse as they stung exposed skin and buzzed around our faces. We were all panting, scratching and soaked in sweat by the time we had travelled past the first few bends.

We slid slowly past a sheer rock-face to the west, its upper reaches shining in the sunlight. The water was fast here and deeper than it had been close to the lake. Back near the river's mouth, the boat's hull had scraped against rocks more than once and Ingvar had cursed. But he knew the ways of the river, and guided us through waters deep enough for *Gullbringa*'s draught. When we left the cliff behind us and came out into the sunshine again, we were met by a pervasive roar.

Peering over my shoulder, I saw that the river widened. There were many rocks here, and the water churned and boiled over them. Beyond the stretch of white water that surged over the boulders, the earth rose in a massive step, perhaps the height of four men. The river flowed over this, dropping with a crashing thunder in a great waterfall. The air was cool on my face with the mist thrown up by the falls. One glance at the obstacle told me there was no way we could get *Gullbringa* beyond this point.

"Pull now!" shouted Ingvar and, trusting his command, we heaved on the oars hard, and soon we had beached the boat on the eastern shore.

"Come on now," Ingvar yelled. "Get it up and onto land."

We all leapt out of the boat. Eadmaer held a rope and Ingvar sent him to loop it around the thick bole of a birch. The bark was scraped and worn smooth at the height of a man's chest, showing where this operation had been performed many times before. Then, with much cursing and shouting, we tugged and heaved on the rope and soon we had the boat out of the water.

We stopped to drink and catch our breath and I looked about us. To the north, running beside the waterfall, a broad path had been cut through the trees. On the loamy soil, that had been kept clear of vegetation by the regular passage of boats and men, lay several smooth logs that had no doubt come from trees that had once grown in the now-cleared path.

The noise from the river reverberated between the rocky cliff and the forested slope where we stood, and Ingvar had to shout to make himself heard.

"This is where your strength really counts. We're pushing *Gullbringa* up there." He pointed along the shadowed path through the trees. "It isn't as far as it looks and you should be thankful."

"Thankful of what?" I asked.

"That there are more of you than I normally have with me, and that the boat isn't laden with goods for trade. We'll be at the top and back in the river in no time."

I passed on his words to the others. They groaned, but without delay, half of us placed our shoulders to *Gullbringa*'s sides, while the rest took up the rope that Eadmaer had coiled around a tree partway along the path. It was hard going, just as Ingvar had said it would be, but I was surprised that the boat moved as smoothly as it did. Gersine and I were given the task of collecting the logs from the rear and running them to the prow, where we placed them beneath the keel once more. For a time, I thought it was a better job than manhandling the bulk of the boat, but I soon changed my mind. The logs were heavy and my arms quickly ached from lifting them. I was breathless and drenched in sweat from having to rush back and forth. Even Gersine, always so pleased to help, grumbled after a short time.

As we neared the point where the path we followed drew closest to the waterfall, the air was misted and cool. The crash of the water drowned out all sound, even our angry expletives as our shoulders and backs burnt from the exertion of hauling the boat up the hill.

Such was the absolute smothering of all sound, that none of us heard the attack when it came.

Forty-Three

The first inkling I had that something was wrong was when Gersine failed to appear with the log he had been lugging. I waited for a moment, then called out to him. There was no response. I knew he would not have heard me over the waterfall, so I hurried back to where I had left him. He had been tiring for some time. Perhaps he had chosen just to pause for a time, to catch his breath. God knew I wanted to rest a while. Maybe I should ask Ingvar to give us a moment's respite.

When I saw him, I thought at first he was reaching down to lift his log, for it was at his feet. But as I watched, he staggered backward a couple of paces. His face was twisted in agony.

Still I did not know what had occurred, but clearly, my friend was in trouble, so I began to run towards him, calling his name. Gersine didn't appear to hear me, for he did not look in my direction. Aghast, I watched as he fell onto his side in the mud. As he toppled over, a shaft of light illuminated his leg and at last I saw the object of his pain. An arrow, fletchings bright in the sunlight, jutted from his right calf.

I skidded the last few paces, sliding down next to him where he lay. His face was pale and grimacing, his teeth white. Blood bloomed through his leg wraps.

"Attack!" I shouted as loudly as I could. "To arms!"

I scoured the woods, but could not see the archer.

"Where did it come from?" I shouted in Gersine's ear.

He shook his head.

"I didn't see. By God it hurts!"

Drosten was at the rear of the boat and with relief I saw his tattooed face turn in our direction. With the instincts of a natural warrior and a man who had been on the run for years, he understood what had happened instantly. He touched Hereward's shoulder and they conversed in short shouts. Drosten pointed at me and Gersine. Hereward nodded. As if to punctuate what they were talking about an arrow struck *Gullbringa*'s top strake, between the two of them. Lesser men might have ducked down, but both Drosten and Hereward calmly turned to look in the direction from which the arrow had flown. I followed their gaze and was rewarded by seeing movement in the trees. There were at least three men there.

"Don't attempt to remove the arrow," I said.

Gersine looked up at me as if I was mad to suggest such a thing.

"Leofstan will know what to do. Stay there."

Without waiting for a response, I pushed myself to my feet and sprinted up the hill towards the men in the trees.

The world was filled with the roar of the cataract and the rush of blood in my ears. I was glad my byrnie yet rested inside the boat. Running uphill was hard enough without being further burdened. But as an arrow flashed by my face, I realised how exposed I was with neither armour nor shield. I lowered my head and powered on. I would be on them soon. I chose not to think about what would happen then.

Sensing movement to my left, I turned to see Gwawrddur close behind me. He grinned wolfishly, drawing his sword as he ran. With the Welsh swordsman at my side, my confidence grew and I let out a roar of defiance, tugging my own simple blade from its scabbard.

Another white-feathered arrow streaked towards me. Without thinking I dodged to the right and I felt the breath of it against my cheek. And then I was on them. There were six enemies I saw now, but there was no time for fear or trepidation.

I rounded the broad bole of a birch tree and, with a bellow, I rushed at the closest of them. He was a slender man, young, with sinewy arms and a straggly beard. He held a bow and was fumbling to nock another arrow. There was a small axe in his belt, and seeing me hurtling towards him, he dropped the bow and arrow and reached for the weapon. His indecision cost him his life. I was upon him before he could free the axe's head from his belt. His eyes widened and he tried to fling himself out of my path, but I swept down with my sword. The blade bit deeply into the base of his neck. Dark blood spurted from a severed artery and he collapsed with a moaning wail.

With the heightened alertness that always came over me in combat, I saw Gwawrddur parry a poorly timed sword blow, then strike down his opponent with a backhanded cut to the throat. The dying man fell to his knees, clutching at his neck in a pathetic attempt at halting the flow of his lifeblood.

Gwawrddur ignored the dying man and carried on beside me, towards the remaining four attackers. None of the men wore armour, but three of those left standing carried shields and they formed a small shieldwall, blocking our path between two trees. Behind them, the fourth man turned and ran northward, into the gloom of the forest.

Cursing in his people's musical tongue, Gwawrddur sprang forward. Without hesitation, I joined him. The men before us were brave and strong, but in those first instants, as we probed with our blades for signs of weakness, it became clear that our adversaries were no warriors. With incredible audacity, Gwawrddur moved in close to the shields. Sending a feint high to draw the left-most defender's attention up, the Welshman reached with his left hand for the hide-covered wooden board. Without pause, he yanked it to the side, uncovering his opponent's body, and plunged his sword into the man's belly.

With the litheness of a cat, Gwawrddur quickly skipped back out of the reach of the central man in the crumbling shieldwall.

Trusting that Gwawrddur would keep the second man occupied, I took the third. He was armed with a spear and he prodded and jabbed at my face over his shield rim. For a heartbeat, I watched the wicked spear-point, then, the instant he made another lunge, I darted forward, catching the spear haft in my left hand and pushing it off line, away from my body. At the same moment, I shoved hard. The man staggered, perhaps colliding with a root or a stone behind him. Stumbling backwards, he fell onto his back, holding his shield over his chest and midriff for protection. Still gripping tightly to the spear, I rammed its butt into the earth, and jumped forward, both feet landing hard on the shield, driving the air from the man's lungs.

His face was white. He stared up at me with terror in his eyes. But I was caught in the joyful, sinful ecstasy that comes from killing, and without hesitation, I smashed my sword blade into the top of his skull. Blood flowed, bright in the woodland shadows. His mouth opened in a scream I could barely hear over the waterfall's constant roar. For an instant, I stared into his eyes, as the light dimmed and the life left him, then I scanned the forest for the last man.

There was no sign of him. But Drosten and Os, the first to reach us, had seen the running figure and I watched their backs as they sped after him as fast as they were able. I was too far away now to stand any chance of catching him, and watching them run, I knew that neither the Pict nor the Northumbrian were fast enough to stop him escaping.

Spinning to my left I was just in time to see Gwawrddur step aside as the last man aimed a swiping overarm blow at him. If it had connected, it would have cut the Welshman from crown to belly, but the blade only met air, and the attacker, off-balance, staggered forward. Gwawrddur hacked down with his sword, severing the man's sword hand. The man's shriek was almost utterly engulfed in the growl of the falls. A heartbeat later he was silenced completely as Gwawrddur, with unerring sword-skill, sliced his head from his shoulders.

The man's head rolled to a halt on the soft loam before me, his unseeing eyes wide with the shock of how quickly his life had been snatched from him. Blood oozed from the neck, but the face was clean, as if he had scrubbed it in the river that morning. There was not a drop of blood on his features.

Only then did the reality of the action hit me. There had been no time to think before, but now I swallowed down the acid taste of bile. I looked away from the dead man's face, and the other corpses, and stared off through the trees. Drosten's black plait bobbed against his sweat-stained kirtle as he ran. Os was a few steps behind him. They were both already slowing their pace.

Gwawrddur wiped his blade on the clothes of the last man he had slain. Sheathing his sword, he took my weapon from my trembling hands and cleaned that too. Handing it back to me, he clapped me on the back, turning me around towards *Gullbringa*.

"You did well, Killer," he said.

I spat, trying to clean the taste from my mouth. I hated the name he had given me. But what other name would be better? I was a killer. And the worst of it was, I knew the truth of it. I enjoyed the killing.

It took me several attempts to slide my sword back into its scabbard.

Leofstan was kneeling beside Gersine. He looked up at me, his expression grave.

"Will he live?" I asked, my stomach churning at the thought of losing my friend.

"If we can get this arrow out soon, and if no evil has entered the wound, he will live. With God's grace."

Letting out a long, steadying breath, I nodded, glad of that news.

Drosten and Os returned shortly after. They were soaked in sweat, and their cheeks and foreheads were streaked with lichen, where they had pulled themselves through the trees and later rubbed the sweat from their eyes.

"Well?" snapped Hereward.

Drosten shook his head.

"He was too fast," he said, breathing hard. "We followed him to the top of the hill, but he'd already got into a log boat and was paddling fast upriver. There is another boat at the top of the falls. They must have been the boats we saw on the lake, north of Gudrun's island."

Hereward looked up through the canopy of the trees to the bright sky above, as if he was searching for an answer to a question there. Perhaps he was praying, I thought, with a pang of guilt at my own lack of prayer for those I had killed.

"Drosten, Os," Hereward said, his mind clearly made up. "Help Leofstan get Gersine into *Gullbringa*. It will make the boat a bit heavier, but he'll be safe there. We cannot stay here. Hunlaf, you have keen eyes. Go to the top of the falls and keep watch. We cannot afford to be attacked again. If you see anyone, come running."

Drosten moved to do Hereward's bidding, but I pulled him back. There was something that nagged at my mind.

"How did you hear me when I called over the noise of the

waterfall?" I asked, raising my voice and speaking close into his ear.

Drosten frowned.

"I didn't hear you," he said, shaking his head. "I thought you and Gersine were shirking your work. I was simply looking to find out where you were hiding instead of carrying those logs."

Forty-Four

Gersine let out a howl of pain that echoed from the steep slopes at either side of the valley. Ingvar flinched at the sound, his eyes darting and flicking, looking for threats in the trees or along the river.

"Keep the boy quiet," he hissed. He had been nervous ever since the attack. But now that we had camped, surrounded by the quiet sounds of the forest, he was as taut as a bowstring.

"Easy, Gersine," I said. He gripped my hand tightly. His face was wet with a sheen of sweat.

"Bite on this," said Leofstan, looking up from where he worked on the arrow jutting from Gersine's leg. The monk passed me a stick of birch wood from which he had stripped the bark.

"Try not to make too much noise," I said, placing the stick in Gersine's mouth. He stared at me with wide eyes and nodded. "Make it quick," I said to Leofstan, pleading with my eyes. Gersine was feeling the pain, but I was suffering too, helpless to do anything to alleviate his anguish.

"I am doing my best," said Leofstan. His face was pale, with colour high on his cheeks as he stooped again to the arrow head. "Hold this."

I could see what he wanted. Taking a deep breath, I released my hold on Gersine's hand and moved to the other side of his leg. I grasped the arrow shaft firmly, while Leofstan, having already cut into the wood with his knife, snapped off the fletchings.

I did my best to hold the arrow still, but Gersine shook and whimpered around the birch stick in his mouth as the arrow moved in his flesh.

"Are the knives hot enough?" asked Leofstan, flicking his glance towards Beorn, who was crouched by the fire.

Beorn, his hands wrapped in strips of cloth, pulled each of the two knives in turn from the embers and inspected their blades. They both glowed a dull red. He replaced them in the fire and nodded, his expression sombre.

"Good," said Leofstan. He began to recite the paternoster quietly. I joined him. When we had finished, he said, "Hold his leg still, Hunlaf. And Gersine, prepare yourself for the worst."

I took a firm hold on my friend's ankle and knee, ready to add my weight to holding the limb in place while Leofstan worked.

"Ready?" he asked.

I nodded, as did Beorn. Gersine groaned something unintelligible.

Without waiting any further, Leofstan took a tight grip of the arrow just below the iron head and pulled it hard. Gersine's moaning intensified and I struggled to hold his leg still as Leofstan tugged on the arrow that was grasped by the muscle and sinew it had passed through. For what seemed a long time Leofstan wrestled with the arrow and Gersine moaned and cried, biting down so hard into the wood that it splintered. Then, with a glut of dark blood, the arrow came free, sliding from Gersine's flesh.

Gersine trembled. His face was white and his eyes were scrunched shut. Blood seeped from the corner of his mouth where the splintered wood had cut his gums. More blood flowed from either side of his leg, from both where the arrow had entered and where it had left his flesh.

Beorn made to pull the hot knives from the fire, but Leofstan held up his hand.

"Let it bleed. The blood will help flush out any dirt that came in with the arrow."

We sat silently for several heartbeats, the only sound Gersine's shallow breathing, interspersed with his grunting moans of pain. Blood pumped from his wounds, dripping down his leg and into the earth.

"Now," said Leofstan, when he deemed enough time had passed and sufficient blood had flowed.

Beorn snatched up the blades from the fire. Each glowed dimly in the shadows of the trees and the great rock that shaded our campsite. The warrior dropped to his knees beside me and I could feel the heat washing off the knives. Beorn hesitated for the briefest of moments and then clamped the blades against the two puncture marks, enclosing Gersine's calf in a burning metallic grip.

Gersine screamed, his voice gurgling behind the splintered birch wood, before turning to weak sobbing. His body bucked and shook with the pain and Leofstan added his own weight and strength to mine to hold him still. The dusk air was filled with the scent of cooking meat and burnt hair. When the smoke stopped rising from the leg, Beorn pulled the blades away, pushing them back into the flames to burn off any remnants of Gersine's skin.

Gersine had gone limp, and I helped Leofstan to bandage his leg in clean cloths and then to wrap Gersine in a blanket.

I left Gersine to rest and walked a few paces away from the fire, down to the edge of the river beside *Gullbringa*. Kneeling, I splashed some of the cool water on my face.

Ingvar had climbed aboard his boat again and was staring

upstream. His nervousness was infectious and I peered upriver, but saw nothing apart from water, trees and rocks. Ingvar hadn't stopped looking northward since we had rejoined the river after the falls.

He had helped the others to heave *Gullbringa* up the rest of the slope without incident, while I'd kept watch as Hereward had ordered. Nothing had moved in the forest while I waited there. It had been strangely peaceful after the sudden violence. The sounds of the forest were hidden by the distant roar of the falls. The cascading water was much quieter up there. The mist hung, damp and cool over the calm water before it tumbled down over the ledge of rock.

I scrubbed Gersine's blood from my hands, then, when they were clean, dipped them into the water and drank from them like a cup. Looking at my hands, I thought back to waiting alone at the top of the falls. My hands had trembled for a time as I'd relived the fight. I had revelled in my prowess with a blade and the joy of besting my opponents, but worse than that was something that I barely admitted to myself. I had enjoyed the act of killing itself. I told myself that I was merely exalted at not having been killed, but deep down, I knew the truth of it. And so did God. I prayed for forgiveness, and not for the first time, and certainly not for the last, I wondered whether I was truly repentant. If I was, the Scriptures said that the Lord would forgive me. But could I continue living this life without becoming lost to the thrill of battle and the ecstasy of spilling blood?

As I stood there, waiting for the others to haul the boat through the forest, a sound and a sudden movement startled me. For a heartbeat, I thought an arrow was arcing overhead towards me and I flinched. But looking up, I saw a great white swan, wings wide and beating forcefully. It flew over the falls and soared upriver. It flew low to the water, its reflection mirroring its flight, until it vanished round the bend, lost behind the trees. I wondered at the sudden appearance of the white bird. Had it been a sign from God Himself? Had He sent the swan to show me that He forgave me?

I had thought about that swan several times that afternoon, as we'd rowed further up the river until Ingvar found the place he was looking for.

"It would be better if we did not stop," he'd said. "That log boat won't have been able to reach Ljósberari yet, but he might reach him tonight, if he doesn't halt. If not, he will be there by tomorrow."

Hereward had consulted briefly with Runolf.

"We will make camp here. Gersine needs to be treated, and Leofstan needs a fire."

Ingvar had shaken his head.

"We're dead already," he'd grumbled under his breath. "What difference does it make if the boy lives one more night?"

But he had steered us into the shade of an overhanging rock. Aspen sprouted from the soil atop the boulder, further shielding the river below.

We had eaten sparingly and Hereward had set guards in the trees around the camp. He'd placed Gwawrddur, whom he trusted most, atop the rock, where he could see any boat approaching down the river.

We had made camp earlier than we would have liked, but Hereward was right. If we had carried on, Gersine might well not have survived. I glanced at his blanket-wrapped form, still and pale beside the fire. As it was, it was not certain he would make it. But with Leofstan's care, at least he stood a chance.

It had taken some time to get the fire lit and hot enough to heat the knives, and now the sun had sunk beyond the mountains in the west and the river valley had been plunged into shadow. I stared up through the leaves of the aspens. There was yet some light in the sky beyond the mountains, but it would be dark soon enough. If what Ingvar had said was true, tomorrow we might well reach our destination.

I was suddenly overcome with a wave of tiredness. I would be called on to stand watch in the night, and if I didn't get any rest, I might disgrace myself by falling asleep at my post. Such a thing filled me with dread. I recalled Hereward's fury at Drosten when he had found the Pict asleep in Werceworthe when he was supposed to be on guard.

Making my way back to the fire, I shook out my blanket, preparing to lie down beside Gersine. Now that I had begun to contemplate sleep, my body responded. My eyelids grew heavy and I could barely keep them open as I stretched out on the ground. I placed my rolled up cloak beneath my head and closed my eyes.

I worried about what the next day would bring, but I was too exhausted to think of it now. Whatever came, I would face it as bravely as I could, but for now, I craved sleep like a thirsty man in a desert yearns for water. I could feel the welcome embrace of slumber enveloping me and I let out a long sigh.

But I never found the respite of sleep that evening. Where the dusk had been tranquil after the long day, the only sounds the rustle of the leaves, the fire's crackle, birdsong, and the trickle of the river against the hull of *Gullbringa*, lulling me to sleep, the gloaming was suddenly filled with a chaotic cacophony.

My eyes flicked open as a huge sound echoed over the river. It was unlike anything I had heard before, a resonant, rumbling growl that set the hair on my neck on end. It had the dark power of nightmare, like the scream of a devil in a fever dream. Pigeons shot into the sky, frightened from their perches in the forest.

I sat up, my hand dropping to the hilt of my sword. I was not certain I had truly heard the dreadful sound. Had I dreamt it?

Then I heard it again and the sound, deep, booming and filled with inhuman malice, made me leap to my feet. The next sound I heard reinforced the reality of this waking nightmare. The forest reverberated with the ululating cries of a man in terrible agony and fear for his life.

Forty-Five

The forest was loud with shouts and yells and the terrible, sonorous roars that sent fingers of dread scratching down my spine. Ulf was barking, adding his incessant yelping anxiety to the din. I surged up from my blanket, my weariness forgotten. Following Beorn and Hereward, I hurried into the twilight, tugging my sword from its scabbard.

Branches snapped ahead of us. A man howled in a paroxysm of pain. Another growling roar was followed by snarling and grunting and the sound of something large crashing through the undergrowth.

Runolf and Gwawrddur ran into our path, almost colliding with us in the gloom. For the first time I could recall, I saw fear on both of their faces. The shock of their fright heightened the terror I felt building within me.

"What is it?" shouted Hereward.

"Bear," was all Runolf could manage. He made to push past us, heading for the boat.

"A bear?" I asked.

"Run," screamed Gwawrddur. "There is nothing we can do now. We must flee."

I saw through the trees to either side of us, Os and Eadmaer leaping and bounding over bracken and brambles, hurrying down to the river.

We hesitated. Hereward looked set to carry on towards the noise.

Runolf shoved me aside.

"If you stay there, it will kill you. Bealdwulf tried to hold it off for a moment, but he's dead now. Nothing can stop a beast of that size. It is a monster."

Only moments earlier we had sat side-by-side next to the fire and chewed our dried fish in companionable silence. As ever, he had been quiet and serious, but he was a good man, strong and brave.

"Dead?" I said, my voice timid and almost lost in the clash and roar of the angry bear. I shook my head stupidly, trying to make sense of this madness. "Bealdwulf can't be dead." Surely Runolf must have been mistaken.

"Come on," shouted Runolf, tugging on my arm.

I could not move. The forest canopy ahead of us shuddered, and I wondered at the power needed to tremble the leaves of such massive trees.

The stocky figure of Bealdwulf staggered backwards into the clearing ahead of us. My heart lifted. He was yet alive! But then, with a twisting in my gut, I made out more details. Bealdwulf's face was awash with blood, his eyes gleaming white from a mask of red. His clothes were in tatters and even his iron byrnie had been rent in great gashes that exposed pallid flesh and bubbling blood. How he was still standing with such wounds, I will never know. He raised his sword, screaming defiantly, hurling abuse into the shadows beneath the trees.

And then I saw the bear and I knew Runolf was right. We could not hope to defeat this beast.

The bear's bulk was prodigious, its dark fur shaking and rippling as it lumbered forward, running on all fours. Rising up on its hind legs before Bealdwulf, the animal dwarfed the warrior. With a flick of a great paw, it swatted his sword away. Then, with a bellowing roar that made its snout quiver, its dagger-like fangs dripping with drool, it pounced with uncanny, terrifying speed. Bealdwulf was crushed beneath the huge creature. The bear bit down, closing its cavernous mouth over Bealdwulf's face. It shook the thickset warrior, worrying at his body like a dog shaking a rat and for a sickening moment, I hoped that the warrior was already dead.

For another heartbeat, I watched, unmoving. Then, with a hideous, crunching snap, Bealdwulf's skull shattered in the bear's maw.

I turned on my heel, and fled with the others.

Twigs and branches snapped and cracked behind us. The bear let out another deafening roar, followed by a series of deep grunting snorts. It sounded so close I imagined I could feel the animal's hot foetid breath on the nape of my neck. I was overcome with terror. The image and sound of Bealdwulf's skull splintering in the jaws of the bear filled my mind. I could think of nothing else save escape from this demonic beast of the forest.

I was the fastest runner in the company, and I sped past Hereward and the others, skidding down the leaf-strewn bank to where our small camp nestled beneath the great rock.

"Get into the boat!" I yelled as I ran. "Into the boat!"

I was welcomed by Ulf's barking. The small dog had not left his master's side and was now yapping from inside the boat, his paws resting atop the wale.

Leofstan and Ingvar had evidently not waited to be told what to do and had already lifted Gersine into *Gullbringa*. Now they both waited anxiously as, one by one, we tumbled into the camp. I scrabbled up the bark-covered side of the boat and without pause was at the foremost thwart, pulling an oar from where it lay. I was sliding the loom into the thole when

Gwawrddur and Runolf clambered aboard and took their places.

The bear's growls and groans had lessened now, but the monstrous creature was still close, and I scanned the tree line for any sign of it. I wondered whether it was feasting on Bealdwulf's flesh, tearing off great chunks of his face, licking the marrow and brains from the warrior's splintered bones.

Ingvar hurried to his place at the stern, while Leofstan helped the others to climb aboard. The fire still burnt in the small patch of clear ground beneath the towering, tree-clad rock.

Hereward remained on the riverbank until everyone was on *Gullbringa*. When Drosten had leapt over the strakes, Hereward accepted Leofstan's hand and allowed him to haul him up.

"Go! Go!" he shouted.

Leofstan touched his shoulder.

"Bealdwulf?" the monk asked.

Hereward shook his head and slumped down.

The bear roared once more, voicing its victory over the interlopers in its realm. None of us spoke as we heaved on the oars, and Ingvar steered us into the middle of the river. Silence wrapped around us, and we slid away upstream on the black waters as night fell, engulfing the river valley in darkness.

Forty-Six

"Why would a bear attack like that? With such ferocity?"

Os put words to a question that plagued all of our minds as we rowed in silent shock upriver. The sounds of the bear had long since been lost in the distance. We rounded a bend in the river, Ingvar navigating by the cold, pale light of the stars that were strewn across the night sky. A long time had passed since I could make out the glimmer from our abandoned campfire. For a time I had watched its glow, flickering on the water and, when we were far off, I fancied that I saw a great shadow there by the water's edge. I shivered at the memory, the fear of the bear bedded deep into my being. I could still not believe what had happened. Bealdwulf had been a stolid, steadfast companion, a constant presence in my life for months, and now he was gone, just as sure as if he had never been.

"Perhaps it was drawn by the scent of my blood," whispered Gersine, from where he sat, wrapped in a blanket, near to Ingvar. Ulf was curled up on Gersine's lap. The dog seemed to have already forgotten the commotion and now slept contentedly while Gersine stroked his head.

"Maybe," said Beorn, "but I think there was something else. I wonder if perhaps that was a mother protecting her cub."

"You think that was a she-bear?" asked Os, his tone incredulous. "I would not like to meet her husband then."

"Beorn is right," said Gwawrddur. "There are few things on this earth that will fight with more ferocity than a mother defending her child."

"But we saw no cub," said Os. He let out a long breath. "I think it was a spirit of the forest. This journey has felt cursed from the beginning."

"Shut your foolish mouth," snarled Runolf. Os fell silent, and we rowed on.

I suspected that Beorn and Gwawrddur were right. I thought of Wulfwaru back at Werceworthe. She had been willing to kill to protect her family. If there had been a cub somewhere nearby and the bear thought we were a threat, then the savagery of its attack made sense. But there was still a part of me that couldn't shake off Os' words. He was right. This journey had been beset by many difficulties, and, as we pulled *Gullbringa* ever closer to the heart of our quest, it seemed as though we were not rowing on a river, but gliding through a nightmare towards death and fire.

I sensed that the others felt it too. The mood was gloomy and dejected. I stared into the darkness and thought of Bealdwulf.

"We should not have run," I whispered. "If we had stood together against the bear, surely we would have prevailed."

"Hush, Hunlaf," said Gwawrddur. "We cannot change the past."

Shame flooded me like a cold tide and I wondered whether Os' talk of spirits and curses was his way of ameliorating his own feelings of guilt.

We carried on upriver, pulling on the looms without another word, the only sounds the drip of water and the occasional knock of the oars against the strakes. We rowed on like that for some time before Hereward called a halt.

"We need rest," he said.

This time Ingvar did not argue. He steered us towards the eastern riverbank. We had travelled a long way from the attack, and whilst I was sure that a bear of that size could cross the river, I was glad for the water between us and the huge beast.

We moored the boat and climbed ashore. There was even less clear ground than in our previous campsite and the men stamped down areas of bracken and weeds, making hollows in which they could sleep.

"No fire now," said Hereward, his voice not much more than a whisper. We were all subdued and hushed, but each sound we made echoed back from the trees and slope across the river. "We keep quiet tonight. How close are we, Ingvar?"

"We will reach Ljósberari's steading tomorrow."

Hereward crouched down close to the skipper. Runolf sat nearby, leaning his broad back against the bole of an alder.

"What are you thinking?" asked the Norse axeman.

"Tell us all you know of Ljósberari's settlement," Hereward said to Ingvar, who shifted his position, uncomfortable with the request. The two could understand each other well for the most part now, and they only occasionally turned to me to interpret.

"I know nothing really."

"You have been there before, no? To pay your tribute to Ljósberari when you passed by."

"Yes," admitted Ingvar, "but I did not tarry. Who would wish to remain in such a place?"

"My daughter might be there, boatman," Runolf said from the darkness, his voice thick with emotion. "Tell us what you know."

Ingvar took a deep breath.

"There is little to tell. There are a few houses and huts, but they are poorly built things. Shacks really. It is a settlement built by thralls." He paused, as if no further explanation was needed. When nobody responded, he went on. "The buildings, such as they are, will surely not survive once the winter snows come."

"And Ljósberari?"

"He lives in the biggest house. A hall, really, though it is not a grand thing."

"Is there a wharf?"

Ingvar nodded.

"Two. Ljósberari's people came by boat, and they have taken many more from the people hereabouts."

"Can the place be approached without being seen?"

"Not from the water. They have people watching the river to the north and south. The forest reaches close to the cleared area where the buildings are. They will have guards, but you might be able to get to the edge of the woods unseen."

Hereward was quiet for a time. He stared out at the star-dotted black water of the river and we waited for him to speak.

"We will be heavily outnumbered," he said. "It would be best not to fight Ljósberari's people openly."

Runolf grunted.

"We will rest up here during the day," Hereward said at last. "We cannot risk being seen before we reach our goal. Pull *Gullbringa* in close to the bank and do your best to cover it with boughs, in case anyone passes on the river. Our best chance to take Ljósberari will be to go in at night. Ingvar, you will take us as close as possible and await our return. The rest of us will approach quietly through the forest. When we get there, we will take stock of things. Then some of us will untie their boats, sending them downriver. We don't want to kill Ljósberari, only to find we have all his people chasing after us."

We listened intently, trying to imagine putting this simple plan into action. There were so many things that could go wrong. We had never even seen the place and were relying on Ingvar's memory when he had only been there briefly several weeks before. Much could have changed since then. But a simple plan was better than no plan at all.

"While the boats are released, we will create a diversion, something to draw men away from Ljósberari's hall."

"A fire in one of the furthest buildings could work," I said. My dreams had been swirling with flames ever since we had embarked on this journey. Fire followed in Ljósberari's wake, so it seemed fitting that fire would be part of his ultimate downfall.

Hereward nodded.

"Then, in the confusion, we will go in and kill that bastard."

"And Chlotar too," said Runolf, his tone obdurate, brooking no dissent.

"Pray for us, Leofstan," said Hereward. "If there has ever been a time for prayer, it is now."

"Remember," I said, imagining the chaos that would surround us if we managed to enact Hereward's plan, "we have heard that many of Ljósberari's people are children. Innocents. And if Aelfwyn and Revna are amongst them, we cannot leave until they are safe."

Leofstan patted my shoulder, making me flinch at the unexpected touch.

"We must not allow the flames of our attack to consume those who are blameless for Ljósberari's sins," he said. Something in his tone made me wonder if he was concerned for the people or the fate of the book, if we put the buildings to the torch.

Hereward leaned forward, his voice low and sombre. It was so dark under the trees that I could only make out his shape by the absence of the reflected starlight on the river behind him.

"Our quarrel is not with children," he said, "nor lowly thralls who have had no say in this madman's actions. Things will not be simple when the fires are lit and the fighting starts.

We will do our best to avoid killing those who do not deserve death. With God's grace, your kin will be hale and well, and they will come to us when they understand what is happening."

"If Revna is there," said Runolf, "I will find her, and any man who stands in my way will feel the bite of my axe."

"I will not leave without Aelfwyn," said Eadmaer, who had been silent ever since the encounter with the bear.

"We will find her," I said, hoping that would prove to be true. It was hard to imagine any good coming of this venture, but I clung to the possibility that my cousin could be saved. We had come too far to think otherwise.

"Now," said Hereward, "get some rest. Who will take the first watch with me? I need two men."

"I will guard with you," I said.

The exhaustion that had smothered me earlier had fled, driven away by the bear's roars and the vision of Bealdwulf's death. I could not think of sleep yet. I was certain that as soon as I closed my eyes, I would see again Bealdwulf's skull crushed in the jaws of the monstrous forest beast.

"I will watch too," said Gwawrddur.

The men settled down to sleep by the river's edge. Hereward led Gwawrddur and me away from the camp for a few paces. The foliage was dense. Thorns and twigs snagged at my cloak like grasping fingers, tugging at me from the darkness. For a short while, the three of us huddled close beneath a great fir tree.

"I will take the north," Hereward said. This was the closest to Ljósberari's settlement, and therefore, he must have imagined it would be the most dangerous. "Gwawrddur, you take the east. Hunlaf, you watch to the south. When you feel yourself growing tired, head back to the camp and rouse someone to replace you. Do not linger longer than you are able. We are close to the lair of our prey now, and we cannot afford to let our guard down."

Each of us made our way deeper into the woods. Brambles caught in my leg wraps and I had to reach down to free myself. The thorns scratched my fingers and I sucked blood from them as I continued some way south. For a time I could hear Gwawrddur and Hereward moving through the trees, but when I halted by the broad, gnarled trunk of a yew, I listened to the night and heard nothing.

I leaned against the rough bark of the tree and peered into the absolute blackness. Pulling my cloak about me, I settled myself for a long night. After some time alone in the total hush and impenetrable blackness, my eyes began to deceive me. I thought I saw movement in the dark. But when I blinked, there was nothing there apart from the night and the shadowed trees.

When we had been preparing the defences of Werceworthe, Gwawrddur had said that no plan survived the first meeting with the enemy. I have never forgotten that. He was right, of course. Battle is unpredictable, and your foe will often surprise you, sometimes anticipating your moves, at other times making their own move that seems to fly in the face of all logic. The Welshman's adage has been proven correct to me many times over the years. On most of those occasions, there was nothing that I, or indeed anyone, could have done to prevent a sudden change to the plans. But on that dark night in the forest of Rygjafylki, there can be nobody to blame for what happened next, but me. When I think back to that time when I was still young and strong, I am ashamed that I have reached such an old age. For my actions that night ultimately led to the deaths of others, and even now, I wonder why I was spared, when they were not.

I have already written of how tired I was and how sleep had beckoned to me before the bear attacked Bealdwulf. And I have oft told of how I was proud and foolish as a young man, believing myself somehow immortal and free from the weaknesses of others. That night, leaning against the trunk of the yew, enveloped in the cool darkness, I stupidly thought I could remain awake and vigilant. If there was any justice in the world, I would have been killed right there in that forest. And yet here I am, writing this tale decades later and far away, when better men than I have long ago been committed to the earth.

The first moment I knew I had fallen asleep, was when the cold steel of a blade pressed against my throat and a powerful hand clamped down over my mouth.

Forty-Seven

"Not a sound, or you're dead," hissed a strangely accented voice in Norse. The man's breath was warm on my face. It smelt of wild garlic and thyme. The acrid odour of smoke lingered about him too, like a cloud. For a sickening instant I wondered if I was dreaming, but then the knife blade at my throat scratched my skin and rough hands pulled me to my feet. There were shapes in the darkness around me, but I could not make out their faces.

Cursing myself for the weakness that had led to me falling asleep, I instinctively reached for the weapons that hung from my belt. The man who held me slapped my hands away.

"Take his blades," he whispered and someone stepped close. I felt my sword and seaxes tugged from their scabbards.

"Let's kill him," hissed a voice. It sounded like it belonged to an excited child.

"No," said the man holding the knife at my neck. "The master wants them alive."

"He won't know if we kill some of them," moaned the child voice.

"You think you can lie to *him*?" replied the man who held me, his tone mocking. "Do you truly believe he would not know?"

Silence.

They bound my hands behind my back and used one of my own seaxes to cut strips of cloth from my cloak. One of these they rolled into a wad and stuffed into my mouth, another was tied around my head to secure it there. The rough cloth rubbed painfully at the corners of my mouth and the greasy wool on my tongue made me gag. But the discomfort was as nothing compared to the anguish I felt at having been captured so easily.

When I was tied up, the leader of the group removed his knife from my throat and pushed me forward.

"Quietly," he whispered to his comrades.

I could not see how many of them there were. Perhaps a dozen. But they moved off stealthily, heading towards our camp. We were some distance from where my friends were resting beside the river and I knew, as surely as I have ever known anything, that it was my duty to warn them of our approach. The shadowy forms around me rustled through the undergrowth, making little more noise than a breeze through the forest. I walked with them, treading as carefully as I was able. Sound travels far in the stillness of the night, but the thick trunks of the trees and the dense foliage might mask a distant noise. If I attempted to alert Runolf and the others too soon, my signal could be missed entirely, or mistaken for the night-time movements of an animal.

I recited the paternoster silently in my mind and tried to calculate how far we had gone in the gloom, and how much further remained until we would reach my friends. An owl screeched, its pained voice a jolt that ripped the silence asunder. Everybody stopped moving. The leader's hand grasped my shoulder and once again I felt the steel of his knife at my throat. He did not speak. No words were necessary. I stood still, breathing through my nose, pushing my tongue against the cloth in my mouth in an effort to dislodge it.

The night bird called again. We waited. Silence once more

draped like a thick cloak over the forest. With a gentle shove on my back, we set off. The knife was withdrawn from my skin, but the memory of its touch was yet fresh and I imagined its cold metal still.

All about me, I sensed the figures drifting away into the gloom, leaving me with only a handful of captors. I had not heard them speak, so their movements must have been part of a pre-arranged plan. How thoughtlessly we had wandered into Ljósberari's lair. But if I had been watchful, we might have been warned in time to defend ourselves. Again, I cursed my pride and stupidity. I pictured the location of the camp and where we now must be. I imagined Ljósberari's people stealthily sneaking between the shadows of the trees, circling round to come at my friends from all sides. We must be close to *Gullbringa* and the resting men, I thought. If I gave my attackers any more time to move into position, Gwawrddur and Hereward might suffer the same fate as me. Or worse.

I had to act now.

The leader of the band was close behind me. I could smell his breath and the reek of wood smoke on his clothes. I recalled the cold steel of his knife, but fear would not dissuade me from my course.

I offered up a silent prayer, and, with no warning, I threw myself sideways into the undergrowth. At the same moment I let out a moaning wail. My voice was muffled and strained behind the gag, but nonetheless it was loud in the dark hush of the forest. I crashed through the sharp thorns of a bramble. My grunted shouts, still trapped behind the wad of woollen cloth wedged in my mouth, rose in pitch as the briars ripped painfully at my face.

I could hear nothing beyond the noise I was making. I wondered whether any of the others had heard, but this was my only chance and I dared not stop. I thrashed and moaned, kicking my feet out to rattle against twigs and fallen branches.

I churned up the leaf-mould and the scent was rich and thick all around me.

The leader's bulk was suddenly on me, driving the air from my lungs. He punched me in the face, hard, and the dark of the night flared bright for an instant. He hit me again, and I ceased my frantic movements. He didn't waste time with words for me. He just grabbed hold of my gag and my tied arms and yanked me painfully to my feet. The brambles again scratched my cheeks and snagged in my clothes, and my shoulders screamed as my arms were pulled backwards.

I stood, swaying before him.

"I should gut you now," he hissed in my ear.

But he did not. We both stood and listened to the night. For a heartbeat, there was silence, and then my heart leapt as Ulf began barking. A moment later, I heard Runolf's deep voice.

"Who is there?"

The man behind me tensed, and I thought he would not answer. We could hear the men in the camp stirring. Ulf continued barking for a time, until Ingvar snapped at the dog to be silent. It was easy to imagine the men rising from their blankets, alert now, sliding blades from sheaths. There were whispers, too quiet to make out words from this distance. But the urgency in them was clear. We were close enough that they had heard me. I let out a long breath. Whatever else the night held in store for us, my friends would not be taken unawares.

Clearly coming to the conclusion that the moment for stealth was over, the leader once more placed his blade at my neck. With a punch in my kidneys, he propelled me forward.

"I have your man here," he called out, his voice loud and sharp. "Throw down your weapons, or he dies."

"If you have one of ours," said Runolf, his voice eerily calm, "show yourself."

Without prompting from their leader, the remaining men around me slipped into the forest, spreading out.

"If you try anything else," whispered the leader, his lips close to my ear, "I will kill you." To emphasise his words he pressed his blade into my throat, just above my Adam's apple. I felt the sting as the knife broke my skin and the warmth as blood trickled down to my chest. Trusting that his warning would be heeded, he shoved me onward. He held me close, his knife never wavering from my throat. I was in no doubt that if fighting commenced, I would be the first to die.

We stepped into the small clearing beside *Gullbringa*. Ulf growled deep in his throat. Ingvar tapped the beast on the nose and hissed a command. The dog fell silent. There was some starlight here, filtering in from the open sky above the river. I could make out the shadowed shapes of the trees across the water. The dawn must already be colouring the eastern sky. Most of the night had passed. Again, I felt the pang of guilt at failing my comrades.

Although it was still dark, after the absolute blackness beneath the trees, I could see the men clearly enough. Their faces were pale in the gloom as they all turned in our direction. I groaned, trying to warn them that there were more men in the forest. I stared at Runolf, eyes wide and pleading, willing him to understand.

The leader's grasp on me tightened.

"Hunlaf," said Leofstan in Englisc, "are you hurt?"

In the darkness they could not see that my mouth was bound. I moaned behind my gag.

"What have you done to him?" asked Runolf, his tone still calm, but taking on an edge of threat now that he saw he was dealing with only one adversary.

"He is well enough," said the man who held me, "but if you do not drop your weapons, his blood will soak the earth before sunrise."

Before anyone could respond, there was a snapping of twigs from the other side of the clearing. Ulf began to bark again, a cutting yelping that rent the night. Runolf and the others turned to see who approached. Gwawrddur and Hereward hurried out of the forest, their swords drawn.

It only took moments for them to understand what had happened. They joined Runolf and the others. Ingvar again snapped at his dog, silencing it.

I was desperate to make them all understand that there were many more enemies out there in the forest. Even now they must have been creeping quietly towards us from every side. But I could do nothing more than whimper behind my gag, as my captor applied painful pressure to his knife's blade.

"Drop your weapons now," he said, his voice dripping with danger, "or the boy's blood flows. The time for talking has passed."

"You speak strangely," said Runolf. "Are you Ljósberari's lackey? The Frank called Chlotar?"

The man clutching me stiffened.

"I am no man's lackey," he said. "But I am glad my battle-fame precedes me." I felt his chest swell with pride behind me and I wondered what kind of man would respond so when faced with nearly a dozen enemies. But of course, he knew he was not alone. And we had already heard tales of what sort of man Chlotar was. I shuddered now at his touch, imagining all those he had tortured and killed before. Surely my death would mean nothing to such a man.

"So Ljósberari is but a man then?" replied Runolf. "We had heard he was a god."

"He is a great man," spat Chlotar. "You will meet him soon enough. Then you will know the truth of his greatness."

"He cannot be that great if he sends one such as you to do his bidding." Runolf hawked and spat, showing his disdain for the Frank. "A powerful man would command strong warriors, not cowards and weaklings."

To my surprise, Chlotar laughed. I heard madness in his cackling, and I shivered again.

"You think you can taunt me with your pathetic words?" His voice became measured then, calm and resonant, and I was reminded of the tone used by monks when offering up prayers to the Almighty. "I have gazed on the light of truth. I am Ljósberari's instrument amongst mortal men." He paused. "And who, pray, are you?"

"I am Runolf Ragnarsson," the great axeman said, his voice rumbling like a far-off rockfall, "and I will kill you, Chlotar the Frank."

"You are a brave one, I will give you that, Runolf Ragnarsson. But you will not be so bold before the end, I promise you. No man is courageous when his eyes have been plucked out and the purifying fires of light are licking around his limbs. Oh, no." He sounded almost sorry, as if remembering the suffering he had caused brought him pain. "No man is brave then." He stared at Runolf, and I wondered how much Chlotar had pieced together from his name. "And no woman either." He laughed again. Runolf snarled and took a pace closer. His huge axe was in his hand and I wondered if he might throw it at Chlotar. Perhaps I could allow myself to fall, presenting Runolf with an open target. But Chlotar's knife was still hard against my skin and I could not move.

Runolf must have seen the futility of the situation. He held his ground, glowering at Chlotar, his eyes burning with a hatred that made the Frank chuckle. Without warning, perhaps sparked by Chlotar's disturbing, throaty laughter, Ulf broke free from his master and rushed towards us, yapping and growling. The dog flew at us fast, but to my amazement, Chlotar was even faster. With a kick to the back of my legs behind my knees, he sent me sprawling forward into the mud. I could do nothing to halt my fall. I twisted my face to the side, but still my right cheek hit the earth hard enough to rattle my teeth. Before I had finished falling, without hesitation, Chlotar drew a sword from its scabbard and in a single fluid motion hacked down at the snapping animal that rushed towards him. Ulf yelped. The dog whined piteously, shuddered and then was still. Chlotar's blade had severed its spine and almost cleaved it in two. My face was only a hand's breadth from the poor creature's snout as it died. It stared at me, as the light left its eyes, and I thought I saw disappointment in its animal gaze.

Ingvar screamed and ran forward. Beorn lunged out, reaching for him in an effort to hold him back, but the boatman was mad with grief and anger, and he escaped the warrior's grasp and rushed at Chlotar. I was certain the Frank would slice him down with as much ease as he had killed the man's dog, but Ingvar never reached the swordsman. He staggered to a halt a few paces from him. He rose up straight, straining on his toes. Making claws of his hands, he reached over his shoulders, as if he had an itch he could not scratch. Stumbling forward a step, he fell to his knees and from where I lay in the muck, looking over Ulf's still form, I saw the bright white feathers of two arrows jutting from between Ingvar's shoulder blades. As Ingvar collapsed forward, Chlotar pounced on me, hauling me to my feet, and placing his bloodied sword to my neck.

"Drop your weapons now, or you all die," he shouted, all calm gone from his voice. "And the boy will be first."

I saw the pale faces of my sword-brothers turn as they glanced about them, taking in the dark figures that now surrounded us. I counted at least twenty adversaries, and perhaps half of them had white-fletched arrows nocked to the strings of their bows.

With a sinking in my stomach, I watched as, one by one, the men with whom I had travelled from Northumbria dropped their weapons on the ground and allowed themselves to be bound.

Forty-Eight

Once we all had our hands tied tightly behind our backs, Chlotar ordered a couple of his men to make a fire. With practised speed, they struck sparks to tinder, and quickly had a small blaze burning. The flickering light danced over Ingvar and Ulf, giving the impression that they both yet breathed and moved. Panic began to rise within me. Did they plan to burn us here, beside the river? I swallowed back my anxiety with difficulty, almost choking on the wool that filled my mouth. To prevent myself thinking too much on our fate, I scanned the faces of our captors, searching for any sign of weakness. I saw none. Chlotar was lithe and strong, his face scarred and hard. He licked his lips as the flames leapt up. His small eyes seemed not to reflect the growing blaze, but rather to swallow the light from the fire, making his gaze black and cold.

The rest of the dark-clad people around us were a motley throng, no doubt made up of escaped thralls and perhaps some of the children Ljósberari was said to have taken from the places he had destroyed. Several were boys, too young even to have straggly fluff growing on their lips or chins, but I was soon reminded that no matter their youth, they were deadly.

One sauntered over to Ingvar's corpse.

"Look," he said, laughing. "I told you my arrow was the one to slay the old fool."

He dropped down beside the body and proceeded to cut the arrows out of the cooling flesh.

Another young archer joined him and they began arguing heatedly over who had landed the better shot.

I turned away, sickened.

There were a couple of women amongst them, and I noticed the youngest looking at me with open interest. Her face was stern, her lips set in a scowl, but her eyes were wide and expressive, and even though her fair hair was covered with a hood, and her body was hidden beneath a drab cloak, her beauty could not be completely hidden. I met her gaze and she looked away. She was little more than a girl I realised, and I wondered at the things she had seen in her short life.

"Well might you look," sneered Chlotar.

I thought he was addressing me, but when I turned, I saw he was staring at Runolf. The massive axeman was scowling at the girl.

"She is no longer yours, Runolf Ragnarsson," said Chlotar, reaching for her and pulling her close. "Oh yes," the Frank went on with a dark chuckle, "do not think I did not recognise your name. But do not imagine for an instant that you will be spared. You have lived too long in the darkness and the master will watch your soul purified soon enough."

With a glance at Runolf's face I understood.

"Revna," he muttered. "Daughter."

Pulling away from Chlotar's grasp, the girl moved to stand before Runolf. For a time she stared up at him, her expression impassive, inscrutable. Then, with the speed I had witnessed in Runolf when he fought, she lashed out and struck him across the cheek. The sound was shockingly loud in the pre-dawn dark of the forest. The chorus of birds that had begun to call and sing with the coming of the day, fell silent once more, frightened by the sudden slap.

"Do not speak to me, old man," she said, her eyes narrowing with loathing. "You abandoned us." Hot emotion bubbled beneath the surface of her words. For a heartbeat, her expression softened. She sighed as she looked up at her father. But then her features hardened once more and she hissed, "You are to blame for all of it. Mother is dead because of you."

Runolf reeled, her words clearly hurting him much more than the slap.

"I did not..." he stammered. "I... I'm sorry."

"I care nothing for your apology," she said. "It comes much too late." She hesitated, seemingly unsure what to say now. Her anger had flared up and died down as quickly as a drop of fat falling into a fire. She drew in a deep breath. "I am Chlotar's now."

The Frank giggled from where he watched the exchange.

With a last look into her father's face, Revna said, "I will enjoy watching you burn." Done now with Runolf, she strode back to Chlotar, who wrapped an arm around her and grinned.

Runolf's face crumpled and his shoulders slumped. He had smouldered with a simmering rage ever since learning of his wife's death. The thought of vengeance and of possibly finding his daughter alive had given him focus and a reason to live. Now, with Revna's damning rejection, his anger had been snuffed out like a rush light pinched between thumb and forefinger.

On seeing Runolf's abject sorrow, Chlotar laughed again. My heart twisted for my friend. I wanted to offer him a word of comfort, but my mouth was still filled with the rough, grease-laden wool.

"Don't worry," Chlotar said, "you will not need to live with the knowledge of your failure for long, and you will see your wife again soon enough." Chlotar paused, as if expecting a response. Runolf did not meet his stare. He did not look away from his daughter. His cheeks glistened wetly in the flame light. Chlotar sighed, apparently disappointed at the lack of reaction. "Burn the boat," he said.

Gullbringa had already been emptied of our provisions. Anything we had left inside was now piled on the earth beside the river. The two men who had lit the fire took branches and, using them like tongs, flicked the burning brands into the belly of the boat. A couple of the logs fizzled out, hissing with steam as they fell into the puddles in the bilge of the sexæringr. I prayed that the fire would not catch, but it was pointless. If Chlotar wanted to destroy the boat, there was nothing that would stop him.

"Put him inside the boat," said Runolf, surprising us all by speaking.

"What?" asked Chlotar, frowning.

"Ingvar," said Runolf, indicating the bloody corpse that was sprawled beside Ulf. "His dog too. You have killed them, now at least send them on their way to the afterlife together."

Chlotar stared down at the bodies. The young men had finished their discussion and, having plucked the arrows from Ingvar's back, they now looked with excitement at the boat that had begun to smoke where some of the coals had caught.

"You are a fool," Chlotar said, shaking his head. "Cut the boat free," he snapped. "We don't want the forest to burn around our ears."

Gullbringa was ablaze now and we watched in silence as the last vestige of Ingvar's life was untied and pushed into the river. It drifted slowly, the heat from the flames hot on our backs, as we headed into the forest prodded on by the sharp points of spears. Ingvar and Ulf remained where they had died, blood-streaked and unmoving in the trembling shadows of the boat's pyre.

The birds once again began their chorus to the dawn and

soon the crackling and hissing of the burning boat was lost in the distance. The scent of its smoke was heavy in the air long after we lost sight or sound of its burning.

When we walked out from beneath the shadows of the trees, the sky was already light with the sun that had risen behind the mountains in the east. My mouth was stuffed with the strip of cloth cut from my cloak and I longed to be rid of it. I wanted to be able to offer comfort to Runolf, though what I would have said, I have no idea. But more than that, I remember feeling the utter despair of one who has let down those who trusted him. We were captives of our enemy because I had fallen asleep, and I yearned for a glance from Leofstan or Gwawrddur, or one of the others. Perhaps a word of consolation that would allow me to assuage my guilt. But none of my friends spoke or even looked at me, and we trudged on in dejected silence, as the sun rose over Ljósberari's domain.

Forty-Nine

I have faced danger many times in my life. I have stood in shieldwalls, vastly outnumbered by raving tribesman on the steppes of the Oguz il. I have fought howling pirates of the Kingdom of Kush under the harsh sun of the sea they called the Great Green. I have been attacked by cut-purses and brigands in the shadowy night streets of Byzantion, Roma and Išbīliya. I have done all these perilous things and more. And when standing before armed foes, only a madman would feel no fear. My bowels would turn to water, and the sound of my heart thumped in my ears. But at such times, it was my sword-skill, courage, God's will, and some would say, luck, that decided who would survive and who would end their life in the swift clash of blades.

I have been held captive more than once, and the fear I have felt at such times does not compare to what I ever felt when fighting. To be bound and defenceless, at the mercy of one who means you harm, eats away at your nerve like a rat gnawing at apples stored for the winter.

As we were led into the small settlement where Ljósberari was the ruler, the terror I had managed to keep at bay as we plodded through the dawn forest gripped me in a painful embrace. I could barely breathe as the rising sun picked out details of the erstwhile thrall's dominion.

The path we followed was lined with the twisted, blackened husks of men and women. The earth at either side of the track was dark with the ashes of countless bonfires. At some, the stakes that had supported the victims had collapsed, perhaps burnt through by the ferocity of the conflagration. On those heaps of ashes, the charred corpses were mercifully more difficult to make out. They were blackened humps of burnt bones and flesh, and it was possible to pretend they had not once belonged to people. But many of the stakes yet stood, and on several of them, the remains of Ljósberari's victims could be seen clearly enough. Contorted and gnarled like old trees, the dead watched our passing, their empty eye sockets staring down.

Ljósberari's people had talked to each other as we walked northward. The two young men still bickered and boasted about their prowess with a bow, while some of the others talked of inconsequential things, such as what food there might be on their return. Even the most talkative of them fell silent as we walked between the rows of burnt bodies.

A light wind rustled the boughs of the trees, lifting flakes of ash into the air, to drift about us like grey snow. The sun was warm, but I trembled as if caught in the coldest of blizzards.

"Looks like my father won't secure that trading agreement with fat King Hjorleif after all," said Gersine, breaking the silence. He winced as he put weight on his leg. On seeing Gersine's injury by the light from the flames that consumed *Gullbringa*, Chlotar had ordered his hands to be untied.

"I told you I had struck one of them at the waterfall," one of the brash archers had said.

"Before you ran away," replied the other.

"If I had not run," snapped the first, anger colouring his voice, "you would not have been warned of their coming. The master was pleased that I brought word."

"Ljósberari would have known whether you had fled or not, Naddod," Chlotar had said then with a knowing smile. "But you did right to bring us word. Better to hear of things from two messengers than none." Chlotar had signalled to Gersine, who tottered with difficulty, favouring his left leg. "Hold on to two of your companions. And if you try anything, I will kill you."

"At least then this damned leg will stop hurting," Gersine had replied. Chlotar had raised his eyebrows at the young man's display of bravado. I too was surprised by Gersine's courage, but I have learnt over the years that some men discover their courage when confronted with danger and adversity. Others, who you had thought would be stalwart in a time of crisis, lose their strength the way water trickles from a cracked pot, leaving a hollow vessel that is good for nothing.

Gersine offered me a thin smile now as he stumbled along between Beorn and Os. The two warriors scowled at me, less forgiving than their lord's son. I did not blame them.

The settlement was as Ingvar had described it. A collection of ramshackle buildings strewn about a cleared area of land bounded by the river on the west, forest to the north and south, and a soaring, wooded slope to the east. At the centre of the settlement was a long hall. Its roof was shingled in timber and in the bright light of the morning I could see that it was well-maintained. It was older and more solid than the rest of the constructions and must surely have been built before the coming of Ljósberari and his people. For a heartbeat I wondered who it had belonged to and what had become of them. Then the shadow of one of the grisly totems fell over me and I shook my head at my foolishness.

From the buildings came dozens of people, streaming out into the day to see their master's latest victims. I counted perhaps a score of adults, both men and women. They walked towards us slowly, warily, their faces forbidding and dark.

Before them ran a throng of children. There were perhaps more than a hundred, of all ages. From tiny snivelling, snot-nosed toddlers, to rangy youths, all gangly arms and willowy legs. They swarmed about us, shouting questions to our captors and hurling insults at us. Podgy fingers tugged at our clothing and pinched our exposed skin.

Hereward, Gwawrddur, Leofstan and Drosten kept their gaze ahead of them, walking in a dignified silence. Eadmaer shouted at the children, screaming at them in Englisc, his fear coalescing into a furious impotent rage. The children laughed and one, a stocky boy with soot-stained cheeks and hair as black as ink rushed forward and punched the Northumbrian in the stomach. Eadmaer doubled over, winded.

A jab from a spear made him stagger on, his face red with his pent-up fury, but he ceased his shouting.

Runolf moved with his head lowered and shoulders slumped, more like an ox being led to slaughter, than the powerful warrior I knew. He did not acknowledge the children's presence. The adults stared at him, taking in his bulk with a mixture of awe and contempt. None of the children approached the tall Norseman.

Os and Beorn, half-carrying Gersine, appeared barely to notice the crowd around them, but Os had clearly been biding his time. When a slender boy with plaited fair hair darted forward, a stone in hand to strike at one of the trio, Os exploded into action, catching the youth unawares. Waiting until the boy was close enough, Os pulled away from Gersine's hold on his neck and took a quick pace forward. At the same time, he swung his right foot in a powerful kick that connected with the incoming boy's groin. Such was the force of the blow, that the boy was lifted from his feet. He collapsed on the ash-speckled ground, crying and coughing from the pain.

"That'll teach him," said Os with a vicious grin of victory.

His triumph was short-lived. An instant later he was

sprawled on the earth. One of the captors struck the back of his skull with the butt of his spear and in a seething rush, the children fell on Os, howling and wailing like wild animals. We were held back by the threat of the wicked spear-points and there was nothing we could do but watch as the children kicked and pummelled the warrior. Os tried to push himself to his feet, snarling and shouting at his attackers, but with his hands tied behind his back, it was impossible.

Audun had described the sound of the attack at Sørbø as like the voices of devils. On hearing the ululating howling that emanated from the pack of children, I thought the description apt. With savage abandon, they punished Os for his audacity at having struck one of their own and I watched helplessly as the warrior's struggles lessened. Eventually, he grew still, his limbs limp, his head flopping on his neck when one of the larger boys kicked his blood-streaked face.

When it seemed Os must surely be dead, Chlotar pulled the children away. He shouted at them to make way, and had some of his band of warriors drag Os' limp and bloodied form as we were driven towards the river.

There were more bodies there, perhaps as a warning to anyone approaching on the water. Some, like those lining the path from the forest, had been burnt. Others hung naked and obscene from the branches of a great ash tree that jutted out over the river. They reminded me of the tokens left on the boughs of the trees at Gudrun's glade.

Dragging my gaze from the vile fruit of the tree, I saw our destination. Down by the wharfs where several log boats and large craft were moored, was what looked like a sizeable storage building. When Chlotar pulled the stout door open, the miasma of human waste that assailed our nostrils made the nature of what had been stored there clear.

We were shoved unceremoniously inside. The stench was overwhelming, unbearable. Beorn and Gersine tripped at the threshold and both tumbled into the churned mud of the floor. It was a thick quagmire of ordure and piss, a reeking memory of the building's previous inhabitants. Gersine cried out in pain at the jolt in his leg and I prayed that when we had sealed his wounds, we had done enough. If the cuts were yet open, it would be a miracle if his leg did not fester in here.

Os' limp form followed us into the noisome hut that would serve as our cage. They tossed him into the shadowed interior and he plummeted onto Beorn and Gersine. He made no effort to break his fall, and again I wondered if he was dead. But as Gersine and Beorn struggled up, moving Os as they did so, the battered warrior let out a small moan.

The door was slammed shut and we heard a bar drop into place on the outside. The hut's walls were fashioned of thick pine planks, the door of solid oak. There was no way we could break out. We were imprisoned as surely as if the building had been made of stone. The sounds of the chattering children and our captors drifted away. We were left in the filth and stink, the only sound the droning buzz of the flies that circled in the darkness.

Gersine was the only one of us whose hands were not tied, and he set about freeing us. With each unbound prisoner, there was another pair of hands, so it was not long before my wrists were untied and we were all free to move about our small cell. I pulled the gag from my mouth, spitting to rid myself of the taste of the dirty wool. Now that I could breathe more easily, I took in deep breaths. I quickly regretted it. The cloth in my mouth had prevented me from experiencing the full depth of the smell of our prison and now, as the pungent stink hit the back of my throat, I retched. I rubbed at where the rope had chafed my wrists, but the discomfort was nothing compared to my sorrow and guilt.

It was Leofstan who had untied me, and he placed a hand on my shoulder.

"You must not blame yourself," he said in a whisper.

"Then who is to blame, brother monk?" snarled Eadmaer, overhearing Leofstan's words. "It seems to me that had Hunlaf done his duty, we would not have been captured."

Beorn, who was busy untying the knots that bound Os' hands, growled, agreeing with Eadmaer. They were not wrong, and I slumped down in the corner furthest from the door.

It was dark inside the hut, but enough light leaked through the cracks between the planks and under the door to allow us to see. It was only early in the morning, and the sun that beat down on the roof was rapidly heating the building. The stink grew ever stronger, if that were possible, as the temperature rose. It soon felt as though the dark interior of the building was thick with a warm fog of shit and piss.

"Do not sit there feeling sorry for yourself, Hunlaf," said Hereward. "Help Leofstan with Os."

"I am not sure what we can do," said the old monk, moving to Os' side. "We have no water, nothing with which to clean and bind his injuries."

"Do what you can," said Hereward. "And the rest of you," he swept the gloom with his gaze, "it does us no good to place the blame of our predicament on Hunlaf. The past is the past, and there are many others who are at fault. I, for one, should not have allowed us to camp so close to this place. And I should have seen that Hunlaf was too tired to stand watch."

"I told you I would not fall asleep," I said. "I am sorry."

"I am as much to blame as you," he said, swatting away a fly that had landed on his forearm. "I know better than to merely listen to what a man says. I do not doubt that you meant to keep watch, but I should have weighed up the truth of your words against the strength of your body."

His comments, well-meaning though they were, further reminded me of my weakness. I shuffled over to Os and, with

Beorn's assistance, Leofstan and I managed to lie him down along one wall of the hut. I tore off the cleanest part of my kirtle I could find and used it to wipe the worst of the blood and muck from his face. His eyes were bruised and swollen shut, and one of his teeth had been knocked out. Blood trickled from his broken nose and oozed from his split lips. Os' breathing was shallow and his sallow skin was cold to the touch. He did not awaken as we moved him. I could find no bones broken on his body, but my greatest concern was with the battering he had taken to the head. I feared that his skull had been cracked, and I looked up at Leofstan in dismay. Our eyes met and I could see he had the same thought. He gave a small shake of his head. We said nothing.

"How bad is he?" asked Beorn.

"We will pray for him," replied Leofstan.

"Pray for us all," said Gwawrddur, rapping his knuckles against one of the posts that supported the roof. It was a thick as a man's leg. "As I see it, we will have little chance of escape from here."

"Little chance is better than no chance," said Drosten. He looked over at me with a sad smile. "As we have seen before."

"That's the spirit," said Hereward, clapping the Pict on the back. "We must prepare for whatever opportunity might present itself. As I see it, our best chance will be when they open the door, before they have had time to tether us again."

They continued to debate the possibilities in hushed tones. They spoke of contingencies, such as the time of day or night that our captors might open the door, how many of them there might be, and how they might go about entering the prison or getting us to leave. For all of these scenarios they came up with differing plans of action, but none felt truly possible to me. We had failed. I would not rescue Aelfwyn, if she yet lived. Nothing we had done to get here amounted to anything. We were trapped and we would die, as those who had occupied this hut before us. All too soon it would be our corpses that would adorn the path, or hang over the river.

Drosten beckoned me over to join them, but I shook my head and stayed with Os, doing the only thing I thought might help us. I knelt beside Leofstan, and joined him in whispering the words found in the book of Isaiah.

"Fear thou not; for I am with thee: be not dismayed; for I am thy God: I will strengthen thee; yea, I will help thee; yea, I will uphold thee with the right hand of my righteousness."

Together, we then recited the words of the paternoster and continued to pray over the injured man for some time. I drew a kernel of comfort from the familiar words and my feeling of dejection abated somewhat, in the way that the sun will force its warmth and light through a bank of storm clouds. Perhaps God was watching over us after all, I thought, gladdened by the small ember of faith that had come to me in the dark of the hut. I clutched onto it, blowing life into it with my prayers.

Glancing over at the rest of the men, I saw they were huddled together, deep in conversation, still planning how we might overpower our captors and break free of this shit-filled prison. I marvelled at their attitude. There seemed little chance that we might escape from this place, but what else could we do but plot and scheme? Runolf, I noted, was not engaged with them. He sat off to one side, his back against the wall, his brow resting on his drawn-up knees.

As often before, I was reminded of Hereward's wisdom as a leader of men. Left without focus, we would have bickered and then fallen into despondency just like Runolf, waiting for the time to pass until our inevitable death in Ljósberari's purifying flames. Looking about me at the shadowed forms of my companions, I could not deny that was the most likely outcome. We were unarmed, Gersine was crippled from his injury, Os might not recover from the beating he had received, and Runolf, the strongest and most fearsome of warriors in our band, had had his spirit broken and now sat in morose silence.

"Do you believe we can escape?" whispered Leofstan.

I thought for a moment, watching Drosten and Gwawrddur deep in conversation.

"Anything is possible," I said with a grim smile. "I don't think they know when they have been beaten."

"And you, Hunlaf? Do you think we have been beaten?"

I pondered all that we had heard and seen on our journey here. The torture and murders in the name of this Ljósberari's perverse faith, his twisted bastardised notions of good and bad, light and dark, that were almost certainly spawned from somehow reading *The Treasure of Life*. The stench of this prison sickened me, as did the thought of those who had languished here before us; the countless men and women who lined the path, and dangled from gibbets over the river's dark waters.

"I think the Almighty has brought us here for a reason," I said. "While I yet draw breath, I will not give up hope of finding Aelfwyn alive." I shuddered now to imagine what horrors she must have witnessed. Runolf's mind was surely teeming with thoughts of what Revna, little more than a child, had been forced to endure here. "And if anyone can get us out of this, it is those men there." I nodded at Hereward and the others, who were oblivious of our conversation.

"Do you think we might yet find it?"

"The book?" I asked, incredulous.

Leofstan nodded.

"It will be a miracle if we are able to escape this place with our lives," I said, my anger rising like a tide within me. "And you still speak of the book! Are you mad?"

"It is dangerous," he replied, his tone even and measured, as if it were perfectly normal to yet seek out the tome. "You have seen what this man has done."

"I do not need you to remind me of the dangers in the heresy within the pages of Mani's teachings," I hissed. "It would be best if it were burnt. But I care nothing now for the book. Ljósberari, though," I said, spitting the words, my fury searing now, "if we somehow succeed in getting out of this and I get the chance, I will gladly kill the bastard that has ordered these atrocities."

"You speak so readily of killing. Does life mean so little to you now?"

I looked down at Os' mottled and swollen face.

"I care for life," I replied. "More than you perhaps."

"How so?" He sounded shocked.

"You seem to find more importance in this book than in the lives this Ljósberari has ruined."

He shook his head sadly.

"No, that is not so. But the book is unique. We know of no other copy. It would be a disaster if it were lost for ever." He hesitated, looking askance at me. "Or destroyed."

"I would destroy it in a heartbeat, if it meant I could rescue Aelfwyn."

"And then you would slay this Ljósberari?"

"In an instant."

"So you have judged him unworthy of life. Is that not for God to decide? They say this Ljósberari calls himself a god. Such pride is ever the undoing of men."

"There is only one true God," I said, glaring at Leofstan. "And He will judge the man when he stands before Him at the gates of heaven. But I have made up my mind. I would put him down as I would kill a moon-touched dog."

"You no longer have any qualms with killing then?"

I sighed. I was in no mood to debate the moral implications of my decisions. I had chosen the way of the sword, and some men deserved death. I believed it then, and I believe it now, though I know such a thought would be rejected by my brothers and sisters in Christ. I have oft thought on this, and prayed for the strength to be merciful. There are far greater men and women than I – holy folk who are able to forgive their enemies as Christ would have done – but I have never found that fortitude of spirit. That is why, despite my sharp mind and steady hand with a quill, I am more suited to the shieldwall than the scriptorium. For me, there comes a point when a man's deeds can longer be forgiven. Let God forgive, for I cannot.

"If a man tries to kill me or my kin," I said to Leofstan, flicking away a fly that buzzed at my ear, "I will do whatever I can to defeat him. I have never killed a man in cold blood, and if you had asked me before now, I would have told you that I thought that was the coward's way, without honour. But now, if I am able, I would choke the life from the man that has overseen so much horror. If Ljósberari lives, how many more innocents will he kill? We have all seen what he has wrought. The man's kingdom is a hell of fire and death." I rubbed at the raw skin of my wrists and thought of the men and women who had been bound thus before being burnt alive, their eyes plucked out by Ljósberari's Frank. "The ruler of Hell is the Devil." I looked directly into my old mentor's eyes. "Would the Almighty not wish one of His servants to kill the Devil if he could?"

Leofstan had no answer to that and we lapsed into silence. After a time, he said he thought it must be time for Sext. I nodded and together we set about reciting the prayers and songs of the office. Our voices worked well together and blended into a powerful, melodious music that filled the fly-infested, cloying, foetid interior of the hut. When at last we had finished, we slumped down either side of Os. There was little change in him. I lowered my head to his face and could barely feel the butterfly flutter of his breath on my cheek.

"Any better?" asked Beorn, his tone anxious. He sat with

the others. They had stopped their talking when we began to sing. But all except Runolf seemed to have been buoyed by their planning and perhaps too by hearing us singing praises to God.

If anything, Os' state had worsened, but I could not bring myself to say as much. Morale was a fickle and fragile thing, easily crushed.

"No change," I said.

Not wanting the mood to sour, I asked what they had planned. Hereward told me and it was simple enough, but relied on good fortune. Without the grace of God we would not be escaping, but I nodded and smiled. There was really nothing else to say, and we soon all fell silent.

Despite the heat and the foulness that rose like a mist from the mud we sat in, the tribulations of the days behind us had taken a great toll on us all and, one by one, our heads nodded and the shadows were filled with the sawing sounds of snores. From time to time, one of the flies that flitted between the shafts of light lancing through the chinks in the walls would settle on an exposed piece of skin and we would slap it away, half waking from our doze and disturbing the others, who grumbled in the dark.

I would not have believed it possible, but soon I was deeply asleep. The drone of flies and the tickle of their scurrying feet punctuated my dreams, but I slept for a large part of the day in spite of them, and when I was awoken, the light had shifted around the walls of our prison to slant in from the other side.

None of us had heard anyone approach, so it was impossible for any of the plans Hereward and the others had devised to be put into practice before the solid timber door scraped on the packed earth outside. I blinked at the bright light that streamed in. The day was on the wane, the sun low in the west, touching the mountains over the river.

"You and you, are to come with me."

I squinted at the dark figure in the doorway. He was in shadow, but I recognised the voice as that of Chlotar. I noticed that neither the Frank nor any of his men ventured into the disgusting hut. Several sharp spears glinted around Chlotar, the men clearly ready for a rushed attack from the prisoners. We would have been hard pressed to force our way from the cell. No matter how brave and strong were the men of our band, they would be no match for a thicket of spear-points jabbing at them from outside.

"Did you not hear me?" growled Chlotar. "Or are you asleep again?"

Some of the men outside chuckled at that. I felt my face grow hot as I realised he was addressing me. My eyes were growing accustomed to the new brightness, and I saw now that he was pointing in my direction. "Bring the old one too. The master would meet you both."

I pushed myself to my feet, my body complaining at the battering it had taken these last days.

"He wants you too," I said to Leofstan.

"Why?" he croaked, his voice hoarse. "What does he want?"

"Best not to keep the master waiting," barked Chlotar, snapping his fingers impatiently.

I pulled Leofstan to his feet.

"Perhaps I will get my chance after all," I whispered, then more loudly. "We are to be guests of Ljósberari."

Fifty

We were taken to the water's edge, Leofstan and I blinking in the bright afternoon sunlight. My gaze kept flicking to the shapes of the corpses that hung like putrid pears from the trees along the riverbank. As well as the dozen or so armed warriors that Chlotar commanded, we were followed by a great throng of Ljósberari's people, mostly children. This time they did not taunt and strike us, but walked in an uncanny silence, their eyes wide and fixed on our every movement. I wondered if we were to be Ljósberari's next victims. Were we being led to the pyres where we would be consumed by flames? I suppressed a shudder and offered up a prayer that God would grant me the strength to die with honour. I did not wish to disgrace myself, weeping and puking with pain and fear, but I could already feel the terror of what was to come coiling within me, gnawing at my guts.

When we reached the first wharf, Chlotar shoved me forward.

"Strip and wash."

I stared at him in disbelief. The children were amassed along the shore. Scores of dark gazes stared back from behind the Frank.

"Your soul cannot be cleansed with water," he said, by way

of explanation, "but the master would like you to have a clean body before he meets you." He threw a pale linen robe to me. "You will wear this."

I looked down at the cloth in my hand. It was lightweight, and undyed. It made me think of a funeral shroud.

"Get washing," Chlotar growled, grabbing Leofstan and pulling him close. "And don't get any ideas. If you try to swim away, I will slice this old one from ear to ear."

Quickly I began to undress. I could feel the gaze of the onlookers roving across my pallid skin and I shivered. When I was naked, I did not tarry on the wharf for all to see. I took a deep breath and jumped into the river. I had expected it to be deep and I was surprised when my feet hit the muddy riverbed before my body was fully submerged. My right leg twisted painfully and I stumbled forward, disappearing beneath the surface. I came up sputtering and coughing. I thought I heard a sprinkling of childish laughter from the crowd, but they were soon eerily silent once more.

The water held the memory of ice, mountains and deep lakes. It was freezing after the warmth of the hut and my breath caught in my throat at the shock of it. But as I scoured the grime and sweat from my body, so my head cleared of the terror that had threatened to overwhelm me. I must be alert and ready for any opportunity that God might give me. I understood then that I had no hope of surviving, surrounded as we were by so many, but if I was given a sliver of a chance of taking Ljósberari's life, I would be ready to act. If I was to die anyway, I could at least rid the land of this evil before my end.

Hauling myself out of the water, I pulled the linen robe over my head. It clung to my dripping body. It was similar to the habit I had worn as a monk, though I was given nothing with which to cinch it. I stood there, skin pimpled with the cold, and waited for Leofstan to clean himself of the muck from the hut. Having watched my ignominious fall, after shedding his travel-stained and torn habit, Leofstan lowered himself more carefully into the water. He pulled his discarded rope belt from where he had left it and cleaned that as well as he could too. Chlotar, knife in hand, moved close to me, but did not feel the need to place the blade at my throat. I contemplated snatching the weapon from him. I was fast, and it might be possible, but then what? Perhaps I would kill the Frank, but I would surely be slain, and it was the head of the snake that needed to be severed if this evil was to be ended.

When Leofstan had finished, I helped him out of the water. He thanked me with a nod and donned the pale robe, tying his wet rope belt about his waist.

"Move," said Chlotar, pushing us towards the land.

"What of our shoes?" I asked, not sure how far we were to walk and wanting to prolong the moment before we reached the place of our execution.

"Leave them," said Chlotar, impatiently shoving me along the wharf towards the crowd.

The watchers parted as we walked between them, their eyes wide and dark. No longer silent, they whispered and murmured with excitement like a vast beehive as we left the river behind us. The atmosphere was tense and charged, the way the air is before a thunderstorm, but there were no clouds in the late afternoon sky.

"Now we know how Isaac must have felt," said Leofstan, his voice a whisper.

I looked at him sidelong.

"But God stayed Abraham's hand," I said. "He sacrificed a goat instead. I don't see any burnt goats hanging from stakes."

Leofstan shrugged and made an approximation of a smile.

"Anything is possible," he said.

"Silence," snarled Chlotar, pushing me forward with a vicious punch to my back.

I stumbled and we walked on without speaking further. My

skin was cool as the moisture from the river dried. It felt good to be clean and I glanced back at the hut where our friends were trapped. I wondered whether Os would survive the night.

And then our destination became apparent when we stopped before the wide doors of the great hall. There was no more time for wondering what the future held. It awaited us within. It was dark inside, and I was gripped with a sudden, dreadful fear, my recent bravery having fled like a miser when asked for alms. The crowd that had followed us hushed. They stood, swaying and silent. Waiting. Expectant. I scanned the land around the hall and saw no bonfire piled with kindling and timber. There was no stake awaiting us as far as I could make out.

"Perhaps they do not mean to burn us right away," I whispered.

"Hush," said Chlotar, his tone sharp. I realised with a start that he too was frightened. He had a sword strapped to his belt and I had seen him use it with skill and savagery. His face and arms bore the scars of many fights, and yet, standing here before Ljósberari's hall, the Frank was subdued and on edge.

"Show my guests in," said a mellifluous voice from deep within the shadowed bowels of the hall.

Chlotar did not reply, but placed a hand on our backs and pushed us through the threshold. I resisted for a moment, leaning against the Frank's strength, testing him.

He growled.

Leofstan made the sign of the cross in the air before him.

"May God be with us both," he said.

And with that, I allowed Chlotar to usher us both forward into the heart of the darkness.

Fifty-One

"Come closer," said the voice from the gloom. Tentatively, Leofstan and I took a couple of paces. The far end of the hall was shrouded in shadows.

"Closer," the voice insisted.

We shuffled forward. Chlotar stepped inside and pulled the door shut. The murmurings of the crowd were silenced behind the thick oak planking. A little light filtered in through several windows dotted along the length of the building. They appeared to be covered with tight, translucent skins. On the brightest of days, the windows would provide enough illumination for the hall's inhabitants to carry out their chores, but now, with the sun low in the sky, the hall was dark.

My eyes took some time to adjust to the darkness. It was warm inside the hall, the air thick with the scent of what smelt to me like burning juniper berries, some sort of resin, and something else. I sniffed. Perhaps mugwort leaves or yew needles. Candles and lamps flickered at the end of the building, and I began to make out the features of the man who waited there. I don't rightly know what I had expected. I was young, but I knew that the evil within a man's soul cannot be seen on his face, and I have since learnt that oftentimes the most handsome of men have the most twisted and corrupted minds.

And yet the figure in the dark hall was the infamous Ljósberari, the bearer of light. A man we had heard so much about; whose murderous deeds we had witnessed all too frequently. This man was feared by kings and jarls. He was the murderer of countless Norse men and women, liberator of thralls, and a man we had been told believed himself to be a god, and who was worshipped as such by those who followed him. I suppose I had thought he would possess a powerful physique, with the strength and size to see his will obeyed. I did not expect such a man to look like a scribe. But the figure who sat on the carved high-backed seat at the head of the hall, was slender and balding, with a sharp nose, a long, almost feminine neck, and graceful, delicate fingers that now reached for a jug. I watched his precise movements as he poured liquid into two cups, before gently returning the pitcher to the board. I could easily imagine him sitting at a desk in a scriptorium, bent over the vellum, quill in hand, much as I am now as I write this. It was hard to believe that such a seemingly weak man could do so much harm; that he could command killers like Chlotar to do his bidding.

We passed a censer that wafted out clouds of pungent-smelling smoke. Ljósberari rose from his seat, a cup in each hand. He walked into the puddle of light surrounding a guttering oil lamp and his blue eyes flashed. In that instant I understood. To stare into his eyes was to gaze into the abyss of madness. But this was no gibbering fool, that drools and raves at the world. Ljósberari's eyes shone with a cool intelligence. He smiled, lips drawing back from a neat row of white teeth, but his eyes remained distant and as cold as a winter night. He did not blink as he moved forward, and his penetrating gaze unnerved me. He walked with a strange elegance, appearing to glide, his head and shoulders barely moving.

Within a heartbeat, he was close before us and I found myself taking the simple wooden cup he thrust towards me. The contents were dark, and I sniffed.

"It is wine," Ljósberari said, laughing suddenly in a cackle that reminded me of Chlotar. "Fine, Frankish wine. Would you like some," he called out to Chlotar, who still hovered by the door, in the shadows.

"No, master," he replied without leaving his post, his tone soft, subservient.

"Master! Master!" said Ljósberari, raising his hands in seemingly feigned fury. Turning, he glided back to his chair. "How many times must I tell you? I am a teacher, not your master."

Chlotar did not answer, and Ljósberari did not appear to care. Sitting once more on the finely carved chair, he beckoned to us both.

"No matter the number of times I tell them, they will insist on calling me 'master'." He shook his head and poured more wine from the pitcher into a cup for himself. Leofstan glanced at me in surprise, for Ljósberari had addressed us in Englisc, and from the tone and his ease with the words, it was clear it was the tongue he had learnt as a child at his mother's side. "I am master of nothing," he went on. "I am but the bearer of truth. It is my honour to help pave the way of light. I am a comforter, a *paracletus*, if you will." He spoke in the tone of a priest giving a sermon and I glanced at Leofstan. His use of the Latin word for helper left me in no doubt now that this man was learned and that somehow, he had read *The Treasure of Life*, for *paracletus* was how Mani described himself in his teachings.

"Come, come, be seated," he said, his teeth flashing in a mirthless grin. Cautiously, we made our way closer. The dry rushes on the floor scratched at my bare feet. "You look startled to hear me speak," Ljósberari said with another bark of laughter. "Did you not know I came from the fair shores of Albion? I have to say, it feels good to speak so freely. There are so few amongst us with whom I can speak Englisc."

"Is Aelfwyn one such?" I asked, scanning the table for any sign of a weapon. A small eating knife rested close to our host's hand. The blade was short. It might be enough to slay the man before Chlotar could stop me. But it was on the other side of the board and I would need to fling myself across the table to reach it. My chances of snatching it up before Ljósberari were slim. He looked at me sharply and picked up the knife. The moment was gone, and I slid onto the bench.

Ljósberari used the knife to skewer a ripe raspberry from a bowl on the table. He popped it into his mouth and chewed with relish. Despite myself, my stomach growled. We had not eaten for a long time and my body had not forgotten how ravenous I was, even if I did not wish to show weakness before this man. While bathing at the river, I had quenched my thirst with a few mouthfuls of water, but my stomach was yet hollow and painfully empty.

"You are hungry," Ljósberari said, pushing the bowl towards me. Leofstan sat at my side. I glanced at the door, feeling exposed and vulnerable with my back to Chlotar. But the Frank had not moved. I looked down at the fruit for a long while, unsure of myself. Guilt scratched at me as I thought of Hereward, Runolf and the others with no water or food. "Eat. Eat," Ljósberari said. At last, with a sigh, I took some of the berries.

The flesh was juicy and soft. I felt the strength returning to my limbs as the sweetness filled my mouth. Ljósberari watched me, unblinking. I sipped the wine. It was good. The warmth of the drink spread through me, lifting my morale, giving me courage.

"You did not answer my question," I said. "Do you speak Englisc with Aelfwyn?"

"Perhaps," he replied, waving his long-fingered hand airily. "Who can say? I speak to any who would listen. It is my duty to speak in whatever language best suits the listener, if I am able. God has blessed me with an ear for languages, and the word of truth must be heard by all."

"*Quid est veritas, paracletus?*" asked Leofstan, in the language of old Roma.

Ljósberari clapped his hands in glee.

"Wonderful!" he replied. "Your Latin is excellent. You would know what truth is, I see. What jubilation I feel to hear you speak with such knowledge." He leaned over the table conspiratorially and signalled for us to move closer. Hesitantly, we both bent towards him. "You know, Chlotar told me you came here to do me harm," he whispered. "He said you were sent to kill me." He stared into our faces in turn, perhaps searching for a sign of our guilt. I wondered then how much he knew or suspected, but I kept my expression impassive. "But no, quoth I. A bird told me that you were coming, you see? And I told Chlotar that you are men of the Lord and surely He has sent you here for another purpose. If it had been up to Chlotar, you would all be dead already. He does so loathe the people of these lands, you see."

"Then why do we yet live?" asked Leofstan.

Ljósberari smiled.

"Firstly, because it was my wish to speak with you. I am not his master, but he does obey me as faithfully as a hound."

"And secondly?"

"I reminded him that you were not from these lands and so he should not hate you. Now tell me, why have you come here?" His smile vanished and his unblinking gaze took on a malevolent air. I struggled not to shudder at the sudden change in his demeanour.

"We came seeking the truth," I said, uttering the first thing I could think of.

"Indeed? You have come so far to speak to me that I might enlighten you?"

"We have," said Leofstan. "Word of your exploits and fame reached us as far away as Northumbria."

Ljósberari frowned now.

"Exploits?" he said, pronouncing the word as if it tasted of poison. "Exploits! I do not do these things for my own gain!" He slammed his fist into the table, shaking the cups. His face was crimson, his ire coming with such force and savagery that I slid back on the bench to distance myself from his madness. "I bring the truth of the light, and you speak of fame and exploits as though I am engaged in a mere dispute over land. I am no warlord. I bring freedom and light."

"Forgive us," I said, the words catching in my throat. "We do not understand. We have studied much. The Scriptures, Primasius, Jerome, Cassiodorus and Beda. But nowhere have we been satisfied that we have found the truth."

"And yet this man wears the tonsure." Ljósberari's voice was flat.

"I do," admitted Leofstan, self-consciously rubbing his hand over the stubble on his shaved scalp. "But I see much in the world that I cannot reconcile with the word of God. I..." He hesitated, seeming to choke on his emotion. Whether feigned or real, I could not tell. "I have lost my faith," he went on, "and I wish to learn the truth. We heard you were the Ljósberari, the bringer of light. I want to see that light."

Ljósberari stared at Leofstan for several heartbeats. His sudden fury had abated and after a time, he nodded slowly, and reached for his wine.

"Perhaps you have more light within you than you know," he said, sipping from his cup. "Perhaps..." His voice trailed off. "Perhaps..."

"Perhaps what?" I asked, scared to interrupt his thoughts, but unable not to ask, such was the power of his character and the pull of my curiosity.

"They call me Ljósberari," he said, ignoring my question.

"But it is not true. I do not bring the light. Each man and woman has the light within them. They have darkness too. So much darkness. And the two battle within their souls, vying for victory over the other, just as God is constantly battling against the Devil, fighting for triumph over this earth."

"So why do they call you Ljósberari?"

He shifted his gaze to me and fixed me with his unflinching stare. I felt like a mouse looking into the eyes of a serpent.

"Because of the fires, I would say," he said, with a strangely warm smirk that sent a chill shivering down my spine. "Little people must put a name to everything. It helps them believe they control it."

"But they don't control you," said Leofstan. "You are clearly too clever for that."

Ljósberari's eyes narrowed. I tensed, worried that Leofstan's clumsy flattery would send him into another rage. But after a moment, he let out a long sigh.

"They controlled my body for a long while," he said, his voice far away as he looked into the past. "But never my mind. No, never my mind." I longed to ask him more questions, but I sensed that the tale he was weaving could all too easily unravel. Leofstan was silent too, and we both waited patiently for him to carry on.

"Can you imagine what it is like to be a thrall?" Ljósberari asked suddenly. "You are both men of learning, I can sense it. You were not always a warrior, eh?" he said to me, and I nodded, not wishing to break the flow of his thoughts with my words. "I would read and pray every day. I did not know the truth then. Oh no. But like you, I studied, and I was always searching. And then the foul devils came from the sea. In their wyrm-prowed longships." He fell silent and his gaze darkened. I remembered what had happened at Lindisfarnae and wondered where this man had been before he was enthralled.

"They did things..." he said, and his voice cracked. "They..."

"We were at Lindisfarnae when they came," said Leofstan, and I was worried that he would cause Ljósberari to halt his tale. "Where were you?"

Ljósberari shuddered and reached a hand out across the table. Leofstan raised his cup to avoid him taking hold of his hand.

"I knew you understood," Ljósberari said. "I could see it in you. We are alike, you and I."

Leofstan said nothing.

"Before they called me Ljósberari, my name was Scomric." He nodded thoughtfully at his memories. "I was at the Abbey of Saint Bertin, in the land of the Franks. A quiet place of peace and great learning. I was blessed to have had my time there and I wonder sometimes what would have become of me, if I had remained there." He sighed. "But such was not to be. The abbot sent me, along with Chlotar, who served the monastery, to Quentovic to oversee the purchase of some lead for the roof of the new chapel. Who could have known that the Norse would be so bold as to attack the port? They came with the dawn." His voice trembled as he relived that dark day. "There was so much blood. More horror than any man should have to witness." I thought of the horrors inflicted on Scomric's victims, but said nothing. "And yet I lived," Scomric went on and a hard edge entered his tone. "As did faithful Chlotar. And I knew then, as I know now, that we had been spared for a reason. Even in the blackest of times, when we were beaten and almost starving, I would pray with Chlotar for a sign." He closed his eyes, as if picturing the two of them kneeling in prayer. "Eventually the sign came to us."

Fifty-Two

"What sign?" asked Leofstan.

"A book," said Scomric, his voice tinged with awe and sorrow. Leofstan glanced at me. "I had been for so long without anything to read, imagine my joy at finding such an exquisite thing in these pagan lands that had been hitherto devoid of all learning and education. Our masters had no comprehension of the thing's value. They tore the gems and gold from the cover, and discarded the pages. Can you believe such a thing? As if the worth of a book can be discerned by its cover!" He shook his head in disbelief. "They did not care when I carried the book back to where we thralls slept. If any of them saw me reading, they laughed, not understanding that God had sent me the tome. For what other reason could such a precious thing have fallen into my hands out of all the people in this accursed land?"

"Tell me of the book," said Leofstan, but the eagerness in his tone betrayed him and Scomric scowled.

"You would like to know about the book, wouldn't you?" he snapped, instantly furious. He surged to his feet, sending his chair toppling over with a crash. "So, that is what you have come for! You wish to steal the *Treasure* from me." Scomric screamed these last words and again I saw in him the power of his passion and madness that led people to follow him.

Leofstan raised his hands in a placatory gesture.

"No, no. I merely wish to learn of this sacred text that you said had been sent to you by God Himself. Did you learn the truth from this book?"

Scomric glowered at the monk for a time. His nostrils flared and his chest heaved with his fervour, but at last he calmed himself, righted his chair and sat down once more.

"Indeed, the book held the truth," he said, still slightly breathless. "The truth of ten heavens and eight hells. The truth of the battle between the darkness and the light. How the Father of Greatness is locked in conflict with Satan, the King of Darkness. All these things and so many more I learnt from the writings of the divine painter, Mani. That most holy Paraclete of the Truth. For long nights I read the pages of that book, over and over, unravelling its mysteries and opening my mind and soul to the truth therein." He reached across the table and gripped Leofstan's hand. Leofstan tensed and I could see that he wanted to be free of the madman's grasp, but he held himself still and met his gaze.

"You would like to read what was inside those pages, wouldn't you?" asked Scomric.

Leofstan did not reply immediately, no doubt weighing up how his words might reignite Scomric's rage. At last he nodded.

"Well, you cannot!" yelled Scomric, making us both jump.

"Will you not share the truth then?" asked Leofstan, his voice surprisingly firm in the face of such crazed ire.

"You think I am jealous of the Mani's writings? That I would keep them for myself?" Scomric shook his head, exasperated with our lack of comprehension of his motives. "But have I not done my best to impart the truth of his teachings throughout this land? The truth is here." He tapped his temple. "And here." He slapped his chest. "I would share it with everyone."

"I would rather read of the truth than be burnt to learn it," said Leofstan, his voice quiet, measured. My stomach turned. Surely he had gone too far now.

Scomric grew very still and I thought he would launch himself at my mentor for his audacity. But then, he threw his head back and cackled. His laughter echoed about the empty hall. I noticed a movement by the door, and saw with a sensation of dread like the uncoiling of a snake within my stomach, that Chlotar was moving closer, as if summoned by his master by some secret signal. My skin crawled at the sound of Ljósberari's demented laughter, and again I cast about for any weapon that might help me. I saw none.

"I am sure you would," Scomric said, when his laughter subsided. "And I would surely let you, if it were not too late."

"Too late?" Leofstan asked, confused.

"Too late for you to steal *The Treasure of Life* from me."

"That was not—" began Leofstan, but Scomric quickly cut him off.

"Or to read it," he said, holding up his left hand, "if that is truly what you came here for."

"Why is it too late?" I asked.

"Because it has been stolen already!"

"Stolen?" asked Leofstan, his disappointment clear in his tone.

"Taken far away," Scomric said, his shoulders slumping. "It was God who brought the book to me, but in the battle between the light and the darkness, the Devil never rests. Before God showed me the way to escape my bonds of slavery, Satan sent a man to the hall of our Norse master. They are heathens, the people of this land, uneducated and uncouth. But they have a knack for three things. Battle, sailing and trade. It is astounding to me that such…" He paused, searching for a term that would sum up these people he so despised. "That such barbarians," he said at last, "should have fine wine from the sunny hills of the south of Frankia. You can find here cinnamon, cloves and cardamom from beyond great Byzantion, silver coins from ar-Raqqah, olive oil and sweet dates from Al-Andalus. These Norsemen's ships can reach as far as the world is wide, it seems. But I was still shocked when a man came to the hall where Chlotar and I were prisoners. He was dark-skinned from the land of the Moors far, far to the south. He was a heathen, of course, but he was a learned man, and I watched him as he conversed with our master. He spoke with great deference, but I could see that he felt nothing but contempt for these people. They were too stupid to see it, or perhaps they did not care, for he paid them good silver for several treasures he unearthed from things they had plundered from minsters in Frankia and Britain. He bought a bejewelled pendant that contained a thorn, from the very crown Christ wore during his passion. There was also a silver reliquary that housed the finger of Saint Walaric. They were pretty enough, but of course, the power they contained was far more valuable than the silver. When the Moor asked about books, my master did not understand to begin with. But when the foreigner explained that they were leaves of parchment where knowledge is recorded in writing, he remembered the stack of vellum I had taken. He had already sold the jewels from the cover, but now he saw a way to profit from the pages that had seemed meaningless to him." Scomric grew still and quiet for a time then. He stared into his cup, lost in his dark memories. I felt Chlotar's presence close behind us, and I looked around at him. I was met with a sneer from the Frank. The hairs on my neck prickled and I longed to be able to stand, to put some space between myself, Scomric and Chlotar. But I knew that if I moved, the Frank would only push me back onto the bench, so I remained where I was, watching and listening, my panic building within me.

Scomric rubbed a hand across his face and sighed.

"I knew better than to speak to my master without being addressed, especially when he was conversing with an honoured guest, but I could not remain silent. I pleaded with him not to sell the book. Stupidly, I told him it was of great importance to me. He laughed, and when I would not stop speaking, he beat me." Scomric hesitated, running his hand over his greying hair, pausing from time to time, as if feeling the scars of that beating. "He hit me until I was senseless. When I awoke, the Moor was gone and so was the book." He reached into his robe and produced a folded piece of parchment. "To taunt me, the Devil left behind this scrap of writing." He shook it out to show the strange flowing script that covered it. I had never seen anything like it before. It was clearly writing, but nothing like any language I had ever studied. "One day I will decipher this thing," he said. "Perhaps then I will learn where the Moor took the book."

"What did you do after you found the book had gone?" asked Leofstan in a small voice.

Folding the parchment, Scomric secreted it away within his robes, close to his heart once more.

"When I was strong enough, Chlotar and I rose up in the night. We liberated the other thralls. I knew the truth and I had waited too long to act. Satan had sent his emissary and I had lost the book that God had given into my hands."

"So you killed your master?"

Scomric smiled at the memory.

"Yes, I killed him. His wife too." He licked his lips, as if the memory of their deaths tasted good. "And we slew all those who had shown me that the darkness had already triumphed within their souls."

Leofstan was horrified.

"I understand that you had suffered. You had been mistreated, and you needed to escape. But you are a man of God. Jesus tells us 'love your enemies, bless them that curse you, do good to them that hate you, and pray for them which despitefully use you, and persecute you.'"

"Christ is weak!" Scomric screamed, his face darkening with anger. "He is pathetic! 'Whosoever shall smite thee on thy right cheek, turn to him the other also.'" He spoke in a singsong, mocking tone. "'Love thy neighbour as thyself.' No! The darkness must be destroyed and the light ushered in. It is the only way."

"But... but..." stammered Leofstan. "To burn people alive... We have seen the corpses. Are those things not the work of Satan? Are they not the darkness you seek to conquer, rather than the light?"

I had watched the tension rising within Leofstan for some time. He could not sit silently by and listen to this twisted portrayal of good and evil. But my heart sank to hear him openly confront Scomric, for there was no doubting that the man was mad. And we had seen what he was capable of.

"I am Ljósberari!" Scomric shouted, rising to his feet again. He appeared to grow in stature, to tower over us. His eyes gleamed with the flames of the candles and I thought of all those he had burnt, all those bonfires his eyes had watched. All those screams he must have listened to. "I bring the light to these damned people. I had hoped that God had sent you to help me in my quest. But now I see the truth." Lashing out across the table with a speed I did not expect, he grabbed a handful of Leofstan's linen robe, dragging him forward. Then, without pause, Scomric flicked his right hand. There was a flash of metal in the gloom and Leofstan jerked, overturning the bowl of berries, his hands flailing and scratching at Scomric's arm.

That arm was slick with blood, bright and terrible, and with a dreadful shudder of horror, I saw that Scomric had slit Leofstan's throat. I lurched forwards, not knowing whether I would try to help my friend or attack the madman who had cut him, but Chlotar's strong hands gripped me, and I felt the cold of a knife at my neck.

"Sit," he hissed.

The blood gushed from Leofstan's neck, bubbling over Scomric's forearm and hand, pouring onto the table, to smother the raspberries that lay there. Leofstan was making a gurgling, mewling sound, trying to speak, but I could make out no words. His skin was pale and already the flow, pumping with each beat of his heart, was slowing. Ljósberari, dark eyes glowing with excitement, snatched up his empty cup and held it beneath Leofstan's trembling form. The blood splashed into the vessel, quickly filling it. When it was full, Scomric, the mad light bearer, released his hold on the monk and Leofstan slid from the bench, to lie, blinking and gasping, in the rushes at my feet. Our eyes met for the briefest of moments, and then all movement ceased, and my friend and mentor was gone.

I could not move. I had come expecting death at the hands of these men, but nothing had prepared me for this sudden, vicious slaughter. It had come too quickly, without warning, and I sat stunned, barely feeling now the metal of the knife at my throat.

Chlotar's sniggering laughter penetrated my clouded mind and a shiver racked my body.

Aghast, I watched as Ljósberari lifted the brimming cup to his lips. My gorge rose, stinging the back of my throat as he drank deeply, the viscous liquid trickling down his chin.

"There is much light in the blood of a Christian," he said when he had finished, grinning at me and Chlotar with reddened teeth. "It would not do to let it go to waste."

I wanted to look away, or even to force Chlotar to slay me too, that I would not have to watch this horror any longer. We were all going to die here. That much was clear to me, so why not end it now, before I had time to grieve the man who had been like a father to me? Better that, than wither and weaken in the prison with the others, only to then be burnt alive. If I could rise and fight, Chlotar might be compelled to kill me quickly. But still I could not move. My body refused to obey me and instead of springing up, I watched the blood spreading around the fruit on the table, dripping down onto the rush-strewn floor where Leofstan lay, the light of life gone from his eyes, blood still oozing from the deep slash in his throat. I watched as Ljósberari emptied the cup of my friend's lifeblood, and as he began to laugh, adding his maniacal cackle to Chlotar's giggle, a great roaring, like a waterfall or a gale, filled my ears. I started to shake uncontrollably and the world darkened around me. I could feel my grip on consciousness slipping away. For a few heartbeats, I willed myself to remain awake, to push my body up, to fight.

But as I watched Ljósberari dipping his finger into his cup, scraping it around the rim and then sucking it clean of the last precious drops of Leofstan's blood, something snapped within my mind and I swooned. As I tumbled down into darkness, I was glad to be free from this nightmare. The rushing sound drowned out all noise and I could feel myself falling, falling. The last thing I saw were Leofstan's shocked, unseeing eyes, and I hoped I would never awaken again.

Fifty-Three

When I awoke, I was cold. Shivering, I opened my eyes. I still wore the thin linen robe and I wished I had my kirtle, breeches and cloak to keep me warm. All about me was darkness. Slowly, I began to make out details, shapes picked out by thin silvered slivers of light that forced themselves between the slats and planks of the walls and beneath the solid door. Figures were huddled on the floor and propped against the wall. The grating buzz of snores, loud in the gloom, was the only sound. I sniffed, and the noxious stench left me in no doubt that I was back in the hut with my friends.

All except Leofstan.

My mind lurched at the memories that flooded back in. I let out a sobbing cry at my loss and longed once more to be plunged into the hidden land of dreams and not this waking nightmare, where I was sure to find only more blood and death.

"Hunlaf?"

I pushed myself up. Gwawrddur sat close by, his face a pale smudge in the gloom, his anxiety evident in his whispered tone. There was movement, a shuffling and rustling of cloth. Three more faces peered at me from the dark. From their shapes and builds I knew the first two to be Hereward and Drosten. The huge shadow of the third told me it was Runolf. I was pleased to see that he had shaken off his lethargy. With a pang I recalled his shock at Revna's reaction to him. He had focused on nothing but rescuing her since finding out about Estrid's murder and she had spurned him. Each one of us was living his own personal hell, it seemed. At least I was not alone.

"Are you well?" asked Hereward.

Well? Mad laughter bubbled up within me at the question. I bit it back and it turned into a choked sob.

"I am not hurt," I said, my voice bitter and hollow. I stretched my back and rolled my shoulders. I was stiff and bruised, but nothing worse than that.

"Leofstan?"

Tears stung my eyes, his name threatening to unman me. Unprepared for the power of my emotions, I sniffed and shook my head. I could not be sure if they saw my movement, but they must have already suspected the worst, for they did not press me further.

"How long have I been senseless?" I asked.

"They brought you back shortly after nightfall," said Hereward. "It must be past midnight now."

"What did they do to you?" asked Runolf, his rumbling in the gloom. "We could find no wound, but we could not awaken you." I heard real concern in his tone, and it gladdened me, despite everything.

"To me?" I asked, with a snort. "They did nothing to me." I felt a dreadful shame. "And I did nothing to stop them..." I could not bring myself to complete the thought, to recount how Ljósberari had slit Leofstan's throat as easily as if he had been a hog ready for roasting. And how I had sat by motionless and watched as he drank the old monk's blood. I closed my eyes, trying to rid myself of the image, but it was burnt into my mind. I would never be free of it. I still see it now sometimes, when my nightmares are particularly bad. On such nights I sleep no further. I use up more fuel than I should, stoking the fire until it blazes, so that I can sit in the firelight and await the dawn. I pray for forgiveness and to be rid of the memory of Leofstan's dying eyes. Perhaps God has forgiven me, but in His infinite wisdom He has not seen fit to remove the vision from my mind, and I am sure that it will haunt me till I follow my old mentor into the vale of death.

Runolf placed a strong hand on my shoulder. I flinched and made to shrug it off, but he gripped me firmly.

"Do not blame yourself," he said.

"That is easy to say, but not so easy to do," I hissed. "I should have saved him."

"You cannot walk again the path already trod," Hereward said with a sigh. "None of us can. All you can do is live the rest of your life well. Do not despair, Hunlaf. Live. For Leofstan, and Os, and the others."

At the mention of Os, I shivered.

"Os?" I said. "Has he...?" I could not bring myself to say the words.

There was a brief silence, and then Hereward's voice came quietly from the shadows.

"He breathed his last shortly after sunset."

I had never been close to the warrior. His brash humour and loud jesting was often annoying. But he was one of us, and to learn of his death in this stinking hovel, hit me with almost physical force. The tears I had been holding back flowed freely down my cheeks now, and I was glad it was dark so that the warriors around me would not witness my weakness.

Nobody spoke for a long while. I wept as quietly as I could, but as the tears rolled down my face, the pain of my grief and self-pity swelled like a tide. I thought of all I had lost and all the mistakes that had led us to this point. Cwenswith and the hólmgang with Wistan. Thurid. Now Leofstan and Os were dead. All because I had been desperate to chase after Aelfwyn. And I didn't even know if she yet lived. It was a simple thing to say I should not blame myself, but I wondered how much of the blame for our ills could truly be laid at my feet? As I wept, Runolf never let go of my shoulder, and I drew comfort from the strength of his grasp. At last my tears were spent and I cuffed at my cheeks.

Runolf squeezed my shoulder.

"Better?" he asked.

I wanted to scream that I would never be well again. My mentor and friend was dead, and we were all doomed to follow him. But as I opened my mouth, I realised with a shock that Runolf was right. My tears had gone some way to washing away my sorrow. In its place I could feel the beginnings of a different emotion: anger. Hard and obdurate, deep within me nestled the ore of my fury that over time the heat of my grief would forge into a blade of righteous vengeance. I recalled Leofstan's last words to Scomric and knew he would disapprove of my desire for blood to pay for his murder. Christ taught that we should love our enemies and turn the other cheek when smitten. But Leofstan was no longer there to rebuke me, and I could pray for forgiveness for my sins later. If I survived. I shook my head at my foolishness. I would not live long enough to seek revenge. My hatred and anger would be of no more use than my weeping and self-pity. We were still captives and I could see no way out of this place with our lives.

"When they come for us again," said Drosten, speaking for the first time, "we must be ready. I would rather die rushing at their spears, than be burnt alive with my eyes put out by that Frankish bastard."

There was a murmur of assent and just as the previous afternoon, the men talked of how best to overcome the armed guards when they next opened the door. I listened, but said little. There was no way we could truly hope to survive such an attack, let alone escape, but I sensed that they needed to speak as if such things were possible. The alternative would be to accept the cruel fate that awaited us. These were not men to stand by and watch as death approached. They were warriors, killers of men, and they would rail against their wyrd, and spit in Death's eye as he stalked towards them.

It was agreed that two of our number would remain awake at all times and they would alert the others the instant they heard people approaching.

"I will keep watch first," said Drosten.

"I will join you," I said. Silence greeted my comment, and I could imagine what they were thinking. "I have slept already," I went on. "I will not let you down again." I could not bear more shame.

After a brief hesitation, Hereward said, "Very well, Hunlaf. But both of you watch the other too. When you need sleep, awaken Runolf and Eadmaer. Gwawrddur and I need to rest, for we have barely slept these last two nights."

"Not that we will be able to sleep in this stinking pit," grumbled the Welshman.

They settled themselves down to rest as best they could. Drosten and I took up our position close to the door. Without comment, we both rose to our feet and stood shoulder-to-shoulder, leaning against the rough-hewn timber of the door frame. The earth beneath my feet was cool and damp. It squeezed between my bare toes and I tried not to think of how much shit and piss was mingled with it. I wrapped my arms around my chest. Gone now was the blistering heat of the summer's day, and all warmth had leached from the building into the cool, cloudless night.

"You think they will come for us before daybreak?" whispered Drosten.

I listened, straining to hear anything from outside the hut. There was nothing but the stillness of the night.

"I doubt it," I said. "I imagine Ljósberari prefers an

audience for his burnings. And nobody is awake to see a fire."

I thought of the great throng of children who had followed Leofstan and I up to the hall. The sea of staring eyes and the sighing of countless rapturous voices. "No, I think he'll wait for tomorrow at least."

"But why wait at all?"

It was true that he had killed Leofstan without an audience. But that felt different somehow. A moment of passionate rage, not a ritual purification. I sighed. I did not wish to put myself into the mind of that madman.

"Who can say? Perhaps he truly believed that Leofstan and I had been sent to aid him."

"He said that?"

I nodded.

"The man is quite insane. God alone can predict his actions."

"Or the Devil," Drosten said.

I shuddered.

"Yes," I agreed. "Perchance the Devil too."

We fell silent for a long time and the breathing of the resting men slowed. Once more the sound of snores filled the interior of our prison, Runolf's the loudest of all. I listened intently for signs of movement outside whenever the Norseman exhaled, for in that instant there was the briefest respite from the noise of his snoring. I heard nothing. The night beyond the walls of the hut appeared silent and peaceful.

My thoughts meandered in the dark. I wondered what they had done with Leofstan's body. He had died unshriven, and again I felt a wave of shame at not preventing his murder.

I prayed silently for his soul then, asking God to welcome him, to offer him a place at His side in heaven. Leofstan was a good man and deserved to find peace in death. I wished that I had asked him more of his life before he became a monk. I knew nothing of his kin, or even where he came from, and I berated myself for my childish selfishness. I vowed I would never again make such a mistake. I would never take friends for granted, for you never know when they will be snatched away from you. Sadly, as with many promises I have made in my life, that was another I would fail to keep. But that is part of another tale.

Drosten's hand on my arm broke me out of my reverie. He leaned in close and whispered so faintly that I barely heard the word he uttered.

"Listen."

I held my breath, straining to hear anything over Runolf's stertorous snoring. For a time, I heard nothing, then, just when I thought Drosten had been mistaken, I made out the slightest scratch at the door. Could that be a whispered voice outside?

There was no time to alert the others without giving away our readiness and losing the element of surprise. I cursed silently. Neither Drosten nor I had fallen asleep. We had both been listening, ready to warn the others, and yet still we had failed. The scrape of the stout timber bar being lifted was clear now, but still too quiet to awaken Runolf or the others.

"Ready," I breathed into Drosten's ear, my lips brushing his skin, as close as a lover's. I sensed more than saw him nod in reply, and we drew apart, standing ready at either side of the doorway, prepared to attack whoever came through.

I clenched and unclenched my fists, tensing and turning my neck and shoulders, working the aches and stiffness from my muscles. I listened intently as the bar was removed and quietly set aside. Stealthily, the door was pulled open. I breathed through my mouth, willing whoever was outside not to detect Drosten and me beside the opening door. If we could overpower our captors, the Pict and I might yet still be able to redeem ourselves.

The door was half open now. Its movement halted. Nobody stepped into the darkness and I readied myself for the shout to come from outside. The moment Chlotar or whoever was outside called for us to rouse ourselves, I would rush through the open door. I was faster than Drosten, but I knew the massively muscled Pict would follow me into the breach, with no thought of the spears or the danger to himself. We were sword-brothers and we would stand together. Our only chance was to attack them without warning and hope that Runolf, Hereward and the others could leap up and join us before we were slain. I drew in a long calming breath, readying myself for action.

But no shout came from without. Instead, a shadowy form slipped through the partially open door. I had no time to think. Action was key to success now, so I leapt forward wrapping my forearm around the intruder's throat, pulling them close in a tight grip that would soon choke the life from them. They were shorter than me, but possessed a wiry strength and they struggled against my hold, scratching fingernails down my arm, reaching back to try to gouge at my eyes. I ignored the pain, turning my head. My opponent gurgled, their words muffled and choked. Though they were strong, they were no match for me. My pent-up rage roared in my ears and I spun around, forcing my adversary back towards the door, using their body as a shield for the spear thrusts I was certain would come slicing out of the darkness.

"Awaken," I called out, loud enough for the others to hear, but not shouting. I did not want to rouse more of Ljósberari's people. I could scarcely believe what was happening. Surely God must have been smiling on me, for I was shoving my way towards the door and no steel had found me yet. Drosten was beside me and in that instant I began to believe that we might actually make it out of the stinking hut, out into the cool air of the night. Out to freedom. Or at least, to be freed from this prison. We would still need to face Ljósberari, Chlotar and his murderous band of thralls and children, but that would have to wait. For now, all that mattered was getting out of our cell.

We passed the threshold, the air fresh and cool on my face. The light from the stars and moon were bright after the inky darkness within the hut and I scanned the night for threats, ready to swing my captive into the path of any weapon that might come hurtling towards me. If I could trap a blade in their flesh, I might even be able to wrest it away and thus arm myself.

But still, no attack came.

Drosten pushed into the moonlight, moving quickly to one side to split us up and divide our enemies. Behind us, I could hear the rest of our band surging to their feet, their whispers and grunts loud in the night as they began to force their way out of the hut.

I moved further into the night, away from the building. Confused at the lack of resistance, I peered into the gloom, but I only spied one other figure there.

"Hunlaf?"

My mind spun. There was something familiar about the voice, but I was filled with rage and horror. I had believed men had come to slay us, and so my mind did not immediately grasp whose voice it was I heard beneath the northern stars of Hǫrðaland. As the truth of it finally penetrated through the fog of my battle-fury, I relaxed my grip on my captive. I was suddenly aware of how slender the body was that was pressed against me, how unlike the brawny shoulders and chest of a warrior.

I gawped, staring into the darkness at the face of the woman before me, searching for proof that it was indeed her. The wide eyes glimmered. The full lips, always so quick to smile, were set in a sombre scowl, but there could be no doubt. At last, I was certain, and a great shuddering breath left me in a rush. I grew weak, releasing the figure I had been clutching so tightly, choking with my arm. I opened my mouth to speak, but before I could utter a sound, another figure stepped from the hut and rushed past me.

"Aelfwyn," Eadmaer said, and an instant later, he had enclosed my cousin in a tight embrace.

Fifty-Four

Eadmaer clung to Aelfwyn for what seemed a long time.

She was alive! After all this time I had finally found her. A wave of elation washed through me, where it mingled with the other swirling powerful emotions. Grief and despair battled against the surge of joy at finding my cousin alive in this strange and dangerous land. I had not allowed myself to admit it, but I knew the truth then. Until that moment, I had long since ceased to believe I would ever find her. It had seemed certain to me that we would all be slain, and, if she yet lived, the closest I would ever come to Aelfwyn again would be to see her as we were led to the place of our execution. But now, the angle of her neck and curve of her cheek unmistakable, her skin pale in the gloom, there she stood, a shadowy vision, close enough to touch.

Eadmaer was whispering to her, holding her tightly and she responded by nuzzling into his neck. Aelfwyn murmured words to the fisherman, but I could not make them out. I felt a stab of a new emotion then: jealousy. It was an ugly feeling, but I could not be rid of it. Aelfwyn was my kin and I wanted her to know how much I had striven to come to her aid. How much danger I had faced and what I had sacrificed.

"There's no time for tears," whispered Hereward, his voice pulling me away from my petty thoughts and back to the predicament in which we found ourselves.

My companions were all outside the hut now, and they crowded around us. I glanced up the slope at the settlement. All was still there, but I noticed a sliver of warm light shining from beneath the hall's great doors, no doubt from the oil lamps and candles Ljósberari favoured. We were close to the river, and the dark waters beckoned. Freedom lay in that direction. The wharfs were nearby and we could be away, paddling downstream in moments.

"Revna," growled Runolf, shouldering past me and stooping to the slender form I had grappled with. Dismayed, I realised I had been choking the Norseman's daughter. He swept her up from where she had fallen after I had released my grip on her.

"Is she well?" I asked, horrified at what I had done and terrified of what answer he might give.

"I am well enough," hissed Revna, rubbing at her neck.

"It is good for you that she is," snarled Runolf.

"Enough, Father," she said, her tone sharp.

He held her at arm's length, staring at her in the gloom.

"I thought I had lost you, child. As I have lost everything else."

"I am no child," Revna replied, and there was a dreadful sadness in the words. "But I am not lost yet. And your man is right. There is no time for this. Take those two and put them inside." She nodded to the shadowed shapes of two men who lay slumped near the entrance to the hut. I had not noticed them before, for they were quite still.

"Are they dead?" I asked.

"No," she replied, "and they will not remain silent for long. More guards will be sent soon, and they will raise the alarm. We must get to the boats." There was fear in her voice, but she did not allow it to control her. Her steely determination reminded me of her father.

Beorn and Gwawrddur dragged the limp guards into the hut. I wondered what Aelfwyn and Revna had done to incapacitate them, but now was not the moment for questions.

Aelfwyn freed herself at last from Eadmaer's grasp and embraced me.

"You came for me," she whispered. As well as gratitude, her tone carried awe. She must have been certain that she would never see me or anyone she knew ever again. I held her tightly, making sure that she was really there and not a spectre from a dream.

"You are kin," I said, simply.

She stepped back and looked me up and down in the pale light of the moon.

"You no longer wear the tonsure," she said.

My face grew hot in the darkness. I was garbed in the linen robe and nothing more. My feet were yet bare, my toes encased in drying mud and shit from the hut's squelching floor.

" I am a monk no more," I said. "Much has changed since last we met."

She let out a long breath. Both of our lives had been ripped apart in this last year. I could scarcely recall what life had been like before the Norse came to Lindisfarnae.

"We have many stories to tell, I am sure, cousin," she said, her tone tight with sorrow and memories that were best left for the daylight. But for that, I thought, we would have to survive beyond the dawn.

"Wait there," said Revna, her voice not much louder than the passing of an owl in the night. She slipped away and was instantly lost in the shadows. Still, there was no sound from the settlement, but my skin prickled with the feeling of being in the open. It could only be a matter of time before we were spotted and all would be lost.

"Where is she going?" asked Gersine, pointing with his chin into the gloom after Revna. He had hobbled out of our cell and now stood leaning against Drosten.

Nobody answered him and we stood in tense silence, listening for any sound. A scuffed footfall close by startled me. It was Beorn and Gwawrddur stepping out of the hut.

"Those guards will not be alerting anyone of our escape," the Welshman said.

Aelfwyn flinched at his ominous words, and I wondered how well she knew the men who had been watching our prison. I reached out to her and squeezed her hand.

"I cannot believe you are here," she murmured. I smiled, despite the dark circumstances of our meeting, thrilled to hear her voice again. "But I am more surprised that you brought Eadmaer with you. You really do have much to tell."

I sensed Eadmaer would not be happy with her words. He was quick to take offence, but I knew Aelfwyn well and recognised the warmth in her tone when she mentioned her husband's brother. But before either of us could say anything, Revna returned. She lugged a large sack over her slim shoulder. She must have hidden it nearby, for she had not been gone long. Swinging it down, she placed the sack gingerly on the ground. Heavy metallic items clattered together despite her care, the sounds terrifyingly loud.

"I could not carry your shields, helms or byrnies," she whispered, "but most of your arms should be there."

Stooping to the sack, we quickly retrieved our things. My plain sword was there and I thanked God that my belt was yet wrapped about its scabbard. I fastened the leather about my waist and immediately felt stronger and less vulnerable. The others pulled their weapons from the sack. Runolf hoomed deep in his throat as he withdrew his huge axe. The crescent of its blade gleamed in the cold light; a reflection of the moon.

All of my companions had found a weapon, and I sensed I was not alone in the feeling of my morale lifting. I rummaged in the sack once more, but I could already see that it was empty now. Neither of my seaxes were inside. The old, antler-handled one that I had taken from a brigand in Northumbria was no great loss, but I was saddened not to find the carved ivory-handled knife I had won on Orkneyjar. It was a thing of wonder and I was sorry to lose such a valuable thing.

I shook my head at the stupidity of my greed. To own a fine seax would matter nought if we did not escape.

"Come, we can tarry no longer," said Hereward.

Revna led the way. We followed as quietly as we could, Gersine limping beside Drosten. We were moving slowly, so he was able to keep up, but I did not wish to think what would occur if we were called upon to run.

The shadows of the scattered buildings were black against the darkness of the mountain slopes in the east. With a start I saw that the sky beyond was already lightening. Dawn was still some way off, but the grey wolf-light of its approach was the harbinger of sunrise.

As we made our way stealthily along the shore towards the wharfs where Leofstan and I had bathed that afternoon, my joy at finding Aelfwyn began to subside. I was still exultant that she lived, but now that I had a sword at my hip once again, and we were free of the stinking hut, my mind turned to Leofstan, and thoughts of vengeance. Scomric had caused so much pain and suffering, had slain so many innocents. I could not bear the thought of fleeing into the night, leaving the madman behind to continue his reign of fire and death.

It seemed Runolf, now that his precious daughter was no longer his enemy, had similar thoughts. For he touched Hereward's shoulder, halting our progress.

"Stick to the original plan," he whispered. "Scatter the boats and keep just enough for us. Stay quiet for as long as you can and wait for me as long as you are able. I will join you at the wharf, if I can."

He turned to head into the settlement. Hereward pulled him back.

"We came here together," he said. "Let us end this as we started."

Gwawrddur too stepped in close. His teeth flashed in the darkness. He thrived on danger and seemed more relaxed than any of us.

"I too would wet the steel of my sword."

Runolf shook his great mane of hair.

"No. I need to know that you will take Revna safely from this place."

"Do that yourself, axeman," said Gwawrddur.

"I will, if I live. But I cannot leave behind the man who put out my wife's eyes and..." His voice trailed away. "That Frank whoreson defiled my daughter," Runolf hissed, his voice sounding like a blade drawn across a whetstone. "I will kill him, if the gods smile on me."

"We need Ljósberari's head," said Gersine. "My father is awaiting our return. Without that head, God knows what King Hjorleif will do."

"I will bring back Ljósberari's head too, then," Runolf said. "If I do not return, promise me you will keep Revna safe."

I looked to where Eadmaer walked close to Aelfwyn. I understood now. He was besotted with his brother's widow. He had risked everything to rescue her. He would die rather than allow further harm to come to her.

But I had watched Scomric drink Leofstan's blood and like Runolf, I could not run without seeking revenge.

"I will go with you," I said. Anticipating Runolf's objections, I added, "I can speak the tongue of the Norse. With God's grace, if we are questioned, in the dark we can pass for Ljósberari's people and get close to our enemies. You stand more chance of success with me."

"No, Hunlaf," he said. "Take care of Aelfwyn. This is my fight."

My anger sprang to life, white-hot and searing.

"Your fight? Ljósberari cut Leofstan's throat as if he were a kine. He..." It was all I could do to keep my voice low, but my words trembled with the force of my wrath. "He drank Leofstan's blood while I watched. I must see him slain." I had never been so certain of anything in my life. Now, decades later, I can recall the power of that terrible emotion as it coursed through my veins like molten iron. Vengeance is a sin, and Leofstan would have wanted me to turn away from that path, but Leofstan was dead and revenge is the warrior's way. And I had chosen the life of a warrior.

After a moment, Runolf patted my shoulder.

"Very well," he said, understanding my need. "You come, but no others."

"Father," whispered Revna, moving close. For a moment I thought she was going to implore Runolf not to go, to instead go with them to the boats without delay. But she grasped her father's arm tightly and her words again reminded me that she was Runolf's daughter. "Chlotar sleeps in the chamber at the rear of the great hall," she hissed. "Avenge my mother."

Runolf nodded.

Aelfwyn reached out in the darkness and took my hand in hers, sending a shiver through me at her touch.

"There are other women and girls there, Hunlaf," she said. "They are not your enemy. Cause them no harm."

"My fight is not with the womenfolk," I said, giving her hand a squeeze. "Eadmaer," I whispered, "look after her."

"There's no more time for talk," said Runolf, interrupting us. "If we dawdle here, we will lose our chance and I do not think Óðinn, or Christ for that matter, will provide us with another. Ljósberari's folk still think we are prisoners. Let us not make them aware of our escape by standing here talking until we are discovered."

He embraced Revna, and then, one by one, the warriors gripped first Runolf's forearm, and then mine.

"Hurry back," said Gwawrddur, his grasp firm in the warrior's grip. "And remember all I have taught you."

I swallowed down the emotion that lumped in my throat.

"I'll see you soon," I said, and I prayed it was true.

For a few heartbeats, we stood in silence and watched the group of them move along the river's edge towards the timber jetties where the log boats and other vessels were moored.

"Come on, then," said Runolf at last, his whispered voice gruff. "Let's kill that accursed Ljósberari and his fucking Frank lackey."

Fifty-Five

I followed Runolf's massive shadow, amazed that a man so large could move with such stealth. He bent low and loped across the open ground to the first of the dark houses clustered at the foot of the slope. I followed, keeping up with him easily. Glancing over my shoulder, I could just make out the dark shapes of the others moving as silently as wraiths along the water line. I shivered. The night air was cold, and despite the solidity of the plain wooden grip of the sword in my hand, and the familiar tightness of the belt cinched at my waist, I felt horribly vulnerable. Grass whipped at my bare legs and muddy feet as I ran and I prayed nobody was awake and looking towards the river from the houses. They might not see our companions heading towards the boats, but they would have to be blind not to see me, wearing nothing more than a pale robe that flapped about me like a luffing sail.

Runolf had halted in the moon shadow of the closest building, and I slid to a halt behind him. My breath was ragged, though we had not covered much distance. My blood rushed in my ears. In an effort to calm my nerves, I breathed slowly through my mouth as quietly as possible, listening for any sound out there in the dark.

Silence.

We walked on, slowly now, flitting from shadow to shadow, moving ever closer to the looming presence of the great hall. The red glow of light that spilt beneath the doors conjured the image in my mind of a dragon's mouth, slowly opening, ready to breath fiery death on its prey.

Off to the south, the pre-dawn light began to illuminate the shapes of the rows of burnt and skewered corpses. Soon it would be light and the bodies were a stark reminder of the fate that awaited us if we were caught by Ljósberari's people.

A noise made Runolf halt without warning and I collided with his back. We both held our breath and stood unmoving. Behind the thin wall of the hut beside us, an infant was crying. Its wailing anguish grew in pitch, so loud that it must have woken everyone within the hut and also those in surrounding buildings. We did not move, and the crying continued, rising in pitch. After what seemed an age, a female voice muttered something and the child's weeping subsided to a snivelling grizzle as the woman cooed and sang to it. The singing continued for some time, the voice beautiful and at odds with the darkness and the horrific shapes of the dead that lined the path to the south.

Runolf tugged at my robe and we set off once more. We could not afford to wait in the shadows. Our only chance was to reach the hall before the settlement awoke. Fleetingly, I wondered how we would escape, if we were able to complete our quest for vengeance, but I pushed my concerns away. Fear was my enemy now and would only serve to cloud my judgement.

We moved on, the singing still clear in the cool air of the night. No other sound came to us as we reached the houses closest to the hall.

Without warning, a door opened beside us and a figure almost stumbled directly into Runolf. In the dim light I saw bleary eyes and tousled hair. Shocked by the hulking shape of

Runolf, the man hesitated, then opened his mouth to sound the alarm. Runolf dropped his axe and in the same movement wrapped his brawny left arm around the man's neck, clamping his broad hand over his mouth before he could utter a sound. Runolf was a head taller than the man and much stronger. As the figure flailed and scratched against Runolf's thick forearms, the axeman dragged him away from the doorway. They struggled together in the darkness for a few heartbeats, Runolf applying counter pressure to the man's head with his right hand. There was a sickening crack, as the man's neck snapped and he went limp.

"Vermund?" a woman's voice, blurred and fuzzy with sleep, called quietly through the open doorway from the darkness within.

Runolf, still holding the dead man, looked at me and nodded towards the hut. I thought of Aelfwyn's words and did not move. How many of those in this settlement were guilty of the same crimes as Ljósberari, and how many had been taken by force, just as Revna and Aelfwyn? I had not come here to fight womenfolk and innocent children.

"Vermund?" came the call again, this time clearer, more urgent.

Runolf let go of the man with his right hand and pointed furiously at the open door. His meaning was clear, but still I did not move. A heartbeat later, Runolf dropped the body and vanished inside the hut.

There was a muffled cry, a thud, then silence. My heart hammered against my ribs and I was breathless again as I stood there in the dark. Distant and thin sounding now, I could just discern the strains of the lullaby we had heard. Surely someone must have heard the scuffle or the woman calling out. But there was no further sound.

Runolf stepped from the hut, his movements stiff. He stooped for his axe.

"Drag his body into the hut so that it won't be discovered," he hissed, his tone clipped and angry.

I did as he asked. I could barely make out anything in the gloom inside and I cursed as I knocked into what might have been a stool. I pulled the man in by his feet, dropping them down on the packed earth when his head and shoulders had cleared the doorway. The hut smelt of stale breath, sweat, ash and the sharp, battlefield tang of voided bowels. There was a woman somewhere in the dark, but I did not look into the far corners of the room where the bed must surely have been. I did not wish to see what Runolf had done to her.

I pushed the door shut behind me and let out a long breath.

"You cannot hesitate, Hunlaf," Runolf growled, leaning down so that he could speak into my ear. "If we are discovered, we will die and all this will be for nothing. You want to avenge Leofstan, no? You would see Ljósberari slain for what he has done and to prevent further killings?"

I nodded.

"Then when the moment comes, act. To hesitate is death."

He did not wait for me to respond, but turned back towards the great hall. After the black of the hut's interior and the gloom of the night, the warm light creeping beneath the door made me blink.

Runolf was about to make his way across the open ground, when my keen, youthful eyes saw something amiss. Catching hold of Runolf's kirtle, I yanked him back. I crouched in the shadow of the hut, pulling him down beside me. Without speaking, I pointed towards the hall doors.

A long moment passed and then, just when I had begun to doubt myself and I could sense Runolf was preparing to shrug me off, I saw the smallest of movements. To the right of the doors, hidden in the shadow of the carved door jamb, there stood a man.

Runolf grew very still, and I knew he too had seen him.

There was only one way into the hall, but we could not hope to approach the doors without being seen by the guard who loitered there. If the hut where the man had stepped into our path had been positioned differently, the door ward would surely have already seen us, but thankfully that building's door, like the hall's, also pointed towards the river, meaning the hut had obscured us from sight.

Pulling again on Runolf's sleeve, not daring to speak, I led him away southward. He followed and when we had gone some distance, he lowered his head to speak to me.

"We must get through those doors. Day will be upon us soon."

"If we approach directly, he will raise the alarm. If we come in from the south side of the hall, and then slip around the corner to the west, we might take him by surprise."

Runolf grunted, and I took that for agreement. Leading the way now, I threaded my way past several buildings. A dog began barking far-off and we halted. Someone shouted and the dog fell silent.

"We are running out of time," grumbled Runolf.

He was right. The sky was noticeably lighter, though the dawn was still some way off. We hurried on as quickly as we could without abandoning caution completely. But we could both sense it now. It was only a matter of time before we were seen and then all would be lost.

At last, breath ragged with tension, we reached the long southern wall of the hall. Slowly, with as much stealth as we could muster, we slid along towards the corner where we knew the guard stood. I used my hands to feel my way along the rough wall. At one point my fingers brushed against something smooth and strangely pliant. I drew my hand back, unsure what I had touched, but it was just one of the windows I had noticed before. It was covered in a thin membrane, some kind of stretched hide. Its touch reminded me of vellum.

I drew in a deep breath and pulled my sword silently from its fur-lined scabbard. It stuck for a moment, but the blade came free easily enough with a tug. Runolf raised his axe, the metal blade dully gleaming in the wolf-pelt grey light. His eyes glimmered and he offered me a nod to show that he was ready.

At that precise moment, a cockerel crowed loudly to the west, its harsh call tearing at the calm of the night. There was nothing for it now. Soon the settlement would be awake. As if the bird's cry had been our signal, we slipped around the corner of the hall and rushed towards the guard.

I had hoped that the door ward might be dozing, drowsy after a long night of staring silently into the darkness. But the luck we had enjoyed until this moment now left us. Maybe he had heard us, or perhaps the baby's crying had roused him, or the dog's barking and now the cock's crowing had warned him of danger. Mayhap he was just a better guard than I, and did not allow his weariness to overcome him. Whatever the reason, the man was alert, and to his credit, he was fast too. He stepped from the shadow of the door as if he had expected us. Still, even with fast reflexes and a sharp awareness of our headlong sprint towards him, he was no match for Runolf's lengthy strides and the reach of his huge battle axe. The sentry's sword had not cleared its scabbard when Runolf's axe bit deep into his skull with a thudding crunch. The man wore no armour, but even if he had worn a helm, no iron could have saved him from that hammering blow. He made a strange, strangled sound, and collapsed into a heap of tangled limbs. He was dead before he hit the ground.

I could barely believe that our plan had worked. For a heartbeat there was silence, and then a voice shouted out, loud and very close.

"Alarm!" it cried.

A chill washed over me as if I had plunged once more into the cold waters of the river. I understood our mistake, an error that would now see the populace of Ljósberari's realm descend upon us. On the far side of the hall doors, there was a second guard. Like the first, he had been silent and hidden in the shadows and we had failed to see him in the gloom. It was his voice that now rent the night's stillness.

I had learnt my lesson earlier, so without hesitation, I sprang forward before Runolf had wrenched his axe free of the first man's skull. The second sentry bore a spear and a shield. He lunged towards me, but he was no match for my speed. I deflected the spear haft with my left hand, pushing the point away from me and down. Stepping close, I feinted a blow at his shins. His shield dipped to protect his legs, and then his eyes widened as I buried my blade in his throat, silencing his yelling. I twisted the sword, tugging it free with a shower of dark gore.

He fell to the earth and I turned to stand, panting beside Runolf, our backs to the doors as if we had taken the place of the sentries and now stood watch there. Shouts echoed around the settlement as men, women and children awoke, rudely roused from their slumber by the sound of fighting and the sentry's calls of warning.

"Well," said Runolf, not bothering to whisper any longer, "we came for vengeance. Let us get what we came for before we are killed."

I watched as lights spilled from open doors, and figures began to tumble into the pre-dawn dark. Runolf was right. I could see no way that we might escape this place, but I would avenge Leofstan and all those others who hung from stakes along the river and path. I would exact vengeance for Ingvar and Os, and all the nameless men and women the madman had tortured and killed.

"Let's find those whoresons," I said, turning to heave open the doors. "They owe us more blood-price than they can ever pay."

The scent of incense and burning whale oil was strong as we slipped into the flickering flame light within. Hurriedly, seeing people streaming out of their houses now and running towards the hall, I shouldered the doors shut. Runolf picked up a stout beam from where it leaned against the wall. Dropping it into place, he barred the doors.

"That will hold them for a while," he said.

Together, we turned our back on the doors and the angry people outside, and strode into Ljósberari's lair.

Fifty-Six

Candlelight glimmered at the far end of the hall, illuminating empty benches and boards. Just as earlier that day, the hall was devoid of Ljósberari's followers. The lord of a hall kept his hearth-warriors close, always wary of an attack from his adversaries. But Scomric was no lord and there were no figures sleeping on the floor here. Perhaps Scomric did not fear any earthly enemy, or maybe he wished to maintain his mystery, keeping himself separate from those ignorant fools who followed him so blindly. Whatever the reason, there were no warriors in our path.

The noise from outside was rising in pitch as men, women and children shouted in the night.

"We don't have much time," said Runolf, hefting his axe and hurrying forward as the people began to hammer on the doors behind us.

Clutching my sword tightly, I followed the axeman as he passed the cold hearth. I glanced down at the dark stain in the rushes where Leofstan had died. My stomach clenched and I shuddered as I recalled his eyes, the light dimming as I watched on, unable to prevent his death or to mete out vengeance for his killing. I turned my head away, ashamed and sickened at the memory. The clamour outside was building and I vowed that, no matter what happened to me, Scomric would pay.

Without warning, Runolf stopped walking, and I was brought up short, barely avoiding a collision. I peered past him, expecting to see our enemy, but there was no movement at the end of the hall. The door to the rear partition was closed, though if Scomric and Chlotar were indeed inside, there was no way they would not have been roused by the shouting coming from without. As if to emphasise the point, the banging on the barred doors increased in intensity.

Momentarily confused, I glanced at Runolf, wondering what had caused him to halt. The doors would soon be breached and there was no time to waste. The giant Norseman was looking up and to the left. I followed his gaze and gasped, taking an involuntary step backwards.

Leofstan was naked and had been hung upside down, like a pig at slaughter. A rope had been tied about his ankles and thrown over a beam. He had been hauled off the ground, the rope secured to a pillar, leaving him to dangle, head down. Beneath the old monk was a large cauldron. I did not need to look into it to know that it would be full of his congealing blood. Bile burnt the back of my throat. To capture his body's blood, they must have done this to him while I yet lay insensate in the hall. At the sight of his dead, pale skin, his face a mask of dried blood that had run down from the gaping wound in his throat, something shifted within me. The tethers that held my reason had been frayed and stretched to their limits, but now they snapped, and for a time, I believe I lost my mind.

I growled, deep in the back of my throat, an animal sound that made Runolf turn away from Leofstan's butchered corpse and stare at me.

The pounding was loud now as those outside took up something heavy and solid in an attempt to break down the doors. But the sounds were distant to me as my blood rushed in my ears like a gale, and a scream of fury ripped my throat.

"Scomric," I bellowed, "I am Death and I am come for you."

Runolf was pale, whether at the vision of Leofstan's bleddry body or at the change in me, I did not know, nor care. I barged past him, making my way towards the door that led to the sleeping quarters at the rear of the hall. Runolf hurried after me.

"Scomric!" I screamed again, revelling in the power of my fury that burnt away all fear and uncertainty. Gone was thought for the past or the future. All that existed was the present and an incandescent hatred that demanded Scomric's death. "I will kill you!" I bellowed.

Before my hand touched the door, it was flung open.

"Not if I kill you first," Chlotar said. He filled the doorway. He must have been awake for some time for he had donned full battle-harness, no doubt stolen from some of Ljósberari's victims. He wore a great helm. Iron covered his skull, encircling his eyes and protruding down to protect his nose. His body was encased in a well-fitting byrnie, its links of iron burnished so that they gleamed in the flickering lamp light. In his left hand he held a shield that looked new, the hide that was stretched over its boards was unblemished and stained a deep wine-red. In his right hand he brandished his fine sword.

Despite being unarmoured, wearing only a thin linen robe and bearing no shield or helm, I felt no dread. I sprang to meet the Frank, holding my sword ready to parry and watching Chlotar's body for a warning of his intention. Even in my rage-filled state, I had not forgotten Gwawrddur's lessons. But I did not manage to close the distance with my opponent. After a single step, Runolf grabbed my robe and, with his prodigious strength, pulled me back, sending me sprawling to the rush-covered floor.

I sprang up, snarling like a wolf, furious at his intervention.

"The Frank is mine," he shouted. "Find Ljósberari."

He bounded forward, swiping his great axe at Chlotar, who was barely able to block the cut with his shield. The Frank had held me back while Leofstan breathed his last and I longed to throw myself at him, to plunge my blade into his flesh. I watched as Runolf retreated, stepping out of the reach of Chlotar's blade as the Frankish warrior counter-attacked. I knew the Norse axeman's skill well, and I could see that he was deliberately feigning weakness, allowing himself to be pushed back by Chlotar's determined attack. He was drawing Chlotar away from the door, freeing it for me.

Shaking my head to rid it of some of the battle-madness that had engulfed me, I ran past the battling warriors. Runolf scythed a blow at Chlotar's legs, but the Frank was fast and agile. He stepped back and flicked out with his sword's blade. Blood bloomed on Runolf's arm and I hesitated to leave him.

"Go!" shouted Runolf, noticing me tarrying by the door. Chlotar's blow had not slowed him, and he stormed forward, sending a flurry of strikes at the Frank, who soaked them up with a clatter on his shield. The red hide there was now scored and cut from the axe's sharp blade.

I took in a deep breath. Outside the hall, the crowd was growing, their shouts and yells raucous, the booming crash of something being rammed into the doors echoing like thunder in the hall's cavernous interior. The timber was beginning to splinter. They would be inside the hall soon, and then our chance for revenge would be lost.

I glanced once more at Leofstan's pallid, grisly form, then, abandoning Runolf to his wyrd and praying that God would watch over me until I had delivered justice for my friend, I rushed through the doorway.

Fifty-Seven

I stepped into a small antechamber that was flanked by two doors. The door on the right was open and light spilt out from the room beyond it. This must be where Chlotar had come from, I surmised, so I turned to the left-hand door, which was closed and dark.

In the main hall, Runolf and Chlotar exchanged blows and insults, while further away, outside in the night, the throng of Ljósberari's folk howled and clamoured, battering at the doors to get to their master's aid. The hall reverberated with noise, so I did not hear Scomric's approach. But as I stood outside the closed door, readying myself to push it open and leap inside, a shadow rippled over me, alerting me of my mistake in thinking that Ljósberari would be to the left.

I flung myself to the side and careened into the thin whitewashed wall that separated the sleeping quarters from the hall. The mud-covered wattle wall shook, dust showering down on me. And a searing pain lanced into my shoulder. I spun around, swinging my sword wildly.

Scomric, eyes feral and hair dishevelled from sleep, jumped away with a yelp. He stumbled back into the room. Scowling, I followed him. In his hand, he brandished the small knife that had taken Leofstan's life. It was red with my blood. My shoulder was agony and I could already feel hot liquid pouring down my back, soaking the linen robe I wore.

Scomric looked about the room, desperate for another weapon perhaps, or anything that might help him escape. There was a large, wooden-framed bed. A chair and a table, upon which rested a small earthenware oil lamp that provided the only light. There was a stoutly built chest against one wall, but there was nothing that Scomric might use to prevent me exacting the revenge I so craved.

"Not so brave now, are you?" I snarled, lunging at him with my sword.

He whimpered and took a quick step back.

"You are not sent by God," he hissed. "The Devil sent you. Isn't that so?"

"You can ask him yourself soon enough," I said, closing on him and raising my sword. It was clear Scomric was no warrior. He was clumsy and slow, and I marvelled that he had lived so long without someone slaying him, surrounded by violence as he was. Perhaps fear of being killed by one of his followers was why he slept in the hall alone, save for his most trusted man.

He backed away, his terror plain on his face. The room darkened as his body blocked out much of the light from the lamp. He collided with the small table. There was nowhere else for him to go. I stepped in, but before I could deliver the killing blow, he reached behind him and snatched up the lamp. Its flame guttered and danced, painting his face in writhing shadows and light. His eyes blazed with madness and malice.

"Back," he shouted, waving the lamp in front of him. "I will burn us both," he sneered, a triumphant glimmer in his eyes.

I stared at him for a heartbeat. Did he truly believe I feared death?

The splintering as the hall doors cracked was loud in the distance. Ljósberari's crazed followers bayed like hounds scenting blood. They would all too soon be inside. No, in that moment I was certain I would die. All I wanted, so help me God, was to be sure that Scomric went before me.

I slashed down with my sword into Scomric's wrist. His hand, and the lamp it held, spun in the air. Hot oil splattered my right arm, stinging and burning. The lamp hit the ground and shattered, spilling oil onto the rushes and over much of the bed. A heartbeat later, the oil ignited with a sound like a great sigh.

The straw-filled mattress caught, and flames shot up, licking the rafters high above. The heat from the blaze was intense and I blinked, shocked by the sudden consequences of my actions. Scomric looked down in horror at his wrist. Blood spurted with each beat of his heart. He stared into my face, aghast. He saw nothing but death in my gaze. Even as the fire began to rage, the heat becoming intolerable, I stepped forward, to finish him; to send his murderous soul to hell.

Scomric glanced back at the flames and a change came over him. His shoulders relaxed and his eyes took on the mesmeric calm I had witnessed before.

"If I am to die here," he said, his tone filled with awe and wonder, "I will join the light." He spun around and I saw what he meant to do. I could not allow him to decide the manner of his death. Springing forward, I thrust my sword into his side, plunging the blade deep into his chest. He staggered, still moving towards the fire. The flames roared, sucking the air from the room. The heat singed my hair. Tears streamed from my eyes and smoke burnt my lungs.

"There is no light in you," I shouted over the sound of the inferno that was rapidly engulfing the room, "only darkness." I twisted the sword and wrenched it free. Blood gushed from the wound and Scomric collapsed, quivering. He was reaching with his remaining hand towards the flames when his body shook, and he died.

I looked down at his still form, incredulous that this small man, so weak and pathetic, had managed to carve such a swathe of destruction and death through this land. The heat was unbearable now and it was becoming hard to breathe. Something fluttered on the table where the lamp had stood, catching my attention. It was the scrap of parchment that Scomric had shown me. A possible clue as to the whereabouts of *The Treasure of Life*. I was sure then that I would never be able to study the meaning of the scrawled writing on it, for within moments I too would be dead, consumed by fire, or killed by Ljósberari's faithful, but on a whim, I snatched up the paper, stuffing it into my belt. Perhaps even in that moment I was unable to see knowledge destroyed, or mayhap I heard the voice of Leofstan in my mind reminding me how I loathed to think of all those scrolls that had been turned to ash at the Mouseion of Alexandria.

Turning away from the fire, I made to leave, when a sudden thought struck me. There was something else I must do. Holding my left arm over my face to shield my eyes from the flames, I hacked down. It took me two blows of my sword, but at the second attempt, Scomric's head came free of his neck. I did not wish to touch it, but now was not the moment to be squeamish. I grabbed the head by the hair and hurried out into the hall, bearing my dripping trophy.

Fifty-Eight

It was noticeably cooler in the main hall, but already I could feel the heat pressing on my back. Wind rushed through the doorway, feeding the flames in Scomric's quarters. It was as if the building itself was breathing. Again I was reminded of a great dragon readying itself to spout fire on those who dared confront it.

Runolf turned to me. He was grinning, his expression at odds with our surroundings and situation. Blood streaked his face, and his kirtle was dark in several places from slashes he had received from Chlotar.

"He didn't want to die," he said, stooping to the body slumped at his feet.

Runolf had not merely killed Chlotar. In his rage, he had continued to hack into the man's body long after death. The fine helm was cleaved in two, the head inside smashed like an overripe apple. A hand was severed and lay nearby like a fat, pale, blood-spattered spider. There was a deep gash in the man's iron-knit coat. Blood oozed from his many wounds and pooled around his body.

"It looks like you convinced him in the end," I said.

"I can be persuasive," Runolf said with a savage chuckle.

He had retrieved something from Chlotar's corpse and now he rose to his full height and tossed it to me. "Yours, I believe."

My hands were full and I had barely any time to react, so, not wishing to be bereft of my sword, I dropped Scomric's head and snatched the object from the air with my left hand.

Runolf stepped to where Ljósberari's severed head had thudded to the rushes.

"Perhaps not a fair exchange," he said, picking up the head, "but I will take it."

I looked down at what Runolf had thrown to me. With a surge of pointless pleasure, given our predicament, I saw that it was the finely carved, ivory-handled seax. It was smeared with Chlotar's blood, but otherwise unscathed.

"Thank you," I said. "I never thought to see it again. Though I doubt I will own it for much longer."

The heat from the fire was growing, and a glance at the double doors showed me they were splintering. A gap had been opened in the timber and I could see movement through it. Axes bit into the wood, widening the opening.

"Anything is possible," Runolf said, striding down the hall towards the fracturing doors and the waiting horde outside.

I hurried after him, gazing up at Leofstan's inverted corpse as I passed. The breeze tugged at the old monk and he spun slowly at the end of the rope, as if he watched our progress. I shuddered. There was no time to see to his body, or to pray for his soul.

"I'm sorry, my friend," I whispered. It seemed that soon enough we would all be killed, our bodies destroyed by the same fire that had turned the sleeping quarters into an inferno and was even now consuming the light bearer himself, just as flames had licked at the bodies of his countless victims.

Shards of wood were flung into the hall where a heavy axe-head dug into the doors. Outside the hall, Ljósberari's folk were howling. Perhaps there were words in their wails, but I could not make them out.

"What are we going to do?" I asked Runolf.

He flicked the blood from his war axe.

"Fight them, if we have to."

"There are too many," I said, but I could think of no better suggestion and so resigned myself to the truth of it. "But better to die fighting, than to burn to death."

"We are not dead yet," Runolf said. "Perhaps we will not need to fight."

"How so? Listen to them. They want our blood, and they will have it. Still," I said, forcing a thin smile, "at least we got our revenge." The thought of it now did little to lift my spirits. The moment of elation at seeing Scomric's corpse had been replaced by sorrow. There was so much I would never do, so many books I would never have the chance to read. *The Treasure of Life* had driven Scomric mad and called to Leofstan like a siren's song over the waves of the North Sea, and now I would not be able to unravel its mysteries. I would never again see my friends or kin. After striving to find Aelfwyn for the last year, I would not lay eyes on her again, but I could draw some comfort in knowing she was safe.

"Before we fight," said Runolf, with a smile, "let us talk to them." He was infuriatingly calm now, as if by slaying Chlotar he had found inner peace and feared nothing. But then again, had Runolf ever truly been afraid of anything?

"They will never allow us to speak," I said. "They will kill us instantly." Perhaps a quick death was all we could hope for now.

"Anything is possible," Runolf said again and, grinning at me, he raised Ljósberari's head and pushed the madman's dead face into the shattered gap between the doors. "Stand back from the doors!" Runolf bellowed, his voice loud enough to cut through the howls of the crowd and the roaring crackle of the flames that had now spread to the main hall, where they ran hungrily along the beams and rafters.

The axe blows on the doors halted. Shouts and screams echoed in the night as the people saw the face of their master. In a few heartbeats, the crowd's wailing subsided, replaced by a hushed sigh of muttering. Runolf looked at me.

"Ready?" he mouthed.

"No," I replied, in barely a whisper, but I raised my sword and clutched the seax in my left hand.

"Good," Runolf said, and kicked the beam away from the doors and dragged them open.

I expected the throng outside to rush at us, but they had fallen back from the entrance and Runolf, holding Ljósberari's head high, his great axe dripping with gore low at his side, stepped out into the dawn gloom.

Taking in great lungfuls of the cool fresh air, I followed him. Smoke billowed out of the doors behind us. The air inside the hall would soon be too thick to breathe. Before us stood dozens of people. Pale faces glowered at us, their eyes glimmering in the light of the flames that had begun to fill the hall. I scanned those gathered there, quickly calculating the odds against us. They were not good.

There were some two dozen men, all bearing weapons and some wearing byrnies. A few carried shields and the firelight glinted from more than one helm. These men were freed thralls, and if they had once been warriors, and knew how to wield those weapons, we stood no chance, no matter how skilled or brave we might be. Beyond the men, there was yet another score of youths and children who had taken up arms, mainly spears. The rest of the throng was comprised of women, the elderly, and children too young and scared to fight. But even without counting those who would flee at the first sign of combat, sheer weight of numbers would see us killed in moments. I had witnessed what untrained villagers were capable of at Werceworthe and I did not underestimate the folk who crowded the open ground before us.

My faith was sorely tested then. I believed in God and His miracles, but I could truly see no way we would survive the night.

"Ljósberari is dead!" shouted Runolf, shaking Scomric's head to reinforce his words. Blood spattered his forearm and added fresh blotches to his already stained kirtle. "You are free now. You can live in peace. We have no quarrel with any of you. Our fight was with Ljósberari and the Frank, Chlotar."

There was a stunned silence for a time and then a young man stepped forward. He was tall and wore a shirt of iron. The sword in his hand flashed as he raised it to point at us.

"The Master is dead!" he howled. "They have killed the Master."

A rumble of anger ran through the crowd, their awe and fear of us dissipating as quickly as morning mist on a warm day.

"You have no need of him any more," yelled Runolf, raising his voice over the growing anger of the crowd. "You are free of the burnings and torture."

"The Master has been taken into the light," shouted the tall warrior, his eyes blazing with the same madness I had seen in Scomric's face. "It is a sign."

The unrest amongst them grew, and they began shuffling forward, growing in confidence, their fury building as rapidly as the fire in the hall.

The heat at our backs was scorching now, as hot as a bread oven, but I could see that the throng would soon find their courage. Goaded by the fervent warrior's words, their anger and devotion to Ljósberari would soon outweigh their temerity. Reaching for Runolf's kirtle, I tugged him back through the doors and into the stifling, smoke-filled heat of the hall. The crowd surged forward, snarling and howling again, their voices demonic and terrifying, just as Audun had described them. Runolf and I leaned on the partially broken doors and once again he slammed the beam into place.

My eyes stung from the smoke. The flames at the rear of the hall singed my hair and stubbly beard. I started to cough as the smoke filled my lungs. The angry crowd hacked at the doors with renewed rage, their new leader screaming them into a frenzy.

"Now what?" Runolf asked. "I thought you said you would rather fight than burn."

"And you said anything was possible," I replied. "Follow me." I pulled him away from the door and we stumbled further into the burning building.

Fifty-Nine

We ran past boards and benches until we reached the southern wall. Flames had engulfed the eastern portion of the building and the smoke was thick and choking, swirling above us in the rafters. Leofstan's body was already invisible from where we stood, smoke and flames obscuring our view of the old monk's corpse. I shoved away thoughts of my dead mentor. There was no time for sadness now, only action. And that part of my mind that has made me so deadly in battle over the years came to the fore. I could see just what we needed to do and I would allow nothing to distract me from my goal.

It was already getting difficult to see, and the acrid hot air stung my throat, eyes and lungs. But after a few moments of groping and feeling along the wall, I found what I was looking for. One of the small windows I had noticed earlier yawned dark before us. I stabbed the thin membrane that covered it, and cool air blew inward, sucked from outside by the ravenous flames. Both Runolf and I pushed our faces close and gulped down breaths of the fresh air. I had thought the window larger when we had passed by outside the hall, but it was there nonetheless, and it might yet prove to be our salvation.

At the doors, in the hazed distance of a few paces away, the crowd's axes were biting into the beam. It would be only heartbeats before they realised they could reach in and unbar the door.

"I'll never fit through there," said Runolf. It was true. I was much slimmer and less heavily muscled, and it was doubtful if I would be able to wriggle through. Runolf would not be able to fit more than his head and one shoulder in without becoming wedged.

"Use your axe," I hissed, glancing at the door. There might still be just enough time for us to slip into the night. If Runolf hurried. But he hesitated. "Come on!" I urged him. "What are you waiting for?"

"So many of them are children," he replied. "I cannot..."

"What?" I snapped. "Would you rather die than fight children who would see you burn?"

"I do not make war on women or children," he said, his tone hollow and full of anguish.

"I know, Runolf," I said. "I know. But if we remain here, we will both die, as sure as the sun rises in the east." He shook his head and I could see that my words were not reaching him. "Your own daughter is down there by the river," I said, panic from the heat and the crashing from the door sharpening my tone. "Her mother was killed by these people. Some of those children and women watched while that bastard, Chlotar, put out Estrid's eyes." I saw the pain my words caused him, but now was not the time for softness. "Would you make Revna an orphan?"

Finally, these words hit their target and Runolf shoved me aside. He swung his great axe into the sill of the window, snapping timber and crumbling whitewashed daub. Behind us, the doors opened. The crowd hesitated in the face of the smoke-filled conflagration that met them.

"Find them!" screamed the young warrior who now led them. "Find them and put out their eyes that they might not see the light where the Master now resides."

Runolf wrenched his axe free and took another swing at the window. He was determined now, and the wall would not hold him for long. A third and then a fourth stroke fell, hammering through the lattice of branches, dried mud and manure. Runolf lifted his foot and kicked the wall, further broadening the rent his axe had made.

"There they are!" the young warrior screeched from the doors, and, the sight of us impelling them at last into action, several of the armed men rushed into the hall.

Seeing the urgency, Runolf pushed me through the gash he had made with his axe. Splinters and shattered twigs caught at my linen robe and tore at my flesh. Then I was outside, sprawling into the dew-wet grass.

"Come on!" I shouted, and Runolf flung himself through the jagged opening. I grabbed hold of his arms and heaved. It was a tight fit, and his bulk snagged on the debris, but he was one of the strongest men I have ever known, and where the wall still impeded his movement, he smashed through it with brute force, kicking and hacking his way out of the smoke and into the cool air of the dawn.

As he cleared the gap, the warriors arrived and I slashed my sword at their faces. My blade connected, cutting one man across the nose. He fell back with a scream of pain, toppling and tripping his comrades.

Runolf hauled me away.

"Time to run," he shouted, and we turned and sprinted down the slope towards the river, the burning hall and the fire of the rising sun lighting the sky at our backs.

Sixty

We had barely gone twenty paces when the young leader screamed a warning to the mass of people gathered before the hall. He had remained at the entrance to the burning building, hanging back and sending the bravest of the warriors inside. Such is the way with most men who lead others, I have found. The leader who will risk his life with those who follow him is rare indeed. But his lack of bravery did not appear to dissuade the majority of the throng from listening to him, and, craven or hero, his eyesight was keen. He bellowed orders and Ljósberari's folk turned and, to my dismay, many of them ran after us.

"Hurry," I yelled, increasing my pace. I sprinted between the shadows of the first buildings, before glancing over my shoulder at our pursuers.

Several of the younger armed men were running parallel to our position, clearly intending to intercept us before we could reach the river. I wondered if the others would still be there. Had they set off when they saw the first flames at the hall? Or had they encountered more of Ljósberari's crazed disciples before they were able to reach the boats?

I prayed they were still there, waiting for us. We would know soon enough. Our only hope was to beat our pursuers to the water's edge and hope that our friends were still there. I ran on, my bare feet slipping on the dewy grass. A sharp pebble dug into the sole of my left foot, but I did not falter, pushing myself to greater speed. My shoulder burnt where Scomric's blade had slashed me, but I ignored the pain. That too was something for later. If we survived past the dawn.

Even as I thought this, my heart sank. I was fast, and with our head start, I believed I would comfortably reach the wharf before Ljósberari's howling followers, but a glance told me that Runolf would never make it. He was tall, with a long stride, but he was hugely muscled and though he was fast in a fight, he was no runner. And he had taken many wounds from Chlotar that were sapping his strength, further slowing him down. He had already fallen some way behind me and when he saw me looking back he waved his axe frantically, urging me on.

"Run, Hunlaf!" he said. "Run!"

But I was already slowing my pace, returning to his side. Tugging at his kirtle, I tried to pull him along, but it was no good. He could go no faster than a trundling lope, and I could see the young warriors bounding and leaping down the incline at the other side of the buildings we were passing.

"If you stay with me," Runolf panted, "we will both be killed."

"Anything is possible," I replied, but I could see no way out of this. Already it was too late. Perhaps a dozen men had raced ahead and were now turning to face us, blocking our path.

"Don't give them time to think," growled Runolf. "Don't stop!"

What he was saying was madness. There could be no way that we could triumph over so many, but I could think of no better course of action, so, with a roar, I flung myself forward towards the waiting warriors.

They were not well-disciplined and only a few had shields

between them. All of them were watching our careening approach, and they had not had time to prepare themselves to receive our charge. By the light in the dawn sky I picked out my target: a wiry, short man with a straggly beard and pocked cheeks. He gripped a spear and snarled like an animal. He thrust his spear at my face, his eyes bright and filled with the certainty that his spear-point would slay me. It did not connect with my flesh and he had no time to look surprised. With the unusual calmness I felt in battle, I pushed the spear haft away with my seax and slammed my sword into his face. He fell back and I ran on, suddenly no longer facing the line of armed opponents, but surrounded by them.

The man beside the dying spear-man was even less prepared. He tried to twist his shield around to defend himself, but before he was able to turn, I slashed my sword backhanded into his neck. Blood flowed like a waterfall and he staggered away.

The men about me fell back, suddenly wary. Dropping my precious seax, I reached down and pulled the shield from the first warrior's weakening grip. All my fears and concerns had burnt away now. Perhaps it was God's will that I was to die there in that far off land, but I was certain of the righteousness of slaying Leofstan's killer, and now I welcomed the coolness and simplicity of the fight. I would not leave Runolf and I would kill our enemies until I was slain, or we had fought our way to freedom. I drew in a breath and cast about for my next victim.

Runolf had hit them like *Brymsteda* smashing through a wave. Two more men already lay dead or dying at his feet, and as I watched his great axe fell again, splintering a shield. An instant later Runolf dispatched the shield bearer with a savage blow to the man's shoulder, crushing bone as easily as he had cut through the wattled twigs and daub of the wall.

The shock of our initial collision had passed now, and even whilst our brutal attack caused our opponents to become more cautious, falling back out of range of our blades, so their numbers grew as more of them arrived from the hall.

Runolf's axe hacked into a man's thigh and he fell. I could see that Runolf wished to finish the man sprawled on the earth, but with a growl at the enemies surrounding us, and the thicket of spears that now threatened from all sides, the axeman was forced to retreat.

There were well over a score of warriors around us now. Several of them were the seasoned armoured men we had seen at the hall. A quick look showed me what I had suspected. We were cut off from the river, and the path behind us was blocked.

"It seems this is the end of the path, Killer," Runolf said, glowering at the warriors who had not yet worked up enough nerve to attack us. I looked at their sharp spears and the long blades of their swords and axes that gleamed in the grey dawn light. The smell of the smoke on the air brought back memories of the battle of Werceworthe. We had been through much, Runolf and I.

"I am glad God sent you into my life, Runolf Ragnarsson," I said.

"Whether it was your Christ, or Óðinn, I too am glad to have called you my friend, Hunlaf of Ubbanford. I hope we meet again in the afterlife."

Runolf's voice was thick with emotion and I glanced askance at him. His eyes brimmed with tears, gleaming like gems in the early morning light and the flicker of the flames that now tore through the roof of the hall.

"Going soft, are you?" I asked, grinning despite the knowledge that death awaited us both in moments. At least I would not die alone.

Runolf smiled, his teeth bright in his thatch of fire-red beard.

"Anything is possible," he said, and then, with a scream from their young leader, the circle of men around us surged forward.

***

We were certain we would die, but neither Runolf nor I would go easily. Back-to-back we stood. I could feel his movements behind me, hear his grunts and the sounds of his axe connecting with weapons, armour and flesh. But I could not turn to see how he fared.

A tall, strong man with a full beard stepped towards me, brandishing a long sword and a shield, and crowding out the spears of his comrades that would have proven an easier method with which to slaughter me. If he had hung back and allowed them to stab with their long ash-hafted weapons, I would have been unable to defend against them all at once, armed as I was with only a sword and a shield. But oftentimes a warrior's pride will lead to his downfall, and so it was for this swordsman. Perhaps he wanted to prove himself to their new leader, or maybe I had killed one of his friends and he sought revenge. Mayhap he simply saw an easy moment of glory and battle-fame for himself. He was strong and from the way he moved and held his weapon and shield, he was not unfamiliar with fighting. I must have looked puny and weak in his eyes. Young and slender of build, wearing nothing but a stained and ripped pale linen robe. He was not the first to underestimate me, and he would not be the last.

I feigned exhaustion, panting and lowering my head, waiting until he believed he would slay me easily. He drew close, then finally made his move, swinging a cut towards my head. Using all of my youthful speed and everything I had learnt from Gwawrddur, I raised my shield, taking his blow on the rim and in the same moment, I sent a scything cut into his extended right leg. My sword caught him in the shin and he screamed with pain. It was not a killing blow, but it was enough to send him reeling back, further confounding the attack of several of his comrades, their weapons snagging and tangling together in the press.

Capitalising on their momentary confusion, I lashed out, taking one unarmoured man in the bicep of his sword arm. He dropped his blade and staggered away from me, pushing into others. I could sense that behind me, Runolf was giving his own assailants much to contend with. There were screams of pain and he bellowed insults at them, goading them, jeering at their cowardice.

For a moment, I wondered if perhaps, beyond all reason, we might be able to turn this tide. Could it be that God in all His wisdom would allow us to conquer against so many? I made to attack once more, raising my shield against the spears that were now being lowered to prod and jab at me.

And then Runolf grunted, and his bulk crashed into my back. He fell and collided with my legs, tripping me. I lost my balance and landed atop him. I managed to keep hold of my shield and my sword, but I knew that a prone enemy was soon to be a dead foe.

"Get up," I yelled, scrambling in an effort to regain my footing. "Get up!" But Runolf did not move. I looked down and saw his face was awash with blood. He lay quite still where he had fallen.

I wanted to give up then, to curl into a ball and cry for all I had lost, all the death and all the suffering that surrounded me. But I heard Gwawrddur's voice screaming inside my mind.

"On your feet, Killer!" he yelled. "I didn't train you to give up. Fight! Fight!"

Pushing myself to my feet with a groan, I turned to face my enemies. Very well, I thought. I would try to make Gwawrddur proud. So, this was the moment of my death. I offered my soul to God and hoped that Runolf's spirit was looking down and would see that I died well.

Sixty-One

Turning my back on those I had been facing, I jumped over Runolf's still form. I vowed to his shade that I would make those who had killed him pay with their blood, before I too fell. A spear blade flickered towards my face, and I swayed to one side, lunging under the reach of the haft and cutting into the fingers of the man who held it. Screaming now, howling and raging as incoherently as Ljósberari's warriors, I slashed and hacked, my sword again biting deep into flesh.

I was sure that at any moment a spear would take me between my shoulder blades. And yet I could not face all of my opponents at once, and so I bellowed and roared my fury at the men before me and carried on my savage assault. Soon I would be struck down, but by the Almighty, I would make them remember this night.

A short man with huge hands and broad shoulders and a neck as thick as an ox's found enough courage to step towards me. He swung a war axe as large and deadly as Runolf's. I caught his downward strike on my shield. The willow wood splintered, and my hand and forearm throbbed from the force of the blow. I took a swipe at the axeman, but he was nimble and he stepped away.

There was a sudden commotion behind me, and I tensed,

certain that I would feel the bitter bite of steel in my back. But the stocky warrior before me came on again, swinging his axe low and I could not turn to see who would kill me from behind without allowing the axeman to kill me from the front. I danced away from the axe-head and it missed my knee by less than a hand's breadth. The men around him were stepping back, seeming to make room for their man to fight me without them impeding his movements.

I stepped towards him, sending a fast strike at his midriff. He parried my blade on his axe's haft as I had known he would, and I twisted my wrist. I was going to cut into his hand, but before I could complete the movement, something flashed past my face, making me flinch away.

I could not believe it. The spear had missed me when all the men behind me had to do was to plunge their weapons into my back. How could they have missed? How was such a thing possible? Then I saw that not only had the spear missed me, but it had struck the short axeman square in the chest. He stumbled back and I shook my head. Was this the miracle I had needed? Could this truly be happening?

"Don't look so surprised, Killer," said Gwawrddur's familiar voice. "Did you truly believe we would leave you two to face this horde of maniacs alone?"

For a time I was stunned, unable to speak. I watched as the Welshman leapt forward, his sword appearing to fly into his hand from the scabbard at his belt. The blade flickered, slicing open the throat of the axeman. Two more warriors closed in and before I could move to assist him, Gwawrddur had slain them both. He stepped back to my side.

I finally risked a glance over my shoulder. The men who had blocked our path to the west were now engaged in a new fight. My heart swelled with joy at seeing my friends. Drosten, his tattooed face a mask of fury, parried a blow with a shield he must have picked up from one of the fallen. Surging forward, using the board as a ram, he barged over two men, hacking down with his sword into their exposed flesh. Hereward and Beorn stood shoulder-to-shoulder, shields interlocking. They fought with the calm efficiency of trained killers, stepping forward as they dispatched those who stood before them. With a shock, I saw that even Eadmaer was there. Spear in hand, he walked beside Hereward and defended their flank, jabbing and thrusting to keep the howling enemies at bay.

Looking back towards the burning hall, I saw the young man who now led these people. He stood at the periphery on the edge of the fighting, safely away from the swinging swords and hacking axes. He was screaming, inciting the people to renewed urgency now that the others had come up from the river to our aid.

"Slay them! Slay them all! They bring the darkness. They are the servants of the Devil. Slay th—"

His voice died. His hands reached up to his throat to claw at the knife that was buried there. With a start, I recognised the ivory hilt of my seax.

Turning, I saw Gwawrddur lowering his hand. He had snatched up my seax from the ground and thrown it with his unerring accuracy.

"I don't know who he is," Gwawrddur said in his lilting, sing-song voice, "and I didn't understand what he was saying. But I could tell that he would be better off dead."

With the death of their new leader, and so many of their number slain, the desire to fight fled, and the men around us began to back away, slinking off into the smoke-hazed dawn light. The hall was an inferno now, its flames lighting the whole settlement and the grisly reminders of Ljósberari's reign that still hung on stakes along the path and down by the river.

"We cannot tarry here," said Hereward, not taking his eyes from the warriors that were still moving away. "They will soon realise that we are few and they are yet many more than us."

"Help me carry Runolf," I said, hurrying to the giant Norseman's body. "I cannot bear him alone, but I will not leave him here." I reached my hands beneath his arms, preparing to lift his bulk. To my amazement, he sat up with a groan. Wiping the blood from his face with one of his huge hands, he looked about him, blinking.

"What did I miss?" he asked.

I saw that the blood came from a cut on his forehead. His skull was strong, for whatever had struck him had only knocked him senseless for a short time.

"You missed us rescuing you," replied Hereward. "Next time you decide to run off, you're on your own."

Runolf snorted and spat.

"Can you stand?" I asked, offering him my hand.

"I'm not dead, am I?" he replied, allowing me to pull him to his feet.

I retrieved his axe and handed it to him, relief running through me at seeing him alive.

"Don't forget that," he said, pointing to Ljósberari's head. "We've come a long way to leave it behind now."

Drosten picked it up, looking at the features with disdain.

"This is the mighty Ljósberari?"

"The same," said Runolf, "though after a talk with Hunlaf he is a little less mighty."

"And shorter," observed Drosten drily.

We hurried down to the river. I was astonished at what had happened, and I could scarcely believe I yet lived.

"Yours, I believe," said Gwawrddur, dragging my attention away from the boats and the two figures that awaited us on the water. I looked at him with a frown.

In his hand he held the ornately-handled seax that he had taken from the young warrior's corpse. That blade had a way of finding its way back to me no matter how many times I lost it. I took it and slipped it into my belt.

"I had prayed for a miracle," I said. "I should just have called for you. My friends."

Gwawrddur sniffed.

"What's the difference?" he said.

Sixty-Two

I am exhausted. To write these words each day is a struggle. My eyes strain and my fingers cramp, but I am gripped by a pain much worse than that of my decrepit body. It was my wish to recount these tales of my life before I face God's judgement for my sins, but to recollect the past is to relive it, and over these recent months I have often wondered at the wisdom of inflicting such hurt upon myself. To live again through the agony of Leofstan's death was terrible. I longed to set aside my quill then and write no more, but Coenric, God bless the boy, brought me warm tisanes of woundwort and all-heal. He prayed with me and convinced me to carry on. But now I feel the weight of time resting heavy on my mind and body. Outside, the monks are sowing the winter barley, and the smoke from burning leaves tells me that another summer has passed since first I put quill to parchment for this record of my life.

There is still much to tell. But I am tired and every book, just as every life, must come to an end. And this seems as likely a place to pause my story as any. Ever since we had arrived in Rygjafylki and found the first burnt buildings and charred corpses left by Ljósberari, we had travelled under a cloud. Even when the skies had been clear and the days warm, it had felt as though we had been cursed, and when we had boarded

Gullbringa and begun our journey upriver, travelling ever closer to the dark soul that hid beneath the guise of bringing light to those who followed him, I often felt that we would never survive; that our corpses would be added to those we saw on the stakes beside the river. Even the land itself seemed to be against us, and I still feel a deep sorrow when I think of brave Bealdwulf and how he was sacrificed to the spirit of the forest, and Os, with his easy grin and quick jests, reduced to a wheezing wreck in that stinking hut where we were imprisoned. It had been a truly dark time, but with Ljósberari's death, it seemed that our luck had changed, or perhaps, having fulfilled the Almighty's plan by ridding the world of Scomric's evil, He once more looked upon us with favour.

As difficult as our voyage upriver had been, so our trip downriver was smooth and uninterrupted by further tragedy or strife. Eadmaer had cut loose the boats from the wharfs, sending them out into the river, where the current took them away. Revna and Aelfwyn awaited us in the two remaining log boats. Each vessel could bear five or six people, but they were light enough that we could carry them beside the river when we reached treacherous rapids or the waterfall. Runolf grumbled that they were even less worthy than *Gullbringa*, or *Skítrbringa*, as he still referred to Ingvar's boat. But he did not protest too much as we clambered aboard and paddled away from the burning hall. The sun rose above the mountains in the east, and as we drifted away on the dark waters, the shore became clogged with Ljósberari's people. They did not howl any longer, nor did they make any attempt to prevent us leaving. Eadmaer, taking charge of steering the foremost boat, took us as close to the far bank as possible, perhaps fearing that the people would loose arrows or throw spears. And yet no projectiles flew towards us, and the silent throng was still standing there, silhouetted against the flames and the fiery dawn sky, when we rounded a bend in the river and they were lost to sight from us forever. I never learnt what happened to them, those children of the damned and freed thralls, but I have never less regretted taking a life than that of Ljósberari. The man's soul had been warped beyond reason and I would like to think that with him gone, his evil spell was broken and those who had been faithful to him were able to find a life of peace.

I wondered what it had been like to live there, surrounded by zealous followers, guided by the hand of a madman whose mind had been twisted beyond all reckoning by the traumas he had suffered, and the words of a long-dead prophet. When it seemed clear that none of his people had come after us, I asked Aelfwyn of her time with Ljósberari. She would say little about it, save that there had been others who, like Revna and her, had not been taken in by his teachings. But they had not known how to escape, and so they had remained, living each day in fear.

Aelfwyn spent most of those days staring at the river banks sliding by, trailing her fingers in the cool water. She spoke little and I thought of the girl I had grown up with, and how she would talk incessantly, laughing often. I was overjoyed that my cousin yet lived, but I was saddened to see how her suffering had changed her. I knew not what words of comfort to say, so I found myself avoiding her company around the campfire at night. The only one who seemed able to reach her was Eadmaer and he sat close to her in the dark, just on the edge of the firelight where the two of them would whisper quietly.

His closeness to her infuriated me, making me jealous. I pushed such petty, resentful thoughts away, for I was truly pleased that Aelfwyn was able to find solace with her husband's brother.

The other woman in our small company was as different from Aelfwyn as lead is to gold. Revna held herself proudly, helping to row when the men tired. She looked so unlike

Runolf, with her black hair and slender form, it would be easy to forget that he was her father. But when she spoke, she was clearly accustomed to being obeyed. I could easily see why Chlotar, with so many other womenfolk available, would have sought her out. She was young and beautiful, of course, but there was an unwavering certainty in all her actions, an obvious strength that made her seem many years her senior.

Even when she was nursing Runolf's wounds, she did so in an efficient, yet impatient manner, as if his injuries were an inconvenience to her. The only time I saw her demeanour soften was on that first day, when she went to her father's side.

"I am sorry for what I said to you," she said, her voice as meek as I ever heard from her.

Runolf brushed away her apology, but I saw his eyes fill with tears at her words.

"You did what you needed," he said gruffly. She was his last living kin, and to have found her alive had gone some way to restoring Runolf's spirit. To have avenged Estrid's death and at the same time slain his daughter's abuser, had brought back the spring in his step that I had not seen since he had completed the construction of *Brymsteda*. Runolf walked tall once more and I was gladdened to see it. In that flame-flicked night of terror, I had been certain the Norseman had been killed, so to see him hale and smiling again helped to alleviate the ache in my heart at the loss of Leofstan.

As we glided along the river and then slipped out into the great lake, it seemed we had truly managed to escape, but there was something else that worried me. Gersine had a fever and I feared the wound-rot had set in to his leg. His limb was red and swollen and, as Leofstan was no longer with us to impart his wisdom about healing, it was left to me to tend to Lord Mancas' son. I fretted and prayed over him, but I had no clean bandages and nothing with which to make poultices or anything that might draw the poison from his leg. So, as Gersine's fever grew in intensity and he began to mumble nonsense in his half-sleep, all we could do was hurry on towards Gudrun's isle, hoping that she would be able to help him.

We were not sure what reception we would find there and we worried that the cunning woman might have cut Sygbald's throat, despite her hospitality when we had stayed on her island. This notion was strengthened when Revna told us how Gudrun sent messages to Ljósberari with runes scratched into the thinnest of birch bark tied to the legs of pigeons. The men were furious when they heard this. Eadmaer cursed and said the witch should be killed. He raved and said that if not for her, we might well have reached Ljósberari without incident. Aelfwyn placed a hand on his arm, stilling him and calming his anger.

"It is no easy thing for a woman in this land," she reminded him. "Gudrun, like Revna and I, did what she must to live."

Eadmaer said no more, but I could see he still carried a simmering bitterness towards Gudrun. He was not alone, and I think Hereward and Beorn might well have agreed to kill her for what she had done, if they had seen her again. As it was, when we arrived at her island and made our way up to her small hut in the clearing, carrying Gersine between us, Gudrun had gone. To our great joy, Sygbald was there and much recovered. He was pleased to see us too, though he wept when he heard of the fate of Os and Bealdwulf. We asked him about the cunning woman, and he said she had treated him well, tending to his hurts and feeding him. The previous morning, when he had awoken, she was nowhere to be seen. She would sometimes disappear in search of wyrts, but she had not returned that night, which was unusual.

"She must have known we were coming," Eadmaer said.

He might have been right, but given that she had looked after our friend, none of us was anxious to search for her and punish her for warning Ljósberari of our approach. There was plenty of food in her house and while Sygbald prepared us the first proper meal we had eaten since fleeing from Ljósberari's hellish domain, I went about preparing a poultice of stale bread, honey and wild garlic for Gersine. I applied it to his leg and prayed over the wound and, when we awoke the following morning, his fever had broken and the swelling had gone down. God was indeed smiling upon us, and we left Gudrun's isle in good spirits. Even Eadmaer seemed to have forgotten his hatred of the pale cunning woman.

Eldgrim was awaiting us at Sand and we were glad to be quickly away from Olvir's hall. It was a grim and unhappy place, and I could not shake the sense that Olvir had hoped for Ingvar's death on the journey upriver. The jarl had been surprised to see us, but had seemed to breathe a sigh of relief when we told him how Ingvar had been slain.

"That is sad," he had said, sounding anything but sorrowful. "And his dog too, you say." He shook his head in a mockery of sadness and I wanted to launch myself at him across the board and its meagre fare. Ingvar was a good man, and brave, and it angered me to see his jarl profiting from his death. With Ingvar gone, not only had his debts been cleared, but his land returned to Olvir's possession. Runolf placed his hand on my shoulder and shook his head. He was right. There was nothing we could do, but it pained me to see the jarl happy to hear of his man's death.

Eldgrim took us back to King Hjorleif Hjorsson's hall aboard *Grágás*. We sailed down the fjords and between the islands without incident. The seas were calm and the winds pleasant and favourable. Hjorleif seemed so amazed that we had been successful in our mission and so shocked when Runolf pulled Scomric's head from the sack, that he choked on a mouthful of venison. His face went as red as Runolf's beard and the king would surely have died if not for Lord Mancas' well-timed blows to his back. The slender Northumbrian struck the massive king three times hard between the shoulders and with the third blow, a gobbet of half-chewed meat flew across the hall. Two hounds began to snarl and fight over the morsel, and when Hjorleif had got his breath back, he laughed at the sight.

The king was a gluttonous pig and disgusting, but he was true to his word. He agreed that he would tell his people to no longer raid Northumbria's coast, but they should begin to trade between our kingdoms. Mancas was delighted. He was also overjoyed to see Gersine again. He frowned when he saw his son limping, but when he heard of our adventures and how close Gersine had been to death, Mancas thanked me for keeping his son alive.

"There is no need to thank me," I said. I too was pleased that my friend was well, and also that I would not need to impart the knowledge of his death to Lord Mancas. My soul had borne all the grief it could that summer and I think any more heartache would have broken me.

Mancas wished to set sail forthwith and we were pleased to be leaving. We introduced the women to him when we were safely aboard *Brymsteda* and we had put out to sea. Neither Revna nor Aelfwyn had entered the hall, instead staying on *Grágás* until our departure. This had been Eldgrim's suggestion when we arrived at the king's steading. Eldgrim was a good man.

"There is no need to burden the king with the presence of the women," he'd said, as *Grágás* was being moored to the wharf. "There will be quite enough tidings to keep him occupied."

We understood the words Eldgrim did not say, and Runolf nodded his thanks to the warmaster. I remembered the cries of the thrall in the night and shivered at the memory. Revna and Aelfwyn had surely suffered enough without falling foul of the king's lustful appetites.

It was on the second day of our journey homeward when Ahmad came to speak to me. The wind had dropped out of the sky and we had become becalmed. Runolf had ordered us to row to a small island where we moored *Brymsteda* and made camp on the beach. There we would wait out the calm, for we would not risk trying to row across the North Sea.

I missed Leofstan terribly, and it was only then, when I was able to rest, with nothing to trouble my mind and no enemies seeking my death, that I could begin to truly take in how lonely I felt without my old mentor. The men around me were my friends, family even. They would fight for me, give their lives for me. And yet none of them understood me as Leofstan had. When there was a moment of peace I would pray alone, reciting the familiar words of the different offices of the day, but it was not the same without Leofstan's voice blending with mine.

That night, the sun had set and I was sitting beside the fire, using its light to look at the scrap of parchment I had taken from Ljósberari. As I had many times before, I stared at the flowing script but, without a reference to help me interpret the symbols, no matter how easily I could learn new languages, the marks meant nothing to me. I was certain that they held a clue that would lead me to *The Treasure of Life* and now, even though I truly wanted nothing more to do with the book that had caused so much suffering, I could think of little else. Leofstan had been obsessed with finding it and I felt that I owed it to his memory to keep searching.

A movement beside me caught my attention and I looked up to see Ahmad gazing down at me. His face was dark, framed in his black hair and beard. As always, he carried himself with a haughty assurance, but where he normally ignored me and the others unless given an order, now he crouched at my side and reached out his hand.

For a time I was confused, then I understood.

"You can read it?" I asked, handing him the parchment. And such was my foolish, youthful pride that, despite Ahmad's bearing and his actions aboard *Brymsteda* when he had brought Gwawrddur back to life, I was still amazed at the thought that a slave might possess knowledge that I did not.

"I am not an animal," he said in his thick accent. "If you had bothered to speak to me as Leofstan had, you would know this. I studied Law, Theology, Philosophy and Alchemy under the best teachers in Išbīliya. Of course I can read." He plucked the parchment away from me.

"I did not know," I said, feeling chastened and stupid and wondering how this man came to be a thrall in Northumbria.

"How would you?" he said, scanning the lines scratched there. "To you, I am nothing but a slave. A man to do your bidding, just as you would command a horse, or an ox."

His words shamed me and I felt my face grow hot. I had no words to offer him, and to apologise seemed pointless, so instead, I said, "What does it say?"

He sniffed and handed back the paper.

"It says that a book was purchased by Abu Jafar Yusuf ibn Sa'īd al-Zarqālluh, servant of the great and holy Hisham Al-Reda, Emir of Cordova."

"That is all it says? Just a record of the purchase?" I had hoped for more, but perhaps a name would help me to find the book. Surely it was a step closer. Ahmad was looking at me strangely.

"What?" I asked.

"I had thought you might thank me," he said, and again I flushed.

"You have my thanks," I said, awkward under his dark gaze.

"And once again, you do not think I can offer you more, despite me showing you that I am more than just a beast of burden."

"What more? What do you mean?" I squirmed and thought of all the times I had snapped at this man, ordering him without thinking.

"I know this al-Zarqālluh."

"Truly?" I could scarcely believe it, but there were many things I had once not believed that I now knew to be true.

"Well," Ahmad shrugged, "I have not met him. But I know of him. He is one of the richest men in the world, and his appetite for learning is insatiable. They say his madrasa," he thought a moment for the word in Englisc, "his school, in Išbīliya teems with students and has more books than the ancient library of Alexandria."

I was astounded by his words; amazed that a man whom I had barely thought of should know of the great library of the Mouseion at Alexandria. And I imagined such a place as he described, filled with books and scrolls, and of the character of the man who would possess such a library. The power of vision that would have this man of learning send out men to acquire tomes from far flung reaches of pagan lands. How Leofstan would have loved to meet such a man, I thought.

Ahmad could see some of the thoughts behind my eyes. Perhaps Leofstan had spoken to him about the book, or he had listened to my mentor and I discussing it, for now Ahmad's eyes narrowed.

"I can guide you to the book you seek," he said. "For a price."

"A price?" I asked, but I knew what he would ask before he spoke, and I could not blame him.

"My freedom," Ahmad said.

Ahmad's freedom would be hard-bought. The search for *The Treasure of Life* would lead us far to the south, to the torrid lands of the Moors, to Al-Andalus and even beyond the great rock of Jabal Ṭāriq. But that is for another day. I am weary. The weather is closing in around the minster and I can smell snow on the wind. I must rest now, and pray that, if it be God's will,

He will give me the strength to continue my story. Until then, I commend my soul to the Lord. May His blessings be upon all who read this tome.

And thus ends the second volume of the Annals of the life of Hunlaf of Ubbanford.

Author's Note

A Night of Flames, just like the first book in the series, *A Time for Swords*, is historical fiction with a capital F. The world that Hunlaf, Runolf and friends inhabit is based on the real world of the early Viking Age of the late eighth century. The kings and kingdoms are grounded in fact and many of the events described historically occurred. Likewise, the culture, lifestyle, technology, clothing and weapons are all as accurate as I can make them.

But just as with the first story in Hunlaf's tale, there is also much of this book that has sprung from my imagination. There was no rogue thrall who led a brutal uprising in Rogaland, but hopefully after reading this story you can believe there could have been.

The journey up the river aboard *Gullbringa* owes much to Joseph Conrad's *Heart of Darkness* and Francis Ford Coppola's seminal film, *Apocalypse Now*, the script of which John Milius had loosely based on Conrad's nineteenth-century novella. Where in Conrad's story they sail along the Congo River, Milius transposes the action to the Vietnam War. The story is so timeless that I was instantly drawn to it and the idea that *The Treasure of Life* might corrupt the mind of someone already broken by circumstance and trauma to become a murderous, Kurtz-like figure.

The Anglo-Saxon Chronicle states that in the year 794, the year after the first Viking attack on Lindisfarne, Vikings attacked the monastery at the mouth of the Wear, but "some of their leaders were slain; and some of their ships also were shattered to pieces by the violence of the weather; many of the crew were drowned; and some, who escaped alive to the shore, were soon dispatched at the mouth of the river".

When I read this entry, it seemed inevitable that Hunlaf and his companions should be at the scene of such an event. Following the attack on Jarrow and Monkwearmouth, there is a hiatus of decades where no more Viking raids are described as taking place on the Northumbrian coastline. The fact they had been beaten soundly at Jarrow may well have had something to do with that, or perhaps other attacks did not involve such prominent locations and so were omitted from the records, or, as I have postulated here, perhaps the Northumbrian king brokered a deal with the Norse kingdoms from which the raiders came.

Much of the novel takes place around and aboard ships and river vessels. The techniques Runolf employs to build *Brymsteda* are as authentic as I could ascertain. While researching I was surprised to learn that new, unseasoned wood was commonly used and even preferred for the strakes. It also surprised me that sails were made from wool. It didn't immediately strike me as a textile suited to holding the wind and not becoming waterlogged. However, remnants of Viking sails have been found and they were indeed made from wool. Sheep and wool were a major commodity in the early medieval period, with it being estimated that the wool from four hundred sheep would be needed to manufacture all the textiles required to fit out a typical Viking ship, including the sail and all the clothes and blankets. Making the sail was a laborious process, with rooing (basically pulling the fleece out by hand), separating the under coat wool from the outer coat, carding, spinning, weaving the two types of yarn together, fulling and drying, stretching, and finally coating with oil or fat to act as a sealant and waterproofing layer. The whole process from collecting the wool to finished sailcloth took about two years, so you can see why Runolf would be pleased to find a sail and rope he could reuse following the destruction of the raiders' ships after their failed attack on the monasteries of Jarrow and Monkwearmouth.

Lots of the details about sailing a Viking longship came from a wonderful documentary I found about the Sea Stallion of Glendalough, a reconstruction of the great longship *Skuldelev* 2, built by the Viking Ship Museum in Roskilde, Denmark, and then sailed to Ireland and later back again in 2007/2008. There are several other such practical archaeology projects, with reconstructions of traditionally made Viking Age craft, and as a novelist, I get a lot more out of seeing and hearing how people interact with the real thing than just reading about it in a dry archaeological report.

I have not stuck to the tradition of referring to ships and boats as females. It is not clear where this tradition comes from, but there is no evidence that ships were referred to as feminine in the early medieval period. In fact there are documented instances of Vikings referring to their ships as masculine. In the end I decided to refer to ships as neutral objects, despite the powerful spiritual connection their owners had with them.

Orkney became part of Norway in 875 when Harold Hårfagre ("Fair Hair") annexed the islands along with Shetland. In 794 the islands were still part of Pictland, and it is unlikely, though not impossible, that the Vikings would have had a permanent base there. The name, Tannskári, comes from the possible derivation of the place name Tankerness. A ness is a promontory.

There are no standing stones at Tankerness, but Neolithic henges and stone circles are found all over the northern islands.

The circle of stones where Hunlaf and the crew of *Brymsteda* pit themselves against Tannskári's people is based on the Ring of Brodgar, some sixteen miles away.

The Royal line of succession of the Picts is confusing. It is matrilineal, meaning that the Royal blood is carried through the mother's line, even though they were ruled by kings and not queens! Also, strangely there are no recorded Pictish women's names. One Royal Pictish lady is mentioned by name in the Annals of Ulster. However, her name, Eithne, is Irish or Gaelic. It could be that Pictish women used names the same as those given to the men, or perhaps the women were commonly given Irish names. Whatever the reason behind the dearth of female Pictish names, I have decided to use Irish names for the Pictish women I've mentioned.

As with Britain in the early medieval period, Norway was made up of several petty kingdoms. The names of the kings of these petty realms and when they ruled are sketchy, but I must admit that when I saw the name Hjorleif Hjorsson the Fornicator on a list of the kings of Rogaland, even though he was probably the ruler some decades earlier, I could not resist adding him into the story. He is probably a semi-fictional, legendary character anyway, but with such an epithet as "the Fornicator" I thought he definitely deserved a mention.

Kaun Solvason, the king of Hordaland, actually ruled earlier too, but I liked his name, and it was sufficiently different from Hjorleif not to be confusing.

The route Hunlaf and company travel along in Norway takes them through fjords, rivers and vast lakes. Much of western Norway is water and the history of the people there is inextricably intertwined with boats and ships. In recent years many of the waterways have been altered to generate hydroelectricity. This has meant that modern maps differ drastically from how things would have been in the eighth century. I believe the route I have chosen for Hunlaf would have been navigable by boat, but if I am mistaken, there would definitely have been other rivers that would have allowed them to head deep into the wilderness of mountains and forests.

Gullbringa, with its birch bark sewn outer covering, is actually based on a ship found in a burial at Sand, where the adventurers set off upriver. The ship burial has been dated to the seventh or eighth century AD. Log boats, whilst perhaps more likely to conjure up images of primitive tribesmen in tropical climates, were in fact common in Scandinavia and in use until well into the second millennium AD. There is even conjecture that they were used because they could double up as sledges during the winter months or on higher ground above the snow line.

Quentovic, the Frankish emporium where Scomric and Chlotar were captured by the Norsemen, no longer exists. It is thought to have been situated near the mouth of the Canche River with access to the English Channel, but its exact location is unknown. Anglo-Saxon monks would cross the English Channel and travel through Quentovic on their pilgrimage to Rome. During King Charlemagne's reign, many monasteries owned warehouses in or around Quentovic. It is not known exactly what happened to the emporium. The last written reference of Quentovic was in 864, but as the rich trade post was attacked by Vikings earlier in the ninth century, that could certainly have had an impact on its decline. It also makes it a possible candidate for a location where an Anglo-Saxon monk could have been captured in an early, undocumented Norse raid.

This period also sees the flourishing of the Abbasid Caliphate with its capital in the new circular city of Baghdad. There were many other Islamic dynasties, including the Umayyad Emirate of Cordoba in the Iberian Peninsula, which all saw a blossoming in education and writing, and an incredible thirst for knowledge.

We have the writings of Ahmad Ibn Fadlan from the tenth century to show us that emissaries from as far south as Baghdad travelled to the land of the Bulghars on the banks of the Volga far to the north, and there are countless artefacts found in Scandinavia that come from all corners of the known world. Who is to say that wealthy and enterprising Muslim nobles were not sending their servants into northern kingdoms in search of valuable items? If one such emissary had travelled to Rogaland and discovered a book such as *The Treasure of Life*, he might well have paid good silver to take it back to his master in Seville, Cordoba or Baghdad. And he might just have written a proof of such a purchase on a piece of parchment. Written receipts have a long history and have been found in Egypt on papyrus dating back to the time of Ramses II.

It seems that this particular receipt will lead Hunlaf far to the south in search of the book that has taken such a hold on his life. He has already hinted at some of the adventures that await him, but whatever stories he has yet to tell, and whether he will survive to write them, they will be for another day.

And other books.

Acknowledgements

Firstly, thank you, dear reader, for setting aside the time to read this book. I know how many things compete for your time and attention, so I am delighted that my writing has made its way to the top of your to-do list. If you have enjoyed the story, please spread the word to others who haven't yet discovered my writing. And if you have a moment, please consider leaving a short review on your online store of choice. Reviews really do help readers find new writers and decide on a book they might otherwise not take a chance on.

Extra special thanks to Jon McAfee, Mary Faulkner and Emma Stone, for their generous patronage. To find out more about becoming a patron, and what rewards you can receive for doing so, please go to www.matthewharffy.com.

Thanks to my test readers, Gareth Jones, Alex Forbes, Shane Smart and Simon Blunsdon. Their input into the early draft is always invaluable.

Special thanks to Christopher Monk for his help with the Old English. And special thanks to Phil Lavender for helping with Old Norse terms. Any linguistic errors in the final text are mine alone.

No book is published without a lot of work from many people besides the author, so thank you to my editors, Nicolas

Cheetham and Holly Domney, and all of the wonderful team at Aries and Head of Zeus. I do my best with the words, but the talented professionals at Head of Zeus are responsible for designing and producing the beautiful books that end up on bookshelves and in your hands.

I wrote all of this book during the numerous, lengthy lockdowns in the UK in 2020 and 2021. It was a very strange time and all too easy to let the seemingly constant barrage of bad news, and the lengthy isolation from friends and family get me down, so thanks to the incredibly supportive online community of historical fiction authors and readers who connect with me regularly on Facebook, Twitter and Instagram. There are many negatives about the modern world and the relentless nature of social media, but the ability to connect with like-minded people via the Internet is certainly a positive, and even more so during a pandemic that saw us unable to travel and meet other people.

And finally, but of course not least, my undying thanks and love to my family. To my daughters for their patience and for keeping me grounded, and to my wonderful wife, Maite (Maria to her work colleagues). There is nobody I would rather have been locked down with!

Matthew Harffy
Wiltshire, August 2021

About the author

MATTHEW HARFFY grew up in Northumberland where the rugged terrain, ruined castles and rocky coastline had a huge impact on him. Matthew is the author of *Wolf of Wessex* and the Bernicia Chronicles series. He now lives in Wiltshire with his wife and their two daughters.

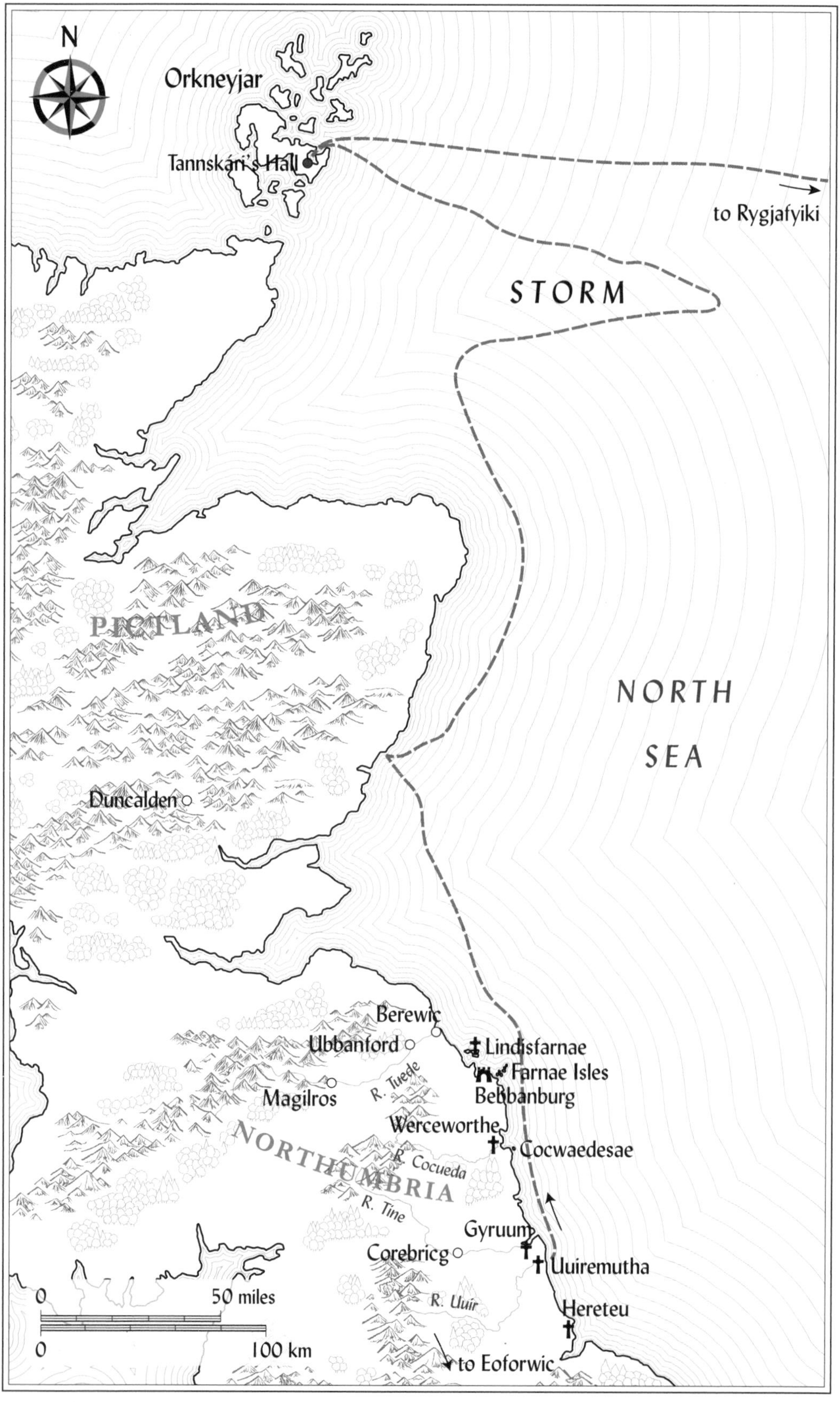
N
Orkneyjar
Tannskári's Hall
to Rygjafyiki
STORM
PICTLAND
NORTH
SEA
Duncalden
Berewic
Ubbanford
Lindisfarnae
Farnae Isles
Magilros
R. Tuede
Bebbanburg
Werceworthe
NORTHUMBRIA
Cocwaedesae
R. Cocueda
R. Tine
Gyruum
Corebricg
Uuiremutha
0
50 miles
R. Uuir
Hereteu
0
100 km
to Eoforwic